L. Maria Child

A Romance of the Republic

l. Maria Child

A Romance of the Republic

ISBN/EAN: 9783337065256

Printed in Europe, USA, Canada, Australia, Japan

Cover: Foto ©Andreas Hilbeck / pixelio.de

More available books at **www.hansebooks.com**

A

ROMANCE OF THE REPUBLIC.

BY

L. MARIA CHILD.

BOSTON:
TICKNOR AND FIELDS.
1867.

UNIVERSITY PRESS: WELCH, BIGELOW, & CO.,
CAMBRIDGE.

TO

THE FATHER AND MOTHER

OF

COL. R. G. SHAW,

THE EARLY AND EVER-FAITHFUL FRIENDS OF FREEDOM AND
EQUAL RIGHTS,

THIS VOLUME

IS MOST RESPECTFULLY AND AFFECTIONATELY
INSCRIBED

BY

THE AUTHOR.

A ROMANCE OF THE REPUBLIC.

PART FIRST.

CHAPTER I.

"WHAT are you going to do with yourself this evening, Alfred?" said Mr. Royal to his companion, as they issued from his counting-house in New Orleans. "Perhaps I ought to apologize for not calling you Mr. King, considering the shortness of our acquaintance; but your father and I were like brothers in our youth, and you resemble him so much, I can hardly realize that you are not he himself, and I still a young man. It used to be a joke with us that we must be cousins, since he was a King and I was of the Royal family. So excuse me if I say to you, as I used to say to him, What are you going to do with yourself, Cousin Alfred?"

"I thank you for the friendly familiarity," rejoined the young man. "It is pleasant to know that I remind you so strongly of my good father. My most earnest wish is to resemble him in character as much as I am said to resemble him in person. I have formed no plans for the evening. I was just about to ask you what there was best worth seeing or hearing in the Crescent City."

"If I should tell you I thought there was nothing better worth seeing than my daughters, you would perhaps excuse a father's partiality," rejoined Mr. Royal.

1   A

"Your daughters!" exclaimed his companion, in a tone of surprise. "I never heard that you were married."

A shadow of embarrassment passed over the merchant's face, as he replied, "Their mother was a Spanish lady, — a stranger here, — and she formed no acquaintance. She was a woman of a great heart and of rare beauty. Nothing can ever make up her loss to me; but all the joy that remains in life is centred in the daughters she has left me. I should like to introduce them to you; and that is a compliment I never before paid to any young man. My home is in the outskirts of the city; and when we have dined at the hotel, according to my daily habit, I will send off a few letters, and then, if you like to go there with me, I will call a carriage."

"Thank you," replied the young man; "unless it is your own custom to ride, I should prefer to walk. I like the exercise, and it will give a better opportunity to observe the city, which is so different from our Northern towns that it has for me the attractions of a foreign land."

In compliance with this wish, Mr. Royal took him through the principal streets, pointing out the public buildings, and now and then stopping to smile at some placard or sign which presented an odd jumble of French and English. When they came to the suburbs of the city, the aspect of things became charmingly rural. Houses were scattered here and there among trees and gardens. Mr. Royal pointed out one of them, nestled in flowers and half encircled by an orange-grove, and said, "That is my home. When I first came here, the place where it stands was a field of sugar-canes; but the city is fast stretching itself into the suburbs."

They approached the dwelling; and in answer to the

bell, the door was opened by a comely young negress, with a turban of bright colors on her head and golden hoops in her ears. Before the gentlemen had disposed of their hats and canes, a light little figure bounded from one of the rooms, clapping her hands, and exclaiming, " Ah, Papasito!" Then, seeing a stranger with him, she suddenly stood still, with a pretty look of blushing surprise.

" Never mind, Mignonne," said her father, fondly patting her head. " This is Alfred Royal King, from Boston; my namesake, and the son of a dear old friend of mine. I have invited him to see you dance. Mr. King, this is my Floracita."

The fairy dotted a courtesy, quickly and gracefully as a butterfly touching a flower, and then darted back into the room she had left. There they were met by a taller young lady, who was introduced as " My daughter Rosabella." Her beauty was superlative and peculiar. Her complexion was like a glowing reflection upon ivory from gold in the sunshine. Her large brown eyes were deeply fringed, and lambent with interior light. Lustrous dark brown hair shaded her forehead in little waves, slight as the rippling of water touched by an insect's wing. It was arranged at the back of her head in circling braids, over which fell clusters of ringlets, with moss-rose-buds nestling among them. Her full, red lips were beautifully shaped, and wore a mingled expression of dignity and sweetness. The line from ear to chin was that perfect oval which artists love, and the carriage of her head was like one born to a kingdom.

Floracita, though strikingly handsome, was of a model less superb than her elder sister. She was a charming little brunette, with laughter always lurking in ambush

within her sparkling black eyes, a mouth like " Cupid's
bow carved in coral," and dimples in her cheeks, that well
deserved their French name, *berceaux d'amour*.

These radiant visions of beauty took Alfred King so
much by surprise, that he was for a moment confused.
But he soon recovered self-possession, and, after the usual
salutations, took a seat offered him near a window over-
looking the garden. While the commonplaces of conversation were interchanged, he could not but notice the floral
appearance of the room. The ample white lace curtains
were surmounted by festoons of artificial roses, caught up
by a bird of paradise. On the ceiling was an exquisitely
painted garland, from the centre of which hung a tasteful
basket of natural flowers, with delicate vine-tresses droop-
ing over its edge. The walls were papered with bright
arabesques of flowers, interspersed with birds and butter-
flies. In one corner a statuette of Flora looked down upon
a geranium covered with a profusion of rich blossoms. In
the opposite corner, ivy was trained to form a dark back-
ground for Canova's " Dancer in Repose," over whose arm
was thrown a wreath of interwoven vines and orange-
blossoms. On brackets and tables were a variety of natural flowers in vases of Sevres china, whereon the best
artists of France had painted flowers in all manner of
graceful combinations. The ottomans were embroidered
with flowers. Rosabella's white muslin dress was trailed
all over with delicately tinted roses, and the lace around
the corsage was fastened in front with a mosaic basket of
flowers. Floracita's black curls fell over her shoulders
mixed with crimson fuchsias, and on each of her little slippers was embroidered a bouquet.

" This is the Temple of Flora," said Alfred, turning to

his host. "Flowers everywhere! Natural flowers, artificial flowers, painted flowers, embroidered flowers, and human flowers excelling them all," — glancing at the young
ladies as he spoke.

Mr. Royal sighed, and in an absent sort of way answered, "Yes, yes." Then, starting up, he said abruptly,
"Excuse me a moment; I wish to give the servants some
directions."

Floracita, who was cutting leaves from the geranium,
observed his quick movement, and, as he left the room,
she turned toward their visitor and said, in a childlike,
confidential sort of way: "Our dear Mamita used to
call this room the Temple of Flora. She had a great
passion for flowers. She chose the paper, she made the
garlands for the curtains, she embroidered the ottomans,
and painted that table so prettily. Papasito likes to have
things remain as she arranged them, but sometimes they
make him sad; for the angels took Mamita away from us
two years ago."

"Even the names she gave you are flowery," said Alfred,
with an expression of mingled sympathy and admiration.

"Yes; and we had a great many flowery pet-names
beside," replied she. "My name is Flora, but when she
was very loving with me she called me her Floracita, her
little flower; and Papasito always calls me so now. Sometimes Mamita called me *Pensée Vivace.*"

"In English we call that bright little flower Jump-up-
and-kiss-me," rejoined Alfred, smiling as he looked down
upon the lively little fairy.

She returned the smile with an arch glance, that seemed
to say, "I sha' n't do it, though." And away she skipped
to meet her father, whose returning steps were heard.

"You see I spoil her," said he, as she led him into the room with a half-dancing step. "But how can I help it?"

Before there was time to respond to this question, the negress with the bright turban announced that tea was ready.

"Yes, Tulipa, we will come," said Floracita.

"Is *she* a flower too?" asked Alfred.

"Yes, she's a flower, too," answered Floracita, with a merry little laugh. "We named her so because she always wears a red and yellow turban; but we call her Tulee, for short."

While they were partaking of refreshments, she and her father were perpetually exchanging badinage, which, childish as it was, served to enliven the repast. But when she began to throw oranges for him to catch, a reproving glance from her dignified sister reminded her of the presence of company.

"Let her do as she likes, Rosa dear," said her father. "She is used to being my little plaything, and I can't spare her to be a woman yet."

"I consider it a compliment to forget that I am a stranger," said Mr. King. "For my own part, I forgot it entirely before I had been in the house ten minutes."

Rosabella thanked him with a quiet smile and a slight inclination of her head. Floracita, notwithstanding this encouragement, paused in her merriment; and Mr. Royal began to talk over reminiscences connected with Alfred's father. When they rose from table, he said, "Come here, Mignonne! We won't be afraid of the Boston gentleman, will we?" Floracita sprang to his side. He passed his arm fondly round her, and, waiting for his guest and his elder daughter to precede them, they returned to the room they had left. They had scarcely entered it, when Flora-

cita darted to the window, and, peering forth into the twilight, she looked back roguishly at her sister, and began to
sing : —

> " Un petit blanc, que j'aime,
> En ces lieux est venu.
> Oui ! oui ! c'est lui même !
> **C'est** lui ! je l'ai **vue** !
> Petit blanc ! mon bon frère !
> Ha ! ha ! petit blanc si doux ! "

The progress of her song was checked by the **entrance**
of a gentleman, who was introduced to Alfred as Mr. Fitzgerald from Savannah. His handsome person reminded
one of an Italian tenor singer, and his manner was a graceful mixture of *hauteur* and insinuating courtesy. After a
brief interchange of salutations, he said to Floracita, "I
heard some notes of a lively little French tune, that went
so trippingly I should be delighted to hear more of it."

Floracita had accidentally overheard some half-whis-
pered words which Mr. Fitzgerald had addressed to her
sister, **during his last visit, and,** thinking she had discovered
an important secret, she was disposed to use her power
mischievously. Without waiting for a repetition of his
request, she sang : —

> " Petit blanc, mon bon frère !
> Ha ! ha ! petit blanc si doux !
> Il n'y a rien sur la terre
> De si joli que vous."

While she was singing, she darted roguish glances at her
sister, whose cheeks glowed like the sun-ripened side of a
golden apricot. Her father touched her shoulder, and said
in a tone of annoyance, " Don't sing that foolish song,
Mignonne!" She turned to him quickly with a look of
surprise; for she was accustomed only to endearments from

him. In answer to her look, he added, in a gentler tone, "You know I told you I wanted my friend to see you dance. Select one of your prettiest, *ma petite*, and Rosabella will play it for you."

Mr. Fitzgerald assiduously placed the music-stool, and bent over the portfolio while Miss Royal searched for the music. A servant lighted the candelabra and drew the curtains. Alfred, glancing at Mr. Royal, saw he was watching the pair who were busy at the portfolio, and that the expression of his countenance was troubled. His eyes, however, soon had pleasanter occupation; for as soon as Rosa touched the piano, Floracita began to float round the room in a succession of graceful whirls, as if the music had taken her up and was waltzing her along. As she passed the marble Dancing Girl, she seized the wreath that was thrown over its arm, and as she went circling round, it seemed as if the tune had become a visible spirit, and that the garland was a floating accompaniment to its graceful motions. Sometimes it was held aloft by the right hand, sometimes by the left; sometimes it was a whirling semicircle behind her; and sometimes it rested on her shoulders, mingling its white orange buds and blossoms with her shower of black curls and crimson fuchsias. Now it was twined round her head in a flowery crown, and then it gracefully unwound itself, as if it were a thing alive. Ever and anon the little dancer poised herself for an instant on the point of one fairy foot, her cheeks glowing with exercise and dimpling with smiles, as she met her father's delighted gaze. Every attitude seemed spontaneous in its prettiness, as if the music had made it without her choice. At last she danced toward her father, and sank, with a wave-like motion, on the ottoman at his feet.

He patted the glossy head that nestled lovingly on his knee, and drawing a long breath, as if oppressed with happiness, he murmured, " Ah, Mignonne!"

The floating fairy vision had given such exquisite pleasure, that all had been absorbed in watching its variations. Now they looked at each other and smiled. " You would make Taglioni jealous," said Mr. Fitzgerald, addressing the little dancer; and Mr. King silently thanked her with a very expressive glance.

As Rosabella retired from the piano, she busied herself with rearranging a bouquet she had taken from one of the vases. When Mr. Fitzgerald stationed himself at her side, she lowered her eyes with a perceptibly deepening color. On her peculiar complexion a blush showed like a roseate cloud in a golden atmosphere. As Alfred gazed on the long, dark, silky fringes resting on those warmly tinted cheeks, he thought he had never seen any human creature so superbly handsome.

" Nothing but music can satisfy us after such dancing," said Mr. Fitzgerald. She looked up to him with a smile; and Alfred thought the rising of those dark eyelashes surpassed their downcast expression, as the glory of morning sunshine excels the veiled beauty of starlight.

" Shall I accompany you while you sing, ' How brightly breaks the morning'?" asked she.

" That always sings itself into my heart, whenever you raise your eyes to mine," replied he, in a low tone, as he handed her to the piano.

Together they sang that popular melody, bright and joyful as sunrise on a world of blossoms. Then came a Tyrolese song, with a double voice, sounding like echoes from the mountains. This was followed by some tender,

1 *

complaining Russian melodies, novelties which Mr. Fitzgerald had brought on a preceding visit. Feeling they were too much engrossed with each other, she said politely, "Mr. King has not yet chosen any music."

"The moon becomes visible through the curtains," replied he. "Perhaps you will **salute** her with 'Casta **Diva.**'"

"That is a favorite with us," she replied. "Either **Flora or I sing** it almost every moonlight night."

She sang it in very pure Italian. Then turning round on the music-stool she looked at her father, and said, "Now, *Papasito querido,* what shall I sing for you?"

"You **know, dear, what** I always love to hear," answered he.

With gentle touch, she drew from the keys a plaintive prelude, which soon modulated itself into "The Light of other Days." She played and sang it with so much feeling, that it seemed the **voice** of memory floating with softened sadness over the far-off waters of the past. The tune was familiar to Alfred, but it had never sung **itself** into his heart, as now. "**I felt as** I did in Italy, listening to a vesper-bell sounding from a distance in the stillness of twilight," said he, turning toward his host.

"**All** who hear Rosabella sing notice a bell in her voice," rejoined her father.

"Undoubtedly it is the voice of a belle," said Mr. Fitzgerald.

Her father, **without** appearing to notice the **common-place pun, went on** to say, "You don't know, Mr. King, what tricks she can play with her voice. I call her a musical ventriloquist. If you want to hear the bell to perfection, ask her to sing 'Toll the bell for lovely Nell.'"

"Do give me that pleasure," said Alfred, persuasively.

She sang the pathetic melody, and with voice and piano imitated to perfection the slow tolling of a silver-toned bell. After a short pause, during which she trifled with the keys, while some general remarks were passing, she turned to Mr. Fitzgerald, who was leaning on the piano, and said, "What shall I sing for *you*?" It was a simple question, but it pierced the heart of Alfred King with a strange new pain. What would he not have given for such a soft expression in those glorious eyes when she looked at *him!*

"Since you are in a ventriloqual mood," answered Mr. Fitzgerald, "I should like to hear again what you played the last time I was here, — Agatha's Moonlight Prayer, from *Der Freyschütz*."

She smiled, and with voice and instrument produced the indescribably dreamy effect of the two flutes. It was the very moonlight of sound.

"This is perfectly magical," murmured Alfred. He spoke in a low, almost reverential tone; for the spell of moonlight was on him, and the clear, soft voice of the singer, the novelty of her peculiar beauty, and the surpassing gracefulness of her motions, as she swayed gently to the music of the tones she produced, inspired him with a feeling of poetic deference. Through the partially open window came the lulling sound of a little trickling fountain in the garden, and the air was redolent of jasmine and orange-blossoms. On the pier-table was a little sleeping Cupid, from whose torch rose the fragrant incense of a nearly extinguished *pastille*. The pervasive spirit of beauty in the room, manifested in forms, colors, tones, and motions, affected the soul as perfume did the senses. The visitors felt they had stayed too long, and yet they lingered. Alfred examined the reclining Cupid, and praised the gracefulness of its outline.

"Cupid could never sleep here, nor would the flame of his torch ever go out," said Mr. Fitzgerald; "but it is time *we* were going out."

The young gentlemen exchanged parting salutations with their host and his daughters, and moved toward the door. But Mr. Fitzgerald paused on the threshold to say, "Please play us out with Mozart's 'Good Night.'"

"As organists play worshippers out of the church," added Mr. King.

Rosabella bowed compliance, and, as they crossed the outer threshold, they heard the most musical of voices singing Mozart's beautiful little melody, "Buena Notte, amato bene." The young men lingered near the piazza till the last sounds floated away, and then they walked forth in the moonlight, — Fitzgerald repeating the air in a subdued whistle.

His first exclamation was, "Is n't that girl a Rose Royal?"

"She is, indeed," replied Mr. King; "and the younger sister is also extremely fascinating."

"Yes, I thought you seemed to think so," rejoined his companion. "Which do you prefer?"

Shy of revealing his thoughts to a stranger, Mr. King replied that each of the sisters was so perfect in her way, the other would be wronged by preference.

"Yes, they are both rare gems of beauty," rejoined Fitzgerald. "If I were the Grand Bashaw, I would have them both in my harem."

The levity of the remark jarred on the feelings of his

companion, who answered, in a grave and somewhat cold tone, "I saw nothing in the manners of the young ladies to suggest such a disposition of them."

"Excuse me," said Fitzgerald, laughing. "I forgot you were from the land of Puritans. I meant no indignity to the young ladies, I assure you. But when one amuses himself with imagining the impossible, it is not worth while to be scrupulous about details. I am *not* the Grand Bashaw; and when I pronounced them fit for his harem, I merely meant a compliment to their superlative beauty. That Floracita is a mischievous little sprite. Did you ever see anything more roguish than her expression while she was singing 'Petit blanc, mon bon frère'?"

"That mercurial little song excited my curiosity," replied Alfred. "Pray what is its origin?"

"I think it likely it came from the French West Indies," said Fitzgerald. "It seems to be the love-song of a young negress, addressed to a white lover. Floracita may have learned it from her mother, who was half French, half Spanish. You doubtless observed the foreign sprinkling in their talk. They told me they never spoke English with their mother. Those who have seen her describe her as a wonderful creature, who danced like Taglioni and sang like Malibran, and was more beautiful than her daughter Rosabella. But the last part of the story is incredible. If she were half as handsome, no wonder Mr. Royal idolized her, as they say he did."

"Did he marry her in the French Islands?" inquired Alfred.

"They were not married," answered Fitzgerald. "Of course not, for she was a quadroon. But here are my lodgings, and I must bid you good night."

These careless parting words produced great disturbance in the spirit of Alfred King. He had heard of those quadroon connections, as one hears of foreign customs, without any realizing sense of their consequences. That his father's friend should be a partner in such an alliance, and that these two graceful and accomplished girls should by that circumstance be excluded from the society they would so greatly ornament, surprised and bewildered him. He recalled that tinge in Rosa's complexion, not golden, but like a faint, luminous reflection of gold, and that slight waviness in the glossy hair, which seemed to him so becoming. He could not make these peculiarities seem less beautiful to his imagination, now that he knew them as signs of her connection with a proscribed race. And that bewitching little Floracita, emerging into womanhood, with the auroral light of childhood still floating round her, she seemed like a beautiful Italian child, whose proper place was among fountains and statues and pictured forms of art. The skill of no Parisian *coiffeur* could produce a result so pleasing as the profusion of raven hair, that *would* roll itself into ringlets. Octoroons! He repeated the word to himself, but it did not disenchant him. It was merely something foreign and new to his experience, like Spanish or Italian beauty. Yet he felt painfully the false position in which they were placed by the unreasoning prejudice of society.

Though he had had a fatiguing day, when he entered his chamber he felt no inclination to sleep. As he slowly paced up and down the room, he thought to himself, " My good mother shares the prejudice. How could I introduce them to *her?* " Then, as if impatient with himself, he murmured, in a vexed tone, " Why should I *think* of introducing them to my mother? A few hours ago I did n't know of their existence."

He threw himself on the bed and tried to sleep; but memory was too busy with the scene of enchantment he had recently left. A catalpa-tree threw its shadow on the moon-lighted curtain. He began to count the wavering leaves, in hopes the monotonous occupation would induce slumber. After a while he forgot to count; and as his spirit hovered between the inner and the outer world, Floracita seemed to be dancing on the leaf shadows in manifold graceful evolutions. Then he was watching a little trickling fountain, and the falling drops were tones of "The Light of other Days." Anon he was wandering among flowers in the moonlight, and from afar some one was heard singing "Casta Diva." The memory of that voice,

> "While slept the limbs and senses all,
> Made everything seem musical."

Again and again the panorama of the preceding evening revolved through the halls of memory with every variety of fantastic change. A light laugh broke in upon the scenes of enchantment, with the words, "Of course·not, for she was a quadroon." Then the plaintive melody of "Toll the bell" resounded in his ears; not afar off, but loud and clear, as if the singer were in the room. He woke with a start, and heard the vibrations of a cathedral bell subsiding into silence. It had struck but twice, but in his spiritual ear the sounds had been modulated through many tones. "Even thus strangely," thought he, "has that rich, sonorous voice struck into the dream of my life."

Again he saw those large, lustrous eyes lowering their long-fringed veils under the ardent gaze of Gerald Fitzgerald. Again he thought of his mother, and sighed. At last a dreamless sleep stole over him, and both pleasure and pain were buried in deep oblivion.

CHAPTER II.

THE sun was up before he woke. He rose hastily
and ordered breakfast and a horse; for he had resolved the day before upon an early ride. A restless,
undefined feeling led him in the same direction he had
taken the preceding evening. He passed the house that
would forevermore be a prominent feature in the landscape of his life. Vines were gently waving in the morning air between the pillars of the piazza, where he had
lingered entranced to hear the tones of " Buena Notte."
The bright turban of Tulipa was glancing about, as she
dusted the blinds. A peacock on the balustrade, in the
sunshine, spread out his tail into a great Oriental fan, and
slowly lowered it, making a prismatic shower of topaz,
sapphires, and emeralds as it fell. It was the first of
March; but as he rode on, thinking of the dreary landscape and boisterous winds of New England at that season, the air was filled with the fragrance of flowers, and
mocking-birds and thrushes saluted him with their songs.
In many places the ground was thickly strewn with oranges,
and the orange-groves were beautiful with golden fruit and
silver flowers gleaming among the dark glossy green foliage. Here and there was the mansion of a wealthy planter, surrounded by whitewashed slave-cabins. The negroes
at their work, and their black picaninnies rolling about on
the ground, seemed an appropriate part of the landscape,
so tropical in its beauty of dark colors and luxuriant
growth.

He rode several miles, persuading himself that he was enticed solely by the healthy exercise and the novelty of the scene. But more alluring than the pleasant landscape and the fragrant air was the hope that, if he returned late, the young ladies might be on the piazza, or visible at the windows. He was destined to be disappointed. As he passed, a curtain was slowly withdrawn from one of the windows and revealed a vase of flowers. He rode slowly, in hopes of seeing a face bend over the flowers; but the person who drew the curtain remained invisible. On the piazza nothing was in motion, except the peacock strutting along, stately as a court beauty, and drawing after him his long train of jewelled plumage. A voice, joyous as a bobolink's, sounded apparently from the garden. He could not hear the words, but the lively tones at once suggested, "Petit blanc, mon bon frère." He recalled the words so carelessly uttered, "Of course not, for she was a quadroon," and they seemed to make harsh discord with the refrain of the song. He remembered the vivid flush that passed over Rosa's face while her playful sister teased her with that tuneful badinage. It seemed to him that Mr. Fitzgerald was well aware of his power, for he had not attempted to conceal his consciousness of the singer's mischievous intent. This train of thought was arrested by the inward question, "What is it to *me* whether he marries her or not?" Impatiently he touched his horse with the whip, as if he wanted to rush from the answer to his own query.

He had engaged to meet Mr. Royal at his counting-house, and he was careful to keep the appointment. He was received with parental kindness slightly tinged with embarrassment. After some conversation about business, Mr. Royal said: "From your silence concerning your visit

to my house last evening, I infer that Mr. Fitzgerald has
given you some information relating to my daughters' history. I trust, my young friend, that you have not suspected me of any intention to deceive or entrap you. I
intended to have told you myself; but I had a desire to
know first how my daughters would impress you, if judged
by their own merits. Having been forestalled in my purpose, I am afraid frankness on your part will now be difficult."

"A feeling of embarrassment did indeed prevent me
from alluding to my visit as soon as I met you this morning," replied Alfred; "but no circumstances could alter
my estimate of your daughters. Their beauty and gracefulness exceed anything I have seen."

"And they are as innocent and good as they are beautiful," rejoined the father. "But you can easily imagine
that my pride and delight in them is much disturbed by
anxiety concerning their future. Latterly, I have thought
a good deal about closing business and taking them to
France to reside. But when men get to be so old as I am,
the process of being transplanted to a foreign soil seems
onerous. If it were as well for *them*, I should greatly prefer returning to my native New England."

"They are tropical flowers," observed Alfred. "There
is nothing Northern in their natures."

"Yes, they are tropical flowers," rejoined the father,
"and my wish is to place them in perpetual sunshine. I
doubt whether they could ever feel quite at home far away
from jasmines and orange-groves. But climate is the
least of the impediments in the way of taking them to New
England. Their connection with the enslaved race is so
very slight, that it might easily be concealed; but the con-

sciousness of practising concealment is always unpleasant. Your father was more free from prejudices of all sorts than any man I ever knew. If he were living, I would confide all to him, and be guided implicitly by his advice. You resemble him so strongly, that I have been involuntarily drawn to open my heart to you, as I never thought to do to so young a man. Yet I find the fulness of my confidence checked by the fear of lowering myself in the estimation of the son of my dearest friend. But perhaps, if you knew all the circumstances, and had had my experience, you would find some extenuation of my fault. I was very unhappy when I first came to New Orleans. I was devotedly attached to a young lady, and I was rudely repelled by her proud and worldly family. I was seized with a vehement desire to prove to them that I could become richer than they were. I rushed madly into the pursuit of wealth, and I was successful; but meanwhile they had married her to another, and I found that wealth alone could not bring happiness. In vain the profits of my business doubled and quadrupled. I was unsatisfied, lonely, and sad. Commercial transactions brought me into intimate relations with Señor Gonsalez, a Spanish gentleman in St. Augustine. He had formed an alliance with a beautiful slave, whom he had bought in the French West Indies. I never saw her, for she died before my acquaintance with him; but their daughter, then a girl of sixteen, was the most charming creature I ever beheld. The irresistible attraction I felt toward her the first moment I saw her was doubtless the mere fascination of the senses; but when I came to know her more, I found her so gentle, so tender, so modest, and so true, that I loved her with a strong and deep affection. I admired her, too, for other reasons than her beauty ; for she had many elegant accomplishments, procured by her father's fond indulgence during two years' residence in Paris. He was wealthy at that time ; but he afterward became entangled in pecuniary difficulties, and his health declined. He took a liking to me, and proposed that I should purchase Eulalia, and thus enable him to cancel a debt due to a troublesome creditor whom he suspected of having an eye upon his daughter. I gave him a large sum for her, and brought her with me to New Orleans. Do not despise me for it, my young friend. If it had been told to me a few years before, in my New England home, that I could ever become a party in such a transaction, I should have rejected the idea with indignation. But my disappointed and lonely condition rendered me an easy prey to temptation, and I was where public opinion sanctioned such connections. Besides, there were kindly motives mixed up with selfish ones. I pitied the unfortunate father, and I feared his handsome daughter might fall into hands that would not protect her so carefully as I resolved to do. I knew the freedom of her choice was not interfered with, for she confessed she loved me.

"Señor Gonsalez, who was more attached to her than to anything else in the world, soon afterward gathered up the fragments of his broken fortune, and came to reside near us. I know it was a great satisfaction to his dying hours that he left Eulalia in my care, and the dear girl was entirely happy with me. If I had manumitted her, carried her abroad, and legally married her, I should have no remorse mingled with my sorrow for her loss. Loving her faithfully, as I did to the latest moment of her life, I now find it difficult to explain to myself how I came to neglect such an obvious duty. I was always thinking that I would do it at some future time. But marriage with a quadroon would have been void, according to the laws of Louisiana; and, being immersed in business, I never seemed to find time to take her abroad. When one has taken the first wrong step, it becomes dangerously easy to go on in the same path. A man's standing here is not injured by such irregular connections; and my faithful, loving Eulalia meekly accepted her situation as a portion of her inherited destiny. Mine was the fault, not hers; for I was free to do as I pleased, and she never had been. I acted in opposition to moral principles, which the education of false circumstances had given her no opportunity to form. I had, remorseful thoughts at times, but I am quite sure she was never troubled in that way. She loved and trusted me entirely. She knew that the marriage of a white man with one of her race was illegal; and she quietly accepted the fact, as human beings do accept what they are powerless to overcome. Her daughters attributed her olive complexion to a Spanish origin; and their only idea was, and is, that she was my honored wife, as indeed she was in the inmost recesses of my heart. I gradually withdrew from the few acquaintances I had formed in New Orleans; partly because I was satisfied with the company of Eulalia and our children, and partly because I could not take her with me into society. She had no acquaintances here, and we acquired the habit of living in a little world by ourselves, — a world which, as you have seen, was transformed into a sort of fairy-land by her love of beautiful things. After I lost her, it was my intention to send the children immediately to France to be educated. But procrastination is my besetting sin; and the idea of parting with them was so painful, that I have deferred and deferred it. The suffering I experience on their account is a just punishment for the wrong I did their mother. When I think how beautiful, how talented, how affectionate, and how pure they are, and in what a cruel position I have placed them, I have terrible writhings of the heart. I do not think I am destined to long life; and who will protect them when I am gone?"

A consciousness of last night's wishes and dreams made Alfred blush as he said, "It occurred to me that your eldest daughter might be betrothed to Mr. Fitzgerald."

"I hope not," quickly rejoined Mr. Royal. "He is not the sort of man with whom I would like to intrust her happiness. I think, if it were so, Rosabella would have **told me**, for my children always confide in me."

"I took it for granted that you liked him," replied Alfred; "for you said an introduction to your home was a favor you rarely bestowed."

"I never conferred it on **any** young man but yourself," answered Mr. Royal, "and you owed it partly to my memory of your honest father, and partly to the expression of your face, which so much resembles his." The young man smiled and bowed, and his friend continued: "When I invited you, I was not aware Mr. Fitzgerald was in the city. I am but slightly acquainted with him, but I conjecture him to be what is called a high-blood. His manners, though elegant, seem to me flippant and audacious. He introduced himself into my domestic sanctum; and, as I partook of his father's hospitality years ago, I **find it** difficult to eject him. He came here a few months since, to transact some business connected with the settlement of his father's estate, and, unfortunately, he heard Rosabella singing as he rode past my house. He made inquiries concerning the occupants; and, from what I have heard, I conjecture that he has learned more of my private history than I wished to have him know. He called without asking my permission, and told my girls that his father was my friend, and that he had consequently taken the liberty to call with some new music, which he was very desirous of hearing them sing. When I was informed of this, on my return home, I was exceedingly annoyed; and I have ever since been thinking of closing business as soon as possible, and taking my daughters to France. He called twice again during his stay in the city, but my daughters made it a point to see him only when I was at home. Now he has come again, to increase the difficulties of my position by his unwelcome assiduities."

"Unwelcome to *you*," rejoined Alfred; "but, handsome and fascinating as he is, they are not likely to be unwelcome to your daughters. Your purpose of conveying them to France is a wise one."

"Would I had done it sooner!" exclaimed Mr. Royal. "How weak I have been in allowing circumstances to drift me along!" He walked up and down the room with agitated steps; then, pausing before Alfred, he laid his hand affectionately on his shoulder, as he said, with solemn earnestness, "My young friend, I am glad your father did not accept my proposal to receive you into partnership. Let me advise you to live in New England. The institutions around us have an effect on character which it is difficult to escape entirely. Bad customs often lead well-meaning men into wrong paths."

"That was my father's reason for being unwilling I should reside in New Orleans," replied Alfred. "He said it was impossible to exaggerate the importance of social institutions. He often used to speak of having met a number of Turkish women when he was in the environs of Constantinople. They were wrapped up like bales of cloth, with two small openings for their eyes, mounted on camels, and escorted by the overseer of the harem. The animal sound of their chatter and giggling, as they passed him, affected him painfully; for it forced upon him the idea what different beings those women would have been if they had been brought up amid the free churches and free schools of New England. He always expounded history to me in the light of that conviction; and he mourned that temporary difficulties should prevent lawgivers from checking the growth of evils that must have a blighting influence on the souls of many generations. He considered slavery a cumulative poison in the veins of this Republic, and predicted that it would some day act all at once with deadly power."

"Your father was a wise man," replied Mr. Royal, "and I agree with him. But it would be unsafe to announce it here; for slavery is a tabooed subject, except to talk in favor of it."

"I am well aware of that," rejoined Alfred. "And now I must bid you good morning. You know my mother is an invalid, and I may find letters at the post-office that will render immediate return necessary. But I will see you again; and hereafter our acquaintance may perhaps be renewed in France."

"That is a delightful hope," rejoined the merchant, cordially returning the friendly pressure of his hand. As he looked after the young man, he thought how pleasant it would be to have such a son; and he sighed deeply over the vision of a union that might have been, under other

circumstances, between his family and that of his old
friend. Alfred, as he walked away, was conscious of that
latent, unspoken wish. Again the query began to revolve
through his mind whether the impediments were really in-
surmountable. There floated before him a vision of that
enchanting room, where the whole of life seemed to be
composed of beauty and gracefulness, music and flowers.
But a shadow of Fitzgerald fell across it, and the recollection of Boston relatives rose up like an iceberg between
him and fairy-land.

A letter informing him of his mother's increasing illness
excited a feeling of remorse that new acquaintances had
temporarily nearly driven her from his thoughts. He resolved to depart that evening; but the desire to see Rosabella again could not be suppressed. Failing to find **Mr.**
Royal at his counting-room or his hotel, he proceeded to
his suburban residence. When Tulipa informed him that
"massa" had not returned from the city, he inquired **for**
the young ladies, and was again shown into that parlor
every feature of which was so indelibly impressed upon
his memory. Portions of the music of *Cenerentola* lay
open on the piano, and the leaves fluttered softly in a gentle breeze laden with perfumes from the garden. Near by
was swinging the beaded tassel of a book-mark **between**
the pages of a half-opened volume. He looked at the
title and saw that it was Lalla Rookh. He smiled, as he
glanced **round the** room on the flowery festoons, the graceful tangle of bright arabesques on the walls, the Dancing
Girl, and the Sleeping Cupid. "All is in harmony with
Canova, and Moore, and Rossini," thought he. "The **Lady**
in Milton's Comus *has* been the ideal of my imagination;
and now here I am so strangely taken captive **by ——**"

2

Rosabella entered at that moment, and almost startled him with the contrast to his ideal. Her glowing Oriental beauty and stately grace impressed him more than ever. Floracita's fairy form and airy motions were scarcely less fascinating. Their talk was very girlish. Floracita had just been reading in a French paper about the performance of *La Bayadère*, and she longed to see the ballet brought out in Paris. Rosabella thought nothing could be quite so romantic as to float on the canals of Venice by moonlight and listen to the nightingales; and she should *so* like to cross the Bridge of Sighs! Then they went into raptures over the gracefulness of Rossini's music, and the brilliancy of Auber's. Very few and very slender thoughts were conveyed in their words, but to the young man's ear they had the charm of music; for Floracita's talk went as trippingly as a lively dance, and the sweet modulations of Rosabella's voice so softened English to Italian sound, that her words seemed floating on a liquid element, like goldfish in the water. Indeed, her whole nature seemed to partake the fluid character of music. Beauty born of harmonious sound " had passed into her face," and her motions reminded one of a water-lily undulating on its native element.

The necessity of returning immediately to Boston was Alfred's apology for a brief call. Repressed feeling imparted great earnestness to the message he left for his father's friend. While he was uttering it, the conversation he had recently had with Mr. Royal came back to him with painful distinctness. After parting compliments were exchanged, he turned to say, " Excuse me, young ladies, if, in memory of our fathers' friendship, I beg of you to command my services, as if I were a brother, should it ever be in my power to serve you."

Rosabella thanked him with a slight inclination of her graceful head; and Floracita, dimpling a quick little courtesy, said sportively, "If some cruel Blue-Beard should shut us up in his castle, we will send for you."

"How funny!" exclaimed the volatile child, as the door closed after him. "He spoke as solemn as a minister; but I suppose that's the way with Yankees. I think *cher papa* likes to preach sometimes."

Rosabella, happening to glance at the window, saw that Alfred King paused in the street and looked back. How their emotions would have deepened could they have fore-seen the future!

CHAPTER III.

A YEAR passed away, and the early Southern spring had again returned with flowers and fragrance. After a day in music and embroidery, with sundry games at Battledoor and The Graces with her sister, Floracita heard the approaching footsteps of her father, and, as usual, bounded forth to meet him. Any one who had not seen him since he parted from the son of his early New England friend would have observed that he looked older and more careworn; but his daughters, accustomed to see him daily, had not noticed the gradual change.

"You have kept us waiting a little, Papasito," said Rosabella, turning round on the music-stool, and greeting him with a smile.

"Yes, my darling," rejoined he, placing his hand fondly on her head. "Getting ready to go to Europe makes a deal of work."

"If we were sons, we could help you," said Rosabella.

"I wish you *were* sons!" answered he, with serious emphasis and a deep sigh.

Floracita nestled close to him, and, looking up archly in his face, said, "And pray what would you do, papa, without your nightingale and your fairy, as you call us?"

"Sure enough, what *should* I do, my little flower?" said he, as with a loving smile he stooped to kiss her.

They led him to the tea-table; and when the repast was ended, they began to talk over their preparations for leaving home.

" *Cher papa*, how long before we shall go to Paris?" inquired Floracita.

" In two or three weeks, I hope," was the reply.

" Won't it be delightful!" exclaimed she. " You will take us to see ballets and everything."

" When I am playing and singing fragments of operas," said Rosabella, " I often think to myself how wonderfully beautiful they would sound, if all the parts were brought out by such musicians as they have in Europe. I should greatly enjoy hearing operas in Paris; but I often think, Papasito, that we can never be so happy anywhere as we have been in this dear home. It makes me feel sad to leave all these pretty things, — so many of them ——"

She hesitated, and glanced at her father.

" So intimately associated with your dear mother, you were about to say," replied he. " That thought is often present with me, and the idea of parting with them pains me to the heart. But I do not intend they shall ever be handled by strangers. We will pack them carefully and leave them with Madame Guirlande; and when we get settled abroad, in some nice little cottage, we will send for them. But when you have been in Paris, when you have seen the world and the world has seen you, perhaps you won't be contented to live in a cottage with your old Papasito. Perhaps your heads will become so turned with flattery, that you will want to be at balls and operas all the time."

" No flattery will be so sweet as yours, *cher papa*," said Floracita.

" No indeed!" exclaimed Rosa. But, looking up, she met his eye, and blushed crimson. She was conscious of having already listened to flattery that was at least more intoxicating than his. Her father noticed the rosy confusion, and felt a renewal of pain that unexpected entanglements had prevented his going to Europe months ago. He tenderly pressed her hand, that lay upon his knee, and looked at her with troubled earnestness, as he said, " Now that you are going to make acquaintance with the world, my daughters, and without a mother to guide you, I want you to promise me that you will never believe any gentleman sincere in professions of love, unless he proposes marriage, and asks my consent."

Rosabella was obviously agitated, but she readily replied, " Do you suppose, Papasito, that we would accept a lover without asking you about it? When *Mamita querida* died, she charged us to tell you everything ; and we always do."

" I do not doubt you, my children," he replied ; " but the world is full of snares ; and sometimes they are so covered with flowers, that the inexperienced slip into them unawares. I shall try to shield you from harm, as I always have done ; but when I am gone—"

" O, don't say that!" exclaimed Floracita, with a quick, nervous movement.

And Rosabella looked at him with swimming eyes, as he repeated, " Don't say that, *Papasito querido!* "

He laid a hand on the head of each. His heart was very full. With solemn tenderness he tried to warn them of the perils of life. But there was much that he was obliged to refrain from saying, from reverence for their inexperienced purity. And had he attempted to describe the manners of a corrupt world, they could have had no realizing sense of his meaning ; for it is impossible for youth to comprehend the dangers of the road it is to travel.

The long talk at last subsided into serious silence.

After remaining very still a few moments, Rosabella said softly, " Would n't you like to hear some music before you go to bed, *Papasito mio?* "

He nodded assent, and she moved to the piano. Their conversation had produced an unusually tender and subdued state of feeling, and she sang quietly many plaintive melodies that her mother loved. The fountain trickling in the garden kept up a low liquid accompaniment, and the perfume of the orange-groves seemed like the fragrant breath of the tones.

It was late when they parted for the night. " *Bon soir, cher papa,*" said Floracita, kissing her father's hand.

" *Buenas noches, Papasito querido,*" said Rosabella, as she touched his cheek with her beautiful lips.

There was moisture in his eyes as he folded them to his heart and said, " God bless you! God protect you, my dear ones!" Those melodies of past times had brought their mother before him in all her loving trustfulness, and his soul was full of sorrow for the irreparable wrong he had done her children.

The pensive mood, that had enveloped them all in a little cloud the preceding evening, was gone in the morning. There was the usual bantering during breakfast, and after they rose from table they discussed in a lively manner various plans concerning their residence in France. Rosabella evidently felt much less pleasure in the prospect than did her younger sister; and her father, conjecturing the reason, was the more anxious to expedite their departure. " I must not linger here talking," said he. " I must go and attend to business; for there are many things to be arranged before we can set out on our travels."

" *Hasta luego, Papasito mio,*" said Rosabella, with an affectionate smile.

"*Au revoir, cher papa,*" said Floracita, as she handed him his hat.

He patted her head playfully as he said, " What a polyglot family we are! Your grandfather's Spanish, your grandmother's French, and your father's English, all mixed up in an *olla podrida.* Good morning, my darlings."

Floracita skipped out on the piazza, calling after him, " Papa, what *is* polyglot?"

He turned and shook his finger laughingly at her, as he exclaimed, " O, you little ignoramus!"

The sisters lingered on the piazza, watching him till he was out of sight. When they re-entered the house, Floracita occupied herself with various articles of her wardrobe; consulting with Rosa whether any alterations would be necessary before they were packed for France. It evidently cost Rosa some effort to attend to her innumerable questions, for the incessant chattering disturbed her revery. At every interval she glanced round the room with a sort of farewell tenderness. It was more to her than the home of a happy childhood; for nearly all the familiar objects had become associated with glances and tones, the memory of which excited restless longings in her heart. As she stood gazing on the blooming garden and the little fountain, whose sparkling rills crossed each other in the sunshine like a silvery network strung with diamonds, she exclaimed, " O Floracita, we shall never be so happy anywhere else as we have been here."

" How do you know that, *sistita mia?*" rejoined the lively little chatterer. "Only think, we have never been to a ball! And when we get to France, Papasito will go everywhere with us. He says he will."

"I should like to hear operas and see ballets in Paris," said Rosabella; "but I wish we could come back *here* before long."

Floracita's laughing eyes assumed the arch expression which rendered them peculiarly bewitching, and she began to sing, —

> "Petit blanc, mon bon frère!
> Ha! ha! petit blanc si doux!
> Il n'y a rien sur la terre
> De si joli que vous.

> "Un petit blanc que j'aime —"

A quick flush mantled her sister's face, and she put her hand over the mischievous mouth, exclaiming, "Don't, Flora! don't!"

The roguish little creature went laughing and capering out of the room, and her voice was still heard singing, —

> "Un petit blanc que j'aime."

The arrival of Signor Papanti soon summoned her to rehearse a music lesson. She glanced roguishly at her sister when she began; and as she went on, Rosa could not help smiling at her musical antics. The old teacher bore it patiently for a while, then he stopped trying to accompany her, and, shaking his finger at her, said, "*Diavolessa!*"

"Did I make a false note?" asked she, demurely.

"No, you little witch, you *can't* make a false note. But how do you suppose I can keep hold of the tail of the Air, if you send me chasing after it through so many capricious variations? Now begin again, *da capo.*"

The lesson was recommenced, but soon ran riot again. The Signor became red in the face, shut the music-book with a slam, and poured forth a volley of wrath in Italian.

When she saw that he was really angry, she apologized, and promised to do better. The third time of trying, she acquitted herself so well that her teacher praised her; and when she bade him good morning, with a comic little courtesy, he smiled good-naturedly, as he said, "*Ah, Malizietta!*"

"I knew I should make Signor Pimentero sprinkle some pepper," exclaimed she, laughing, as she saw him walk away.

"You are too fond of sobriquets," said Rosa. "If you are not careful, you will call him Signor Pimentero to his face, some day."

"What did you tell me *that* for?" asked the little rogue. "It will just make me do it. Now I am going to pester Madame's parrot."

She caught up her large straw hat, with flying ribbons, and ran to the house of their next neighbor, Madame Guirlande. She was a French lady, who had given the girls lessons in embroidery, the manufacture of artificial flowers, and other fancy-work. Before long, Floracita returned through the garden, skipping over a jumping-rope. "This is a day of compliments," said she, as she entered the parlor, "Signor Pimentero called me *Diavolessa ;* Madame Guirlande called me *Joli petit diable ;* and the parrot took it up, and screamed it after me, as I came away."

"I don't wonder at it," replied Rosa. "I think I never saw even you so full of mischief."

Her frolicsome mood remained through the day. One moment she assumed the dignified manner of Rosabella, and, stretching herself to the utmost, she stood very erect, giving sage advice. The next, she was impersonating a

negro preacher, one of Tulipa's friends.   Hearing a mocking-bird in the garden, she went to the window and taxed
his powers to the utmost, by running up and down difficult
roulades, interspersed with the talk of parrots, the shrill
fanfare of trumpets, and the deep growl of a contra-fagotto.
The bird produced a grotesque fantasia in his efforts to
imitate her.   The peacock, as he strutted up and down the
piazza, trailing his gorgeous plumage in the sunshine, ever
and anon turned his glossy neck, and held up his ear to
listen, occasionally performing his part in the *charivari* by
uttering a harsh scream.   The mirthfulness of the little
madcap was contagious, and not unfrequently the giggle of
Tulipa and the low musical laugh of Rosabella mingled
with the concert.

Thus the day passed merrily away, till the gilded Flora
that leaned against the timepiece pointed her wand toward
the hour when their father was accustomed to return.

CHAPTER IV.

FLORACITA was still in the full career of fun, when footsteps were heard approaching ; and, as usual, she bounded forth to welcome her father. Several men, bearing a palanquin on their shoulders, were slowly ascending the piazza. She gave one glance at their burden, and uttered a shrill scream. Rosabella hastened to her in great alarm. Tulipa followed, and quickly comprehending that something terrible had happened, she hurried away to summon Madame Guirlande. Rosabella, pale and trembling, gasped out, "What has happened to my father?"

Franz Blumenthal, a favorite clerk of Mr. Royal's, replied, in a low, sympathizing tone, "He was writing letters in the counting-room this afternoon, and when I went in to speak to him, I found him on the floor senseless. We called a doctor immediately, but he failed to restore him."

"O, call another doctor!" said Rosa, imploringly ; and Floracita almost shrieked, "Tell me where to *go* for a doctor."

"We have already summoned one on the way," said young Blumenthal, "but I will go to hasten him" ; — and, half blinded by his tears, he hurried into the street.

The doctor came in two minutes, and yet it seemed an age. Meanwhile the wretched girls were chafing their father's cold hands, and holding sal-volatile to his nose, while Madame Guirlande and Tulipa were preparing hot water and hot cloths. When the physician arrived, they watched his countenance anxiously, while he felt the pulse and laid his hand upon the heart. After a while he shook his head and said, " Nothing can be done. He is dead."

Rosabella fell forward, fainting, on the body. Floracita uttered shriek upon shriek, while Madame Guirlande and Tulipa vainly tried to pacify her. The doctor at last persuaded her to swallow some valerian, and Tulipa carried her in her arms and laid her on the bed. Madame Guirlande led Rosa away, and the two sisters lay beside each other, on the same pillows where they had dreamed such happy dreams the night before. Floracita, stunned by the blow that had fallen on her so suddenly, and rendered drowsy by the anodyne she had taken, soon fell into an uneasy slumber, broken by occasional starts and stifled sobs. Rosabella wept silently, but now and then a shudder passed over her, that showed how hard she was struggling with grief. After a short time, Flora woke up bewildered. A lamp was burning in the farther part of the room, and Madame Guirlande, who sat there in spectacles and ruffled cap, made a grotesque black shadow on the wall. Floracita started up, screaming, "What is that?" Madame Guirlande went to her, and she and Rosa spoke soothingly, and soon she remembered all.

"O, let me go home with *you*," she said to Madame "I am afraid to stay here."

"Yes, my children," replied the good Frenchwoman. "You had better both go home and stay with me to-night."

"I cannot go away and leave *him* alone," murmured Rosa, in tones almost inaudible.

"Franz Blumenthal is going to remain here," replied Madame Guirlande, "and Tulipa has offered to sit up all night. It is much better for you to go with me than to stay here, my children."

Thus exhorted, they rose and began to make preparations for departure. But all at once the tender good-night of the preceding evening rushed on Rosa's memory, and she sank down in a paroxysm of grief. After weeping bitterly for some minutes, she sobbed out, " O, this is worse than it was when Mamita died. Papasito was so tender with us then ; and now we are *all* alone."

" Not all alone," responded Madame. " Jesus and the Blessed Virgin are with you."

" O, I don't know where *they* are ! " exclaimed Flora, in tones of wild agony. " I want my Papasito ! I want to die and go to my Papasito."

Rosabella folded her in her arms, and they mingled their tears together, as she whispered : " Let us try to be tranquil, Sistita. We must not be troublesome to our kind friend. I did wrong to say we were all alone. We have always a Father in heaven, and he still spares us to love each other. Perhaps, too, our dear Papasito is watching over us. You know he used to tell us Mamita had become our guardian angel."

Floracita kissed her, and pressed her hand in silence. Then they made preparations to go with their friendly neighbor ; all stepping very softly, as if afraid of waking the beloved sleeper.

The sisters had lived in such extreme seclusion, that when sorrow came upon them, like the sudden swoop and swift destruction of a tropical storm, they had no earthly friend to rely upon but Madame Guirlande. Only the day before, they had been so rich in love, that, had she passed away from the earth, it would have made no distressing change in their existence. They would have said, " Poor Madame Guirlande ! She was a good soul. How patient she used to be with us!" and after a day or two, they would have danced and sung the same as ever. But one day had so beggared them in affection, that they leaned upon her as their only earthly support.

After an almost untasted breakfast, they all went back to the desolated home. The flowery parlor seemed awfully lonesome. The piano was closed, the curtains drawn, and their father's chair was placed against the wall. The murmur of the fountain sounded as solemn as a dirge, and memories filled the room like a troop of ghosts. Hand in hand, the bereaved ones went to kiss the lips that would speak to them no more in this world. They knelt long beside the bed, and poured forth their breaking hearts in prayer. They rose up soothed and strengthened, with the feeling that their dear father and mother were still near them. They found a sad consolation in weaving garlands and flowery crosses, which they laid on the coffin with tender reverence.

When the day of the funeral came, Madame Guirlande kept them very near her, holding a hand of each. She had provided them with long veils, which she requested them not to remove; for she remembered how anxiously their father had screened their beauty from the public gaze. A number of **merchants**, who had known and respected Mr. Royal, followed his remains to the grave. Most of them had heard of his quadroon connection, and some supposed that the veiled mourners might be his daughters; but such things were too common to excite remark, or to awaken much interest. The girls passed almost unnoticed; having, out of respect to the wishes of their friend, stifled their sobs till they were alone in the carriage with her and their old music-teacher.

The conviction that he was not destined to long life, which Mr. Royal had expressed to Alfred King, was founded on the opinion of physicians that his heart was diseased. This furnished an additional motive for closing his business as soon as possible, and taking his children to France. But the failure of several houses with which he was connected brought unexpected entanglements. Month by month, these became more complicated, and necessarily delayed the intended emigration. His anxiety concerning his daughters increased to an oppressive degree, and aggravated the symptoms of his disease. With his habitual desire to screen them from everything unpleasant, he unwisely concealed from them both his illness and his pecuniary difficulties. He knew he could no longer be a rich man; but he still had hope of saving enough of his fortune to live in a moderate way in some cheap district of France. But on the day when he bade his daughters good morning so cheerfully, he received a letter informing him of another extensive failure, which involved him deeply. He was alone in his counting-room when he read it; and there Franz Blumenthal found him dead, with the letter in his hand. His sudden exit of course aroused the vigilance of creditors, and their examination into the state of his affairs proved anything but satisfactory.

The sisters, unconscious of all this, were undisturbed by any anxiety concerning future support. The necessity of living without their father's love and counsel weighed heavily on their spirits; but concerning his money they took no thought. Hitherto they had lived as the birds do, and it did not occur to them that it could ever be otherwise. The garden and the flowery parlor, which their mother had created and their father had so dearly loved, seemed almost

as much a portion of themselves as their own persons. It
had been hard to think of leaving them, even for the attractions of Paris ; and now *that* dream was over, it seemed a
necessity of their existence to live on in the atmosphere of
beauty to which they had always been accustomed. But
now that the sunshine of love had vanished from it, they
felt lonely and unprotected there. They invited Madame
Guirlande to come and live with them on what terms she
chose ; and when she said there ought to be some elderly
man in the house, they at once suggested inviting their
music-teacher. Madame, aware of the confidence Mr. Royal
had always placed in him, thought it was the best arrangement that could be made, at least for the present. While
preparations were being made to effect this change, her
proceedings were suddenly arrested by tidings that the
house and furniture were to be sold at auction, to satisfy
the demands of creditors. She kept back the unwelcome
news from the girls, while she held long consultations with
Signor Papanti. He declared his opinion that Rosabella
could make a fortune by her voice, and Floracita by
dancing.

"But then they are so young," urged Madame,—"one
only sixteen, the other only fourteen."

"Youth is a disadvantage one soon outgrows," replied
the Signor. "They can't make fortunes immediately, of
course ; but they can earn a living by giving lessons. I
will try to open a way for them, and the sooner you prepare them for it the better."

Madame dreaded the task of disclosing their poverty, but
she found it less painful than she had feared. They had
no realizing sense of what it meant, and rather thought that
giving lessons would be a pleasant mode of making time

pass less heavily. Madame, who fully understood the condition of things, kept a watchful lookout for their interests.
Before an inventory was taken, she gathered up and hid
away many trifling articles which would be useful to them,
though of little or no value to the creditors. Portfolios of
music, patterns for drawings, boxes of paint and crayons,
baskets of chenille for embroidery, and a variety of other
things, were safely packed away out of sight, without the
girls' taking any notice of her proceedings.

During her father's lifetime, Floracita was so continually
whirling round in fragmentary dances, that he often told
her she rested on her feet less than a humming-bird. But
after he was gone, she remained very still from morning till
night. When Madame spoke to her of the necessity of
giving dancing-lessons, it suggested the idea of practising.
But she felt that she could not dance where she had been
accustomed to dance before *him ;* and she had not the heart
to ask Rosa to play for her. She thought she would try, in
the solitude of her chamber, how it would seem to give
dancing-lessons. But without music, and without a specta-
tor, it seemed so like the ghost of dancing that after a few
steps the poor child threw herself on the bed and sobbed.

Rosa did not open the piano for several days after the
funeral ; but one morning, feeling as if it would be a relief
to pour forth the sadness that oppressed her, she began to
play languidly. Only requiems and prayers came. Half
afraid of summoning an invisible spirit, she softly touched
the keys to " The Light of other Days." But remembering it was the very last tune she ever played to her father,
she leaned her head forward on the instrument, and wept
bitterly.

While she sat thus the door-bell rang, and she soon became conscious of steps approaching the parlor. Her heart gave a sudden leap; for her first thought was of Gerald Fitzgerald. She raised her head, wiped away her tears, and rose to receive the visitor. Three strangers entered. She bowed to them, and they, with a little look of surprise, bowed to her. "What do you wish for, gentlemen?" she asked.

"We are here concerning the settlement of Mr. Royal's estate," replied one of them. "We have been appointed to take an inventory of the furniture."

While he spoke, one of his companions was inspecting the piano, to see who was the maker, and another was examining the timepiece.

It was too painful; and Rosa, without trusting herself to speak another word, walked quietly out of the room, the gathering moisture in her eyes making it difficult for her to guide her steps.

"Is that one of the daughters we have heard spoken of?" inquired one of the gentlemen.

"I judge so," rejoined his companion. "What a royal beauty she is! Good for three thousand, I should say."

"More likely five thousand," added the third. "Such a fancy article as that don't appear in the market once in fifty years."

"Look here!" said the first speaker. "Do you see that pretty little creature crossing the garden? I reckon that 's the other daughter."

"They 'll bring high prices," continued the third speaker. "They 're the best property Royal has left. We may count them eight or ten thousand, at least. Some of our rich fanciers would jump at the chance of obtaining *one* of them for that price." As he spoke, he looked significantly at the first speaker, who refrained from expressing any opinion concerning their pecuniary value.

All unconscious of the remarks she had elicited, Rosa retired to her chamber, where she sat at the window plunged in mournful revery. She was thinking of various articles her mother had painted and embroidered, and how her father had said he could not bear the thought of their being handled by strangers. Presently Floracita came running in, saying, in a flurried way, "Who are those men down stairs, Rosa?"

"I don't know who they are," replied her sister. "They said they came to take an inventory of the furniture. I don't know what right they have to do it. I wish Madame would come."

"I will run and call her," said Floracita.

"No, you had better stay with me," replied Rosa. "I was just going to look for you when you came in."

"I ran into the parlor first, thinking you were there," rejoined Floracita. "I saw one of those men turning over Mamita's embroidered ottoman, and chalking something on it. How dear papa would have felt if he had seen it! One of them looked at me in such a strange way! I don't know what he meant; but it made me want to run away in a minute. Hark! I do believe they have come up stairs, and are in papa's room. They won't come here. will they?"

"Bolt the door!" exclaimed Rosa; and it was quickly done. They sat folded in each other's arms, very much afraid, though they knew not wherefore.

"Ah!" said Rosa, with a sigh of relief, "there is Madame coming." She leaned out of the window, and beckoned to her impatiently.

Her friend hastened her steps; and when she heard of the strangers who were in the house, she said, " You had better go home with me, and stay there till they are gone."

" What are they going to do?" inquired Floracita.

" I will tell you presently," replied Madame, as she led them noiselessly out of the house by a back way.

When they entered her own little parlor, the parrot called out, " *Joli petit diable!* " and after waiting for the old familiar response, " *Bon jour, jolie Manon!* " she began to call herself " *Jolie Manon!* " and to sing, " *Ha! ha! petit blanc, mon bon frère!* " The poor girls had no heart for play; and Madame considerately silenced the noisy bird by hanging a cloth over the cage.

" My dear children," said she, " I would gladly avoid telling you anything calculated to make you more unhappy. But you *must* know the state of things sooner or later, and it is better that a friend should tell you. Your father owed money to those men, and they are seeing what they can find to sell in order to get their pay."

" Will they sell the table and boxes Mamita painted, and the ottomans she embroidered?" inquired Rosa, anxiously.

" Will they sell the piano that papa gave to Rosa for a birthday present?" asked Flora.

" I am afraid they will," rejoined Madame.

The girls covered their faces and groaned.

" Don't be so distressed, my poor children," said their sympathizing friend. " I have been trying to save a little something for you. See here!" And she brought forth some of the hidden portfolios and boxes, saying, " These will be of great use to you, my darlings, in helping you to earn your living, and they would bring almost nothing at auction."

They thanked their careful friend for her foresight. But when she brought forward their mother's gold watch and diamond ring, Rosa said, " I would rather not keep such expensive things, dear friend. You know our dear father was the soul of honor. It would have troubled him greatly not to pay what he owed. I would rather have the ring and the watch sold to pay his debts."

" I will tell the creditors what you say," answered Madame, " and they will be brutes if they don't let you keep your mother's things. Your father owed Signor Papanti a little bill, and he says he will try to get the table and box-es, and some other things, in payment, and then you shall have them all. You will earn enough to buy another piano by and by, and you can use mine, you know; so don't be discouraged, my poor children."

" God has been very good to us to raise us up such friends as you and the Signor," replied Rosa. " You don't know how it comforts me to have you call us your chil-dren, for without you we should be all alone in the world."

CHAPTER V.

SUCH sudden reverses, such overwhelming sorrows, mature characters with wonderful rapidity. Rosa, though formed by nature and habit to cling to others, soon began to form plans for future support. Her inexperienced mind foresaw few of the difficulties involved in the career her friends had suggested. She merely expected to study and work hard; but that seemed a trifle, if she could avoid for herself and her sister the publicity which their father had so much dreaded.

Floracita, too, seemed like a tamed bird. She was sprightly as ever in her motions, and quick in her gestures; but she would sit patiently at her task of embroidery, hour after hour, without even looking up to answer the noisy challenges of the parrot. Sometimes the sisters, while they worked, sang together the hymns they had been accustomed to sing with their father on Sundays; and memory of the missing voice imparted to their tones a pathos that no mere skill could imitate.

One day, when they were thus occupied, the door-bell rang, and they heard a voice, which they thought they recognized, talking with Madame. It was Franz Blumenthal. "I have come to bring some small articles for the young ladies," said he. "A week before my best friend died, a Frenchwoman came to the store, and wished to sell some fancy-baskets. She said she was a poor widow; and Mr. Royal, who was always kind and generous, commissioned her to make two of her handsomest baskets, and embroider the names of his daughters on them. She has placed them in my hands to-day, and I have brought them myself in order to explain the circumstances."

"Are they paid for?" inquired Madame.

"I have paid for them," replied the young man, blushing deeply; "but please not to inform the young ladies of that circumstance. And, Madame, I have a favor to ask of you. Here are fifty dollars. I want you to use them for the young ladies without their knowledge; and I should like to remit to you half my wages every month for the same purpose. When Mr. Royal was closing business, he wrote several letters of recommendation for me, and addressed them to well-established merchants. I feel quite sure of getting a situation where I can earn more than I need for myself."

"*Bon garçon!*" exclaimed Madame, patting him on the shoulder. "I will borrow the fifty dollars; but I trust we shall be able to pay you before many months."

"It will wound my feelings if you ever offer to repay me." replied the young man. "My only regret is, that I cannot just now do any more for the daughters of my best friend and benefactor, who did so much for me when I was a poor, destitute boy. But would it be asking too great a favor, Madame, to be allowed to see the young ladies, and place in their hands these presents from their father?"

Madame Guirlande smiled as she thought to herself, "What is he but a boy now? He grows tall though."

When she told her *protégées* that Franz Blumenthal had a message he wished to deliver to them personally, Rosa said, "Please go and receive it, Sistita. I had rather not leave my work."

Floracita glanced at the mirror, smoothed her hair a lit-

tle, arranged her collar, and went out. The young clerk
was awaiting her appearance with a good deal of trepida-
tion. He had planned a very nice little speech to make ;
but before he had stammered out all the story about
the baskets, he saw an expression in Flora's face which
made him feel that it was indelicate to intrude upon her
emotion ; and he hurried away, scarcely hearing her
choked voice as she said, "I thank you."

Very reverently the orphans opened the box which contained the posthumous gifts of their beloved father. The
baskets were manufactured with exquisite taste. They
were lined with quilled apple-green satin. Around the
outside of one was the name of Rosabella embroidered in
flowers, and an embroidered garland of roses formed the
handle. The other bore the name of Floracita in minute
flowers, and the handle was formed of *Pensées vivaces.*
They turned them round slowly, unable to distinguish the
colors through their swimming tears.

" How like Papasito, to be so kind to the poor woman,
and so thoughtful to please us," said Rosabella. " But he
was always so."

" And he must have told her what flowers to put on the
baskets," said Floracita. " You know Mamita often called
me *Pensée vivace.* O, there never *was* such a Papasito !"

Notwithstanding the sadness that invested tokens coming
as it were from the dead, they inspired a consoling consciousness of his presence ; and their work seemed pleasanter all the day for having their little baskets by them.

The next morning witnessed a private conference between Madame and the Signor. If any one had seen them
without hearing their conversation, he would certainly have

3   **D**

thought they were rehearsing some very passionate scene in a tragedy.

The fiery Italian rushed up and down the room, plucking his hair; while the Frenchwoman ever and anon threw up her hands, exclaiming, "*Mon Dieu! Mon Dieu!*"

When the violence of their emotions had somewhat abated, Madame said, "Signor, there must be some mistake about this. It cannot be true. Mr. Royal would never have left things in such a way."

" At your request," replied the Signor, "I went to one of the creditors, to ask whether Mr. Royal's family could not be allowed to keep their mother's watch and jewels. He replied that Mr. Royal left no family; that his daughters were slaves, and, being property themselves, they could legally hold no property. I was so sure my friend Royal would not have left things in such a state, that I told him he lied, and threatened to knock him down. He out with his pistol; but when I told him I had left mine at home, he said I must settle with him some other time, unless I chose to make an apology. I told him I would do so whenever I was convinced that his statement was true. I was never more surprised than when he told me that Madame Royal was a slave. I knew she was a quadroon, and I supposed she was a *placée,* as so many of the quadroons are. But now it seems that Mr. Royal bought her of her father; and he, good, easy man, neglected to manumit her. He of course knew that by law 'the child follows the condition of the mother,' but I suppose it did not occur to him that the daughters of so rich a man as he was could ever be slaves. At all events, he neglected to have manumission papers drawn till it was too late; for his property had become so much involved that he no longer had a legal right to convey any of it away from creditors."

Madame swung back and forth in the vehemence of her agitation, exclaiming, "What *is* to be done? What *is* to be done?"

The Italian strode up and down the room, clenching his fist, and talking rapidly. "To think of that Rosabella!" exclaimed he, — "a girl that would grace any throne in Europe! To think of *her* on the auction-stand, with a crowd of low-bred rascals staring at her, and rich libertines, like that Mr. Bruteman — Pah! I can't endure to think of it. How like a satyr he looked while he was talking to me about their being slaves. It seems he got sight of them when they took an inventory of the furniture. And that handsome little witch, Floracita, whom her father loved so tenderly, to think of her being bid off to some such filthy wretch! But they sha' n't have 'em! They sha' n't have 'em! I swear I'll shoot any man that comes to take 'em." He wiped the perspiration from his forehead, and rushed round like a tiger in a cage.

"My friend," replied Madame, "they have the law on their side; and if you try to resist, you will get yourself into trouble without doing the girls any good. I'll tell you what we must do. We must disguise them, and send them to the North."

"Send them to the North!" exclaimed the Italian. "Why, they'd no more know how to get there than a couple of kittens."

"Then I must go with them," replied Madame; "and they must be got out of this house before another day; for now that we know of it, we shall be watched."

The impetuous Italian shook her hand cordially. "You

have a brave heart, Madame," said he. "I should rather march up to the cannon's mouth than tell them such news as this."

The bewildered Frenchwoman felt the same dread of the task before her; but she bravely said, "What *must* be done, *can* be done."

After some further talk with the Signor concerning ways and means, she bade him good morning, and sat still for a moment to collect her thoughts. She then proceeded to the apartment assigned to the orphans. They were occupied with a piece of embroidery she had promised to sell for them. She looked at the work, praised the exactness of the stitches and the tasteful shading of the flowers; but while she pointed out the beauties of the pattern, her hand and voice trembled.

Rosabella noticed it, and, looking up, said, "What troubles you, dear friend?"

"O, this is a world of trouble," replied Madame, "and you have had such a storm beating on your young heads, that I wonder you keep your senses."

"I don't know as we could," said Rosa, "if the good God had not given us such a friend as you."

"If any *new* trouble should come, I trust you will try to keep up brave hearts, my children," rejoined Madame.

"I don't know of any new trouble that *can* come to us now," said Rosa, "unless you should be taken from us, as our father was. It seems as if everything else had happened that *could* happen."

"O, there are worse things than having *me* die," replied Madame.

Floracita had paused with her thread half drawn through her work, and was looking earnestly at the troubled countenance of their friend. " Madame," exclaimed she, " something has happened. What is it ? "

" I will tell you," said Madame, " if you will promise not to scream or faint, and will try to keep your wits collected, so as to help me think what is best to be done."

They promised ; and, watching her countenance with an expression of wonder and anxiety, they waited to hear what she had to communicate. " **My** dear children," said she, " I have heard something that will distress you very much. Something neither you nor I ever suspected. Your mother was a slave."

" *Our* mother a slave ! " exclaimed Rosa, coloring vehemently. " *Whose* slave could she be, when she was Papasito's wife, and he loved her so ? It is impossible, Madame."

" Your father bought her when she was very young, my dear ; but I know very well **that no** wife **was** ever loved better than she was."

" But she always lived with her own father till she married papa," said **Floracita**. " How then *could* she be his slave ? "

" Her father got into trouble about money, my dear ; and he sold her."

" **Our** Grandpapa Gonsalez sold his daughter ! " exclaimed Rosa. " How incredible ! Dear friend, I wonder **you** can believe such things."

" The world is full of strange things, my child,—stranger than anything you ever **read** in story-books."

" If she was only Papasito's slave," said Flora, " I don't think Mamito **found** *that* any great hardship."

" She did not, my dear. I don't suppose she ever thought **of it** ; but a great misfortune has grown out of it."

" What is it ? " they both asked at once.

Their friend hesitated. "Remember, you have promised to be calm," said she. "I presume you don't know that, by the laws of Louisiana, 'the child follows the condition of the mother.' The consequence is, that *you* are slaves, and your father's creditors claim a right to sell you."

Rosabella turned very pale, and the hand with which she clutched a chair trembled violently. But she held her head erect, and her look and tone were very proud, as she exclaimed, "*We* become slaves! I will die rather."

Floracita, unable to comprehend this new misfortune, looked from one to the other in a bewildered way. Nature had written mirthfulness in the shape of her beautiful eyes, which now contrasted strangely with their startled and sad expression.

The kind-hearted Frenchwoman bustled about the room, moving chairs, and passing her handkerchief over boxes, while she tried hard to swallow the emotions that choked her utterance. Having conquered in the struggle, she turned toward them, and said, almost cheerfully: "There 's no need of dying, my children. Perhaps your old friend can help you out of this trouble. We must disguise ourselves as gentlemen, and start for the North this very evening."

Floracita looked at her sister, and said, hesitatingly: "Could n't you write to Mr. Fitzgerald, and ask *him* to come here? Perhaps he could help us."

Rosa's cheeks glowed, as she answered proudly: "Do you think I would *ask* him to come? I would n't do such a thing if we were as rich and happy as we were a little while ago; and certainly I would n't do it now."

"There spoke Grandpa Gonsalez!" said Madame. "How grand the old gentleman used to look, walking about so erect, with his gold-headed cane! But we must go to work in a hurry, my children. Signor Papanti has promised to send the disguises, and we must select and pack such things as it is absolutely necessary we should carry. I am sorry now that Tulee is let out in the city, for we need her help.

"She must go with **us**," said Flora. "I can't leave Tulee."

"We must do **as** we can," replied Madame. "**In this** emergency we can't do as we would. *We* are all white, and if we can get a few miles from here, we shall have no further trouble. But if we had a negro with us, it would lead to questions, perhaps. Besides, we have n't time to disguise her and instruct her how to perform her part. The Signor will be a good friend **to** her; and as soon as we can earn some money, **we** will send and buy her."

"But where can we go when we get to the North?" asked Rosa.

"I will tell **you**," said Floracita. "**Don't you** remember that Mr. King from Boston, who came to see us a year ago? His father was papa's best friend, you know; and when he went away, he told us if ever we were in trouble, to apply to him, as if he were our brother."

"Did he?" said Madame. "That lets in a gleam of light. I heard your father say he was a very good young man, and rich."

"But Papasito said, some months ago, that Mr. King had **gone to Europe with** his mother, on account of her health," replied Rosa. "Besides, if he were at home, it would be very disagreeable to go to a young gentleman as beggars and runaways, when he was introduced to us as ladies."

"You must put your pride in your pocket for the pres-

ent, Señorita Gonsalez," said Madame, playfully touching
her under the chin. "If this Mr. King is absent, I will
write to him. They say there is a man in Boston, named
William Lloyd Garrison, who takes great interest in slaves.
We will tell him our story, and ask him about Mr. King.
I did think of stopping awhile with relatives in New York.
But it would be inconvenient for them, and they might not
like it. This plan pleases me better. To Boston we will
go. The Signor has gone to ask my cousin, Mr. Duroy, to
come here and see to the house. When I have placed you
safely, I will come back slyly to my cousin's house, a few
miles from here, and with his help I will settle up my
affairs. Then I will return to you, and we will all go to
some secure place and live together. I never starved yet,
and I don't believe I ever shall."

The orphans clung to her, and kissed her hands, as they
said: "How kind you are to us, dear friend! What shall
we ever do to repay you?"

"Your father and mother were generous friends to me,"
replied Madame; "and now their children are in trouble, I
will not forsake them."

As the good lady was to leave her apartments for an
indefinite time, there was much to be done and thought of,
beside the necessary packing for the journey. The girls
tried their best to help her, but they were continually pro-
posing to carry something because it was a keepsake from
Mamita or Papasito.

"This is no time for sentiment, my children," said
Madame. "We must not take anything we can possibly
do without. Bless my soul, there goes the bell! What if
it should be one of those dreadful creditors come here to
peep and pry? Run to your room, my children, and bolt
the door."

A moment afterward, she appeared before them smiling, and said: "There was no occasion for being so frightened, but I am getting nervous with all this flurry. Come back again, dears. It is only Franz Blumenthal."

"What, come again?" asked Rosa. "Please go, Floracita, and I will come directly, as soon as I have gathered up these things that we must carry."

The young German blushed like a girl as he offered two bouquets, one of heaths and orange-buds, the other of orange-blossoms and fragrant geraniums; saying as he did so, "I have taken the liberty to bring some flowers, Miss Floracita."

"My name is Miss Royal, sir," she replied, trying to increase her stature to the utmost. It was an unusual caprice in one whose nature was so childlike and playful; but the recent knowledge that she was a slave had made her, for the first time, jealous of her dignity. She took it into her head that he knew the humiliating fact, and presumed upon it.

But the good lad was as yet unconscious of this new trouble, and the unexpected rebuke greatly surprised him. Though her slight figure and juvenile face made her attempt at majesty somewhat comic, it was quite sufficient to intimidate the bashful youth; and he answered, very meekly: "Pardon me, Miss Royal. Floracita is such a very pretty name, and I have always liked it so much, that I spoke it before I thought."

The compliment disarmed her at once; and with one of her winning smiles, and a quick little courtesy, she said: "Do you think it's a pretty name? You *may* call me Floracita, if you like it so much."

"I think it is the prettiest name in the world," replied

3 *

he. "I used to like to hear your mother say it. She said everything so sweetly! Do you remember she used to call me Florimond when I was a little boy, because, she said, my face was so florid? Now I always write my name Franz Florimond Blumenthal, in memory of her."

"I will always call you Florimond, just as Mamita did," said she.

Their very juvenile *tête-à-tête* was interrupted by the entrance of Madame with Rosa, who thanked him graciously for her portion of the flowers, and told him her father was so much attached to him that she should always think of him as a brother.

He blushed crimson as he thanked her, and went away with a very warm feeling at his heart, thinking Floracita a prettier name than ever, and happily unconscious that he was parting from her.

He had not been gone long when the bell rang again, and the girls again hastened to hide themselves. Half an hour elapsed without their seeing or hearing anything of Madame; and they began to be extremely anxious lest something unpleasant was detaining her. But she came at last, and said, "My children, the Signor wants to speak to you."

They immediately descended to the sitting-room, where they found the Signor looking down and slowly striking the ivory head of his cane against his chin, as he was wont to do when buried in profound thought. He rose as they entered, and Rosa said, with one of her sweetest smiles, "What is it you wish, dear friend?" He dropped a thin cloak from his shoulders and removed his hat, which brought away a grizzled wig with it, and Mr. Fitzgerald stood smiling before them.

The glad surprise excited by this sudden realization of a latent hope put maidenly reserve to flight, and Rosa dropped on her knees before him, exclaiming, "O Gerald, save us!"

He raised her tenderly, and, imprinting a kiss on her forehead, said: "Save you, my precious Rose? To be sure I will. That's what I came for."

"And me too," said Flora, clinging to him, and hiding her face under his arm.

"Yes, and you too, mischievous fairy," replied he, giving her a less ceremonious kiss than he had bestowed on her sister. "But we must talk fast, for there is a great deal to be done in a short time. I was unfortunately absent from home, and did not receive the letter informing me of your good father's death so soon as I should otherwise have done. I arrived in the city this morning, but have been too busy making arrangements for your escape to come here any earlier. The Signor and I have done the work of six during the last few hours. The creditors are not aware of my acquaintance with you, and I have assumed this disguise to prevent them from discovering it. The Signor has had a talk with Tulee, and told her to keep very quiet, and not tell any mortal that she ever saw me at your father's house. A passage for you and Madame is engaged on board a vessel bound to Nassau, which will sail at midnight. Soon after I leave this house, Madame's cousin, Mr. Duroy, will come with two boys. You and Madame will assume their dresses, and they will put on some clothes the Signor has already sent, in such boxes as Madame is accustomed to receive, full of materials for her flowers. All, excepting ourselves, will suppose you have gone North, according to the original plan, in order that

they may swear to that effect if they are brought to trial.
When I go by the front of the house whistling *Ça ira*,
you will pass through the garden to the street in the rear,
where you will find my servant with a carriage, which will
convey you three miles, to the house of one of my friends.
I will come there in season to accompany you on board the
ship."

"O, how thoughtful and how kind you are!" exclaimed
Rosa. "But can't we contrive some way to take poor
Tulee with us?"

"It would be imprudent," he replied. "The creditors
must be allowed to sell her. She knows it, but she has
my assurance that I will take good care of her. No harm
shall come to Tulee, I promise you. I cannot go with you
to Nassau; because, if I do, the creditors may suspect my
participation in the plot. I shall stay in New Orleans a
week or ten days, then return to Savannah, and take an
early opportunity to sail for Nassau, by the way of New
York. Meanwhile, I will try to manage matters so that
Madame can safely return to her house. Then we will
decide where to make a happy home for ourselves."

The color forsook Rosa's cheeks, and her whole frame
quivered, as she said, "I thank you, Gerald, for all this
thoughtful care; but I cannot go to Nassau, — indeed I
cannot!"

"Cannot go!" exclaimed he. "Where *will* you go, then?"

"Before you came, Madame had made ready to take us
to Boston, you know. We will go there with her."

"Rosa, do you distrust me?" said he reproachfully.
"Do you doubt my love?"

"I do not distrust you," she replied; but" — she
looked down, and blushed deeply as she added — "but I

promised my father that I would never leave home with any gentleman unless I was married to him."

"But, Rosa dear, your father did not foresee such a state of things as this. Everything is arranged, and there is no time to lose. If you knew all that I know, you would see the necessity of leaving this city before to-morrow."

"I cannot go with you," she repeated in tones of the deepest distress, — "I *cannot* go with you, for I promised my dear father the night before he died."

He looked at her for an instant, and then, drawing her close to him, he said : " It shall be just as you wish, darling. I will bring a clergyman to the house of my friend, and we will be married before you sail."

Rosa, without venturing to look up, said, **in a** faltering tone: " I cannot bear to bring degradation upon you, Gerald. It seems wrong to take advantage of your generous forgetfulness of yourself. When you first told me you loved me, you did not know I was an octoroon, and a — slave."

"I knew your mother was a quadroon," he replied ; "and as for the rest, no circumstance can degrade *you*, my Rose Royal."

"But if your plan should not succeed, how ashamed you would feel to have us seized!" said she.

"**It** *will* succeed, dearest. But even if it should not, you shall never be the property of any man but myself."

"*Property !*" she exclaimed in the proud Gonsalez tone, striving to withdraw herself from his embrace.

He hastened to say : " Forgive me, Rosabella. I am so intoxicated with happiness that I cannot be careful of my words. I merely meant to express the joyful feeling that you would be surely mine, wholly mine."

While they were talking thus, Floracita had glided out of the room to carry the tidings to Madame. The pressure of misfortune had been so heavy upon her, that, now it was lifted a little, her elastic spirit rebounded with a sudden spring, and she felt happier than she had ever thought of being since her father died. In the lightness of her heart she began to sing, " *Petit blanc, mon bon frère!* " but she stopped at the first line, for she recollected how her father had checked her in the midst of that frisky little song ; and now that she knew they were octoroons, she partly comprehended why it had been disagreeable to him. But the gayety that died out of her voice passed into her steps. She went hopping and jumping up to Madame, exclaiming : " What do you think is going to happen now ? Rosabella is going to be married right off. What a pity she can't be dressed like a bride ! She would look so handsome in white satin and pearls, and a great lace veil ! But here are the flowers Florimond brought so opportunely. I will put the orange-buds in her hair, and she shall have a bouquet in her hand."

" She will look handsome in anything," rejoined Madame. " But tell me about it, little one."

After receiving Flora's answers to a few brief questions, she stationed herself within sight of the outer door, that she might ask Fitzgerald for more minute directions concerning what they were to do. He very soon made his appearance, again disguised as the Signor.

After a hurried consultation, Madame said : " I do hope nothing will happen to prevent our getting off safely. Rosabella has so much Spanish pride, I verily believe she would stab herself rather than go on the auction-stand."

" Heavens and earth! don't speak of that ! " exclaimed

he, impetuously. "Do you suppose I would allow my beautiful rose to be trampled by swine. If we fail, I will buy them if it costs half my fortune. But we shall *not* fail. Don't let the girls go out of the door till you hear the signal."

"No danger of that," she replied. "Their father always kept them like wax flowers under a glass cover. They are as timid as hares." Before she finished the words, he was gone.

Rosabella remained where he had left her, with her head bowed on the table. Floracita was nestling by her side, pouring forth her girlish congratulations. Madame came in, saying, in her cheerly way: "So you are going to be married to night! Bless my soul, how the world whirls round!"

"Is n't God *very* good to us?" asked Rosa, looking up. "How noble and kind Mr. Fitzgerald is, to wish to marry me now that everything is so changed!"

"*You* are not changed, darling," she replied; "except that I think you are a little better, and that seemed unnecessary. But you must be thinking, my children, whether everything is in readiness."

"He told us we were not to go till evening, and it is n't dark yet," said Floracita. "Could n't we go into Papasito's garden one little minute, and take one sip from the fountain, and just one little walk round the orange-grove?"

"It would n't be safe, my dear. There 's no telling who may be lurking about. Mr. Fitzgerald charged me not to let you go out of doors. But you can go to my chamber, and take a last look of the house and garden."

They went up stairs, and stood, with their arms around

each other, gazing at their once happy home. "How many times we have walked in that little grove, hand in hand with Mamita and Papasito! and now they are both gone," sighed Rosa.

"Ah, yes," said Flora; "and now we are afraid to go there for a minute. How strangely everything has changed! We don't hear Mamita's Spanish and papa's English any more. We have nobody to talk *olla podrida* to now. It's all French with Madame, and all Italian with the Signor."

"But what kind souls they are, to do so much for us!" responded Rosa. "If such good friends had n't been raised up for us in these dreadful days, what *should* we have done?"

Here Madame came hurrying in to say, "Mr. Duroy and the boys have come. We must change dresses before the whistler goes by."

The disguises were quickly assumed; and the metamorphosis made Rosa both blush and smile, while her volatile sister laughed outright. But she checked herself immediately, saying: "I am a wicked little wretch to laugh, for you and your friends may get into trouble by doing all this for us. What shall you tell them about us when you get back from Nassau?"

"I don't intend to tell them much of anything," replied Madame. "I may, perhaps, give them a hint that one of your father's old friends invited you to come to the North, and that I did not consider it my business to hinder you."

"O fie. Madame!" said Floricita; "what a talent you have for arranging the truth with variations!"

Madame tried to return a small volley of French pleasantry; but the effort was obviously a forced one. The pulses of her heart were throbbing with anxiety and fear;

and they all began to feel suspense increasing to agony, when at last the whistled tones of *Ça ira* were heard.

"Now don't act as if you were afraid," whispered Madame, as she put her hand on the latch of the door. "Go out naturally. Remember I am my cousin, and you are the boys."

They passed through the garden into the street, feeling as if some rough hand might at any instant seize them. But all was still, save the sound of voices in the distance. When they came in sight of the carriage, the driver began to hum carelessly to himself, "Who goes there? Stranger, quickly tell!"

"A friend. Good night," — sang the disguised Madame, in the same well-known tune of challenge and reply. The carriage door was instantly opened, they entered, and the horses started at a brisk pace. At the house where the driver stopped, they were received as expected guests. Their disguises were quickly exchanged for dresses from their carpet-bags, which had been conveyed out in Madame's boxes, and smuggled into the carriage by their invisible protector. Flora, who was intent upon having things seem a little like a wedding, made a garland of orange-buds for her sister's hair, and threw over her braids a white gauze scarf. The marriage ceremony was performed at half past ten; and at midnight Madame was alone with her *protégées* in the cabin of the ship Victoria, dashing through the dark waves under a star-bright sky.

E

CHAPTER VI.

MR. FITZGERALD lingered on the wharf till the vessel containing his treasure was no longer visible. Then he returned to the carriage, and was driven to his hotel. Notwithstanding a day of very unusual excitement and fatigue, when he retired to rest he felt no inclination to sleep. Rosabella floated before him as he had first seen her, a radiant vision of beauty surrounded by flowers. He recalled the shy pride and maidenly modesty with which she had met his ardent glances and impassioned words. He thought of the meek and saddened expression of her face, as he had seen it in these last hurried interviews, and it seemed to him she had never appeared so lovely. He remembered with a shudder what Madame Guirlande had said about the auction-stand. He was familiar with such scenes, for he had seen women offered for sale, and had himself bid for them in competition with rude, indecent crowds. It was revolting to his soul to associate the image of Rosa with such base surroundings; but it seemed as if some fiend persisted in holding the painful picture before him. He seemed to see her graceful figure gazed at by a brutal crowd, while the auctioneer assured them that she was warranted to be an entirely new and perfectly sound article, — a moss rosebud from a private royal garden, — a diamond fit for a king's crown. And men, whose upturned faces were like greedy satyrs, were calling upon her to open her ruby lips and show her pearls. He turned restlessly on his pillow with a muttered oath. Then he smiled as he thought to himself that, by saving her from such degradation, he had acquired complete control of her destiny. From the first moment he heard of her reverses, he had felt that her misfortunes were his triumph. Madly in love as he had been for more than a year, his own pride, and still more the dreaded scorn of proud relatives, had prevented him from offering marriage; while the watchful guardianship of her father, and her dutiful respect to his wishes, rendered any less honorable alliance hopeless. But now he was her sole protector; and though he had satisfied her scruples by marriage, he could hide her away and keep his own secret; while she, in the fulness of her grateful love, would doubtless be satisfied with any arrangement he chose to make. But there still remained some difficulties in his way. He was unwilling to leave his own luxurious home and exile himself in the British West Indies; and if he should bring the girls to Georgia, he foresaw that disastrous consequences might ensue, if his participation in their elopement should ever be discovered, or even suspected. " It would have been far more convenient to have bought them outright, even at a high price," thought he; "but after the Signor repeated to me that disgusting talk of Bruteman's, there could be no mistake that he had *his* eye fixed upon them; and it would have been ruinous to enter into competition with such a wealthy *roué* as he is. He values money no more than pebble-stones, when he is in pursuit of such game. But though I have removed them from his grasp for the present, I can feel no security if I bring them back to this country. I must obtain a legal ownership of them; but how shall I manage it?" Revolving many plans in his mind, he at last fell asleep.

His first waking thought was to attend a meeting of the

creditors at noon, and hear what they had to say. He found ten or twelve persons present, some of gentlemanly appearance, others hard-looking characters. Among them, and in singular contrast with their world-stamped faces, was the ingenuous countenance of Florimond Blumenthal. Three hundred dollars of his salary were due to him, and he hoped to secure some portion of the debt for the benefit of the orphans. A few individuals, who knew Mr. Fitzgerald, said, " What, are you among the creditors ? "

"I am not a creditor," he replied, " but I am here to represent the claims of Mr. Whitwell of Savannah, who, being unable to be present in person, requested me to lay his accounts before you."

He sat listening to the tedious details of Mr. Royal's liabilities, and the appraisement of his property, with an expression of listless indifference ; often moving his fingers to a tune, or making the motion of whistling, without the rudeness of emitting a sound.

Young Blumenthal, on the contrary, manifested the absorbed attention of one who loved his benefactor, and was familiar with the details of his affairs. No notice was taken of him, however, for his claim was small, and he was too young to be a power in the commercial world. He modestly refrained from making any remarks ; and having given in his account, he rose to take his hat, when his attention was arrested by hearing Mr. Bruteman say : " We have not yet mentioned the most valuable property Mr. Royal left. I allude to his daughters."

Blumenthal sank into his chair again, and every vestige of color left his usually blooming countenance ; but though Fitzgerald was on tenter-hooks to know whether the escape was discovered, he betrayed no sign of interest.

Mr. Bruteman went on to say, "We appraised them at six thousand dollars."

"Much less than they would bring at auction," observed Mr. Chandler, "as you would all agree, gentlemen, if you had seen them; for they are fancy articles, A No. 1."

"Is it certain the young ladies are slaves?" inquired Blumenthal, with a degree of agitation that attracted attention toward him.

"It *is* certain," replied Mr. Bruteman. "Their mother was a slave, and was never manumitted."

"Could n't a subscription be raised, or an appeal be made to some court in their behalf?" asked the young man, with constrained calmness in his tones, while the expression of his face betrayed his inward suffering. "They are elegant, accomplished young ladies, and their good father brought them up with the greatest indulgence."

"Perhaps you are in love with one or both of them," rejoined Mr. Bruteman. "If so, you must buy them at auction, if you can. The law is inexorable. It requires that all the property of an insolvent debtor should be disposed of at public sale."

"I am very slightly acquainted with the young ladies," said the agitated youth; "but their father was my benefactor when I was a poor destitute orphan, and I would sacrifice my life to save *his* orphans from such a dreadful calamity. I know little about the requirements of the law, gentlemen, but I implore you to tell me if there is n't *some* way to prevent this. If it can be done by money, I will serve any gentleman gratuitously any number of years he requires, if he will advance the necessary sum."

"We are not here to talk sentiment, my lad," rejoined Mr. Bruteman. "We are here to transact business."

"I respect this youth for the feeling he has manifested toward his benefactor's children," said a gentleman named Ammidon. "If we *could* enter into some mutual agreement to relinquish this portion of the property, I for one should be extremely glad. I should be willing to lose much more than my share, for the sake of bringing about such an arrangement. And, really, the sale of such girls as these are said to be is not very creditable to the country. If any **foreign** travellers happen **to be** looking on, they will make great capital out of such a story. At all events, the Abolitionists will be sure to get it into their papers, and all Europe will be ringing changes upon it."

"Let 'em ring!" fiercely exclaimed Mr. Chandler. "I don't care a damn about the Abolitionists, nor Europe neither. I reckon we can manage our own affairs in this free country."

"I should judge by your remarks that you were an Abolitionist yourself, Mr. Ammidon," said Mr. Bruteman. "I am surprised to hear a Southerner speak as if the opinions of rascally abolition-amalgamationists were of the slightest consequence. I consider such sentiments unworthy any Southern *gentleman*, sir."

Mr. Ammidon flushed, and answered quickly, "I allow no man to call in question my being a gentleman, sir."

"If you consider yourself insulted, you know your remedy," rejoined Mr. Bruteman. "I give you your choice of place and weapons."

Mr. Fitzgerald consulted his watch, and two or three others followed his example.

"I see," said Mr. Ammidon, "that gentlemen are desirous to adjourn."

"It is time that we did so," rejoined Mr. Bruteman.

"Officers have been sent for these slaves of Mr. Royal, and they are probably now lodged in jail. At our next meeting we will decide upon the time of sale."

Young Blumenthal rose and attempted to go out; but a blindness came over him, and he staggered against the wall.

"I reckon that youngster's an Abolitionist," muttered Mr. Chandler. "At any rate, he seems to think there's a difference in niggers, — and all such ought to have notice to quit."

Mr. Ammidon called for water, with which he sprinkled the young man's face, and two or three others assisted to help him into a carriage.

Another meeting was held the next day, which Mr. Fitzgerald did not attend, foreseeing that it would be a stormy one. The result of it was shown in the arrest and imprisonment of Signor Papanti, and a vigilant search for Madame Guirlande. Her cousin, Mr. Duroy, declared that he had been requested to take care of her apartments for a few weeks, as she was obliged to go to New York on business; that she took her young lady boarders with her, and that was all he knew. Despatches were sent in hot haste to the New York and Boston police, describing the fugitives, declaring them to be thieves, and demanding that they should be sent forthwith to New Orleans for trial. The policeman who had been employed to watch Madame's house, and who had been induced to turn his back for a while by some mysterious process best known to Mr. Fitzgerald, was severely cross-examined and liberally pelted with oaths. In the course of the investigations, it came out that Florimond Blumenthal had visited the house on the day of the elopement, and that toward dusk he had been seen lingering about the premises, watching the windows. The story got abroad that he had been an accomplice in helping off two valuable slaves. The consequence was that he received a written intimation that, if he valued his neck, he had better quit New Orleans within twenty-four hours, signed Judge Lynch.

Mr. Fitzgerald appeared to take no share in the excitement. When he met any of the creditors, he would sometimes ask, carelessly, " Any news yet about those slaves of Royal's?" He took occasion to remark to two or three of them, that, Signor Papanti being an old friend of his, he had been to the prison to see him; that he was convinced he had no idea where those girls had gone; he was only their music-teacher, and such an impetuous, peppery man, that they never would have thought of trusting him with any important secret. Having thus paved the way, he came out with a distinct proposition at the next meeting. " I feel a great deal of sympathy for Signor Papanti," said he. " I have been acquainted with him a good while, and have taken lessons of him, both in music and Italian; and I like the old gentleman. He is getting ill in prison, and he can never tell you any more than he has told you. Doubtless he knew that Madame intended to convey those girls to the North if she possibly could; but I confess I should have despised him if he had turned informer against the daughters of his friend, who had been his own favorite pupils. If you will gratify me by releasing him, I will make you an offer for those girls, and take my chance of ever finding them."

" What sum do you propose to offer?" inquired the creditors.

" I will pay one thousand dollars if you accede to my terms."

" Say two thousand, and we will take the subject under consideration," they replied.

" In that case I must increase my demands," said he. " I have reason to suspect that my friend the Signor would like to make a match with Madame Guirlande. If you will allow her to come back to her business and remain undisturbed, and will make me a sale of these girls, I don't care if I do say two thousand."

" He has told you where they are!" exclaimed Mr. Bruteman, abruptly; " and let me tell you, if you know where they are, you are not acting the part of a gentleman."

" He has not told me, I assure you, nor has he given me the slightest intimation. It is my firm belief that he does not know. But I am rather fond of gambling, and this is such a desperate throw, that it will be all the more exciting. I never tried my luck at buying slaves running, and I have rather a fancy for experimenting in that game of chance. And I confess my curiosity has been so excited by the wonderful accounts I have heard of those nonpareil girls, that I should find the pursuit of them a stimulating occupation. If I should not succeed, I should at least have the satisfaction of having done a good turn to my old Italian friend."

They asked more time to reflect upon it, and to hear from New York and Boston. With inward maledictions on their slowness, he departed, resolving in his own mind that nothing should keep him much longer from Nassau, come what would.

As he went out, Mr. Chandler remarked: " It 's very much like him. He 's always ready to gamble in anything."

4

"After all, I have my suspicion that he's got a clew to the mystery somehow, and that he expects to find those handsome wenches," said Mr. Bruteman. "I'd give a good deal to baffle him."

"It seems pretty certain that *we* cannot obtain any clew," rejoined Mr. Ammidon, "and we have already expended considerable in the effort. If he can be induced to offer two thousand five hundred, I think we had better accept it."

After a week's absence in Savannah and its vicinity, making various arrangements for the reception of the sisters, Mr. Fitzgerald returned to New Orleans, and took an early opportunity to inform the creditors that he should remain a very short time. He made no allusion to his proposed bargain, and when they alluded to it he affected great indifference.

"I should be willing to give you five hundred dollars to release my musical friend," said he. "But as for those daughters of Mr. Royal, it seems to me, upon reflection, to be rather a quixotic undertaking to go in pursuit of them. You know it's a difficult job to catch a slave after he gets to the North, if he's as black as the ace of spades; and all Yankeedom would be up in arms at any attempt to seize such white ladies. Of course, I could obtain them in no other way than by courting them and gaining their good-will."

Mr. Bruteman and Mr. Chandler made some remarks unfit for repetition, but which were greeted with shouts of laughter. After much dodging and doubling on the financial question, Fitzgerald agreed to pay two thousand five hundred dollars, if all his demands were complied with. The papers were drawn and signed with all due formality. He clasped them in his pocket-book, and walked off with an elastic step, saying, "Now for Nassau!"

CHAPTER VII.

THE scenery of the South was in the full glory of June, when Mr. Fitzgerald, Rosa, and Floracita were floating up the Savannah River in a boat manned by negroes, who ever and anon waked the stillness of the woods with snatches of wild melody. They landed on a sequestered island which ocean and river held in their arms. Leaving the servants to take care of the luggage, they strolled along over a carpet of wild-flowers, through winding bridle-paths, where glances of bright water here and there gleamed through the dark pines that were singing their sleepy chorus, with its lulling sound of the sea, and filling the air with their aromatic breath. Before long, they saw a gay-colored turban moving among the green foliage, and the sisters at once exclaimed, "Tulipa!"

"Dear Gerald, you did n't tell us Tulee was here," said Rosa.

"I wanted to give you a pleasant surprise," he replied.

She thanked him with a glance more expressive than words. Tulipa, meanwhile, was waving a white towel with joyful energy, and when she came up to them, she half smothered them with hugs and kisses, exclaiming: "The Lord bless ye, Missy Rosy! The Lord bless ye, Missy Flory! It does Tulee's eyes good to see ye agin." She eagerly led the way through flowering thickets to a small lawn, in the midst of which was a pretty white cottage.

It was evident at a glance that she, as well as the master of the establishment, had done her utmost to make the in-

terior of the dwelling resemble their old home as much as
possible. Rosa's piano was there, and on it were a number
of books which their father had given them. As Floracita
pointed to the ottomans their mother had embroidered, and
the boxes and table she had painted, she said : "Our good
friend the Signor sent those. He promised to buy them."

"He could not buy them, poor man!" answered Fitzgerald, "for he was in prison at the time of the auction;
but he did not forget to enjoin it upon me to buy them."

A pleasant hour was spent in joyful surprises over
pretty novelties and cherished souvenirs. Rosa was full
of quiet happiness, and Floracita expressed her satisfaction
in lively little gambols. The sun was going down when
they refreshed themselves with the repast Tulipa had provided. Unwilling to invite the merciless mosquitoes, they
sat, while the gloaming settled into darkness, playing and
singing melodies associated with other times.

Floracita felt sorry when the hour of separation for the
night came. Everything seemed so fearfully still, except
the monotonous wash of the waves on the sea-shore! And
as far as she could see the landscape by the light of a bright
little moon-sickle, there was nothing but a thick screen of
trees and shrubbery. She groped her way to her sleeping-
apartment, expecting to find Tulee there. She had been
there, and had left a little glimmering taper behind a screen,
which threw a fantastic shadow on the ceiling, like a face
with a monstrous nose. It affected the excitable child like
some kind of supernatural presence. She crept to the
window, and through the veil of the mosquito-bar she
dimly saw the same thick wall of greenery. Presently
she espied a strange-looking long face peering out from its
recesses. On their voyage home from Nassau, Gerald had

sometimes read aloud to them from "The Midsummer
Night's Dream." Could it be that there were such crea-
tures in the woods as Shakespeare described? A closet
adjoining her room had been assigned to Tulee. She
opened the door and said, "Tulee, are you there? Why
don't you come?" There was no answer. Again she gave
a timid look at the window. The long face moved, and
a most unearthly sound was heard. Thoroughly frightened, she ran out, calling, "Tulee! Tulee!" In the darkness, she ran against her faithful attendant, and the sudden
contact terrified her still more.

"It's only Tulee. What is the matter with my little
one?" said the negress. As she spoke, the fearful sound
was heard again.

"O Tulee, what is that?" she exclaimed, all of a
tremble.

"That is only Jack," she replied.

"Who's Jack?" quickly asked the nervous little
maiden.

"Why, the jackass, my puppet," answered Tulee.
"Massa Gerald bought him for you and Missy Rosy to
ride. In hot weather there's so many snakes about in
the woods, he don't want ye to walk."

"What does he make that horrid noise for?" asked
Flora, somewhat pacified.

"Because he was born with music in him, like the rest
of ye," answered Tulee, laughing.

She assisted her darling to undress, arranged her pillows,
and kissed her cheek just as she had kissed it ever since
the rosy little mouth had learned to speak her name. Then
she sat by the bedside talking over things that had happened since they parted.

"So you were put up at auction and sold !" exclaimed
Flora. "Poor Tulee! how dreadfully I should have felt
to see you there ! But Gerald bought you ; and I suppose
you like to belong to *him*."

"Ise nothin' to complain of Massa Gerald," she answered ; "but I'd like better to belong to myself."

"So you'd like to be free, would you ?" asked Flora.

"To be sure I would," said Tulee. "Ye like it yerself,
don't ye, little missy ?"

Then, suddenly recollecting what a narrow escape her
young lady had had from the auction-stand, she hastened
with intuitive delicacy to change the subject. But the
same thought had occurred to Flora ; and she fell asleep,
thinking how Tulee's wishes could be gratified.

When morning floated upward out of the arms of night,
in robe of brightest saffron, the aspect of everything was
changed. Floracita sprang out of bed early, eager to ex-
plore the surroundings of their new abode. The little
lawn looked very beautiful, sprinkled all over with a variety of wild-flowers, in whose small cups dewdrops glistened,
prismatic as opals. The shrubbery was no longer a dismal
mass of darkness, but showed all manner of shadings of
glossy green leaves, which the moisture of the night had
ornamented with shimmering edges of crystal beads. She
found the phantom of the night before browsing among
flowers behind the cottage, and very kindly disposed to
make her acquaintance. As he had a thistle blossom sticking out of his mouth, she forthwith named him Thistle.
She soon returned to the house with her apron full of vines,
and blossoms, and prettily tinted leaves. "See. Tulee," said
she, "what a many flowers ! I'm going to make haste and
dress the table, before Gerald and Rosa come to breakfast."

They took graceful shape under her nimble fingers, and, feeling happy in her work, she began to hum,

" How brightly breaks the morning ! "

" Whisper low ! " sang Gerald, stealing up behind her, and making her start by singing into her very ear ; while Rosa exclaimed, " What a fairy-land you have made here, with all these flowers, *pichoncita mia.*"

The day passed pleasantly enough, with some ambling along the bridle-paths on Thistle's back, some reading and sleeping, and a good deal of music. The next day, black Tom came with a barouche, and they took a drive round the lovely island. The cotton-fields were all abloom on Gerald's plantation, and his stuccoed villa, with spacious veranda and high porch, gleamed out in whiteness among a magnificent growth of trees, and a garden gorgeous with efflorescence. The only drawback to the pleasure was, that Gerald charged them to wear thick veils, and never to raise them when any person **was** in sight. They made no complaint, because he told them that he should be deeply involved in trouble if his participation in their escape should be discovered ; but, happy as Rosa was in reciprocated love, this necessity of concealment was a skeleton ever sitting at her feast ; and Floracita, who had no romantic compensation for it, chafed under the restraint. It was dusk when they returned to the cottage, and the thickets were alive with fire-flies, as if Queen Mab and all her train were out dancing in spangles.

A few days after was Rosa's birthday, and Floracita busied herself in adorning the rooms with flowery festoons. After breakfast, Gerald placed a small parcel in the hand of each of the sisters. Rosa's contained her mother's dia-

mond ring, and Flora's was her mother's gold watch, in
the back of which was set a small locket-miniature of her
father. Their gratitude took the form of tears, and the
pleasure-loving young man, who had more taste for gayety
than sentiment, sought to dispel it by lively music. When
he saw the smiles coming again, he bowed playfully, and
said: "This day is yours, dear Rosa. Whatsoever you
wish for, you shall have, if it is attainable."

"I do wish for one thing," she replied promptly. "Floracita has found out that Tulee would like to be free. I
want you to gratify her wish."

"Tulee is yours," rejoined he. "I bought her to attend
upon you."

"She will attend upon me all the same after she is
free," responded Rosa; "and we should all be happier."

"I will do it," he replied. "But I hope you won't
propose to make *me* free, for I am happier to be your
slave."

The papers were brought a few days after, and Tulee
felt a great deal richer, though there was no outward
change in her condition.

As the heat increased, mosquitoes in the woods and
sand-flies on the beach rendered the shelter of the house
desirable most of the time. But though Fitzgerald had
usually spent the summer months in travelling, he seemed
perfectly contented to sing and doze and trifle away his
time by Rosa's side, week after week. Floracita did not
find it entertaining to be a third person with a couple
of lovers. She had been used to being a person of consequence in her little world; and though they were very
kind to her, they often forgot that she was present, and

never seemed to miss her when she was away. She had
led a very secluded life from her earliest childhood, but she
had never before been so entirely out of sight of houses and
people. During the few weeks she had passed in Nassau,
she had learned to do shell-work with a class of young
girls; and it being the first time she had enjoyed such companionship, she found it peculiarly agreeable. She longed
to hear their small talk again; she longed to have Rosa to
herself, as in the old times; she longed for her father's caresses, for Madame Guirlande's brave cheerfulness, for the
Signor's peppery outbursts, which she found very amusing;
and sometimes she thought how pleasant it would be to
hear Florimond say that her name was the prettiest in the
world. She often took out a pressed geranium blossom,
under which was written "Souvenir de Florimond"; and
she thought *his* name was very pretty too. She sang
Moore's Melodies a great deal; and when she warbled,

> "Sweet vale of Avoca! how calm could I rest
> In thy bosom of shade, with the friend I love best!"

she sighed, and thought to herself, "Ah! if I only *had* a
friend to love best!" She almost learned "Lalla Rookh"
by heart; and she pictured herself as the Persian princess
listening to a minstrel in Oriental costume, but with a very
German face. It was not that the child was in love, but
her heart was untenanted; and as memories walked through
it, it sounded empty.

Tulee, who was very observing where her affections
were concerned, suspected that she was comparing her
own situation with that of Rosa. One day, when she
found her in dreamy revery, she patted her silky curls,
and said: "Does she feel as if she was laid by, like a fifth

4 *   F

wheel to a coach? Never mind! My little one will have a husband herself one of these days."

Without looking up, she answered, very pensively: "Do you think I ever shall, Tulee? I don't see how I can, for I never see anybody."

Tulipa took the little head between her black hands, and, raising the pretty face toward her, replied: "Yes, sure, little missy. Do ye s'pose ye had them handsome eyes for nothin' but to look at the moon? But come, now, with me, and feed Thistle. I'm going to give him a pailful of water. Thistle knows us as well as if he was a Christian."

Jack Thistle was a great resource for Tulee in her isolation, and scarcely less so for Flora. She often fed him from her hand, decorated him with garlands, talked to him, and ambled about with him in the woods and on the seashore. The visits of black Tom also introduced a little variety into their life. He went back and forth from Savannah to procure such articles as were needed at the cottage, and he always had a budget of gossip for Tulee. Tom's Chloe was an expert ironer; and as Mr. Fitzgerald was not so well pleased with Tulee's performances of that kind, baskets of clothes were often sent to Chloe, who was ingenious in finding excuses for bringing them back herself. She was a great singer of Methodist hymns and negro songs, and had wonderful religious experiences to tell. To listen to her and Tom was the greatest treat Tulee had; but as she particularly prided herself on speaking like white people, she often remarked that she could n't understand half their "lingo." Floracita soon learned it to perfection, and excited many a laugh by her imitations.

Tulee once obtained Rosa's permission to ride back with

Tom, and spend a couple of hours at his cabin near "the Grat Hus," as he called his master's villa. But when Mr. Fitzgerald heard of it, he interdicted such visits in the future. He wished to have as little communication as possible between the plantation and the lonely cottage; and if he had overheard some of the confidences between Chloe and Tulee, he probably would have been confirmed in the wisdom of such a prohibition. But Tom was a factotum that could not be dispensed with. They relied upon him for provisions, letters, and newspapers.

Three or four weeks after their arrival he brought a box containing a long letter from **Madame** Guirlande, and the various articles she had saved for the orphans from the wreck of their early home. Not long afterward another letter came, announcing the marriage of Madame and **the** Signor. Answering these letters and preparing bridal presents for their old friends gave them busy days. Gerald sometimes ordered new music **and new novels from** New York, and their arrival caused great **excitement.** Floracita's natural taste for drawing had been cultivated by private lessons from a French lady, and **she** now used the pretty accomplishment to make likenesses of Thistle with and without garlands, of Tulee in her bright turban, and of Madame Guirlande's parrot, inscribed, " *Bon jour, jolie Manon !* "

One day Rosa said : " As soon as the heat abates, so that we can use our needles without rusting, we will do a **good** deal of embroidery, and give it to Madame. She sells **such** articles, you know; and we can make beautiful **things of** those flosses and chenilles the good soul saved **for us.**"

" I like that idea," replied Flora. " I 've been wanting to do something to show our gratitude."

There was wisdom as well as kindness in the plan, though they never thought of the wisdom. Hours were whiled away by the occupation, which not only kept their needles from rusting, but also their affections and artistic faculties.

As the tide of time flowed on, varied only by these little eddies and ripples, Gerald, though always very loving with Rosa, became somewhat less exclusive. His attentions were more equally divided between the sisters. He often occupied himself with Floracita's work, and would pick out the shades of silk for her, as well as for Rosa. He more frequently called upon her to sing a solo, as well as to join in duets and trios. When the weather became cooler, it was a favorite recreation with him to lounge at his ease, while Rosa played, and Floracita's fairy figure floated through the evolutions of some graceful dance. Sometimes he would laugh, and say: "Am I not a lucky dog? I don't envy the Grand Bashaw his Circassian beauties. He 'd give his biggest diamond for such a dancer as Floracita; and what is his Flower of the World compared to my Rosamunda?"

Floracita, whose warm heart always met affection as swiftly as one drop of quicksilver runs to another, became almost as much attached to him as she was to Rosa. "How kind Gerald is to me!" she would say to Tulee. "Papa used to wish we had a brother; but I did n't care for one then, because he was just as good for a playmate. But now it *is* pleasant to have a brother."

To Rosa, also, it was gratifying to have his love for her. overflow upon what was dearest to her; and she would give him one of her sweetest smiles when he called her sister "Mignonne" or "Querida." To both of them the

lonely island came to seem like a happy home. Floracita
was not so wildly frolicsome as she was before those stun-
ning blows fell upon her young life; but the natural buoy-
ancy of her spirits began to return. She was always
amusing them with "quips and cranks." If she was out
of doors, her return to the house would be signalized by
imitations of all sorts of birds or musical instruments; and
often, when Gerald invited her to "trip it on the light, fantastic toe," she would entertain him with one of the negroes' clumsy, shuffling dances. Her sentimental songs fell
into disuse, and were replaced by livelier tunes. Instead
of longing to rest in the "sweet vale of Avoca," she was
heard musically chasing "Figaro here! Figaro there!
Figaro everywhere!"

Seven months passed without other material changes
than the changing seasons. When the flowers faded, and
the leafless cypress-trees were hung with their pretty pen-
dulous seed-vessels, Gerald began to make longer visits to
Savannah. He was, however, rarely gone more than a
week; and, though Rosa's songs grew plaintive in his absence, her spirits rose at once when he came to tell how
homesick he had been. As for Floracita, she felt compen-
sated for the increased stillness by the privilege of having
Rosa all to herself.

One day in January, when he had been gone from home
several days, she invited Rosa to a walk, and, finding her
desirous to finish a letter to Madame Guirlande, she threw
on her straw hat, and went out half dancing, as she was
wont to do. The fresh air was exhilarating, the birds were
singing, and the woods were already beautified with every
shade of glossy green, enlivened by vivid buds and leaflets
of reddish brown. She gathered here and there a pretty

sprig, sometimes placing them in her hair, sometimes in her little black silk apron, coquettishly decorated with cherry-colored ribbons. She stopped before a luxuriant wild myrtle, pulling at the branches, while she sang,

"When the little hollow drum beats to bed,
When the little fifer hangs his head,
When is mute the Moorish flute —"

Her song was suddenly interrupted by a clasp round the waist, and a warm kiss on the lips.

"O Gerald, you 've come back!" she exclaimed. "How glad Rosa will be!"

"And nobody else will be glad, I suppose?" rejoined he. "Won't you give me back my kiss, when I 've been gone a whole week?"

"Certainly, *mon bon frère*," she replied; and as he inclined his face toward her, she imprinted a slight kiss on his cheek.

"That 's not giving me back *my* kiss," said he. "I kissed your mouth, and you must kiss mine."

"I will if you wish it," she replied, suiting the action to the word. "But you need n't hold me so tight," she added, as she tried to extricate herself. Finding he did not release her, she looked up wonderingly in his face, then lowered her eyes, blushing crimson. No one had ever looked at her so before.

"Come, don't be coy, *ma petite*," said he.

She slipped from him with sudden agility, and said somewhat sharply: "Gerald, I don't want to be always called *petite;* and I don't want to be treated as if I were a child. I am no longer a child. I am fifteen. I am a young lady."

"So you are, and a very charming one," rejoined he, giving her a playful tap on the cheek as he spoke.

"I am going to tell Rosa you have come," said she; and she started on the run.

When they were all together in the cottage she tried not to seem constrained; but she succeeded so ill that Rosa would have noticed it if she had not been so absorbed in her own happiness. Gerald was all affection to her, and full of playful raillery with Flora, — which, however, failed to animate her as usual.

From that time a change came over the little maiden, and increased as the days passed on. She spent much of her time in her own room; and when Rosa inquired why she deserted them so, she excused herself by saying she wanted to do a great deal of shell-work for Madame Guirlande, and that she needed so many boxes they would be in the way in the sitting-room. Her passion for that work grew wonderfully, and might be accounted for by the fascination of perfect success; for her coronets and garlands, and bouquets and baskets were arranged with so much lightness and elegance, and the different-colored shells were so tastefully combined, that they looked less like manufactured articles than like flowers that grew in the gardens of the Nereids.

Tulee wondered why her vivacious little pet had all of a sudden become so sedentary in her habits, — why she never took her customary rambles except when Mr. Fitzgerald was gone, and even then never without her sister. The conjecture she formed was not very far amiss, for Chloe's gossip had made her better acquainted with the character of her master than were the other inmates of the cottage; but the extraordinary industry was a mystery to her. One evening, when she found Floracita alone in her room at dusk, leaning her head on her hand and gazing out of the window dreamily, she put her hand on the silky head and said, "Is my little one homesick?"

"I have no home to be sick for," she replied, sadly.

"Is she lovesick then?"

"I have no lover," she replied, in the same desponding tone.

"What is it, then, my pet? Tell Tulee."

"I wish I could go to Madame Guirlande," responded Flora. "She was so kind to us in our first troubles."

"It would do you good to make her a visit," said Tulee, "and I should think you might manage to do it somehow."

"No. Gerald said, a good while ago, that it would be dangerous for us ever to go to New Orleans."

"Does he expect to keep you here always?" asked Tulee. "He might just as well keep you in a prison, little bird."

"O, what's the use of talking, Tulee!" exclaimed she, impatiently. "I have no friends to go to, and I *must* stay here." But, reproaching herself for rejecting the sympathy so tenderly offered, she rose and kissed the black cheek as she added, "Good Tulee! kind Tulee! I *am* a little homesick; but I shall feel better in the morning."

The next afternoon Gerald and Rosa invited her to join them in a drive round the island. She declined, saying the box that was soon to be sent to Madame was not quite full, and she wanted to finish some more articles to put in it. But she felt a longing for the fresh air, and the intense blue glory of the sky made the house seem prison-like. As soon as they were gone, she took down her straw hat and passed out, swinging it by the strings. She stopped on the lawn to gather some flame-colored buds from a Pyrus Japonica, and, fastening them in the ribbons as she went, she walked toward her old familiar haunts in the woods.

It was early in February, but the warm sunshine brought out a delicious aroma from the firs, and golden garlands of the wild jasmine, fragrant as heliotrope, were winding round the evergreen thickets, and swinging in flowery festoons from the trees. Melancholy as she felt when she started from the cottage, her elastic nature was incapable of resisting the glory of the sky, the beauty of the earth, the music of the birds, and the invigorating breath of the ocean, intensified as they all were by a joyful sense of security and freedom, growing out of the constraint that had lately been put upon her movements. She tripped along faster, carolling as she went an old-fashioned song that her father used to be often humming: —

> " Begone, dull care !
> I prithee begone from me !
> Begone, dull care !
> Thou and I shall never agree ! "

The walk changed to hopping and dancing, as she warbled various snatches from ballets and operas, settling at last upon the quaint little melody, " Once on a time there was a king," and running it through successive variations.

A very gentle and refined voice, from behind a clump of evergreens, said, " Is this Cinderella coming from the ball ? "

She looked up with quick surprise, and recognized a lady she had several times seen in Nassau.

" And it is really you, Señorita Gonsalez ! " said the lady. " I thought I knew your voice. But I little dreamed of meeting you here. I have thought of you many times since I parted from you at Madame Conquilla's store of shell-work. I am delighted to see you again."

" And I am glad to see you again, Mrs. Delano," replied

Flora; "and I am very much pleased that you remember me."

"How could I help remembering you?" asked the lady. "You were a favorite with me from the first time I saw you, and I should like very much to renew our acquaintance. Where do you live, my dear?"

Covered with crimson confusion, Flora stammered out: "I don't live anywhere, I'm only staying here. Perhaps I shall meet you again in the woods or on the beach. I hope I shall."

"Excuse me," said the lady. "I have no wish to intrude upon your privacy. But if you would like to call upon me at Mr. Welby's plantation, where I shall be for three or four weeks, I shall always be glad to receive you."

"Thank you," replied Flora, still struggling with embarrassment. "I should like to come very much, but I don't have a great deal of time for visiting."

"It's not common to have such a pressure of cares and duties at your age," responded the lady, smiling. "My carriage is waiting on the beach. Trusting you will find a few minutes to spare for me, I will not say adieu, but *au revoir*."

As she turned away, she thought to herself: "What a fascinating child! What a charmingly unsophisticated way she took to tell me she would rather not have me call on her! I observed there seemed to be some mystery about her when she was in Nassau. What can it be? Nothing wrong, I hope."

Floracita descended to the beach and gazed after the carriage as long as she could see it. Her thoughts were so occupied with this unexpected interview, that she took no notice of the golden drops which the declining sun was

showering on an endless procession of pearl-crested waves;
nor did she cast one of her customary loving glances at the
western sky, where masses of violet clouds, with edges of
resplendent gold, enclosed lakes of translucent beryl, in
which little rose-colored islands were floating. She re-
traced her steps to the woods, almost crying. "How
strange my answers must appear to her!" murmured she.
"How I do wish I could go about openly, like other people! I am so tired of all this concealment!" She neither jumped, nor danced, nor sung, on her way homeward. She seemed to be revolving something in her mind
very busily.

After tea, as she and Rosa were sitting alone in the twilight, her sister, observing that she was unusually silent,
said, "What are you thinking of, Mignonne?"

"I am thinking of the time we passed in Nassau," replied she, "and of that Yankee lady who seemed to take
such a fancy to me when she came to Madame Conquilla's
to look at the shell-work.

"I remember your talking about her," rejoined Rosa.
"You thought her beautiful."

"Yes," said Floracita, "and it was a peculiar sort of
beauty. She was n't the least like you or Mamita. Everything about her was violet. Her large gray eyes sometimes had a violet light in them. Her hair was not exactly
flaxen, it looked like ashes of violets. She always wore
fragrant violets. Her ribbons and dresses were of some
shade of violet; and her breastpin was an amethyst set with
pearls. Something in her ways, too, made me think of a
violet. I think she knew it, and that was the reason she
always wore that color. How delicate she was! She must
have been very beautiful when she was young."

" You used to call her the Java sparrow," said Rosa.

" Yes, she made me think of my little Java sparrow, with pale fawn-colored feathers, and little gleams of violet on the neck," responded Flora.

" That lady seems to have made a great impression on your imagination," said Rosa; and Floracita explained that it was because she had never seen anything like her. She did not mention that she had seen that lady on the island. The open-hearted child was learning to be reticent.

A few minutes afterward, Rosa exclaimed, " There's Gerald coming!" Her sister watched her as she ran out to meet him, and sighed, " Poor Rosa!"

CHAPTER VIII.

A WEEK later, when Gerald had gone to Savannah and Rosa was taking her daily siesta, Floracita filled Thistle's panniers with several little pasteboard boxes, and, without saying anything to Tulee, mounted and rode off in a direction she had never taken, except in the barouche. She was in search of the Welby plantation.

Mrs. Delano, who was busy with her crochet-needle near the open window, was surprised to see a light little figure seated on a donkey riding up the avenue. As soon as Floracita dismounted, she recognized her, and descended the steps of the piazza to welcome her.

"So you have found the Welby plantation," said she. "I thought you would n't have much difficulty, for there are only two plantations on the island, this and Mr. Fitzgerald's. I don't know that there are any other *dwellings* except the huts of the negroes." She spoke the last rather in a tone of inquiry; but Flora merely answered that she had once passed the Welby plantation in a barouche.

As the lady led the way into the parlor, she said, "What is that you have in your hand, my dear?"

"You used to admire Madame Conquilla's shell-work," replied Flora, "and I have brought you some of mine, to see whether you think I succeed tolerably in my imitations." As she spoke, she took out a small basket and poised it on her finger.

"Why, that is perfectly beautiful!" said Mrs. Delano. "I don't know how you could contrive to give it such an air of lightness and grace. I used to think shell-work heavy, and rather vulgar, till I saw those beautiful productions at Nassau. But you excel your teacher, my dear Miss Gonsalez. I should think the sea-fairies made this."

Four or five other articles were brought forth from the boxes and examined with similar commendation. Then they fell into a pleasant chat about their reminiscences of Nassau ; and diverged from that to speak of the loveliness of their lonely little island, and the increasing beauty of the season. After a while, Flora looked at her watch, and said, " I must not stay long, for I didn't tell anybody I was going away."

Mrs. Delano, who caught a glimpse of the medallion inserted in the back, said: "That is a peculiar little watch. Have you the hair of some friend set in it ?"

" No," replied Flora. " It is the likeness of my father." She slipped the slight chain from her neck, and placed the watch in the lady's hand. Her face flushed as she looked at it, but the habitual paleness soon returned.

" You were introduced to me as a Spanish young lady," said she, " but this face is not Spanish. What was your father's name ?"

" Mr. Alfred Royal of New Orleans," answered Flora.

" But *your* name is Gonsalez," said she.

Flora blushed crimson with the consciousness of having betrayed the incognito assumed at Nassau. " Gonsalez was my mother's name," she replied, gazing on the floor while she spoke.

Mrs. Delano looked at her for an instant, then, drawing her gently toward her, she pressed her to her side, and said with a sigh, " Ah, Flora, I wish you were my daughter."

"O, how I wish I was!" exclaimed the young girl, looking up with a sudden glow; but a shadow immediately clouded her expressive face, as she added, "But you would n't want me for a daughter, if you knew everything about me."

The lady was obviously troubled. "You seem to be surrounded by mysteries, my little friend," responded she. "I will not ask you for any confidence you are unwilling to bestow. But I am a good deal older than you, and I know the world better than you do. If anything troubles you, or if you are doing anything wrong, perhaps if you were to tell me, I could help you out of it."

"O, no, I'm not doing anything wrong," replied Floracita, eagerly. "I never did anything wrong in my life." Seeing a slight smile hovering about the lady's lips, she made haste to add: "I did n't mean exactly that. I mean I never did anything *very* wrong. I'm cross sometimes, and I have told some *fibititas;* but then I could n't seem to help it, things were in such a tangle. It comes more natural to me to tell the truth."

" That I can readily believe," rejoined Mrs. Delano. "But I am not trying to entrap your ingenuousness into a betrayal of your secrets. Only remember one thing; if you ever do want to open your heart to any one, remember that I am your true friend, and that you can trust me."

"O, thank you! thank you!" exclaimed Flora, seizing her hand and kissing it fervently.

" But tell **me** one thing, **my** little friend," continued Mrs. Delano. "Is there anything I can do for **you now?**"

" I came to ask you to do something for me," replied Flora; "but you have been so kind to me, that it has made me almost forget my errand. I have very particular reasons for wanting to earn some money. You used to admire the shell-work in Nassau so much, that I thought, if you liked mine, you might be willing to buy it, and that perhaps you might have friends who would buy some. I have tried every way to think how I could manage to sell my work."

"I will gladly buy all you have," rejoined the lady, "and I should like to have you make me some more; especially of these garlands of rice-shells, trembling so lightly on almost invisible silver wire."

"I will make some immediately," replied Flora. "But I must go, dear Mrs. Delano. I wish I could stay longer, but I cannot."

"When will you come again?" asked the lady.

"I can't tell," responded Flora, "for I have to manage to come here."

"That seems strange," said Mrs. Delano.

"I know it seems strange," answered the young girl, with a kind of despairing impatience in her tone. "But please don't ask me, for everything seems to come right out to you; and I don't know what I ought to say, indeed I don't."

"I want you to come again as soon as you can," said Mrs. Delano, slipping a gold eagle into her hand. "And now go, my dear, before you tell me more than you wish to."

"Not more than I wish," rejoined Floracita; "but more than I ought. I *wish* to tell you everything."

In a childish way she put up her lips for a kiss, and the lady drew her to her heart and caressed her tenderly.

When Flora had descended the steps of the piazza, she turned and looked up. Mrs. Delano was leaning against one of the pillars, watching her departure. Vines of gossamer

lightness were waving round her, and her pearly complexion and violet-tinted dress looked lovely among those aerial
arabesques of delicate green. The picture impressed Flora
all the more because it was such a contrast to the warm
and gorgeous styles of beauty to which she had been accustomed. She smiled and kissed her hand in token of
farewell; the lady returned the salutation, but she thought
the expression of her face was sad, and the fear that this
new friend distrusted her on account of unexplained mysteries haunted her on her way homeward.

Mrs. Delano looked after her till she and her donkey
disappeared among the trees in the distance. "What a
strange mystery is this!" murmured she. "Alfred Royal's
child, and yet she bears her mother's name. And why does
she conceal from me where she lives? Surely, she cannot
be consciously doing anything wrong, for I never saw such
perfect artlessness of look and manner." The problem occupied her thoughts for days after, without her arriving at
any satisfactory conjecture.

Flora, on her part, was troubled concerning the distrust
which she felt must be excited by her mysterious position,
and she was continually revolving plans to clear herself from
suspicion in the eyes of her new friend. It would have
been an inexpressible consolation if she could have told
her troubles to her elder sister, from whom she had never
concealed anything till within the last few weeks. But,
alas! by the fault of another, a barrier had arisen between
them, which proved an obstruction at every turn of their daily
intercourse; for while she had been compelled to despise
and dislike Gerald, Rosa was always eulogizing his noble
and loving nature, and was extremely particular to have his
slightest wishes obeyed. Apart from any secret reasons for

wishing to obtain money, Floracita was well aware that it would not do to confess her visit to Mrs. Delano; for Gerald had not only forbidden their making any acquaintances, but he had also charged them not to ride or walk in the direction of either of the plantations unless he was with them.

Day after day, as Flora sat at work upon the garlands she had promised, she was on the watch to elude his vigilance; but more than a week passed without her finding any safe opportunity. At last Gerald proposed to gratify Rosa's often-expressed wish, by taking a sail to one of the neighboring islands. They intended to make a picnic of it, and return by moonlight. Rosa was full of pleasant anticipations, which, however, were greatly damped when her sister expressed a decided preference for staying at home. Rosa entreated, and Gerald became angry, but she persisted in her refusal. She said she wanted to use up all her shells, and all her flosses and chenilles. Gerald swore that he hated the sight of them, and that he would throw them all into the sea if she went on wearing her beautiful eyes out over them. Without looking up from her work, she coolly answered, "Why need you concern yourself about *my* eyes, when you have a wife with such beautiful eyes?"

Black Tom and Chloe and the boat were in waiting, and after a flurried scene they departed reluctantly without her.

"I never saw any one so changed as she is," said Rosa. "She used to be so fond of excursions, and now she wants to work from morning till night."

"She 's a perverse, self-willed, capricious little puss. She 's been too much indulged. She needs to be brought under discipline," said Gerald, angrily whipping off a blossom with his rattan as they walked toward the boat.

As soon as they were fairly off, Flora started on a second visit to the Welby plantation. Tulee noticed all this in silence, and shook her head, as if thoughts were brooding there unsafe for utterance.

Mrs. Delano was bending over her writing-desk finishing a letter, when she perceived a wave of fragrance, and, looking up, she saw Flora on the threshold of the open door, with her arms full of flowers.

"Excuse me for interrupting you," said she, dropping one of her little quick courtesies, which seemed half frolic, half politeness. "The woods are charming to-day. The trees are hung with curtains of jasmine, embroidered all over with golden flowers. You love perfumes so well, I could n't help stopping by the way to load Thistle with an armful of them."

"Thank you, dear," replied Mrs. Delano. "I rode out yesterday afternoon; and I thought I had never seen anything so beautiful as the flowery woods and the gorgeous sunset. After being accustomed to the splendor of these Southern skies, the Northern atmosphere will seem cold and dull."

"Shall you go to the North soon?" inquired Flora, anxiously.

"I shall leave here in ten or twelve days," she replied; "but I may wait a short time in Savannah, till March has gone; for that is a blustering, disagreeable month in New England, though it brings you roses and perfume. I came to Savannah to spend the winter with my friends, Mr. and Mrs. Welby; but I have always taken a great fancy to this island, and when they were suddenly called away to Arkansas by the illness of a son, I asked their permission to come here for a few weeks and watch the beautiful opening of the spring. I find myself much inclined to solitude since I lost a darling daughter, who died two years ago. If she had lived, she would have been about your age."

"I am *so* sorry you are going away," said Flora. "It seems as if I had always known you. I don't know what I shall do without you. But when you go back among your friends, I suppose you will forget all about poor little me."

"No, my dear little friend, I shall never forget you," she replied; "and when I come again, I hope I shall find you here."

"I felt troubled when I went away the other day," said Flora. "I thought you seemed to look sadly after me, and I was afraid you thought I had done something wicked, because I said you would n't wish I were your daughter if you knew everything about me. So I have come to tell you my secrets, as far as I can without betraying other people's. I am afraid you won't care anything more about me after I have told you; but I can't help it if you don't. Even that would be better than to have you suspect me of being bad."

Mrs. Delano drew an ottoman toward her, and said, "Come and sit here, dear, and tell me all about it, the same as if I were your mother."

Floracita complied; and resting one elbow on her knee, and leaning her cheek upon the hand, she looked up timidly and wistfully into the friendly face that was smiling serenely over her. After a moment's pause, she said abruptly: "I don't know how to begin, so I won't begin at all, but tell it right out. You see, dear Mrs. Delano, I am a colored girl."

The lady's smile came nearer to a laugh than was usual with her. She touched the pretty dimpled cheek with her jewelled finger, as she replied: "O, you mischievous little kitten! I thought you were really going to tell me something about your troubles. But I see you are hoaxing me. I remember when you were at Madame Conquilla's you always seemed to be full of fun, and the young ladies there said you were a great rogue."

"But this is not fun; indeed it is not," rejoined Flora. "I *am* a colored girl."

She spoke so earnestly that the lady began to doubt the evidence of her own eyes. "But you told me that Mr. Alfred Royal was your father," said she.

"So he was my father," replied Flora; "and the kindest father that ever was. Rosa and I were brought up like little princesses, and we never knew that we were colored. My mother was the daughter of a rich Spanish gentleman named Gonsalez. She was educated in Paris, and was elegant and accomplished. She was handsomer than Rosa; and if you were to see Rosa, you would say nobody *could* be handsomer than she is. She was good, too. My father was always saying she was the dearest and best wife in the world. You don't know how he mourned when she died. He could n't bear to have anything moved that she had touched. But *cher papa* died very suddenly; and first they told us that we were very poor, and must earn our living; and then they told us that our mother was a slave, and so, according to law, we were slaves too. They would have sold us at auction, if a gentleman who knew us when papa was alive had n't smuggled us away privately to Nassau. He had been very much in love with Rosa for a good while; and he married her, and I live with them.

But he keeps us very much hidden; because, he says, he should get into lawsuits and duels and all sorts of troubles with papa's creditors if they should find out that he helped us off. And that was the reason I was called Señorita Gonsalez in Nassau, though my real name is Flora Royal."

She went on to recount the kindness of Madame Guirlande, and the exciting particulars of their escape; to all of which Mrs. Delano listened with absorbed attention. As they sat thus, they made a beautiful picture. The lady, mature in years, but scarcely showing the touch of time, was almost as fair as an Albiness, with serene lips, and a soft moonlight expression in her eyes. Every attitude and every motion indicated quietude and refinement. The young girl, on the contrary, even when reclining, seemed like impetuosity in repose for a moment, but just ready to spring. Her large dark eyes laughed and flashed and wept by turns, and her warmly tinted face glowed like the sunlight, in its setting of glossy black hair. The lady looked down upon her with undisguised admiration while she recounted their adventures in lively dramatic style, throwing in imitations of the whistling of *Ça ira*, and the tones of the coachman as he sang, " Who goes there?"

" But you have not told me," said Mrs. Delano, " who the gentleman was that married your sister. Ah, I see you hesitate. No matter. Only tell me one thing, — is he kind to you?"

Flora turned red and pale, and red again.

" Let that pass, too," said the lady. " I asked because I wished to know if I could help you in any way. I see you have brought some more boxes of shell-work, and by and by we will examine them. But first I want to tell you that I also have a secret, and I will confide it to you that you may feel assured I shall love you always. Flora, dear, when your father and I were young, we were in love with each other, and I promised to be his wife."

"So you might have been my Mamita!" exclaimed Floracita, impetuously.

"No, not *your* Mamita, dear," replied Mrs. Delano, smiling. "You call me the Java sparrow, and Java sparrows never hatch gay little humming-birds or tuneful mocking-birds. I might tell you a long story about myself, dear; but the sun is declining, and you ought not to be out after dusk. My father was angry about our love, because Alfred was then only a clerk with a small salary. They carried me off to Europe, and for two years I could hear nothing from Alfred. Then they told me he was married; and after a while they persuaded me to marry Mr. Delano. I ought not to have married him, because my heart was not in it. He died and left me with a large fortune and the little daughter I told you of. I have felt very much alone since my darling was taken from me. That void in my heart renders young girls very interesting to me. Your looks and ways attracted me when I first met you; and when you told me Alfred Royal was your father, I longed to clasp you to my heart. And now you know, my dear child, that you have a friend ever ready to listen to any troubles you may choose to confide, and desirous to remove them if she can."

She rose to open the boxes of shell-work; but Flora sprung up, and threw herself into her arms, saying, "My Papasito sent you to me, — I know he did."

After a few moments spent in silent emotion, Mrs. Delano again spoke of the approaching twilight, and with mutual caresses they bade each other adieu.

Four or five days later, Floracita made her appearance at the Welby plantation in a state of great excitement. She was in a nervous tremor, and her eyelids were swollen as if with much weeping. Mrs. Delano hastened to enfold her in her arms, saying: "What is it, my child? Tell your new Mamita what it is that troubles you so."

"O, *may* I call you Mamita?" asked Flora, looking up with an expression of grateful love that warmed all the fibres of her friend's heart. "O, I do so need a Mamita! I am very wretched; and if you don't help me, I don't know what I *shall* do!"

"Certainly, I will help you, if possible, when you have told me your trouble," replied Mrs. Delano.

"Yes, I will tell," said Flora, sighing. "Mr. Fitzgerald is the gentleman who married my sister; but we don't live at his plantation. We live in a small cottage hidden away in the woods. You never saw anybody so much in love as he was with Rosa. When we first came here, he was never willing to have her out of his sight a moment. And Rosa loves him so! But for these eight or ten weeks past he has been making love to me; though he is just as affectionate as ever with Rosa. When she is playing to him, and I am singing beside her, he keeps throwing kisses to me behind her back. It makes me feel so ashamed that I can't look my sister in the face. I have tried to keep out of his way. When I am in the house I stick to Rosa like a burr; and I have given up riding or walking, except when he is away. But there's no telling when he *is* away. He went away yesterday, and said he was going to Savannah to be gone a week; but this morning, when I went into the woods behind the cottage to feed Thistle, he was lurking there. He seized me, and held his hand over my mouth, and said I *should* hear him. Then he told me that Rosa and I were his slaves; that he bought us of papa's creditors, and could sell us any day. And he says he will carry me off to Savannah and sell me if I don't treat him better. He would not let me go till I promised to meet him in Cypress Grove at dusk to-night. I have been trying to earn money to go to Madame Guirlande, and get her to send me somewhere where I could give dancing-lessons, or singing-lessons, without being in danger of being taken up for a slave. But I don't know how to get to New Orleans alone; and if I am his slave, I am afraid he will come there with officers to take me. So, dear new Mamita, I have come to you, to see if you can't help me to get some money and go somewhere."

Mrs. Delano pressed her gently to her heart, and responded in tones of tenderest pity: " Get some money and go somewhere, you poor child! Do you think I shall let dear Alfred's little daughter go wandering alone about the world? No, darling, you shall live with me, and be my daughter."

"And don't you care about my being colored and a slave?" asked Floracita, humbly.

"Let us never speak of that," replied her friend. "The whole transaction is so odious and wicked that I can't bear to think of it."

"I do feel so grateful to you, my dear new Mamita, that I don't know what to say. But it tears my heart in two to leave Rosa. We have never been separated for a day since I was born. And she is so good, and she loves me so! And Tulee, too. I did n't dare to try to speak to her. I knew I should break down. All the way coming here I was frightened for fear Gerald would overtake me

5 *

and carry me off. And I cried so, thinking about Rosa
and Tulee, not knowing when I should see them again,
that I could n't see ; and if Thistle had n't known the way
himself, I should n't have got here. Poor Thistle! It
seemed as if my heart would break when I threw the
bridle on his neck and left him to go back alone; I did n't
dare to hug him but once, I was so afraid. O, I am so
glad that you will let me stay here !"

"I have been thinking it will not be prudent for you to
stay here, my child," replied Mrs. Delano. "Search will
be made for you in the morning, and you had better be out
of the way before that. There are some dresses belonging
to Mrs. Welby's daughter in a closet up stairs. I will
borrow one of them for you to wear. The boat from Beaufort to Savannah will stop here in an hour to take some
freight. We will go to Savannah. My colored laundress
there has a chamber above her wash-room where you will
be better concealed than in more genteel lodgings. I will
come back here to arrange things, and in a few days I will
return to you and take you to my Northern home."

The necessary arrangements were soon made ; and when
Flora was transformed into Miss Welby, she smiled very
faintly as she remarked, "How queer it seems to be always
running away."

"This is the last time, my child," replied Mrs. Delano.
"I will keep my little bird carefully under my wings."

When Flora was in the boat, hand in hand with her new
friend, and no one visible whom she had ever seen before,
her excitement began to subside, but sadness increased.
In her terror the poor child had scarcely thought of anything except the necessity of escaping somewhere. But
when she saw her island home receding from her, she began to realize the importance of the step she was taking.

She fixed her gaze on that part where the lonely cottage was embowered, and she had a longing to see even a little whiff of smoke from Tulee's kitchen. But there was no sign of life save a large turkey-buzzard, like a black vulture, sailing gracefully over the tree-tops. The beloved sister, the faithful servant, the brother from whom she had once hoped so much, the patient animal that had borne her through so many pleasant paths, the flowery woods, and the resounding sea, had all vanished from her as suddenly as did her father and the bright home of her childhood.

The scenes through which they were passing were beautiful as Paradise, and all nature seemed alive and jubilant. The white blossoms of wild-plum-trees twinkled among dark evergreens, a vegetable imitation of starlight. Wide-spreading oaks and superb magnolias were lighted up with sudden flashes of color, as scarlet grosbeaks flitted from tree to tree. Sparrows were chirping, doves cooing, and mocking-birds whistling, now running up the scale, then down the scale, with an infinity of variations between. The outbursts of the birds were the same as in seasons that were gone, but the listener was changed. Rarely before had her quick musical ear failed to notice how they would repeat the same note with greater or less emphasis, then flat it, then sharp it, varying their performances with all manner of unexpected changes. But now she was merely vaguely conscious of familiar sounds, which brought before her that last merry day in her father's house, when Rosabella laughed so much to hear her puzzle the birds with her musical vagaries. Memory held up her magic mirror, in which she saw pictured processions of the vanished years. Thus the lonely child, with her loving, lingering looks upon the past, was floated toward an unknown future with the new friend a kind Providence had sent her.

CHAPTER IX.

ROSA was surprised at the long absence of her sister; and when the sun showed only a narrow golden edge above the horizon, she began to feel anxious. She went to the kitchen and said, "Tulee, have you seen anything of Floracita lately? She went away while I was sleeping."

"No, missy," she replied. "The last I see of her was in her room, with the embroidery-frame before her. She was looking out of the window, as she did sometimes, as if she was looking nowhere. She jumped up and hugged and kissed me, and called me 'Dear Tulee, good Tulee.' The little darling was always mighty loving. When I went there again, her needle was sticking in her work, and her thimble was on the frame, but she was gone. I don't know when she went away. Thistle's come back alone; but he does that sometimes when little missy goes rambling round."

There was no uneasiness expressed in her tones, but, being more disquieted than she wished to acknowledge, she went forth to search the neighboring wood-paths and the sea-shore. When she returned, Rosa ran out with the eager inquiry, "Is she anywhere in sight?" In reply to the negative answer, she said: "I don't know what to make of it. Have you ever seen anybody with Floracita since we came here?"

"Nobody but Massa Gerald," replied Tulee.

"I wonder whether she was discontented here," said Rosa. "I don't see why she should be, for we all loved

her dearly; and Gerald was as kind to her as if she had
been his own sister. But she has n't seemed like herself
lately; and this forenoon she hugged and kissed me ever so
many times, and cried. When I asked her what was the
matter, she said she was thinking of the pleasant times
when *Papasito querido* was alive. Do you think she was
unhappy?"

"She told me once she was homesick for Madame Guirlande," replied Tulee.

"Did she? Perhaps she was making so many things for
Madame because she meant to go there. But she could n't
find her way alone, and she knew it would be very dangerous for either of us to go to New Orleans."

Tulee made no reply. She seated herself on a wooden
bench by the open door, swinging her body back and forth
in an agitated way, ever and anon jumping up and looking
round in all directions. The veil of twilight descended
upon the earth, and darkness followed. The two inmates
of the cottage felt very miserable and helpless, as they sat
there listening to every sound. For a while nothing was
heard but the dash of the waves, and the occasional hoot-
ing of an owl. The moon rose up above the pines, and
flooded earth and sea with silvery splendor.

"I want to go to the plantation and call Tom," said
Rosa; "and there is such bright moonshine we might go,
but I am afraid Gerald would be displeased."

Tulee at once volunteered to bring out Thistle, and to
walk beside her mistress.

Both started at the sound of footsteps. They were not
light enough for Floracita, but they thought it might be
some one bringing news. It proved to be the master of
the house.

"Why, Gerald, how glad I am! I thought you were in Savannah," exclaimed Rosa. "Have you seen anything of Floracita?"

"No. Is n't she here?" inquired he, in such a tone of surprise, that Tulee's suspicions were shaken.

Rosa repeated the story of her disappearance, and concluded by saying, "She told Tulee she was homesick to go to Madame."

"She surely would n't dare to do that," he replied.

"Massa Gerald," said Tulee, and she watched him closely while she spoke, "there 's something I did n't tell Missy Rosy, 'cause I was feared it would worry her. I found this little glove of Missy Flory's, with a bunch of sea-weed, down on the beach; and there was marks of her feet all round."

Rosa uttered a cry. "O heavens!" she exclaimed, "I saw an alligator a few days ago."

An expression of horror passed over his face. "I 've cautioned her not to fish so much for shells and sea-mosses," said he; "but she was always so self-willed."

"*Don't* say anything against the little darling!" implored Rosa. "Perhaps we shall never see her again."

He spoke a few soothing words, and then took his hat, saying, "I am going to the sea-shore."

"Take good care of yourself, dear Gerald!" cried Rosa.

"No danger 'bout that," muttered Tulee, as she walked out of hearing. "There 's things with handsomer mouths than alligators that may be more dangerous. Poor little bird! I wonder where he has put her."

His feelings as he roamed on the beach were not to be envied. His mind was divided between the thoughts that she had committed suicide, or had been drowned accidentally. That she had escaped from his persecutions by flight he could not believe; for he knew she was entirely unused to taking care of herself, and felt sure she had no one to help her. He returned to say that the tide had washed away the footprints, and that he found no vestige of the lost one.

At dawn he started for the plantation, whence, after fruitless inquiries, he rode to the Welby estate. Mrs. Delano had requested the household servants not to mention having seen a small young lady there, and they had nothing to communicate.

He resolved to start for New Orleans as soon as possible. After a fortnight's absence he returned, bringing grieved and sympathizing **letters** from the Signor and Madame; and on the minds of all, except Tulee, the conviction settled that Floracita was drowned. Hope lingered long in her mind. "Wherever the little pet may be, she'll surely contrive to let us know," thought she. "She ain't like the poor slaves when *they*'re **carried off. She can** write." Her mistress talked with her every day about the lost darling; but of course such suspicions were not to be mentioned to her. Gerald, who disliked everything mournful, avoided the subject entirely; and Rosabella, looking upon him only with the eyes of love, considered it a sign of deep feeling, and respected it accordingly.

But, blinded as she was, she gradually became aware that he did not seem exactly like the same man who first won her girlish love. Her efforts to please him were not always successful. He was sometimes moody and fretful. He swore at the slightest annoyance, and often flew into paroxysms of anger with Tom and Tulee. He was more

and more absent from the cottage, and made few professions of regret for such frequent separations. Some weeks
after Flora's disappearance, he announced his intention to
travel in the North during the summer months. Rosabella looked up in his face with a pleading expression, but
pride prevented her from asking whether she might accompany him. She waited in hopes he would propose it;
but as he did not even think of it, he failed to interpret
the look of disappointment in her expressive eyes, as she
turned from him with a sigh.

"Tom will come with the carriage once a week," said
he; "and either he or Joe will be here every night."

"Thank you," she replied.

But the tone was so sad that he took her hand with the
tenderness of former times, and said, "You are sorry to
part with me, Bella Rosa?"

"How can I be otherwise than sorry," she asked,
"when I am all alone in the world without you? Dear
Gerald, are we always to live thus? Will you never acknowledge me as your wife?"

"How can I do it," rejoined he, "without putting myself
in the power of those cursed creditors? It is no fault of
mine that your mother was a slave."

"We should be secure from them in Europe," she replied. "Why couldn't we live abroad?"

"Do you suppose my rich uncle would leave me a cent
if he found out I had married the daughter of a quadroon?" rejoined he. "I have met with losses lately, and
I can't afford to offend my uncle. I am sorry, dear, that
you are dissatisfied with the home I have provided for
you."

"I am not dissatisfied with my home," said she. "I have

no desire to mix with the world, but it is necessary for you, and these separations are dreadful."

His answer was: " I will write often, dearest, and I will send you quantities of new music. I shall always be looking forward to the delight of hearing it when I return. You must take good care of your health, for my sake. You must go ambling about with Thistle every day."

The suggestion brought up associations that overcame her at once. " O how Floracita loved Thistle ! " she exclaimed. " And it really seems as if the poor beast misses her. I am afraid we neglected her too much, Gerald. We were so taken up with our own happiness, that we did n't think of her so much as we ought to have done."

" I am sure I tried to gratify all her wishes," responded he. " I have nothing to reproach myself with, and certainly you were always a devoted sister. This is a morbid state of feeling, and you must try to drive it off. You said a little while ago that you wanted to see how the plantation was looking, and what flowers had come out in the garden. Shall I take you there in the barouche to-morrow ? "

She gladly assented, and a few affectionate words soon restored her confidence in his love.

When the carriage was brought to the entrance of the wood the next day, she went to meet it with a smiling face and a springing step. As he was about to hand her in, he said abruptly, " You have forgotten your veil."

Tulee was summoned to bring it. As Rosa arranged it round her head, she remarked, " One would think you were ashamed of me, Gerald."

The words were almost whispered, but the tone sounded more like a reproach than anything she had ever uttered.

With ready gallantry he responded aloud, " I think so much of my treasure that I want to keep it all to myself."

He was very affectionate during their drive ; and this, combined with the genial air, the lovely scenery, and the exhilaration of swift motion, restored her to a greater sense of happiness than she had felt since her darling sister vanished so suddenly.

The plantation was in gala dress. The veranda was almost covered with the large, white, golden-eyed stars of the Cherokee rose, gleaming out from its dark, lustrous foliage. The lawn was a sheet of green velvet embroidered with flowers. Magnolias and oaks of magnificent growth ornamented the extensive grounds. In the rear was a cluster of negro huts. Black picaninnies were rolling about in the grass, mingling their laughter with the songs of the birds. The winding paths of the garden were lined with flowering shrubs, and the sea sparkled in the distance. Wherever the eye glanced, all was sunshine, bloom, and verdure.

For the first time, he invited her to enter the mansion. Her first movement was toward the piano. As she opened it, and swept her hand across the keys, he said : " It is sadly out of tune. It has been neglected because its owner had pleasanter music elsewhere."

" But the tones are very fine," rejoined she. " What a pity it shouldn't be used !" As she glanced out of the window on the blooming garden and spacious lawn, she said : " How pleasant it would be if we could live here ! It is so delightful to look out on such an extensive open space."

" Perhaps we will some time or other, my love," responded he.

She smiled, and touched the keys, while she sang

snatches of familiar songs. The servants who brought in refreshments wondered at her beauty, and clear, ringing voice. Many dark faces clustered round the crack of the door to obtain a peep; and as they went away they exchanged nudges and winks with each other. Tom and Chloe had confidentially whispered to some of them the existence of such a lady, and that Tulee said Massa married her in the West Indies; and they predicted that she would be the future mistress of Magnolia Lawn. Others gave it as their opinion, that Massa would never hide her as he did if she was to be the Missis. But all agreed that she was a beautiful, grand lady, and they paid her homage accordingly. Her cheeks would have burned to scarlet flame if she had heard all their comments and conjectures; but unconscious of blame or shame, she gave herself up to the enjoyment of those bright hours.

A new access of tenderness seemed to have come over Fitzgerald; partly because happiness rendered her beauty more radiant, and partly because secret thoughts that were revolving in his mind brought some twinges of remorse. He had never seemed more enamored, not even during the first week in Nassau, when he came to claim her as his bride. Far down in the garden was an umbrageous walk, terminating in a vine-covered bower. They remained there a long time, intertwined in each other's arms, talking over the memories of their dawning consciousness of love, and singing together the melodies in which their voices had first mingled.

Their road home was through woods and groves festooned with vines, some hanging in massive coils, others light and aerial enough for fairy swings; then over the smooth beach, where wave after wave leaped up and

tossed its white foam-garland on the shore. The sun
was sinking in a golden sea, and higher toward the zenith
little gossamer clouds blushingly dissolved in the brilliant
azure, and united again, as if the fragrance of roses had
floated into form.

When they reached the cottage, Rosa passed through the
silent little parlor with swimming eyes, murmuring to herself: " Poor little Floracita! how the sea made me think
of her.   I ought not to have been so happy."

But memory wrote the record of that halcyon day in
illuminated manuscript, all glowing with purple and gold,
with angel faces peeping through a graceful network of
flowers.

CHAPTER X.

ROSABELLA had never experienced such loneliness as in the months that followed. All music was saddened by far-off echoes of past accompaniments. Embroidery lost its interest with no one to praise the work, or to be consulted in the choice of colors and patterns. The books Gerald occasionally sent were of a light character, and though they served to while away a listless hour, there was nothing in them to strengthen or refresh the soul. The isolation was the more painful because there was everything around her to remind her of the lost and the absent. Flora's unfinished embroidery still remained in the frame, with the needle in the last stitch of a blue forget-me-not. Over the mirror was a cluster of blush-roses she had made. On the wall was a spray of sea-moss she had pressed and surrounded with a garland of small shells. By the door was a vine she had transplanted from the woods ; and under a tree opposite was a turf seat where she used to sit sketching the cottage, and Tulee, and Thistle, and baskets of wild-flowers she had gathered. The sight of these things continually brought up visions of the loving and beautiful child, who for so many years had slept nestling in her arms, and made the days tuneful with her songs. Then there was Gerald's silent flute, and the silken cushion she had embroidered for him, on which she had so often seen him reposing, and thought him handsome as a sleeping Adonis. A letter from him made her cheerful for days ; but they did not come often, and were generally brief.

Tom came with the carriage once a week, according to his master's orders; but she found solitary drives so little refreshing to body or mind that she was often glad to avail herself of Tulee's company.

So the summer wore away, and September came to produce a new aspect of beauty in the landscape, by tinging the fading flowers and withering leaves with various shades of brown and crimson, purple and orange. One day, early in the month, when Tom came with the carriage, she told him to drive to Magnolia Lawn. She had long been wishing to revisit the scene where she had been so happy on that bright spring day; but she had always said to herself, "I will wait till Gerald comes." Now she had grown so weary with hope deferred, that she felt as if she could wait no longer.

As she rode along she thought of improvements in the walks that she would suggest to Gerald, if they ever went there to live, as he had intimated they might. The servants received her with their usual respectful manner and wondering looks; but when she turned back to ask some question, she saw them whispering together with an unusual appearance of excitement. Her cheeks glowed with a consciousness that her anomalous position was well calculated to excite their curiosity; and she turned away, thinking how different it had been with her mother, — how sheltered and protected she had always been. She remembered how very rarely her father left home, and how he always hastened to return. She stood awhile on the veranda, thinking sadly, "If Gerald loves me as Papasito loved Mamita, how can he be contented to leave me so much?" With a deep sigh she turned and entered the house through an open window. The sigh changed at once to a bright smile. The parlor had undergone a wondrous transformation since she last saw it. The woodwork had been freshly painted, and the walls were covered with silvery-flowered paper. Over curtains of embroidered lace hung a drapery of apple-green damask, ornamented with deep white-silk fringe and heavy tassels. "How kind of Gerald!" murmured she. "He has done this because I expressed a wish to live here. How ungrateful I was to doubt him in my thoughts!"

She passed into the chamber, where she found a white French bedstead, on which were painted bouquets of roses. It was enveloped in roseate lace drapery, caught up at the centre in festoons on the silver arrow of a pretty little Cupid. From silver arrows over the windows there fell the same soft, roseate folds. Her whole face was illuminated with happiness as she thought to herself: "Ah! I know why everything has a tinge of *roses*. How kind of him to prepare such a beautiful surprise for me!"

She traversed the garden walks, and lingered long in the sequestered bower. On the floor was a bunch of dried violets which he had placed in her belt on that happy day. She took them up, kissed them fervently, and placed them near her heart. That heart was lighter than it had been for months. "At last he is going to acknowledge me as his wife," thought she. "How happy I shall be when there is no longer any need of secrecy!"

The servants heard her singing as she traversed the garden, and gathered in groups to listen; but they scattered as they saw her approach the house.

"She's a mighty fine lady," said Dinah, the cook.

"Mighty fine lady," repeated Tom; "an' I tell yer she's married to Massa, an' she's gwine to be de Missis."

Venus, the chambermaid, who would have passed very well for a bronze image of the sea-born goddess, tossed her head as she replied: "Dunno bout dat ar. Massa does a heap o' courtin' to we far sex."

"How yer know dat ar?" exclaimed Dinah. "Whar d' yer git dem year-rings?" And then there was a general titter.

Rosabella, all unconscious in her purity, came up to Tom while the grin was still upon his face, and in her polite way asked him to have the goodness to bring the carriage. It was with great difficulty that she could refrain from outbursts of song as she rode homeward ; but Gerald had particularly requested her not to sing in the carriage, lest her voice should attract the attention of some one who chanced to be visiting the island.

Her first words when she entered the cottage were : "O Tulee, I am *so* happy! Gerald has fitted up Magnolia Lawn beautifully, because I told him I wished we could live there. He said, that day we were there, that he would try to make some arrangement with Papasito's creditors, and I do believe he has, and that I shall not have to hide much longer. He has been fitting up the house as if it were for a queen. Isn't he kind?"

Tulee, who listened rather distrustfully to praises bestowed on the master, replied that nobody could do anything too good for Missy Rosy.

"Ah, Tulee, you have always done your best to spoil me," said she, laying her hand affectionately on the shoulder of her petted servant, while a smile like-sunshine mantled her face. "But do get me something to eat. The ride has made me hungry."

"Ise glad to hear that, Missy Rosy. I begun to think

't want no use to cook nice tidbits for ye, if ye jist turned
'em over wi' yer fork, and ate one or two mouthfuls, without knowing what ye was eatin'."

"I 've been pining for Gerald, Tulee; and I 've been
afraid sometimes that he did n't love me as he used to do.
But now that he has made such preparations for us to live
at Magnolia Lawn, I am as happy as a queen."

She went off singing, and as Tulee looked after her she
murmured to herself: "And what a handsome queen she 'd
make! Gold ain't none too good for her to walk on. But
is it the truth he told her about settling with the creditors?
There 's never no telling anything by what *he* says. Do
hear her singing now! It sounds as lively as Missy Flory.
Ah! that was a strange business. I wonder whether the
little darling *is* dead."

While she was preparing supper, with such cogitations
passing through her mind, Rosa began to dash off a letter,
as follows: —

"DEARLY BELOVED, — I am so happy that I cannot
wait a minute without telling you about it. I have done a
naughty thing, but, as it is the first time I ever disobeyed
you, I hope you will forgive me. You told me never to
go to the plantation without you. But I waited and waited, and you did n't come; and we were so happy there,
that lovely day, that I longed to go again. I knew it
would be very lonesome without you; but I thought it
would be some comfort to see again the places where we
walked together, and sang together, and called each other
all manner of foolish fond names. Do you remember how
many variations you rung upon my name, — Rosabella,
Rosalinda, Rosamunda, Rosa Regina? How you did pelt

6

me with roses! Do you remember how happy we were in
the garden bower? How we sang together the old-fashioned canzonet, 'Love in thine eyes forever plays'? And
how the mocking-bird imitated your guitar, while you were
singing the Don Giovanni serenade?

"I was thinking this all over, as I rode alone over the
same ground we traversed on that happy day. But it was
so different without the love-light of your eyes and the
pressure of your dear hand, that I felt the tears gathering,
and had all manner of sad thoughts. I feared you did n't
care for me as you used to do, and were finding it easy to
live without me. But when I entered the parlor that
overlooks the beautiful lawn, all my doubts vanished.
You had encouraged me to hope that it might be our
future home; but I little dreamed it was to be so soon, and
that you were preparing such a charming surprise for me.
Don't be vexed with me, dearest, for finding out your secret.
It made me *so* happy! It made the world seem like Paradise. Ah! I *knew* why everything was so *rose*-colored.
It was so like *you* to think of that! Then everything is so
elegant! You knew your Rosamunda's taste for elegance.

"But Tulee summons me to supper. Dear, good, faithful Tulee! What a comfort she has been to me in this
lonesome time!

.   .   .   .   .

"Now I have come back to the pretty little writing-desk
you gave me, and I will finish my letter. I feel as if I
wanted to write to you forever, if I can't have you to talk
to. You can't imagine how lonesome I have been. The
new music you sent me was charming; but whatever I
practised or improvised took a solemn and plaintive character, like the moaning of the sea and the whispering of

the pines. One's own voice sounds so solitary when there
is no other voice to lean upon, and no appreciating ear to
listen for the coming chords. I have even found it a relief
to play and sing to Tulee, who is always an admiring listener, if not a very discriminating one; and as for Tom, it
seems as if the eyes would fly out of his head when I play
to him. I have tried to take exercise every day, as you
advised; but while the hot weather lasted, I was afraid of
snakes, and the mosquitoes and sand-flies were tormenting.
Now it is cooler I ramble about more, but my loneliness
goes everywhere with me. Everything is so still here,
that it sometimes makes me afraid. The moonlight looks
awfully solemn on the dark pines. You remember that dead
pine-tree? The wind has broken it, and there it stands in
front of the evergreen grove, with two arms spread out,
and a knot like a head with a hat on it, and a streamer of
moss hanging from it. It looks so white and strange in
the moonlight, that it seems as if Floracita's spirit were
beckoning to me.

"But I did n't mean to write about sad things. I don't
feel sad now; I was only telling you how lonely and
nervous I *had* been, that you might imagine how much
good it has done me to see such kind arrangements at
Magnolia Lawn. Forgive me for going there, contrary
to your orders. I did so long for a little variety! I
could n't have dreamed you were planning such a pleasant
surprise for me. Sha' n't we be happy there, calling one
another all the old foolish pet names? Dear, good Gerald,
I shall never again have any ungrateful doubts of your love.

"*Adios, luz de mes ojos.* Come soon to

"Your grateful and loving

"ROSA."

That evening the plash of the waves no longer seemed like a requiem over her lost sister; the moonlight gave poetic beauty to the pines; and even the blasted tree, with its waving streamer of moss, seemed only another picturesque feature in the landscape; so truly does Nature give us back a reflection of our souls.

She waked from a refreshing sleep with a consciousness of happiness unknown for a long time. When Tom came to say he was going to Savannah, she commissioned him to go to the store where her dresses were usually ordered, and buy some fine French merino. She gave him very minute directions, accompanied with a bird-of-paradise pattern. "That is Gerald's favorite color," she said to herself. "I will embroider it with white floss-silk, and tie it with white silk cord and tassels. The first time we breakfast together at Magnolia Lawn I will wear it, fastened at the throat with that pretty little knot of silver filigree he gave me on my birthday. Then I shall look as bridal as the home he is preparing for me."

The embroidery of this dress furnished pleasant occupation for many days. When it was half finished, she tried it on before the mirror, and smiled to see how becoming was the effect. She queried whether Gerald would like one or two of Madame Guirlande's pale amber-colored artificial nasturtiums in her hair. She placed them coquettishly by the side of her head for a moment, and laid them down, saying to herself: "No; too much dress for the morning. He will like better the plain braids of my hair with the curls falling over them." As she sat, hour after hour, embroidering the dress which was expected to produce such a sensation, Tulee's heart was gladdened by hearing her sing almost continually. "Bless her

dear heart!" exclaimed she; "that sounds like the old
times."

But when a fortnight passed without an answer to her
letter, the showers of melody subsided. Shadows of old
doubts began to creep over the inward sunshine; though
she tried to drive them away by recalling Gerald's promise
to try to secure her safety by making a compromise with
her father's creditors. And were not the new arrangements at Magnolia Lawn a sign that he had accomplished
his generous purpose? She was asking herself that question for the hundredth time, as she sat looking out on the
twilight landscape, when she heard a well-known voice approaching, singing, " C'est l'amour, l'amour, l'amour, qui
fait le monde à la ronde"; and a moment after she was
folded in Gerald's arms, and he was calling her endearing
names in a polyglot of languages, which he had learned
from her and Floracita.

"So you are not very angry with me for going there
and finding out your secret," inquired she.

" I *was* angry," he replied ; " but while I was coming to
you all my anger melted away."

"And you do love me as well as ever," said she. " I
thought perhaps so many handsome ladies would fall in love
with you, that I should not be your Rosa *munda* any more."

" I have met many handsome ladies," responded he,
" but never one worthy to bear the train of my Rosa Regina."

Thus the evening passed in conversation more agreeable
to them than the wittiest or the wisest would have been.
But it has been well said, " the words of lovers are like the
rich wines of the South, — they are delicious in their native
soil, but will not bear transportation."

The next morning he announced the necessity of returning to the North to complete some business, and said he must, in the mean time, spend some hours at the plantation. "And Rosa dear," added he, "I shall really be angry with you if you go there again unless I am with you."

She shook her finger at him, and said, with one of her most expressive smiles : " Ah, I see through you ! You are planning some more pleasant surprises for me. How happy we shall be there ! As for that rich uncle of yours, if you will only let me see him, I will do my best to make him love me, and perhaps I shall succeed."

"It would be wonderful if you did not, you charming enchantress," responded he. He folded her closely, and looked into the depths of her beautiful eyes with intensity, not unmingled with sadness.

A moment after he was waving his hat from the shrubbery ; and so he passed away out of her sight. His sudden reappearance, his lavish fondness, his quick departure, and the strange earnestness of his farewell look, were remembered like the flitting visions of a dream.

CHAPTER XI.

IN less than three weeks after that tender parting, an elegant barouche stopped in front of Magnolia Lawn, and Mr. Fitzgerald assisted a very pretty blonde young lady to alight from it. As she entered the parlor, wavering gleams of sunset lighted up the pearl-colored paper, softened by lace-shadows from the windows. The lady glanced round the apartment with a happy smile, and, turning to the window, said: "What a beautiful lawn! What superb trees!"

"Does it equal your expectations, dear?" he asked. "You had formed such romantic ideas of the place, I feared you might be disappointed."

"I suppose that was the reason you tried to persuade me to spend our honeymoon in Savannah," rejoined she. "But we should be so bored with visitors. Here, it seems like the Garden of Eden, when Adam and Eve had it all to themselves, before the serpent went there to make mischief. I had heard father and mother tell so much about Magnolia Lawn that I was eager to see it."

"They visited it in spring, when it really does look like Paradise," replied he. "It has its beauties now; but this is not the favorable season for seeing it; and after we have been here a few days, I think we had better return to Savannah, and come again when the lawn is carpeted with flowers."

"I see your mind is bent upon not staying here," answered she; "and I suppose it *would* be rather tiresome to have no other company than your stupid little Lily Bell."

She spoke with a pouting affectation of reproach, and he exclaimed, " Lily, darling ! " as he passed his arm round her slender waist, and, putting aside a shower of pale yellowish ringlets, gazed fondly into the blue eyes that were upturned to his.

They were interrupted by the entrance of Venus, who came to ask their orders. " Tell them to serve supper at seven, and then come and show your mistress to her dressing-room," he said. As she retired, he added: " Now she 'll have something to tell of. She 'll be proud enough of being the first to get a full sight of the new Missis; and it *is* a sight worth talking about."

With a gratified smile, she glanced at the pier-glass which reflected her graceful little figure, and, taking his arm, she walked slowly round the room, praising the tasteful arrangements. " Everything has such a bridal look ! " she said.

" Of course," replied he ; " when I have such a fair Lily Bell for a bride, I wish to have her bower pearly and lily-like. But here is Venus come to show you to your dressing-room. I hope you will like the arrangements up stairs also."

She kissed her hand to him as she left the room, and he returned the salute. When she had gone, he paced slowly up and down for a few moments. As he passed the piano, he touched the keys in a rambling way. The tones he brought out were a few notes of an air he and Rosabella had sung in that same room a few months before. He turned abruptly from the instrument, and looked out from the window in the direction of the lonely cottage. Nothing was visible but trees and a line of the ocean beyond. But the chambers of his soul were filled with visions of Rosa.

He thought of the delightful day they had spent together, looking upon these same scenes; of their songs and caresses in the bower; of her letter, so full of love and glad surprise at the bridal arrangements she supposed he had made for her. "I really hope Lily wont insist upon staying here long," thought he; "for it is rather an embarrassing position for me."

He seated himself at the piano and swept his hand up and down the keys, as if trying to drown his thoughts in a tempest of sound. But, do what he would, the thoughts spoke loudest; and after a while he leaned his head forward on the piano, lost in revery.

A soft little hand touched his head, and a feminine voice inquired, "What are you thinking of, Gerald?"

"Of you, my pearl," he replied, rising hastily, and stooping to imprint a kiss on the forehead of his bride.

"And pray what were **you thinking about** *me?*" she asked.

"That you are the greatest beauty in the world, and that I love you better than man ever loved woman," rejoined he. And so the game of courtship went **on, till** it was interrupted by a summons to supper.

When they returned some time later, the curtains were drawn and candles lighted. "You have not yet tried the piano," said he, as he placed the music-stool.

She seated herself, and, after running up and down the keys, and saying she liked the tone of the instrument, she began to play and sing "Robin Adair." She had a **sweet,** thin voice, and her style of playing indicated rather one who had learned music, than one whose soul lived in its element. Fitzgerald thought of the last singing he had heard at that piano; and without asking for another song,

6 *   I

he began to sing to her accompaniment, " Drink to me only
with thine eyes." He had scarcely finished the line, " Leave
a kiss within the cup, and I'll not ask for wine," when clear,
liquid tones rose on the air, apparently from the veranda ;
and the words they carried on their wings were these : —

> " Down in the meadow, 'mong the clover,
>> I walked with Nelly by my side.
> Now all those happy-days are over,
>> **Farewell, my** dark Virginia bride.
>> **Nelly was a lady ;**
>>> Last night she died.
>> Toll the bell for lovely Nell,
>>> My dark Virginia bride."

The bride listened intensely, her fingers resting lightly
on the keys, and when the sounds died away she started
up, exclaiming, " What a voice ! I never heard anything
like it."

She moved eagerly toward the veranda, but was suddenly arrested by her husband. " No, no, darling," said
he. " You mustn't expose yourself to the night air."

" Then do go out yourself and bring her in," urged she.
" I must hear more of that voice. Who is she ? "

" One of the darkies, I suppose," rejoined he. " You
know they all have musical gifts."

" Not such gifts as that, I imagine," she replied. " Do
go out and bring her in."

She was about to draw **the** curtain aside to look out,
when he nervously called her attention to another window.
" See here ! " he exclaimed. " My people are gathering to
welcome their new missis. In answer to Tom's request,
I told him I would introduce you to them to-night. But
you are tired, and I am afraid you will take cold in the

evening air; so we will postpone the ceremony until to-
morrow."

"O, no," she replied, "I would prefer to go now. How
their black faces will shine when they see the glass beads
and gay handkerchiefs I have brought for them! Besides,
I want to find out who that singer is. It's strange you
don't take more interest in such a voice as that, when you
are so full of music. Will you have the goodness to ring
for my shawl?"

With a decision almost peremptory in its tone, he said,
"No; I had rather you would *not* go out." Seeing that
his manner excited some surprise, he patted her head and
added: "Mind your husband now, that's a good child.
Amuse yourself at the piano while I go out."

She pouted a little, but finished by saying coaxingly,
"Come back soon, dear." She attempted to follow him
far enough to look out on the veranda, but he gently put
her back, and, kissing his hand to her, departed. She
raised a corner of the curtain and peeped out to catch the
last glimpse of his figure. The moon was rising, and she
could see that he walked slowly, peering into spots of dense
shadow or thickets of shrubbery, as if looking for some
one. But all was motionless and still, save the sound of a
banjo from the group of servants. "How I wish I could
hear that voice again!" she thought to herself. "It's very
singular Gerald should appear so indifferent to it. What
can be the meaning of it?"

She pondered for a few minutes, and then she tried to
play; but not finding it entertaining without an auditor, she
soon rose, and, drawing aside one of the curtains, looked
out upon the lovely night. The grand old trees cast broad
shadows on the lawn, and the shrubbery of the garden

gleamed in the soft moonlight. She felt solitary without
any one to speak to, and, being accustomed to have her
whims gratified, she was rather impatient under the prohibition laid upon her. She rung the bell and requested
Venus to bring her shawl. The obsequious dressing-maid
laid it lightly on her shoulders, and holding out a white
nubia of zephyr worsted, she said, " P'r'aps missis would
like to war dis ere." She stood watching while her mistress twined the gossamer fabric round her head with careless grace. She opened the door for her to pass out on the
veranda, and as she looked after her she muttered to herself, " She 's a pooty missis ; but not such a gran' hansom
lady as turrer." A laugh shone through her dark face as
she added, " 'T would be curus ef she should fine turrer
missis out dar." As she passed through the parlor she
glanced at the large mirror, which dimly reflected her
dusky charms, and said with a smile : " Massa knows
what 's hansome. He 's good judge ob we far sex."

The remark was inaudible to the bride, who walked up
and down the veranda, ever and anon glancing at the garden walks, to see if Gerald were in sight. She had a little
plan of hiding among the vines when she saw him coming,
and peeping out suddenly as he approached. She thought
to herself she should look so pretty in the moonlight, that
he would forget to chide her. And certainly she was a
pleasant vision. Her fairy figure, enveloped in soft white
folds of muslin, her delicate complexion shaded by curls so
fair that they seemed a portion of the fleecy nubia, were so
perfectly in unison with the mild radiance of the evening,
that she seemed like an embodied portion of the moonlight.
Gerald absented himself so long that her little plan of sur-
prising him had time to cool. She paused more frequently

in her promenade, and looked longer at the distant sparkle
of the sea. Turning to resume her walk, after one of these
brief moments of contemplation, she happened to glance at
the lattice-work of the veranda, and through one of its
openings saw a large, dark eye watching her. She started
to run into the house, but upon second thought she called
out, " Gerald, you rogue, why did n't you speak to let me
know you were there?" She darted toward the lattice,
but the eye disappeared. She tried to follow, but saw only
a tall shadow gliding away behind the corner of the house.
She pursued, but found only a tremulous reflection of vines
in the moonlight. She kept on round the house, and into
the garden, frequently calling out, " Gerald! Gerald!"
" Hark! hark!" she murmured to herself, as some far-off
tones of " Toll the bell" floated through the air. The
ghostly moonlight, the strange, lonely place, and the sad,
mysterious sounds made her a little afraid. In a more
agitated tone, she called Gerald again. In obedience to
her summons, she saw him coming toward her in the garden walk. Forgetful of her momentary fear, she sprang
toward him, exclaiming: " Are you a wizard? How did
you get there, when two minutes ago you were peeping at
me through the veranda lattice?"

" I have n't been there," he replied; " but why are you
out here, Lily, when I particularly requested you to stay
in the house till I came?"

" O, you were so long coming, that I grew tired of being
alone. The moonlight looked so inviting that I went out
on the veranda to watch for you; and when I saw you
looking at me through the lattice, I ran after you, and
could n't find you."

' I have n't been near the lattice," he replied. " If you

saw somebody looking at you, I presume it was one of the servants peeping at the new missis."

"None of your tricks!" rejoined she, snapping her fingers at him playfully. "It was *your* eye that I saw. If it were n't for making you vain, I would ask you whether your handsome eyes could be mistaken for the eyes of one of your negroes. But I want you to go with me to that bower down there."

"Not to-night, dearest," said he. "I will go with you to-morrow."

"Now is just the time," persisted she. "Bowers never look so pretty as by moonlight. I don't think you are very gallant to your bride to refuse her such a little favor."

Thus urged, he yielded, though reluctantly, to her whim. As she entered the bower, and turned to speak to him, the moonlight fell full upon her figure. "What a pretty little witch you are!" he exclaimed. "My Lily Bell, my precious pearl, my sylph! You look like a spirit just floated down from the moon."

"All moonshine!" replied she, with a smile.

He kissed the saucy lips, and the vines which had witnessed other caresses in that same bower, a few months earlier, whispered to each other, but told no tales. She leaned her head upon his bosom, and looking out upon the winding walks of the garden, so fair and peaceful in sheen and shadow, she said that her new home was more beautiful than she had dreamed. "Hark!" said she, raising her head suddenly, and listening. "I thought I heard a sigh."

"It was only the wind among the vines," he replied. "Wandering about in the moonlight has made you nervous."

"I believe I *was* a little afraid before you came," said she. "That eye looking at me through the lattice gave me a start; and while I was running after your shadow, I heard that voice again singing, 'Toll the bell.' I wonder how you can be so indifferent about such a remarkable voice, when you are such a lover of music."

"I presume, as I told you before, that it was one of the darkies," rejoined he. "I will inquire about it to-morrow."

"I should sooner believe it to be the voice of an angel from heaven, than a darky," responded the bride. "I wish I could hear it again before I sleep."

In immediate response to her wish, the full rich voice she had invoked began to sing an air from "Norma," beginning, "O, how his art deceived thee!"

Fitzgerald started so suddenly, he overturned a seat near them. "Hush!" she whispered, clinging to his arm. Thus they stood in silence, she listening with rapt attention, he embarrassed and angry almost beyond endurance. The enchanting sounds were obviously receding.

"Let us follow her, and settle the question who she is," said Lily, trying to pull him forward. But he held her back strongly.

"No more running about to-night," he answered almost sternly. Then, immediately checking himself, he added, in a gentler tone: "It is imprudent in you to be out so long in the evening air; and I am really very tired, dear Lily. To-morrow I will try to ascertain which of the servants has been following you round in this strange way."

"Do you suppose any servant could sing *that?*" she exclaimed.

"They are nearly all musical, and wonderfully imitative," answered he. "They can catch almost anything

they hear." He spoke in a nonchalant tone, but she felt
his arm tremble as she leaned upon it. He had never before made such an effort to repress rage.

In tones of tender anxiety, she said: "I am afraid
you are very tired, dear. I am sorry I kept you out
so long."

"I am rather weary," he replied, taking her hand, and
holding it in his. He was so silent as they walked toward
the house, that she feared he was seriously offended with
her.

As they entered the parlor she said, "I did n't think
you cared about my not going out, Gerald, except on account of my taking cold; and with my shawl and nubia I
don't think there was the least danger of that. It was such
a beautiful night, I wanted to go out to meet you, dear."

He kissed her mechanically, and replied, "I am not
offended, darling."

"Then, if the blue devils possess you, we will try Saul's
method of driving them away," said she. She seated herself at the piano, and asked him whether he would accompany her with voice or flute. He tried the flute, but
played with such uncertainty, that she looked at him with
surprise. Music was the worst remedy she could have
tried to quiet the disturbance in his soul; for its voice
evoked ghosts of the past.

"I am really tired, Lily," said he; and, affecting a drowsiness he did not feel, he proposed retiring for the night.

The chamber was beautiful with the moon shining through
its rose-tinted drapery, and the murmur of the ocean was a
soothing lullaby. But it was long before either of them
slept; and when they slumbered, the same voice went
singing through their dreams. He was in the flowery par-

lor at New Orleans, listening to "The Light of other Days";
and she **was** following a veiled shadow through a strange
garden, hearing the intermingled tones of "Norma" and
"Toll the bell."

It was late in the morning when she **awoke.** **Gerald**
was gone, but a bouquet of fragrant flowers lay on the pillow beside her. Her dressing-gown was on a chair by the
bedside, and Venus sat at the window sewing.

"Where is Mr. Fitzgerald?" she inquired.

"He said he war gwine to turrer plantation on business.
He leff dem flower dar, an' tole me to say he 'd come back
soon."

The fair hair was neatly arranged by the black hands that
contrasted so strongly with it. The genteel little figure
was enveloped in a morning-dress of delicate blue and
white French cambric, and the little feet were ensconced
in slippers of azure velvet embroidered with silver. The
dainty breakfast, served on French porcelain, was slowly
eaten, and still Gerald returned not. She removed to the
chamber window, and, leaning her cheek on her hand, looked
out upon the sun-sparkle of the ocean. Her morning
thought was the same with which she had passed into slumber the previous night. How strange it was that Gerald
would take no notice of that enchanting voice! The inci-
dent that seemed to her a charming novelty had, she knew
not why, cast a shadow over the first evening in their
bridal home.

CHAPTER XII.

MR. FITZGERALD had ordered his horse to be saddled at an earlier hour than Tom had ever known him to ride, except on a hunting excursion, and in his own mind he concluded that his master would be asleep at the hour he had indicated. Before he stretched himself on the floor for the night, he expressed this opinion to the cook by saying, "Yer know, Dinah, white folks is allers mighty wide awake de night afore dey gits up."

To his surprise, however, Mr. Fitzgerald made his appearance at the stable just as he was beginning to comb the horse. "You lazy black rascal," he exclaimed, "did n't I order you to have the horse ready by this time?"

"Yes, Massa," replied Tom, sheering out of the way of the upraised whip; "but it peers like Massa's watch be leetle bit faster dan de sun dis ere mornin'."

The horse was speedily ready, and Tom looked after his master as he leaped into the saddle and dashed off in the direction of the lonely cottage. There was a grin on his face as he muttered, "Reckon Missis don't know whar yer gwine." He walked toward the house, whistling, "Nelly was a lady."

"Dat ar war gwine roun' an' roun' de hus las' night, jes like a sperit. 'Twar dat ar Spanish lady," said Dinah.

"She sings splendiferous," rejoined Tom, "an' Massa liked it more dan de berry bes bottle ob wine." He ended by humming, "Now all dem happy days am ober."

"Better not let Massa hear yer sing dat ar," said Dinah. "He make yer sing nudder song."

"She's mighty gran' lady, an' a bery perlite missis, an' Ise sorry fur her," replied Tom.

Mr. Fitzgerald had no sense of refreshment in his morning ride. He urged his horse along impatiently, with brow contracted and lips firmly compressed. He was rehearsing in his mind the severe reprimand he intended to bestow upon Rosa. He expected to be met with tears and reproaches, to which he would show himself hard till she made contrite apologies for her most unexpected and provoking proceedings. It was his purpose to pardon her at last, for he was far enough from wishing to lose her; and she had always been so gentle and submissive, that he entertained no doubt the scene would end with a loving willingness to accept his explanations, and believe in his renewed professions. "She loves me to distraction, and she is entirely in my power," thought he. "It will be strange indeed if I cannot mould her as I will."

Arrived at the cottage, he found Tulee washing on a bench outside the kitchen. "Good morning, Tulee," said he. "Is your mistress up yet?"

"Missy Rosy ha'n't been asleep," she answered in a very cold tone, without looking up from her work.

He entered the house, and softly opened the door of Rosa's sleeping apartment. She was walking slowly, with arms crossed, looking downward, as if plunged in thought. Her extreme pallor disarmed him, and there was no hardness in his tone when he said, "Rosabella!"

She started, for she had supposed the intruder was Tulee. With head proudly erect, nostrils dilated, and eyes that flashed fire, she exclaimed, "How dare you come here?"

This reception was so entirely unexpected, that it disconcerted him; and instead of the severe reproof he had contemplated, he said, in an expostulating tone: "Rosa, I always thought you the soul of honor. When we parted, you promised not to go to the plantation unless I was with you. Is this the way you keep your word?"

"*You* talk of honor and promises!" she exclaimed.

The sneer conveyed in the tones stung him to the quick. But he made an effort to conceal his chagrin, and said, with apparent calmness: "You must admit it was an unaccountable freak to start for the plantation in the evening, and go wandering round the grounds in that mysterious way. What could have induced you to take such a step?"

"I accidentally overheard Tom telling Tulee that you were to bring home a bride from the North yesterday. I could not believe it of you, and I was too proud to question him. But after reflecting upon it, I chose to go and see for myself. And when I *had* seen for myself, I wished to remind you of that past which you seemed to have forgotten."

"Curse on Tom!" he exclaimed. "He shall smart for this mischief."

"Don't be so unmanly as to punish a poor servant for mentioning a piece of news that interested the whole plantation, and which must of course be a matter of notoriety," she replied very quietly. "Both he and Tulee were delicate enough to conceal it from me."

Fitzgerald felt embarrassed by her perfect self-possession. After a slight pause, during which she kept her face averted from him, he said: "I confess that appearances are against me, and that you have reason to feel offended. But if you knew just how I was situated, you would, perhaps, judge me less harshly. I have met with heavy losses lately, and I was in danger of becoming bankrupt unless I could keep up my credit by a wealthy marriage. The father of this young lady is rich, and she fell in love with me. I have married her; but I tell you truly, dear Rosa, that I love you more than I ever loved any other woman."

"You say she loved you, and yet you could deceive her so," she replied. "You could conceal from her that you already had a wife. When I watched her as she walked on the veranda I was tempted to reveal myself, and disclose your baseness."

Fitzgerald's eyes flashed with sudden anger, as he vociferated, "Rosa, if you ever dare to set up any such claim — "

"If I *dare!*" she exclaimed, interrupting him in a tone of proud defiance, that thrilled through all his nerves.

Alarmed by the strength of character which he had never dreamed she possessed, he said: "In your present state of mind, there is no telling what you may dare to do. It becomes necessary for you to understand your true position. You are not my wife. The man who married us had no legal authority to perform the ceremony."

"O steeped in falsehood to the lips!" exclaimed she. "And *you* are the idol I have worshipped!"

He looked at her with astonishment not unmingled with admiration. "Rosa, I could not have believed you had such a temper," rejoined he. "But why will you persist in making yourself and me unhappy? As long as my wife is ignorant of my love for you, no harm is done. If you would only listen to reason, we might still be happy. I could manage to visit you often. You would find me as affectionate as ever; and I will provide amply for you."

"*Provide* for me?" she repeated slowly, looking him

calmly and loftily in the face. " What have you ever seen
in me, Mr. Fitzgerald, that has led you to suppose I would
consent to sell myself?"

His susceptible temperament could not withstand the
regal beauty of her proud attitude and indignant look.
"O Rosa," said he, "there is no woman on earth to be
compared with you. If you only knew how I idolize you
at this moment, after all the cruel words you have uttered,
you surely would relent. Why will you not be reasonable,
dearest? Why not consent to live with me as your mother
lived with your father?"

" Don't wrong the memory of my mother," responded
she hastily. " She was too pure and noble to be dishon-
ored by your cruel laws. She would never have entered
into any such base and degrading arrangement as you propose. She could n't have lived under the perpetual shame
of deceiving another wife. She could n't have loved my
father, if he had deceived her as you have deceived me.
She trusted him entirely, and in return he gave her his
undivided affection."

" And I give you undivided affection," he replied. " By
all the stars of heaven, I swear that you are now, as you
always have been, my Rosa Regina, my Rosa *munda*."

" Do not exhaust your oaths," rejoined she, with a contemptuous curl of the lip. " Keep some of them for your
Lily Bell, your precious pearl, your moonlight sylph."

Thinking the retort implied a shade of jealousy, he felt
encouraged to persevere. " You may thank your own im-
prudence for having overheard words so offensive to you,"
responded he. " But Rosa, dearest, you cannot, with all
your efforts, drive from you the pleasant memories of our
love. You surely do not hate me?"

"No, Mr. Fitzgerald; you have fallen below hatred. I despise you."

His brow contracted, and his lips tightened. "I cannot endure this treatment," said he, in tones of suppressed rage. "You tempt me too far. You compel me to humble your pride. Since I cannot persuade you to listen to expostulations and entreaties, I must inform you that my power over you is complete. You are my slave. I bought you of your father's creditors before I went to Nassau. I can sell you any day I choose; and, by Jove, I will, if — "

The sudden change that came over her arrested him. She pressed one hand hard upon her heart, and gasped for breath. He sank at once on his knees, crying, "O, forgive me, Rosa! I was beside myself."

But she gave no sign of hearing him; and seeing **her** reel backward into a chair, with pale lips and closing eyes, he hastened to summon Tulee. Such remorse came over him that he longed to wait for her returning consciousness. But he remembered that his long absence must excite surprise in the mind of his bride, and might, perhaps, connect itself with the mysterious singer of the preceding evening. Goaded by contending feelings, he hurried through the footpaths whence he had so often kissed his hand to Rosa in fond farewell, and hastily mounted his horse without one backward glance.

Before he came in sight of the plantation, the perturbation of his mind had subsided, and he began to think himself a much-injured individual. "Plague on the caprices of women!" thought he. "All this comes of Lily's taking the silly, romantic whim of coming here to spend the honeymoon. And Rosa, foolish girl, what airs she assumes! I wanted to deal generously by her; but she rejected all my offers as haughtily as if she had been queen of Spain and all the Americas. There's a devilish deal more of the Spanish blood in her than I thought for. Pride becomes her wonderfully; but it won't hold out forever. She'll find that she can't live without me. I can wait."

Feeling the need of some safety-valve to let off his vexation, he selected poor Tom for that purpose. When the obsequious servant came to lead away the horse, his master gave him a sharp cut of the whip, saying, "I'll teach you to tell tales again, you black rascal!" But having a dainty aversion to the sight of pain, he summoned the overseer, and consigned him to his tender mercies.

CHAPTER XIII.

IF Flora could have known all this, the sisters would have soon been locked in each other's arms ; but while she supposed that Rosa still regarded Mr. Fitzgerald with perfect love and confidence, no explanation of her flight could be given. She did indeed need to be often reminded by Mrs. Delano that it would be the most unkind thing toward her sister, as well as hazardous to herself, to attempt any communication. Notwithstanding the tenderest care for her comfort and happiness, she could not help being sometimes oppressed with homesickness. Her Boston home was tasteful and elegant, but everything seemed foreign and strange. She longed for Rosa and Tulee, and Madame and the Signor. She missed what she called the *olla-podrida* phrases to which she had always been accustomed ; and in her desire to behave with propriety, there was an unwonted sense of constraint. When callers came, she felt like a colt making its first acquaintance with harness. She endeavored to conceal such feelings from her kind benefactress ; but sometimes, if she was surprised in tears, she would say apologetically, "I love you dearly, Mamita Lila ; but it is dreadful to be so far away from anybody that ever knew anything about the old times."

"But you forget that I do know something about them, darling," replied Mrs. Delano. "I am never so happy as when you are telling me about your father. Perhaps by and by, when you have become enough used to your new home to feel as mischievous as you are prone to be, you

will take a fancy to sing to me, ' O, there's nothing half
so sweet in life as love's *old* dream.'"

It was beautiful to see how girlish the sensible and serious lady became in her efforts to be companionable to her
young *protégée*. Day after day, her intimate friends found
her playing battledoor or the Graces, or practising pretty
French romanzas, flowery rondeaux, or lively dances. She
was surprised at herself; for she had not supposed it possible for her ever to take an interest in such things after her
daughter died. But, like all going out of self, these efforts
brought their recompense.

She always introduced the little stranger as " Miss Flora
Delano, my adopted daughter." To those who were curious to inquire further, she said : " She is an orphan, in
whom I became much interested in the West Indies. As
we were both very much alone in the world, I thought the
wisest thing we could do would be to cheer each other's
loneliness." No allusion was ever made to her former
name, for that might have led to inconvenient questions
concerning her father's marriage ; and, moreover, the lady
had no wish to resuscitate the little piece of romance in
her own private history, now remembered by few.

It was contrary to Mrs. Delano's usual caution and de-
liberation to adopt a stranger so hastily; and had she been
questioned beforehand, she would have pronounced it impossible for her to enter into such a relation with one allied
to the colored race, and herself a slave. But a strange
combination of circumstances had all at once placed her in
this most unexpected position. She never for one moment
regretted the step she had taken ; but the consciousness of
having a secret to conceal, especially a secret at war with
the conventional rules of society, was distasteful to her, and

felt as some diminution of dignity. She did not believe in
the genuineness of Rosa's marriage, though she deemed it
best not to impart such doubts to Flora. If Mr. Fitzgerald
should marry another, she foresaw that it would be her
duty to assist in the reunion of the sisters, both of whom
were slaves. She often thought to herself, "In what a
singular complication I have become involved! So strange
for me, who have such an aversion to all sorts of intrigues
and mysteries." With these reflections were mingled anx-
ieties concerning Flora's future. Of course, it would not
be well for her to be deprived of youthful companionship;
and if she mixed with society, her handsome person, her
musical talent, and her graceful dancing would be sure to
attract admirers. And then, would it be right to conceal
her antecedents? And if they should be explained or accidentally discovered, after her young affections were engaged, what disappointment and sadness might follow!

But Flora's future was in a fair way to take care of
itself. One day she came flying into the parlor with her
face all aglow. "O Mamita Lila," exclaimed she, " I
have had such a pleasant surprise! I went to Mr. Goldwin's store to do your errand, and who should I find there
but Florimond Blumenthal!"

"And, pray, who is Florimond Blumenthal?" inquired
Mrs. Delano.

"O, have n't I told you? I thought I had told you all
about everybody and everything. He was a poor orphan,
that papa took for an errand-boy. He sent him to school,
and afterward he was his clerk. He came to our house
often when I was a little girl; but after he grew tall, papa
used to send an old negro man to do our errands. So I
did n't see him any more till *cher papa* died. He was very

kind to us then. He was the one that brought those beautiful baskets I told you of. Is n't it funny? They drove him away from New Orleans because they said he was an Abolitionist, and that he helped us to escape, when he did n't know anything at all about it. He said he heard we had gone to the North. And he went looking all round in New York, and then he came to Boston, hoping to see us or hear from us some day; but he had about done expecting it when I walked into the store. You never saw anybody so red as he was, when he held out his hand and said, in such a surprised way, 'Miss Royal, is it you?' Just out of mischief, I told him very demurely that my name was Delano. Then he became very formal all at once, and said, 'Does this silk suit you, Mrs. Delano?' That made me laugh, and blush too. I told him I was n't married, but a kind lady in Summer Street had adopted me and given me her name. Some other customers came up to the counter, and so I had to come away."

"Did you ask him not to mention your former name?" inquired Mrs. Delano.

"No, I had n't time to think of that," replied Flora; "but I *will* ask him."

"Don't go to the store on purpose to see him, dear. Young ladies should be careful about such things," suggested her maternal friend.

Two hours afterward, as they returned from a carriage-drive, Flora had just drawn off her gloves, when she began to rap on the window, and instantly darted into the street. Mrs. Delano, looking out, saw her on the opposite sidewalk, in earnest conversation with a young gentleman. When she returned, she said to her: "You should n't rap on the windows to young gentlemen, my child. It has n't a good appearance."

"I did n't rap to young gentlemen," replied Flora. "It was only Florimond. I wanted to tell him not to mention my name. He asked me about my sister, and I told him she was alive and well, and I could n't tell him any more at present. Florimond won't mention anything I request him not to, — I know he won't."

Mrs. Delano smiled to herself at Flora's quick, off-hand way of doing things. "But after all," thought she, "it is perhaps better settled so, than it would have been with more ceremony." Then speaking aloud, she said, "Your friend has a very blooming name."

"His name was Franz," rejoined Flora; "but Mamita called him Florimond, because he had such pink cheeks; and he liked Mamita so much, that he always writes his name Franz Florimond. We always had so many flowery names mixed up with our *olla-podrida* talk. *Your* name is flowery too. I used to say Mamita would have called you Lady Viola; but violet colors and lilac colors are cousins, and they both suit your complexion and your name, Mamita Lila."

After dinner, she began to play and sing with more gayety than she had manifested for many a day. While her friend played, she practised several new dances with great spirit; and after she had kissed good-night, she went twirling through the door, as if music were handing her out.

Mrs. Delano sat awhile in revery. She was thinking what a splendid marriage her adopted daughter might make, if it were not for that stain upon her birth. She was checked by the thought: "How I have fallen into the world's ways, which seemed to me so mean and heartless when I was young! Was *I* happy in the splendid marriage they made for *me?* From what Flora lets out occasionally, I judge her father felt painfully the anomalous position of his handsome daughters. Alas! if I had not been so weak as to give him up, all this miserable entanglement might have been prevented. So one wrong produces another wrong; and thus frightfully may we affect the destiny of others, while blindly following the lead of selfishness. But the past, with all its weaknesses and sins, has gone beyond recall; and I must try to write a better record on the present."

As she passed to her sleeping-room, she softly entered the adjoining chamber, and, shading the lamp with her hand, she stood for a moment looking at Flora. Though it was but a few minutes since she was darting round like a humming-bird, she was now sleeping as sweetly as a babe. She made an extremely pretty picture in her slumber, with the long dark eyelashes resting on her youthful cheek, and a shower of dark curls falling over her arm. "No wonder Alfred loved her so dearly," thought she. "If his spirit can see us, he must bless me for saving his innocent child." Filled with this solemn and tender thought, she knelt by the bedside, and prayed for blessing and guidance in the task she had undertaken.

The unexpected finding of a link connected with old times had a salutary effect on Flora's spirits. In the morning, she said that she had had pleasant dreams about Rosabella and Tulee, and that she did n't mean to be homesick any more. "It 's very ungrateful," added she, " when my dear, good Mamita Lila does so much to make me happy."

"To help you keep your good resolution, I propose that we go to the Athenæum," said Mrs. Delano, smiling.

Flora had never been in a gallery of paintings, and she was as much pleased as a little child with a new picture-book. Her enthusiasm attracted attention, and visitors smiled to see her clap her hands, and to hear her little shouts of pleasure or of fun. Ladies said to each other, "It 's plain that this lively little *adoptée* of Mrs. Delano's has never been much in good society." And gentlemen answered, "It is equally obvious that she has never kept vulgar company."

Mrs. Delano's nice ideas of conventional propriety were a little disturbed, and she was slightly annoyed by the attention they attracted. But she said to herself, "If I am always checking the child, I shall spoil the naturalness which makes her so charming." So she quietly went on explaining the pictures, and giving an account of the artists.

The next day it rained; and Mrs. Delano read aloud "The Lady of the Lake," stopping now and then to explain its connection with Scottish history, or to tell what scenes Rossini had introduced in *La Donna del Lago*, which she had heard performed in Paris. The scenes of the opera were eagerly imbibed, but the historical lessons rolled off her memory, like water from a duck's back. It continued to rain and drizzle for three days; and Flora, who was very atmospheric, began to yield to the dismal influence of the weather. Her watchful friend noticed the shadow of homesickness coming over the sunlight of her eyes, and proposed that they should go to a concert. Flora objected, saying that music would make her think so much of Rosabella, she was afraid she should cry in public. But when the programme was produced, she saw nothing associated with her sister, and said, "I will go if you wish

it, Mamita Lila, because I like to do everything you wish."
She felt very indifferent about going ; but when Mr. Wood
came forward, singing, " The sea, the sea, the open sea ! "
in tones so strong and full that they seemed the voice of
the sea itself, she was half beside herself with delight. She
kept time with her head and hands, with a degree of ani-
mation that made the people round her smile. She, quite
unconscious of observation, swayed to the music, and ever
and anon nodded her approbation to a fair-faced young
gentleman, who seemed to be enjoying the concert very
highly, though not to such a degree as to be oblivious of
the audience.

Mrs. Delano was partly amused and partly annoyed.
She took Flora's hand, and by a gentle pressure, now and
then, sought to remind her that they were in public ; but
she understood it as an indication of musical sympathy,
and went on all the same.

When they entered the carriage to return home, she
drew a long breath, and exclaimed, " O Mamita, how I
have enjoyed the concert ! "

" I am very glad of it," replied her friend. " I suppose
that was Mr. Blumenthal to whom you nodded several
times, and who followed you to the carriage. But, my
dear, it is n't the custom for young ladies to keep nodding
to young gentlemen in public places."

" Is n't it? I did n't think anything about it," rejoined
Flora. " But Florimond is n't a gentleman. He 's an old
acquaintance. Don't you find it very tiresome, Mamita, to
be always remembering what is the custom? I 'm sure _I_
shall never learn."

When she went singing up stairs that night, Mrs. Delano
smiled to herself as she said, " What _am_ I to do with this

mercurial young creature? What an overturn she makes in all my serious pursuits and quiet ways! But there is something singularly refreshing about the artless little darling."

Warm weather was coming, and Mrs. Delano began to make arrangements for passing the summer at Newport; but her plans were suddenly changed. One morning Flora wished to purchase some colored crayons to finish a drawing she had begun. As she was going out, her friend said to her, "The sun shines so brightly, you had better wear your veil."

"O, I 've been muffled up so much, I do detest veils," replied Flora, half laughingly and half impatiently. " I like to have a whole world full of air to breathe in. But if you wish it, Mamita Lila, I will wear it."

It seemed scarcely ten minutes after, when the door-bell was rung with energy, and Flora came in nervously agitated.

" O Mamita! " exclaimed she, " I am so glad you advised me to wear a veil. I met Mr. Fitzgerald in this very street. I don't think he saw me, for my veil was close, and as soon as I saw him coming I held my head down. He can't take me here in Boston, and carry me off, can he? "

" He shall not carry you off, darling; but you must not go in the street, except in the carriage with me. We will sit up stairs, a little away from the windows; and if I read aloud, you won't forget yourself and sing at your embroidery or drawing, as you are apt to do. It 's not likely he will remain in the city many days, and I will try to ascertain his movements."

Before they had settled to their occupations, a ring at the door made Flora start, and quickened the pulses of her less excitable friend. It proved to be only a box of flow-

7 *

ers from the country. But Mrs. Delano, uneasy in the presence of an undefined danger, the nature and extent of which she did not understand, opened her writing-desk and wrote the following **note** : —

"MR. WILLARD PERCIVAL.

"Dear Sir, — If you can spare an hour this evening to talk with me on a subject of importance, you will greatly oblige yours,

"Very respectfully,

"LILA DELANO."

A servant was sent with the note, and directed to admit no gentleman during the day or evening, without first bringing **up** his name.

While they were lingering at the tea-table, the door-bell rang, and Flora, with a look of alarm, started to run up stairs. "Wait a moment, till the **name is** brought in," said her friend. "If I admit the visitor, I should like to have you follow me to the parlor, and remain there ten or fifteen minutes. You can then go to your room, and when you are there, dear, be careful not to sing loud. Mr. Fitzgerald shall not take you from me ; but if he were to find out you were here, it might give rise to talk that would be unpleasant."

The servant announced Mr. Willard Percival ; and a few moments afterward Mrs. Delano introduced her *protégée*. Mr. Percival was too well bred to stare, but the handsome, foreign-looking little damsel evidently surprised him. He congratulated them both upon the relation between them, and said he need not wish the young lady happiness in her new home, for he believed Mrs. Delano always created an atmosphere of happiness around her.

After a few moments of desultory conversation, Flora left the room. When she had gone, Mr. Percival remarked, " That is a very fascinating young person."

" I thought she would strike you agreeably," replied Mrs. Delano. " Her beauty and gracefulness attracted me the first time I saw her ; and afterward I was still more taken by her extremely *naïve* manner. She has been brought up in seclusion as complete as Miranda's on the enchanted island ; and there is no resisting the charm of her impulsive naturalness. But, if you please, I will now explain the note I sent to you this morning. I heard some months ago that you had joined the Anti-Slavery Society."

" And did you send for me hoping to convert me from the error of my ways ? " inquired he, smiling.

" On the contrary, I sent for you to consult concerning a slave in whom I am interested."

" *You*, Mrs. Delano ! " he exclaimed, in a tone of great surprise.

" You may well think it strange," she replied, " knowing, as you do, how bitterly both my father and my husband were opposed to the anti-slavery agitation, and how entirely apart my own life has been from anything of that sort. But while I was at the South this winter, I heard of a case which greatly interested my feelings. A wealthy American merchant in New Orleans became strongly attached to a beautiful quadroon, who was both the daughter and the slave of a Spanish planter. Her father became involved in some pecuniary trouble, and sold his daughter to the American merchant, knowing that they were mutually attached. Her bondage was merely nominal, for the tie of affection remained constant between them as long as she lived ; and he would have married her if such marriages

had been legal in Louisiana. By some unaccountable
carelessness, he neglected to manumit her. She left two
handsome and accomplished daughters, who always supposed their mother to be a Spanish lady, and the wedded
wife of their father. But he died insolvent, and, to their
great dismay, they found themselves claimed as slaves under the Southern law, that 'the child follows the condition
of the mother.' A Southern gentleman, who was in love
with the eldest, married her privately, and smuggled them
both away to Nassau. After a while he went there to meet
them, having previously succeeded in buying them of the
creditors. But his conduct toward the younger was so
base, that she absconded. The question I wish to ask of
you is, whether, if he should find her in the Free States,
he could claim her as his slave, and have his claim allowed
by law."

"Not if he sent them to Nassau," replied Mr. Percival.
"British soil has the enviable distinction of making free
whosoever touches it."

"But he afterward brought them back to an island
between Georgia and South Carolina," said Mrs. Delano.
"The eldest proved a most loving and faithful wife, and to
this day has no suspicion of his designs with regard to her
sister."

"If he married her before he went to Nassau, the ceremony is not binding," rejoined Mr. Percival; "for no marriage with a slave is legal in the Southern States."

"I was ignorant of that law," said Mrs. Delano, "being
very little informed on the subject of slavery. But I suspected trickery of some sort in the transaction, because he
proved himself so unprincipled with regard to the sister."

"And where is the sister?" inquired Mr. Percival.

" I trust to your honor as a gentleman to keep the secret from every mortal," answered Mrs. Delano. " You have seen her this evening."

" Is it possible," he exclaimed, "that you mean to say she is your adopted daughter?"

" I did mean to say that," she replied. " I have placed great confidence in you ; for you can easily imagine it would be extremely disagreeable to me, as well as to her, to become objects of public notoriety."

" Your confidence is a sacred deposit," answered he. " I have long been aware that the most romantic stories in the country have grown out of the institution of slavery ; but this seems stranger than fiction. With all my knowledge of the subject, I find it hard to realize that such a young lady as that has been in danger of being sold on the auction-block in this republic. It makes one desirous to conceal that he is an American."

" My principal reason for wishing to consult you," said Mrs. Delano, " is, that Mr. Fitzgerald, the purchaser of these girls, is now in the city, and Flora met him this morning. Luckily, she was closely veiled, and he did not recognize her. I think it is impossible he can have obtained any clew to my connivance at her escape, and yet I feel a little uneasy. I am so ignorant of the laws on this subject, that I don't know what he has the power to do if he discovers her. Can he claim her here in Boston?"

" He could claim her and bring her before the United States Court," replied Mr. Percival ; " but I doubt whether he *would* do it. To claim such a girl as *that* for a slave, would excite general sympathy and indignation, and put too much ammunition into the hands of us Abolitionists. Besides, no court in the Free States could help deciding that, if he sent her to Nassau, she became free. If he should discover her whereabouts, I should n't wonder if attempts were made to kidnap her; for men of his character are very unscrupulous, and there are plenty of caitiffs in Boston ready to do any bidding of their Southern masters. If she were conveyed to the South, though the courts *ought* to decide she was free, it is doubtful whether they *would* do it; for, like Achilles, they scorn the idea that laws were made for such as they."

"If I were certain that Mr. Fitzgerald knew of her being here, or that he even suspected it," said Mrs. Delano, "I would at once take measures to settle the question by private purchase; but the presumption is that he and the sister suppose Flora to be dead, and her escape cannot be made known without betraying the cause of it. Flora has a great dread of disturbing her sister's happiness, and she thinks that, now she is away, all will go well. Another difficulty is, that, while the unfortunate lady believes herself to be his lawful wife, she is really his slave, and if she should offend him in any way he could sell her. It troubles me that I cannot discover any mode of ascertaining whether he deserts her or not. He keeps her hidden in the woods in that lonely island, where her existence is unknown, except to a few of his negro slaves. The only white friends she seems to have in the world are her music teacher and French teacher in New Orleans. Mr. Fitzgerald has impressed it upon their minds that the creditors of her father will prosecute him, and challenge him, if they discover that he first conveyed the girls away and then bought them at reduced prices. Therefore, if I should send an agent to New Orleans at any time to obtain tidings of the sister, those cautious friends would doubtless consider it a trap of the creditors, and would be very secretive."

"It is a tangled skein to unravel," rejoined Mr. Perci-val. "I do not see how anything can be done for the sister, under present circumstances."

"I feel undecided what course to pursue with regard to my adopted daughter," said Mrs. Delano. "Entire seclusion is neither cheerful nor salutary at her age. But her person and manners attract attention and excite curiosity. I am extremely desirous to keep her history secret, but I already find it difficult to answer questions without resorting to falsehood, which is a practice exceedingly abhorrent to me, and a very bad education for her. After this meeting with Mr. Fitzgerald, I cannot take her to any public place without a constant feeling of uneasiness. The fact is, I am so unused to intrigues and mysteries, and I find it so hard to realize that a young girl like her *can* be in such a position, that I am bewildered, and need time to settle my thoughts upon a rational basis."

"Such a responsibility is so new to you, so entirely foreign to your habits, that it must necessarily be perplexing," replied her visitor. "I would advise you to go abroad for a while. Mrs. Percival and I intend to sail for Europe soon, and if you will join us we shall consider ourselves fortunate."

"I accept the offer thankfully," said the lady. "It will help me out of a present difficulty in the very way I was wishing for."

When the arrangement was explained to Flora, with a caution not to go in the streets, or show herself at the windows meanwhile, she made no objection. But she showed her dimples with a broad smile, as she said, "It is written in the book of fate, Mamita Lila, 'Always hiding or running away.'"

CHAPTER XIV.

ALFRED R. KING, when summoned home to Boston by the illness of his mother, had, by advice of physicians, immediately accompanied her to the South of France, and afterward to Egypt. Finding little benefit from change of climate, and longing for familiar scenes and faces, she urged her son to return to New England, after a brief sojourn in Italy. She was destined never again to see the home for which she yearned. The worn-out garment of her soul was laid away under a flowery mound in Florence, and her son returned alone. During the two years thus occupied, communication with the United States had been much interrupted, and his thoughts had been so absorbed by his dying mother, that the memory of that bright evening in New Orleans recurred less frequently than it would otherwise have done. Still, the veiled picture remained in his soul, making the beauty of all other women seem dim. As he recrossed the Atlantic, lonely and sad, a radiant vision of those two sisters sometimes came before his imagination with the distinctness of actual presence. As he sat silently watching the white streak of foam in the wake of the vessel, he could see, as in a mirror, all the details of that flowery parlor; he could hear the continuous flow of the fountain in the garden, and the melodious tones of "Buena Notte, amato bene."

Arrived in Boston, his first inquiry of the merchants was whether they had heard anything of Mr. Royal. He received the news of his death with a whirl of emotions.

How he longed for tidings concerning the daughters! But questions would of course be unavailing, since their existence was entirely unknown at the North. That Mr. Royal had died insolvent, and his property had been disposed of at auction, filled him with alarm. It instantly occurred to him how much power such circumstances would place in the hands of Mr. Fitzgerald. The thought passed through his mind, "Would he marry Rosabella?" And he seemed to hear a repetition of the light, careless tones, "Of course not, — she was a quadroon." His uneasiness was too strong to be restrained, and the second day after his arrival he started for New Orleans.

He found the store of his old friend occupied by strangers, who could only repeat what he had already heard. He rode out to the house where he had passed that never-to-be-forgotten evening. There all was painfully changed. The purchasers had refurnished the house with tasteless gewgaws, and the spirit of gracefulness had vanished. Their unmodulated voices grated on his ear, in contrast with the liquid softness of Rosabella's tones, and the merry, musical tinkling of Floracita's prattle. All they could tell him was, that they heard the quadroons who used to be kept there by the gentleman that owned the house had gone to the North somewhere. A pang shot through his soul as he asked himself whether they remembered his offer of assistance, and had gone in search of him. He turned and looked back upon the house, as he had done that farewell morning, when he assured them that he would be a brother in time of need. He could hardly believe that all the life and love and beauty which animated that home had vanished into utter darkness. It seemed stranger than the changes of a dream.

K

Very sad at heart, he returned to the city and sought out a merchant with whom his father had been accustomed to transact business. "Mr. Talbot," said he, "I have come to New Orleans to inquire concerning the affairs of the late Mr. Alfred Royal, who was a particular friend of my father. I have been surprised to hear that he died insolvent; for I supposed him to be wealthy."

"He was generally so considered," rejoined Mr. Talbot. "But he was brought down by successive failures, and some unlucky investments, as we merchants often are, you know."

"Were you acquainted with him," asked Alfred.

"I knew very little of him, except in the way of business," replied the merchant. "He was disinclined to society, and therefore some people considered him eccentric; but he had the reputation of being a kind-hearted, honorable man."

"I think he never married," said Alfred, in a tone of hesitating inquiry, which he hoped might lead to the subject he had at heart.

But it only elicited the brief reply, "He was a bachelor."

"Did you ever hear of any family not legitimated by law?" inquired the young man.

"There was a rumor about his living somewhere out of the city with a handsome quadroon," answered the merchant. "But such arrangements are so common here, they excite no curiosity."

"Can you think of any one who had intimate relations with him, of whom I could learn something about that connection?"

"No, I cannot. As I tell you, he never mixed with society, and people knew very little about him. Ha!

there's a gentleman going by now, who may be able to give you some information. Hallo, Signor Papanti!"

The Italian, who was thus hailed, halted in his quick walk, and, being beckoned to by Mr. Talbot, crossed the street and entered the store.

"I think you brought a bill against the estate of the late Mr. Alfred Royal for lessons given to some quadroon girls. Did you not?" inquired the merchant.

Having received an answer in the affirmative, he said: "This is Mr. King, a young gentleman from the North, who wishes to obtain information on that subject. Perhaps you can give it to him."

"I remember the young gentleman," replied the Signor. "Mr. Royal did introduce me to him at his store."

The two gentlemen thus introduced bade Mr. Talbot good morning, and walked away together, when Mr. King said, "My father and Mr. Royal were as brothers, and that is the reason I feel interested to know what has become of his daughters."

The Italian replied, "I will tell *you*, sir, because Mr. Royal told me you were an excellent man, and the son of his old friend."

Rapid questions and answers soon brought out the principal features of the sisters' strange history. When it came to the fact of their being claimed as slaves, Mr. King started. "Is such a thing possible in this country?" he exclaimed. "Girls so elegant and accomplished as they were!"

"Quite possible, sir," responded the Signor. "I have known several similar instances in this city. But in this case I was surprised, because I never knew their mother was a slave. She was a singularly handsome and ladylike woman."

"How was it possible that Mr. Royal neglected to manumit her?" inquired the young man.

"I suppose he never thought of her otherwise than as his wife, and never dreamed of being otherwise than rich," rejoined the Signor. "Besides, you know how often death does overtake men with their duties half fulfilled. He did manumit his daughters a few months before his decease; but it was decided that he was then too deeply in debt to have a right to dispose of any portion of his property."

"Property!" echoed the indignant young man. "Such a term applied to women makes me an Abolitionist."

"Please not to speak that word aloud," responded the Italian. "I was in prison several weeks on the charge of helping off those interesting pupils of mine, and I don't know what might have become of me, if Mr. Fitzgerald had not helped me by money and influence. I have my own opinions about slavery, but I had rather go out of New Orleans before I express them."

"A free country indeed!" exclaimed the young man, "where one cannot safely express his indignation against such enormities. But tell me how the girls were rescued from such a dreadful fate; for by the assurance you gave me at the outset that they needed no assistance, I infer that they were rescued."

He listened with as much composure as he could to the account of Mr. Fitzgerald's agency in their escape, his marriage, Rosabella's devoted love for him, and her happy home on a Paradisian island. The Signor summed it up by saying, "I believe her happiness has been entirely without alloy, except the sad fate of her sister, of which we heard a few weeks ago."

"What has happened to her?" inquired Alfred, with eager interest.

"She went to the sea-shore to gather mosses, and never returned," replied the Signor. "It is supposed she slipped into the water and was drowned, or that she was seized by an alligator."

"O horrid!" exclaimed Alfred. "Poor Floracita! What a bright, beaming little beauty she was! But an alligator's mouth was a better fate than slavery."

"Again touching upon the dangerous topic!" rejoined tl.e Signor. "If you stay here long, I think you and the prison-walls will become acquainted. But here is what used to be poor Mr. Royal's happy home, and yonder is where Madame Papanti resides, — the Madame Guirlande I told you of, who befriended the poor orphans when they had no other friend. Her kindness to them, and her courage in managing for them, was what first put it in my head to ask her to be my wife. Come in and have a *tête-à-tête* with her, sir. She knew the girls from the time they were born, and she loved them like a mother."

Within the house, the young man listened to a more prolonged account, some of the details of which were new, others a repetition. Madame dwelt with evident satisfaction on the fact that Rosa, in the midst of all her peril, refused to accept the protection of Mr. Fitzgerald, unless she were married to him; because she had so promised her father, the night before he died.

"That was highly honorable to her," replied Mr. King; "but marriage with a slave is not valid in law."

"So the Signor says," rejoined Madame. "I was so frightened and hurried, and I was so relieved when a protector offered himself, that I did n't think to inquire anything about it. Before Mr. Fitzgerald made his appearance, we had planned to go to Boston in search of you."

"Of *me!*" he exclaimed eagerly. "O, how I wish you had, and that I had been in Boston to receive you!"

"Well, I don't know that anything better could be done than has been done," responded Madame. "The girls were handsome to the perdition of their souls, as we say in France; and they knew no more about the world than two blind kittens. Their mother came here a stranger, and she made no acquaintance. Thus they seemed to be left singularly alone when their parents were gone. Mr. Fitzgerald was so desperately in love with Rosabella, and she with him, that they could not have been kept long apart any way. He has behaved very generously toward them. By purchasing them, he has taken them out of the power of the creditors, some of whom were very bad men. He bought Rosa's piano, and several other articles to which they were attached on their father's and mother's account, and conveyed them privately to the new home he had provided for them. Rosabella always writes of him as the most devoted of husbands; and dear little Floracita used to mention him as the kindest of brothers. So there seems every reason to suppose that Rosa will be as fortunate as her mother was."

"I hope so," replied Mr. King. "But I know Mr. Royal had very little confidence in Mr. Fitzgerald; and the brief acquaintance I had with him impressed me with the idea that he was a heartless, insidious man. Moreover, they are his slaves."

"They don't know that," rejoined Madame. "He has had the delicacy to conceal it from them."

"It would have been more delicate to have recorded their manumission," responded Mr. King.

"That would necessarily involve change of residence,"

remarked the Signor; "for the laws of Georgia forbid the manumission of slaves within the State."

"What blasphemy to call such cruel enactments by the sacred name of law!" replied the young man. "As well might the compacts of robbers to secure their plunder be called law. The walls have no ears or tongues, Signor," added he, smiling; "so I think you will not be thrust in jail for having such an imprudent guest. But, as I was saying, I cannot help having misgivings concerning the future. I want you to keep a sharp lookout concerning the welfare of those young ladies, and to inform me from time to time. Wheresoever I may happen to be, I will furnish you with my address, and I wish you also to let me know where you are to be found, if you should change your residence. My father and Mr. Royal were like brothers when they were young men, and if my father were living he would wish to protect the children of his friend. The duty that he would have performed devolves upon me. I will deposit five thousand dollars with Mr. Talbot, for their use, subject to your order, should any unhappy emergency occur. I say *their* use, bearing in mind the possibility that Floracita may reappear, though that seems very unlikely. But, my friends, I wish to bind you, by the most solemn promise, never to mention my name in connection with this transaction, and never to give any possible clew to it. I wish you also to conceal my having come here to inquire concerning them. If they ever need assistance, I do not wish them to know or conjecture who their benefactor is. If you have occasion to call for the money, merely say that an old friend of their father's deposited it for their use."

"I will solemnly pledge myself to secrecy," answered

the Signor; "and though secrets are not considered very
safe with women, I believe Madame may be trusted to any
extent, where the welfare of these girls is concerned."

"I think you might say rather more than that, my
friend," rejoined Madame. "But that will do. I promise
to do in all respects as the young gentleman has requested,
though I trust and believe that his precautions will prove
needless. Mr. Fitzgerald is very wealthy, and I cannot
suppose it possible that he would ever allow Rosabella to
want for anything."

"That may be," replied Mr. King. "But storms come
up suddenly in the sunniest skies, as was the case with
poor Mr. Royal. If Mr. Fitzgerald's love remains constant, he may fail, or he may die, without making provision
for her manumission or support."

"That is very true," answered the Signor. "How much
forecast you Yankees have!"

"I should hardly deserve that compliment, my friends,
if I failed to supply you with the necessary means to carry
out my wishes." He put two hundred dollars into the
hands of each, saying, "You will keep me informed on the
subject; and if Mrs. Fitzgerald should be ill or in trouble,
you will go to her."

They remonstrated, saying it was too much. "Take it
then for what you *have* done," replied he.

When he had gone, Madame said, "Do you suppose he
does all this on account of the friendship of their fathers?"

"He's an uncommon son, if he does," replied the Signor. "But I'm glad Rosabella has such a firm anchor to
the windward if a storm should come."

Mr. King sought Mr. Talbot again, and placed five thousand dollars in his hands, with the necessary forms and in-

structions, adding: "Should any unforeseen emergency
render a larger sum necessary, please to advance it, and
draw on me. I am obliged to sail for Smyrna soon, on
business, or I would not trouble you to attend to this."

Mr. Talbot smiled significantly, as he said, "These
young ladies must be very charming, to inspire so deep
an interest in their welfare."

The young man, clad in the armor of an honest purpose,
did not feel the point of the arrow, and answered quietly:
"They *are* very charming. I saw them for a few hours
only, and never expect to see them again. Their father
and mine were very intimate friends, and I feel it a duty to
protect them from misfortune if possible." When the business was completed, and they had exchanged parting salutations, he turned back to say, "Do you happen to know
anything of Mr. Fitzgerald of Savannah?"

"I never had any acquaintance with him," replied Mr.
Talbot; "but he has the name of being something of a
roué, and rather fond of cards."

"Can the death of Floracita be apocryphal?" thought
Alfred. "Could he be capable of selling her? No. Surely mortal man could not wrong that artless child."

He returned to his lodgings, feeling more fatigued and
dispirited than usual. He had done all that was possible
for the welfare of the woman who had first inspired him
with love; but O, what would he not have given for such
an opportunity as Fitzgerald had! He was obliged to
confess to himself that the utter annihilation of his hope
was more bitter than he had supposed it would be. He no
longer doubted that he would have married her if he could,
in full view of all her antecedents, and even with his mother's prejudices to encounter. He could not, however, help

8

smiling at himself, as he thought: " Yet how very different
she was from what I had previously resolved to choose!
How wisely I have talked to young men about preferring
character to beauty! And lo! I found myself magnetized
at first sight by mere beauty!"

But manly pride rebelled against the imputation of such
weakness. "No, it was not mere outward beauty," he said
to himself. "True, I had no opportunity of becoming acquainted with the qualities of her soul, but her countenance
unmistakably expressed sweetness, modesty, and dignity,
and the inflexions of her voice were a sure guaranty for
refinement."

With visions of past and future revolving round him, he
fell asleep and dreamed he saw Rosabella alone on a plank,
sinking in a tempestuous sea. Free as he thought himself
from superstition, the dream made an uncomfortable impression on him, though he admitted that it was the natural
sequence of his waking thoughts.

CHAPTER XV.

ROSA came out of her swoon in a slow fever accompanied with delirium. Tulee was afraid to leave her long enough to go to the plantation in search of Tom; and having no medicines at hand, she did the best thing that could have been done. She continually moistened the parched tongue with water, and wiped the hot skin with wet cloths. While she was doing this, tears fell on her dear young mistress, lying there so broken and helpless, talking incoherently about her father and Floracita, about being a slave and being sold. This continued eight or ten days, during which she never seemed to recognize Tulee's presence, or to be conscious where she was. She was never wild or troublesome, but there were frequent restless motions, and signs of being afraid of something. Then such a heavy drowsiness came over her, that it was difficult to arouse her sufficiently to swallow a spoonful of nourishment. She slept, and slept, till it seemed as if she would sleep forever. "Nature, dear goddess," was doing the best she could for the poor weak body, that had been so racked by the torture of the soul.

Three weeks passed before Mr. Fitzgerald again made his appearance at the lonely cottage. He had often thought of Rosa meanwhile, not without uneasiness and some twinges of self-reproach. But considering the unlucky beginning of his honeymoon at Magnolia Lawn, he deemed it prudent to be very assiduous in his attentions to his bride. He took no walks or drives without her, and she seemed

satisfied with his entire devotion; but a veiled singing
shadow haunted the chambers of her soul.   When she and
her husband were occupied with music, she half expected
the pauses would be interrupted by another voice; nor was
he free from fears that those wandering sounds would come
again.   But annoyed as he would have been by the rich
tones of that voice once so dear to him, his self-love was
piqued that Rosa took no steps to recall him.   He had
such faith in his power over her, that he had been daily
hoping for a conciliatory note.   Tom had been as attentive
to the invalid as his enslaved condition would admit; but
as Tulee said very decidedly that she did n't want Massa
Fitzgerald to show his face there, he did not volunteer any
information.   At last, his master said to him one day,
" You 've been to the cottage, I suppose, Tom ? "

" Yes, Massa."

" How are they getting on there ? "

" Missy Rosy hab bin bery sick, but she done better
now."

" Why did n't you tell me, you black rascal ? "

" Massa hab neber ax me," replied Tom.

Mr. Fitzgerald found some food for vanity in this news.
He presumed the illness was caused by love for him, which
Rosa found herself unable to conquer.   This idea was very
pleasant to him; for it was not easy to relinquish the beautiful young creature who had loved him so exclusively.
Making a pretext of business, he mounted his horse and
rode off; throwing a farewell kiss to his bride as he went.
For greater security, he travelled a few moments in another
direction, and then sought the sequestered cottage by a cir-
cuitous route.   Tulee was vexed at heart when she heard
him, as he came through the woods, humming, " *C'est*

l'amour, l'amour "; and when he entered the cottage, she
wished she was a white man, that she could strike him.
But when he said, "Tulee, how is your mistress?" she
civilly answered, "Better, Massa."

He passed softly into Rosa's room. She was lying on
the bed, in a loose white robe, over which fell the long
braids of her dark hair. The warm coloring had entirely
faded from her cheeks, leaving only that faintest reflection
of gold which she inherited from her mother ; and the thinness and pallor of her face made her large eyes seem larger
and darker. They were open, but strangely veiled ; as if
shadows were resting on the soul, like fogs upon a landscape. When Gerald bent over her, she did not see him,
though she seemed to be looking at him. He called her
by the tenderest names ; he cried out in agony, "O Rosa,
speak to me, darling ! " She did not hear him. **He had**
never before been so deeply moved. He groaned aloud,
and, covering his face with **his hands, he wept.**

When Tulee, hearing the sound, crept in **to see** whether
all was well with her mistress, she found him in that pos-
ture. She went out silently, but when she was beyond
hearing she muttered to herself, "Ise glad he's got any
human feelin'."

After the lapse of a few moments, he came to her, saying, "O Tulee, do you think she's going to die? Could n't
a doctor save her?"

"No, Massa, I don't believe she's going to die," replied
Tulee ; "but she'll be very weak for a great while. I
don't think all the doctors in the world could do poor Missy
Rosy any good. It's her soul that's sick, Massa ; and
nobody but the Great Doctor above can cure that."

Her words cut him like a knife ; but, without **any at-**

tempt to excuse the wrong he had done, he said: "I am going to Savannah for the winter. I will leave Tom and Chloe at the plantation, with instructions to do whatever you want done. If I am needed, you can send Tom for me."

The melancholy wreck he had seen saddened him for a day or two; those eyes, with their mysterious expression of somnambulism, haunted him, and led him to drown uncomfortable feelings in copious draughts of wine. But, volatile as he was impressible, the next week saw him the gayest of the gay in parties at Savannah, where his pretty little bride was quite the fashion.

At the cottage there was little change, except that Chloe, by her master's permission, became a frequent visitor. She was an affectionate, useful creature, with good voice and ear, and a little wild gleam of poetry in her fervid eyes. When she saw Rosa lying there so still, helpless and unconscious as a new-born babe, she said, solemnly, "De sperit hab done gone somewhar." She told many stories of wonderful cures she had performed by prayer; and she would kneel by the bedside, hour after hour, holding the invalid's hand, praying, "O Lord, fotch back de sperit! Fotch back de sperit! Fotch back de sperit!" she would continue to repeat in ascending tones, till they rose to wild imploring. Tulee, looking on one day, said, "Poor Missy Rosy don't hear nothin' ye say, though ye call so loud."

"De good Lord up dar, He hars," replied Chloe, reverently pointing upward; and she went on with the vehement repetition. These supplications were often varied with Methodist hymns and negro melodies, of which the most common refrain was, "O glory! glory! glory!" But whether singing or praying, she made it a point to hold the invalid's hand and look into her eyes. For a long while, the spirit that had gone somewhere showed no signs of returning, in obedience to the persevering summons. But after several weeks had elapsed, there was a blind groping for Chloe's hand; and when it was found, Tulee thought she perceived something like a little flickering gleam flit over the pale face. Still, neither of the nurses was recognized; and no one ever knew what the absent soul was seeing and hearing in that mysterious somewhere whither it had flown. At last, Chloe's patient faith was rewarded by a feeble pressure of her hand. Their watchfulness grew more excited; and never did mother welcome the first gleam of intelligence in her babe with more thrilling joy, than the first faint, quivering smile on Rosa's lips was welcomed by those anxious, faithful friends. The eyes began to resume their natural expression. The fog was evidently clearing away from the soul, **and** the sunshine was gleaming through. The process of resuscitation was thenceforth constant, though very slow. It was **three** months after those cruel blows fell upon her loving heart before she spoke and feebly called them by their names. And not until a month later was she able to write a few lines to quiet the anxiety of Madame and the Signor.

A few days before her last ghostly visit to Magnolia Lawn, she had written them a very joyful letter, telling them of Gerald's preparations to acknowledge her as his wife, and make her the mistress of his beautiful home. They received the tidings with great joy, and answered with hearty congratulations. The Signor was impatient to write to Mr. King; but Madame, who had learned precaution and management by the trials and disappointments of a changing life, thought it best to wait till they could

inform him of the actual fact. As Rosa had never been in
the habit of writing oftener than once in four or five weeks,
they felt no uneasiness until after that time had elapsed;
and even then they said to each other, " She delays writing, as we do, until everything is arranged." But when
seven or eight weeks had passed, Madame wrote again,
requesting an immediate answer. Owing to the peculiar
position of the sisters, letters to them had always been sent
under cover to Mr. Fitzgerald; and when this letter arrived,
he was naturally curious to ascertain whether Madame
was aware of his marriage. It so happened that it had not
been announced in the only paper taken by the Signor; and
as they lived in a little foreign world of their own, they
remained in ignorance of it. Having read the letter, Mr.
Fitzgerald thought, as Rosa was not in a condition to read
it, it had better be committed to the flames. But fearing
that Madame or the Signor might come to Savannah in
search of tidings, and that some unlucky accident might
bring them to speech of his bride, he concluded it was best
to ward off such a contingency. He accordingly wrote a
very studied letter to Madame, telling her that, with her
knowledge of the world, he supposed she must be well
aware that the daughter of a quadroon slave could not be
legally recognized as the wife of a Southern gentleman;
that he still loved Rosa better than any other woman, but
wishing for legal heirs to his hereditary estate, it was necessary for him to marry. He stated that Rosa was recov-
ering from a slow fever, and had requested him to say that
they must not feel anxious about her; that she had everything for her comfort, had been carefully attended by two
good nurses, was daily getting better, and would write in a
few weeks; meanwhile, if anything retarded her complete
recovery, he would again write.

This letter he thought would meet the present emergency. His plans for the future were unsettled. He still hoped that Rosa, alone and unprotected as she was, without the legal ownership of herself, and subdued by sickness and trouble, would finally accede to his terms.

She, in her unconscious state, was of course ignorant of this correspondence. For some time after she recognized her nurses, she continued to be very drowsy, and manifested no curiosity concerning her condition. She was as passive in their hands as an infant, and they treated her as such. Chloe sung to her, and told her stories, which were generally concerning her own remarkable experiences ; for she was a great seer of visions. Perhaps she owed them to gifts of imagination, of which culture would have made her a poet ; but to her they seemed to be an objective reality. She often told of seeing Jesus, as she walked to and from the plantation. Once she had met him riding upon Thistle, with a golden crown upon his head. One evening he had run before her all the way, as a very little child, whose shining garments lighted up all the woods.

Four months after the swift destruction of her hopes, Rosa, after taking some drink from Tulee's hand, looked up in her face, and said, " How long have I been sick, dear Tulee ? "

" No matter about that, darling," she replied, patting her head fondly. " Ye must n't disturb your mind 'bout that."

After a little pause, the invalid said, " But tell me how long."

" Well then, darling, I did n't keep no 'count of the time ; but Tom says it 's February now."

" Yer see, Missy Rosy," interposed Chloe, " yer sperit hab done gone somewhar, an' yer did n't know nottin'.

But a booful angel, all in white, tuk yer by de han' an' toted yer back to Tulee an' Chloe. Dat ar angel hab grat hansum eyes, an' she tole me she war yer mudder; an' dat she war gwine to be wid yer allers, cause twar de will ob de Lord."

Rosa listened with a serious, pleased expression in her face; for the words of her simple comforter inspired a vague consciousness of some supernatural presence surrounding her with invisible protection.

A few hours after, she asked, with head averted from her attendant, "Has any one been here since I have been ill?"

Anxious to soothe the wounded heart as much as possible, Tulee answered: "Massa Gerald come to ask how ye did; and when he went to Savannah, he left Tom and Chloe at the plantation to help me take care of ye."

She manifested no emotion; and after a brief silence she inquired for letters from Madame. Being informed that there were none, she expressed a wish to be bolstered up, that she might try to write a few lines to her old friend. Chloe, in reply, whispered something in her ear, which seemed to surprise her. Her cheeks flushed, the first time for many a day; but she immediately closed her eyes, and tears glistened on the long, dark lashes. In obedience to the caution of her nurses, she deferred any attempt to write till the next week. She remained very silent during the day, but they knew that her thoughts were occupied; for they often saw tears oozing through the closed eyelids.

Meanwhile, her friends in New Orleans were in a state of great anxiety. Mr. Fitzgerald had again written in a strain very similar to his first letter, but from Rosa herself nothing had been received.

"I don't know what to make of this," said Madame.
"Rosa is not a girl that would consent to a secondary position where her heart was concerned."

"You know how common it is for quadroons to accede
to such double arrangements," rejoined the Signor.

"Of course I am well aware of that," she replied; "but
they are educated, from childhood, to accommodate themselves to their subordinate position, as a necessity that cannot be avoided. It was far otherwise with Rosa. Moreover, I believe there is too much of Grandpa Gonsalez in
her to submit to anything she deemed dishonorable. I
think, my friend, somebody ought to go to Savannah to inquire into this business. If you should go, I fear you would
get into a duel. You know dear Floracita used to call you
Signor Pimentero. But Mr. Fitzgerald won't fight *me*,
let me say what I will. So I think I had better go."

"Yes, you had better go. You're a born diplomate,
which I am not," replied the Signor.

Arrangements were accordingly made for going in a day
or two; but they were arrested by three or four lines from
Rosa, stating that she was getting well, that she had everything for her comfort, and would write more fully soon.
But what surprised them was that she requested them to
address her as Madame Gonsalez, under cover to her man-
tuamaker in Savannah, whose address was given.

"That shows plainly enough that she and Fitzgerald
have dissolved partnership," said Madame; "but as she
does not ask me to come, I will wait for her letter of explanation." Meanwhile, however, she wrote very affectionately in reply to the brief missive, urging Rosa to come
to New Orleans, and enclosing fifty dollars, with the statement that an old friend of her father's had died and left

a legacy for his daughters. Madame had, as Floracita observed, a talent for arranging the truth with variations.

The March of the Southern spring returned, wreathed with garlands, and its pathway strewn with flowers. She gave warm kisses to the firs and pines as she passed, and they returned her love with fragrant sighs. The garden at Magnolia Lawn had dressed itself with jonquils, hyacinths, and roses, and its bower was a nest of glossy greenery, where mocking-birds were singing their varied tunes, moving their white tail-feathers in time to their music. Mrs. Fitzgerald, who was not strong in health, was bent upon returning thither early in the season, and the servants were busy preparing for her reception. Chloe was rarely spared to go to the hidden cottage, where her attendance upon Rosa was no longer necessary; but Tom came once a week, as he always had done, to do whatever jobs or errands the inmates required. One day Tulee was surprised to hear her mistress ask him whether Mr. Fitzgerald was at the plantation; and being answered in the affirmative, she said, " Have the goodness to tell him that Missy Rosy would like to see him soon."

When Mr. Fitzgerald received the message, he adjusted his necktie at the mirror, and smiled over his self-complacent thoughts. He had hopes that the proud beauty was beginning to relent. Having left his wife in Savannah, there was no obstacle in the way of his obeying the summons. As he passed over the cottage lawn, he saw that Rosa was sewing at the window. He slackened his pace a little, with the idea that she might come out to meet him; but when he entered the parlor, she was still occupied with her work. She rose on his entrance, and moved a chair toward him; and when he said, half timidly, "How do you do now, dear Rosa?" she quietly replied, "Much better, I thank you. I have sent for you, Mr. Fitzgerald, to ask a favor."

"If it is anything in my power, it shall be granted," he replied.

"It is a very easy thing for you to do," rejoined she, "and very important to me. I want you to give me papers of manumission."

"Are you so afraid of me?" he asked, coloring as he remembered a certain threat he had uttered.

"I did not intend the request as any reproach to you," answered she, mildly; "but simply as a very urgent necessity to myself. As soon as my health will permit, I wish to be doing something for my own support, and, if possible, to repay you what you expended for me and my sister."

"Do you take me for a mean Yankee," exclaimed he indignantly, "that you propose such an account of dollars and cents?"

"I expressed my own wishes, not what I supposed you would require," replied she. "But aside from that, you can surely imagine it must be painful to have my life haunted by this dreadful spectre of slavery."

"Rosa," said he earnestly, "do me the justice to remember that I did not purchase you as a slave, or consider you a slave. I expended money with all my heart to save my best-beloved from misfortune."

"I believe those were your feelings then," she replied. "But let the past be buried. I simply ask you now, as a gentleman who has it in his power to confer a great favor on an unprotected woman, whether you will manumit me."

"Certainly I will," answered he, much discomposed by her cool business tone.

She rose at once, and placed the writing-desk before him. It was the pretty little desk he had given her for a birthday present.

He put his finger on it, and, looking up in her face, with one of his old insinuating glances, he said, "Rosa, do you remember what we said when I gave you this?"

Without answering the question, she said, "Will you have the goodness to write it now?"

"Why in such haste?" inquired he. "I have given you my promise, and do you suppose I have no sense of honor?"

A retort rose to her lips, but she suppressed it. "None of us can be sure of the future," she replied. "You know what happened when my dear father died." Overcome by that tender memory, she covered her eyes with her hand, and the tears stole through her fingers.

He attempted to kiss away the tears, but she drew back, and went on to say: "At that time I learned the bitter significance of the law, 'The child shall follow the condition of the mother.' It was not mainly on my own account that I sent for you, Mr. Fitzgerald. I wish to secure my child from such a dreadful contingency as well-nigh ruined me and my sister." She blushed, and lowered her eyes as she spoke.

"O Rosa!" he exclaimed. The impulse was strong to fold her to his heart; but he could not pass the barrier of her modest dignity.

After an embarrassed pause, she looked up bashfully, and said, "Knowing this, you surely will not refuse to write it now."

" I must see a lawyer and obtain witnesses," he replied.

She sighed heavily. " I don't know what forms are necessary," said she. " But I beg of you to take such steps as will make me perfectly secure against any accidents. And don't delay it, Mr. Fitzgerald. Will you send the papers next week?"

" I see you have no confidence in me," replied he, sadly. Then, suddenly dropping on his knees beside her, he exclaimed, " O Rosa, don't call me Mr. again. Do call me Gerald once more! Do say you forgive me!"

She drew back a little, but answered very gently: " I do forgive you, and I hope your innocent little wife will never regret having loved you; for that is a very bitter trial. I sincerely wish you may be happy; and you may rest assured I shall not attempt to interfere with your happiness. But I am not strong enough to talk much. Please promise to send those papers next week."

He made the promise, with averted head and a voice that was slightly tremulous.

" I thank you," she replied; " but I am much fatigued, and will bid you good morning." She rose to leave the room, but turned back and added, with solemn earnestness, " I think it will be a consolation on your death-bed if you do not neglect to fulfil Rosa's last request." She passed into the adjoining room, fastened the door, and threw herself on the couch, utterly exhausted. How strange and spectral this meeting seemed! She heard his retreating footsteps without the slightest desire to obtain a last glimpse of his figure. How entirely he had passed out of her life, he who so lately was *all* her life!

The next day Rosa wrote as follows to Madame and the Signor: —

"DEAREST AND BEST FRIENDS, — It would take days
to explain to you all that has happened since I wrote
you that long, happy letter; and at present I have not
strength to write much. When we meet we will talk
about it more fully, though I wish to avoid the miserable particulars as far as possible. The preparations I
so foolishly supposed were being made for me were for
a rich Northern bride, — a pretty, innocent-looking little
creature. The marriage with me, it seems, was counterfeit. When I discovered it, my first impulse was to
fly to you. But a strange illness came over me, and
I was oblivious of everything for four months. My good
Tulee and a black woman named Chloe brought me back
to life by their patient nursing. I suppose it was wrong,
but when I remembered who and what I was, I felt sorry
they did n't let me go. I was again seized with a longing
to fly to you, who were as father and mother to me and my
darling little sister in the days of our first misfortune.
But I was too weak to move, and I am still far from being
able to bear the fatigue of such a journey. Moreover, I
am fastened here for the present by another consideration.
Mr. Fitzgerald says he bought us of papa's creditors, and
that I am his slave. I have entreated him, for the sake
of our unborn child, to manumit me, and he has promised
to do it. If I could only be safe in New Orleans, it is my
wish to come and live with you, and find some way to support myself and my child. But I could have no peace, so
long as there was the remotest possibility of being claimed
as slaves. Mr. Fitzgerald may not mean that I shall ever
come to harm; but he may die without providing against
it, as poor papa did. I don't know what forms are necessary for my safety. I don't understand how it is that there

is no law to protect a defenceless woman, who has done no wrong. I will wait here a little longer to recruit my strength and have this matter settled. I wish it were possible for you, my dear, good mother, to come to me for two or three weeks in June; then perhaps you could take back with you your poor Rosa and her baby, if their lives should be spared. But if you cannot come, there is an experienced old negress here, called Granny Nan, who, Tulee says, will take good care of me. I thank you for your sympathizing, loving letter. Who could papa's friend be that left me a legacy? I was thankful for the fifty dollars, for it is very unpleasant to me to use any of Mr. Fitzgerald's money, though he tells Tom to supply everything I want. If it were not for you, dear friends, I don't think I should have courage to try to live. But something sustains me wonderfully through these dreadful trials. Sometimes I **think** poor Chloe's prayers bring me help from above; for the good soul is always praying for me.

"Adieu. May the good God bless you both.

"Your loving and grateful

"ROSABELLA."

Week passed after week, and the promised papers did not come. The weary days dragged their slow length along, unsoothed by anything except Tulee's loving care and Madame's cheering letters. The piano was never opened; for all tones of music were draped in mourning, and its harmonies were a funeral march over buried love. But she enjoyed the open air and the fragrance of the flowers. Sometimes she walked slowly about the lawn, and sometimes Tulee set her upon Thistle's back, and led him round and round through the bridle-paths. But out of the woods that concealed their nest they never ventured, lest they should meet Mrs. Fitzgerald. Tulee, who was somewhat proud on her mistress's account, was vexed by this limitation. "I don't see why ye should hide yerself from her," said she. "Yese as good as she is; and ye've nothin' to be shamed of."

"It isn't on my own account that I wish to avoid her seeing me," replied Rosa. "But I pity the innocent young creature. She didn't know of disturbing my happiness, and I should be sorry to disturb hers."

As the weeks glided away without bringing any fulfilment of Fitzgerald's promise, anxiety changed to distrust. She twice requested Tom to ask his master for the papers he had spoken of, and received a verbal answer that they would be sent as soon as they were ready. There were greater obstacles in the way than she, in her inexperience, was aware of. The laws of Georgia restrained humane impulses by forbidding the manumission of a slave. Consequently, he must either incur very undesirable publicity by applying to the legislature for a special exception in this case, or she must be manumitted in another State. He would gladly have managed a journey without the company of his wife, if he could thereby have regained his former influence with Rosa; but he was disinclined to take so much trouble to free her entirely from him. When he promised to send the papers, he intended to satisfy her with a sham certificate, as he had done with a counterfeit marriage; but he deferred doing it, because he had a vague sense of satisfaction in being able to tantalize the superior woman over whom he felt that he no longer had any other power.

CHAPTER XVI.

MADAME'S anxiety was much diminished after she began to receive letters in Rosa's own handwriting; but, knowing the laws of Georgia, and no longer doubtful concerning Fitzgerald's real character, she placed small reliance upon his promise of manumission. "This is another of his deceptions," said she to the Signor. "I have been thinking a good deal about the state of things, and I am convinced there will be no security in this country for that poor girl. You have been saying for some time that you wanted to see your beautiful Italy again, and I have the same feeling about my beautiful France. We each of us have a little money laid up; and if we draw upon the fund Mr. King has deposited, we can take Rosabella to Europe and bring her out as a singer."

"She would have a great career, no doubt," replied the Signor; "and I was going to suggest such a plan to you. But you would have to change your name again on my account, Madame; for I was obliged to leave Italy because I was discovered to be one of the Carbonari; and though fifteen years have elapsed, it is possible the watchful authorities have not forgotten my name."

"That's a trifling obstacle," resumed Madame. "You had better give notice to your pupils at once that you intend to leave as soon as present engagements are fulfilled. I will use up my stock for fancy articles, and sell off as fast as possible, that we may be ready to start for Europe as soon as Rosa has sufficient strength."

This resolution was immediately acted upon; but the fates were unpropitious to Madame's anticipated visit to the lonely island. A few days before her intended departure, the Signor was taken seriously ill, and remained so for two or three weeks. He fretted and fumed, more on her account than his own, but she, as usual, went through the trial bravely. She tried to compensate Rosa for the disappointment, as far as she could, by writing frequent letters, cheerful in tone, though prudently cautious concerning details. Fearing that Mr. Fitzgerald's suspicions might be excited by an apparent cessation of correspondence, she continued to write occasionally under cover to him, in a style adapted to his views, in case he should take a fancy to open the letters. The Signor laughed, and said, "Your talent for diplomacy is not likely to rust for want of use, Madame." Even Rosa, sad at heart as she was, could not help smiling sometimes at the totally different tone of the letters which she received under different covers.

She had become so accustomed to passive endurance, that no murmur escaped her when she found that her only white friend could not come to her, as she had expected. Granny Nan boasted of having nursed many grand white ladies, and her skill in the vocation proved equal to her pretensions. Only her faithful Tulee and the kind old colored mammy were with her when, hovering between life and death, she heard the cry that announced the advent of a human soul. Nature, deranged by bodily illness and mental trouble, provided no nourishment for the little one; but this, which under happier circumstances would have been a disappointment, called forth no expressions of regret from the patient sufferer. When Tulee held the babe before her in its first dress, she smiled faintly, but immediately closed her eyes. As she lay there, day after day, with the helpless little creature nestling in her arms, the one consoling reflection was that she had not given birth to a daughter. A chaos of thoughts were revolving through her mind; the theme of all the variations being how different it was from what it might have been, if the ideal of her girlhood had not been shattered so cruelly. Had it not been for that glimmering light in the future which Madame so assiduously presented to her view, courage would have forsaken her utterly. As it was, she often listened to the dash of the sea with the melancholy feeling that rest might be found beneath its waves. But she was still very young, the sky was bright, the earth was lovely, and she had a friend who had promised to provide a safe asylum for her somewhere. She tried to regain her strength, that she might leave the island, with all its sad reminders of departed happiness. Thinking of this, she rose one day and wandered into the little parlor to take a sort of farewell look. There was the piano, so long unopened, with a whole epic of love and sorrow in its remembered tones; the pretty little table her mother had painted; the basket she had received from her father after his death; Floracita's paintings and mosses; and innumerable little tokens of Gerald's love. Walking round slowly and feebly in presence of all those memories, how alone she felt, with none to speak to but Tulee and the old colored mammy, — she, who had been so tenderly cared for by her parents, so idolized by him to whom she gave her heart! She was still gazing pensively on these souvenirs of the past, when her attention was arrested by Tom's voice, saying: "Dar's a picaninny at de Grat Hus. How's turrer picaninny?"

The thought rushed upon her, " Ah, that baby had a father to welcome it and fondle it ; but *my* poor babe — " A sensation of faintness came over her ; and, holding on by the chairs and tables, she staggered back to the bed she had left.

Before the babe was a fortnight old, Tom announced that he was to accompany his master to New Orleans, whither he had been summoned by business. The occasion was eagerly seized by Rosa to send a letter and some small articles to Madame and the Signor. Tulee gave him very particular directions how to find the house, and charged him over and over again to tell them everything. When she cautioned him not to let his master know that he carried anything, Tom placed his thumb on the tip of his nose, and moved the fingers significantly, saying: " Dis ere nigger ha'n't jus' wakum'd up. Bin wake mos' ob de time sense twar daylight." He foresaw it would be difficult to execute the commission he had undertaken ; for as a slave he of course had little control over his own motions. He, however, promised to try ; and Tulee told him she had great confidence in his ingenuity in finding out ways and means.

" An' I tinks a heap o' ye, Tulee. Ye knows a heap more dan mos' niggers," was Tom's responsive compliment. In his eyes Tulee was in fact a highly accomplished person ; for though she could neither read nor write, she had caught the manners and speech of white people, by living almost exclusively with them, and she was, by habit, as familiar with French as English, beside having a little smattering of Spanish. To have his ingenuity praised by her operated as a fillip upon his vanity, and he inwardly resolved to run the risk of a flogging, rather than fail to do her bidding. He was also most loyal in the service of Rosa, whose beauty and kindliness had won his heart, before his sympathy had been called out by her misfortunes. But none of them foresaw what important consequences would result from his mission.

The first day he was in New Orleans, he found no hour when he could be absent without the liability of being called for by his master. The next day Mr. Bruteman dined with his master, and Tom was in attendance upon the table. Their conversation was at first about cotton crops, the prices of negroes, and other business matters, to which Tom paid little attention. But a few minutes afterward his ears were wide open.

"I suppose you came prepared to pay that debt you owe me," said Mr. Bruteman.

"I am obliged to ask an extension of your indulgence," replied Mr. Fitzgerald. "It is not in my power to raise that sum just now."

"How is that possible," inquired Mr. Bruteman, "when you have married the daughter of a Boston nabob?"

"The close old Yankee keeps hold of most of his money while he lives," rejoined his companion; "and Mrs. Fitzgerald has expensive tastes to be gratified."

"And do you expect me to wait till the old Yankee dies?" asked Mr. Bruteman. "Gentlemen generally consider themselves bound to be prompt in paying debts of honor."

"I'll pay you as soon as I can. What the devil can you ask more?" exclaimed Fitzgerald. "It seems to me it's not the part of a gentleman to play the dun so continually."

They had already drank pretty freely; but Mr. Bruteman took up a bottle, and said, "Let us drink another glass to the speedy replenishing of your purse." They poured full bumpers, touched glasses, and drank the contents.

There was a little pause, during which Mr. Bruteman sat twirling his glass between thumb and finger, with looks directed toward his companion. All at once he said, "Fitzgerald, did you ever find those handsome octoroon girls?"

"What octoroon girls?" inquired the other.

"O, you disremember them, do you?" rejoined he. "I mean how did that bargain turn out that you made with Royal's creditors? You seemed to have small chance of finding the girls; unless, indeed, you hid them away first, for the purpose of buying them for less than half they would have brought to the creditors, — which, of course, is not to be supposed, because no gentleman would do, such a thing."

Thrown off his guard by too much wine, Fitzgerald vociferated, "Do you mean to insinuate that I am no gentleman?"

Mr. Bruteman smiled, as he answered: "I said such a thing was not to be supposed. But come, Fitzgerald, let us understand one another. I'd rather, a devilish sight, have those girls than the money you owe me. Make them over to me, and I'll cancel the debt. Otherwise, I shall be under the necessity of laying an attachment on some of your property."

There was a momentary silence before Mr. Fitzgerald answered, "One of them is dead."

"Which one?" inquired his comrade.

"Flora, the youngest, was drowned."

"And that queenly beauty, where is she? I don't know that I ever heard her name."

"Rosabella Royal," replied Fitzgerald. "She is living at a convenient distance from my plantation."

"Well, I will be generous," said Bruteman. "If you will make *her* over to me, I will cancel the debt."

"She is not in strong health at present," rejoined Fitzgerald. "She has a babe about two weeks old."

"You know you have invited me to visit your island two or three weeks hence," replied Bruteman; "and then I shall depend upon you to introduce me to your fair Rosamond. But we will draw up the papers and sign them now, if you please."

Some jests unfit for repetition were uttered by the creditor, to which the unhappy debtor made no reply. When he called Tom to bring paper and ink, the observing servant noticed that he was very pale, though but a few moments before his face had been flushed.

That night, he tried to drown recollection in desperate gambling and frequent draughts of wine. Between one and two o'clock in the morning, his roisterous companions were led off by their servants, and he was put into bed by Tom, where he immediately dropped into a perfectly senseless sleep.

As soon as there was sufficient light, Tom started for the house of the Signor; judging that he was safe from his master for three hours at least. Notwithstanding the earliness of the hour, Madame made her appearance in a very few moments after her servant informed her who was in waiting, and the Signor soon followed. In the course of the next hour and a half an incredible amount of talking was done in negro "lingo" and broken English. The

9   M

impetuous Signor strode up and down, clenching his fists,
cursing slavery, and sending Fitzgerald to the Devil in a
volley of phrases hard enough in their significance, though
uttered in soft-flowing Italian.

"Swearing does no good, my friend," said Madame; "besides, there is n't time for it. Rosabella must be brought
away immediately. Bruteman will be on the alert, you
may depend. She slipped through his fingers once, and he
won't trust Fitzgerald again."

The Signor cooled down, and proposed to go for her
himself. But that was overruled, in a very kind way, by
his prudent wife, who argued that he was not well enough
for such an exciting adventure, or to be left without her
nursing, when his mind would be such a prey to uneasiness. It was her proposition to send at once for her
cousin Duroy, and have him receive very particular directions from Tom how to reach the island and find the cottage. Tom said he did n't know whether he could get
away for an hour again, because his master was always
very angry if he was out of the way when called; but if
Mr. Duroy would come to the hotel, he would find chances
to tell him what to do. And that plan was immediately
carried into effect.

While these things were going on in New Orleans, Mrs.
Fitzgerald was taking frequent drives about the lovely
island with her mother, Mrs. Bell; while Rosa was occasionally perambulating her little circuit of woods on the
back of patient Thistle. One day Mrs. Fitzgerald and her
mother received an invitation to the Welby plantation, to
meet some Northern acquaintances who were there; and
as Mrs. Fitzgerald's strength was not yet fully restored,
Mrs. Welby proposed that they should remain all night.

Chloe, who had lost her own baby, was chosen to nurse her master's new-born heir, and was consequently tied so closely that she could find no chance to go to the cottage, whose inmates she had a great longing to see. But when master and mistress were both gone, she thought she might take her freedom for a while without incurring any great risk. The other servants agreed to keep her secret, and Joe the coachman promised to drive her most of the way when he came back with the carriage. Accordingly, she made her appearance at the cottage quite unexpectedly, to the great joy of Tulee.

When she unwrapped the little black-haired baby from its foldings of white muslin, Tulee exclaimed: "He looks jus' like his good-for-nothing father; and so does Missy Rosy's baby. I'm 'fraid 't will make poor missy feel bad to see it, for she don't know nothin' 'bout it."

"Yes I do, Tulee," said Rosa, who had heard Chloe's voice, and gone out to greet her. "I heard Tom tell you about it."

She took up the little hand, scarcely bigger than a bird's claw, and while it twined closely about her finger, she looked into its eyes, so like to Gerald's in shape and color. She was hoping that those handsome eyes might never be used as his had been, but she gave no utterance to her thoughts. Her manner toward Chloe was full of grateful kindness; and the poor bondwoman had some happy hours, playing free for a while. She laid the infant on its face in her lap, trotting it gently, and patting its back, while she talked over with Tulee all the affairs at the "Grat Hus." And when the babe was asleep, she asked and obtained Rosa's permission to lay him on her bed beside his little brother. Then poor Chloe's soul took wing and soared aloft among sun-lighted clouds. As she prayed, and sang her fervent hymns, and told of her visions and revelations, she experienced satisfaction similar to that of a troubadour, or palmer from Holy Land, with an admiring audience listening to his wonderful adventures.

While she was thus occupied, Tulee came in hastily to say that a stranger gentleman was coming toward the house. Such an event in that lonely place produced general excitement, and some consternation. Rosa at once drew her curtain and bolted the door. But Tulee soon came rapping gently, saying, "It's only I, Missy Rosy." As the door partially opened, she said, "It's a friend Madame has sent ye." Rosa, stepping forward, recognized Mr. Duroy, the cousin in whose clothes Madame had escaped with them from New Orleans. She was very slightly acquainted with him, but it was such a comfort to see any one who knew of the old times that she could hardly refrain from throwing herself on his neck and bursting into tears. As she grasped his hand with a close pressure, he felt the thinness of her emaciated fingers. The paleness of her cheeks, and the saddened expression of her large eyes, excited his compassion. He was too polite to express it in words, but it was signified by the deference of his manner and the extreme gentleness of his tones. He talked of Madame's anxious love for her, of the Signor's improving health, of the near completion of their plan for going to Europe, and of their intention to take her with them. Rosa was full of thankfulness, but said she was as yet incapable of much exertion. Mr. Duroy went on to speak of Tom's visit to Madame; and slowly and cautiously he prepared the way for his account of the conversation between Mr. Fitzgerald and Mr. Bruteman. But

careful as he was, he noticed that her features tightened
and her hands were clenched. When he came to the interchange of writings, she sprung to her feet, and, clutching
his arm convulsively, exclaimed, " Did he do that ? " Her
eyes were like a flame, and her chest heaved with the
quick-coming breath.

He sought to draw her toward him, saying in soothing
tones, " They shall not harm you, my poor girl. Trust to
me, as if I were your father." But she burst from him
impetuously, and walked up and down rapidly ; such a
sudden access of strength had the body received from the
frantic soul.

" Try not to be so much agitated," said he. " In a very
short time you will be in Europe, and then you will be
perfectly safe."

She paused an instant in her walk, and, with a strange
glare in her eyes, she hissed out, " I hate him."

He laid his hand gently upon her shoulder, and said : " I
want very much that you should try to be calm. Some
negroes are coming with a boat at daybreak, and it is
necessary we should all go away with them. You ought
to rest as much as possible beforehand."

" Rest ! " repeated she with bitter emphasis. And
clenching her teeth hard, she again said, " I hate him ! "

Poor Rosa ! It had taken a mountain-weight of wrong
so to crush out all her gentleness.

Mr. Duroy became somewhat alarmed. He hastened to
the kitchen and told Chloe to go directly to Miss Rosa.
He then briefly explained his errand to Tulee, and told her
to prepare for departure as fast as possible. " But first go
to your mistress," said he ; " for I am afraid she may
go crazy."

The sufferer yielded more readily to Tulee's accustomed influence than she had done to that of Mr. Duroy. She allowed herself to be laid upon the bed; but while her forehead and temples were being bathed, her heart beat violently, and all her pulses were throbbing. It was, however, necessary to leave her with Chloe, who knelt by the bedside, holding her hand, and praying in tones unusually low for her.

"I'm feared for her," said Tulee to Mr. Duroy. "I never see Missy Rosy look so wild and strange."

A short time after, when she looked into the room, Rosa's eyes were closed. She whispered to Chloe: "Poor Missy's asleep. You can come and help me a little now."

But Rosa was not in the least drowsy. She had only remained still, to avoid being talked to. As soon as her attendants had withdrawn, she opened her eyes, and, turning toward the babes, she gazed upon them for a long time. There they lay side by side, like twin kittens. But ah! thought she, how different is their destiny! One is born to be cherished and waited upon all his days, the other is an outcast and a slave. My poor fatherless babe! He would n't manumit us. It was not thoughtlessness. He *meant* to sell us. "He *meant* to sell us," she repeated aloud; and again the wild, hard look came into her eyes. Such a tempest was raging in her soul, that she felt as if she could kill him if he stood before her. This savage paroxysm of revenge was followed by thoughts of suicide. She was about to rise, but hearing the approach of Tulee, she closed her eyes and remained still.

Language is powerless to describe the anguish of that lacerated soul. At last the storm subsided, and she fell into a heavy sleep.

Meanwhile the two black women were busy with arrangements for the early flight. Many things had been already prepared with the expectation of a summons to New Orleans, and not long after midnight all was in readiness. Chloe, after a sound nap on the kitchen floor, rose up with the first peep of light. She and Tulee hugged each other, with farewell kisses and sobs. She knelt by Rosa's bedside to whisper a brief prayer, and, giving her one long, lingering look, she took up her baby, and set off for the plantation, wondering at the mysterious ways of Providence.

They deferred waking Rosa as long as possible, and when they roused her, she had been so deeply sunk in slumber that she was at first bewildered. When recollection returned, she looked at her babe. " Where 's Chloe ? " she asked.

" Gone back to the plantation," was the reply.

" O, I am so sorry ! " sighed Rosa.

" She was feared they would miss her," rejoined Tulee. " So she went away as soon as she could see. But she prayed for ye, Missy Rosy ; and she told me to say poor Chloe would never forget ye."

" O, I 'm so sorry ! " repeated Rosa, mournfully.

She objected to taking the nourishment Tulee offered, saying she wanted to die. But Mr. Duroy reminded her that Madame was longing to see her, and she yielded to that plea. When Tulee brought the same travelling-dress in which she had first come to the cottage, she shrunk from it at first, but seemed to remember immediately that she ought not to give unnecessary trouble to her friends. While she was putting it on, Tulee said, " I tried to remember to put up everything ye would want, darling."

" I don't want *anything*," she replied listlessly. Then,

looking up suddenly, with that same wild, hard expression, she added, "Don't let me ever see anything that came from *him!*" She spoke so sternly, that Tulee, for the first time in her life, was a little afraid of her.

The eastern sky was all of a saffron glow, but the golden edge of the sun had not yet appeared above the horizon, when they entered the boat which was to convey them to the main-land. Without one glance toward the beautiful island where she had enjoyed and suffered so much, the unhappy fugitive nestled close to Tulee, and hid her face on her shoulder, as if she had nothing else in the world to cling to.

*   *   *   *   *

A week later, a carriage stopped before Madame's door, and Tulee rushed in with the baby on her shoulder, exclaiming, "*Nous voici!*" while Mr. Duroy was helping Rosa to alight. Then such huggings and kissings, such showers of French from Madame, and of mingled French and Italian from the Signor, while Tulee stood by, throwing up her hand, and exclaiming, "Bless the Lord! bless the Lord!" The parrot listened with ear upturned, and a lump of sugar in her claw, then overtopped all their voices with the cry of "*Bon jour, Rosabella! je suis enchantée.*"

This produced a general laugh, and there was the faint gleam of a smile on Rosa's face, as she looked up at the cage and said, "*Bon jour, jolie Manon!*" But she soon sank into a chair with an expression of weariness.

"You are tired, darling," said Madame, as she took off her bonnet and tenderly put back the straggling hair. "No wonder, after all you have gone through, my poor child!"

Rosa clasped her round the neck, and murmured, "O my dear friend, I *am* tired, *so* tired!"

Madame led her to the settee, and arranged her head comfortably on its pillows. Then, giving her a motherly kiss, she said, " Rest, darling, while Tulee and I look after the boxes."

When they had all passed into another room, she threw up her hands and exclaimed : " How she's changed ! How thin and pale she is ! How large her eyes look ! But she's beautiful as an angel."

" I never see Missy Rosy but once when she was n't beautiful as an angel," said Tulee ; " and that was the night Massa Duroy told her she was sold to Massa Bruteman. Then she looked as if she had as many devils as that Mary Magdalene Massa Royal used to read about o' Sundays."

" No wonder, poor child ! " exclaimed Madame. " But I hope the little one is some comfort to her."

" She ha'n't taken much notice of him, or anything else, since Massa Duroy told her that news," rejoined Tulee.

Madame took the baby and tried to look into its face as well as the lopping motions of its little head would permit. " I should n't think she'd have much comfort in looking at it," said she ; " for it's the image of its father ; but the poor little dear ain't to blame for that."

An animated conversation followed concerning what had happened since Tulee went away, — especially the disappearance of Flora. Both hinted at having entertained similar suspicions, but both had come to the conclusion that she could not be alive, or she would have written.

Rosa, meanwhile, left alone in the little parlor, where she had listened so anxiously for the whistling of Ça ira, was scarcely conscious of any other sensation than the luxury of repose, after extreme fatigue of body and mind.

9 *

There was, indeed, something pleasant in the familiar surroundings. The parrot swung in the same gilded ring in
her cage. Madame's table, with its basket of chenilles,
stood in the same place, and by it was her enamelled snuff-
box. Rosa recognized a few articles that had been purchased at the auction of her father's furniture ; — his arm-
chair, and the astral lamp by which he used to sit to read
his newspaper ; a sewing-chair that was her mother's ; and
one of Flora's embroidered slippers, hung up for a watch-
case. With these memories floating before her drowsy
eyes, she fell asleep, and slept for a long time. As her
slumbers grew lighter, dreams of father, mother, and sister
passed through various changes ; the last of which was that
Flora was puzzling the mocking-birds. She waked to the
consciousness that some one was whistling in the room.

"Who is that!" exclaimed she ; and the parrot replied
with a tempest of imitations. Madame, hearing the noise,
came in, saying : "How stupid I was not to cover the
cage! She is *so* noisy! Her memory is wonderful. I
don't think she'll ever forget a note of all the *mélange*
dear Floracita took so much pains to teach her."

She began to call up reminiscences of Flora's incessant
mischief ; but finding Rosa in no mood for anything gay,
she proceeded to talk over the difficulties of her position,
concluding with the remark : "To-day and to-night you
must rest, my child. But early to-morrow you and the
Signor will start for New York, whence you will take passage to Marseilles, under the name of Signor Balbino and
daughter."

"I wish I could stay here, at least for a little while,"
sighed Rosa.

"It's never wise to wish for what cannot be had," rejoined Madame. " It would cause great trouble and expense to obtain your freedom; and it is doubtful whether we could secure it at all, for Bruteman won't give you up if he can avoid it. The voyage will recruit your strength, and it will do you good to be far away from anything that reminds you of old troubles. I have nothing left to do but to dispose of my furniture, and settle about the lease of this house. You will wait at Marseilles for me. I shall be uneasy till I have the sea between me and the agents of Mr. Bruteman, and I shall hurry to follow after you as soon as possible."

" And Tulee and the baby?" asked Rosa.

"Yes, with Tulee and the baby," replied **Madame.** **"** But I shall send them to my cousin's to-morrow, to be out of the way of being seen by the neighbors. He lives off the road, and three miles out. **They'll be nicely out** of the way there."

It was all **accomplished as** the energetic Frenchwoman had planned. Rosa was whirled away, without time **to** think of anything. **At parting,** she embraced Tulee, and looked earnestly in the baby's face, while she stroked his shining black hair. " Good by, dear, kind Tulee," said she. " Take good care of the little one."

At Philadelphia, her strength broke down, and they were detained three days. Consequently, when they arrived in **New** York, they found that the Mermaid, in which they expected to take passage, had sailed. The Signor considered it imprudent to correspond with his wife on the subject, and **concluded to go out of the city and** wait for the next vessel. When they went on board, they found Madame, and explained to her **the circumstances.**

" I am glad I did n't **know of** the delay," said she; "for

I was frightened enough as it was. But, luckily, I got off without anybody's coming to make inquiries."

"But where are Tulee and the baby? Are they down below?" asked Rosa.

"No, dear, I did n't bring them."

"O, how came you to leave them?" said Rosa. "Something will happen to them."

"I have provided well for their safety," rejoined Madame. "The reason I did it was this. We have no certain home or prospects at present; and I thought we had better be settled somewhere before the baby was brought. My cousin is coming to Marseilles in about three months, and he will bring them with him. His wife was glad to give Tulee her board, meanwhile, for what work she could do. I really think it was best, dear. The feeble little thing will be stronger for the voyage by that time; and you know Tulee will take just as good care of it as if it were her own."

"Poor Tulee!" sighed Rosa. "Was she willing to be left?"

"She did n't know when I came away," replied Madame.

Rosa heaved an audible groan, as she said: "I am so sorry you did this, Madame! If anything should happen to them, it would be a weight on my mind as long as I live."

"I did what I thought was for the best," answered Madame. "I was in such a hurry to get away, on your account, that, if I had n't all my wits about me, I hope you will excuse me. But I think myself I made the best arrangement."

Rosa, perceiving a slight indication of pique in her tone, hastened to kiss her, and call her her best and dearest friend. But in her heart she mourned over what she considered, for the first time in her life, a great mistake in the management of Madame.

*   *   *   *   *

After Tom's return from New Orleans, he continued to go to the cottage as usual, and so long as no questions were asked, he said nothing; but when his master inquired how they were getting on there, he answered that Missy Rosy was better. When a fortnight had elapsed, he thought the fugitives must be out of harm's way, and he feared Mr. Bruteman might be coming soon to claim his purchase. Accordingly he one day informed his master, with a great appearance of astonishment and alarm, that the cottage was shut up, and all the inmates gone.

Fitzgerald's first feeling was joy; for he was glad to be relieved from the picture of Rosa's horror and despair, which had oppressed him like the nightmare. But he foresaw that Bruteman would suspect him of having forewarned her, though he had solemnly pledged himself not to do so. He immediately wrote him the tidings, with expressions of surprise and regret. The answer he received led to a duel, in which he received a wound in the shoulder, that his wife always supposed was occasioned by a fall from his horse.

When Mr. Bruteman ascertained that Madame and the Signor had left the country, he at once conjectured that the fugitive was with them. Having heard that Mr. Duroy was a relative, he waited upon him, at his place of business, and was informed that Rosabella Royal had sailed for France, with his cousin, in the ship Mermaid. Not long after, it was stated in the ship news that the Mermaid had foundered at sea, and all on board were lost.

CHAPTER XVII.

WHILE Rosabella had been passing through these dark experiences, Flora was becoming more and more accustomed to her new situation. She strove bravely to conceal the homesickness which she could not always conquer; but several times, in the course of their travels, Mrs. Delano noticed moisture gathering on her long black eyelashes when she saw the stars and stripes floating from the mast of a vessel. Once, when a rose was given her, she wept outright; but she soon wiped her eyes, and apologized by saying: " I wonder whether a *Pensee - Vivace* makes Rosa feel as I do when I see a rose? But what an ungrateful child I am, when I have such a dear, kind, new Mamita!" And a loving smile again lighted up her swimming eyes, — those beautiful April eyes of tears and sunshine, that made rainbows in the heart.

Mrs. Delano wisely kept her occupied with a succession of teachers and daily excursions. Having a natural genius for music and drawing, she made rapid progress in both during a residence of six months in England, six months in France, and three months in Switzerland. And as Mr. and Mrs. Percival were usually with them, she picked up, in her quick way, a good degree of culture from the daily tone of conversation. The one drawback to the pleasure of new acquisitions was that she could not share them with Rosa.

One day, when she was saying this, Mrs. Delano replied: "We will go to Italy for a short time, and then we will return to live in Boston. I have talked the matter over a good deal with Mr. Percival, and I think I should know how to guard against any contingency that may occur. And as you are so anxious about your sister, I have been revolving plans for taking you back to the island, to see whether we can ascertain what is going on in that mysterious cottage."

From that time there was a very perceptible increase of cheerfulness in Flora's spirits. The romance of such an adventure hit her youthful fancy, while the idea of getting even a sly peep at Rosa filled her with delight. She imagined all sorts of plans to accomplish this object, and often held discussions upon the propriety of admitting Tulee to their confidence.

Her vivacity redoubled when they entered Italy. She was herself composed of the same materials of which Italy was made ; and without being aware of the spiritual relationship, she at once felt at home there. She was charmed with the gay, impulsive people, the bright costumes, the impassioned music, and the flowing language. The clear, intense blue of the noonday sky, and the sun setting in a glowing sea of amber, reminded her of her Southern home ; and the fragrance of the orange-groves was as incense waved by the memory of her childhood. The ruins of Rome interested her less than any other features of the landscape ; for, like Bettini, she never asked who any of the ancients were, for fear they would tell her. The play of sunshine on the orange-colored lichens interested her more than the inscriptions they covered ; and while their guide was telling the story of mouldering arches, she was looking through them at the clear blue sky and the soft outline of the hills.

One morning they rode out early to spend a whole day
at Albano; and every mile of the ride presented her with
some charming novelty. The peasants who went dancing
by in picturesque costumes, and the finely formed women
walking erect with vases of water on their heads, or drawing an even thread from their distaffs, as they went singing
along, furnished her memory with subjects for many a
picture. Sometimes her exclamations would attract the
attention of a group of dancers, who, pleased with an exuberance of spirits akin to their own, and not unmindful of
forthcoming coin, would beckon to the driver to stop, while
they repeated their dances for the amusement of the Sig-
norina. A succession of pleasant novelties awaited her at
Albano. Running about among the ilex-groves in search
of bright mosses, she would come suddenly in front of an
elegant villa, with garlands in stucco, and balconies gracefully draped with vines. Wandering away from that, she
would utter a little cry of joy at the unexpected sight of
some reclining marble nymph, over which a little fountain
threw a transparent veil of gossamer sparkling with diamonds. Sometimes she stood listening to the gurgling and
dripping of unseen waters ; and sometimes melodies floated
from the distance, which her quick ear caught at once, and
her tuneful voice repeated like a mocking-bird. The childlike zest with which she entered into everything, and made
herself a part of everything, amused her quiet friend, and
gave her even more pleasure than the beauties of the landscape.

After a picnic repast, they ascended Monte Cavo, and
looked down on the deep basins of the lakes, once blaz-
ing with volcanic fire, now full of water blue as the sky
it reflected ; like human souls in which the passions have

burned out, and left them calm recipients of those divine truths in which the heavens are mirrored. As Mrs. Delano pointed out various features in the magnificent panorama around them, she began to tell Flora of scenes in the Æneid with which they were intimately connected. The young girl, who was serious for the moment, dropped on the grass to listen, with elbows on her friend's lap, and her upturned face supported by her hands. But the lecture was too grave for her mercurial spirit; and she soon sprang up, exclaiming: "O Mamita Lila, all those people were dead and buried so long ago! I don't believe the princess that Æneas was fighting about was half as handsome as that dancing Contadina from Frascati, with a scarlet bodice and a floating veil fastened among her black braids with a silver arrow. How her eyes sparkled, and her cheeks glowed! And the Contadino who was dancing with her, with those long streamers of red ribbon flying round his peaked hat, he looked almost as handsome as she did. How I wish I could see them dance the saltarello again! O Mamita Lila, as soon as we get back to Rome, do buy a tambourine." Inspired by the remembrance, she straightway began to hum the monotonous tune of that grasshopper dance, imitating the hopping steps and the quick jerks of the arms, marking the time with ever-increasing rapidity on her left hand, as if it were a tambourine. She was so aglow with the exercise, and so graceful in her swift motions, that Mrs. Delano watched her with admiring smiles. But when the extempore entertainment came to a close, she thought to herself: "It is a hopeless undertaking to educate her after the New England pattern. One might as well try to plough with a butterfly, as to teach her ancient history."

N

When they had wandered about a little while longer, happy as souls newly arrived in the Elysian Fields, Mrs. Delano said: "My child, you have already gathered mosses enough to fill the carriage, and it is time for us to return. You know twilight passes into darkness very quickly here."

"Just let me gather this piece of golden lichen," pleaded she. "It will look so pretty among the green moss, in the cross I am going to make you for Christmas."

When all her multifarious gleanings were gathered up, they lingered a little to drink in the beauty of the scene before them. In the distance was the Eternal City, girdled by hills that stood out with wonderful distinctness in the luminous atmosphere of that brilliant day, which threw a golden veil over all its churches, statues, and ruins. Before they had gone far on their homeward ride, all things passed through magical changes. The hills were seen in vapory visions, shifting their hues with opaline glances; and over the green, billowy surface of the broad Campagna was settling a prismatic robe of mist, changing from rose to violet. Earth seemed to be writing, in colored notes, with tenderest modulations, her farewell hymn to the departing God of Light. And the visible music soon took voice in the vibration of vesper-bells, in the midst of which they entered Rome. Flora, who was sobered by the solemn sounds and the darkening landscape, scarcely spoke, except to remind Mrs. Delano of the tambourine as they drove through the crowded Corso; and when they entered their lodgings in Via delle Quattro Fontane, she passed to her room without any of her usual skipping and singing. When they met again at supper her friend said: "Why so serious? Is my little one tired?"

"I have been thinking, Mamita, that something is going

to happen to me," she replied; "for always when I am very merry something happens."

" I should think something would happen very often then," rejoined Mrs. Delano with a smile, to which she responded with her ready little laugh. " **Several visitors** called while we were gone," said Mrs. Delano. " Our rich Boston friend, Mr. Green, has left his card. He follows us very diligently." She looked at Flora as she spoke; but though the light from a tall lamp fell directly on her face, she saw no emotion, either of pleasure or embarrassment.

She merely looked up with a smile, as she remarked: " He always seems to be going round very leisurely in search of something to entertain him. I wonder whether he has found it yet."

Though she was really tired with the exertions of the day, the sight of the new tambourine, after supper, proved too tempting; and she was soon practising the saltarello again, with an agility almost equal to that of the nimble Contadina from whom she had learned it. She was whirling round more and more swiftly, as if fatigue were a thing impossible to her, when Mr. Green was announced; and a very stylishly dressed gentleman, with glossy shirt-bosom and diamond studs, entered the room. She had had scarcely time to seat herself, and her face was still flushed with exercise, while her dimples were revealed by a sort of shy smile at the consciousness of having been so nearly caught in her rompish play by such an exquisite. The glowing cheek and the dimpling smile were a new revelation to Mr. Green; for he had never interested her sufficiently to call out the vivacity which rendered her so charming.

Mrs. Delano noticed his glance of admiration, and the thought occurred, as it had often done before, what an embarrassing dilemma she would be in, if he should propose marriage to her *protegée*.

"I called this morning," said he, "and found you had gone to Albano. I was tempted to follow, but thought it likely I should miss you. It is a charming drive."

"Everything is charming here, I think," rejoined Flora.

"Ah, it is the first time you have seen Rome," said he. "I envy you the freshness of your sensations. This is the third time I have been here, and of course it palls a little upon me."

"Why don't you go to some new place then?" inquired Flora.

"Where *is* there any new place?" responded he languidly. "To be sure, there is Arabia Petræa, but the accommodations are not good. Besides, Rome has attractions for me at present; and I really think I meet more acquaintances here than I should at home. Rome is beginning to swarm with Americans, especially with Southerners. One can usually recognize them at a glance by their unmistakable air of distinction. They are obviously of porcelain clay, as Willis says."

"I think our New England Mr. Percival is as polished a gentleman as any I have seen," observed Mrs. Delano.

"He is a gentleman in manners and attainments, I admit," replied Mr. Green; "but with his family and education, what a pity it is he has so disgraced himself."

"Pray what has he done?" inquired the lady.

"Did n't you know he was an Abolitionist?" rejoined Mr. Green. "It is a fact that he has actually spoken at their meetings. I was surprised to see him travelling with you in England. It must be peculiarly irritating to the

South to see a man of his position siding with those vulgar
agitators. Really, unless something effectual can be done
to stop that frenzy, I fear Southern gentlemen will be unable to recover a fugitive slave."

Flora looked at Mrs. Delano with a furtive, sideway
glance, and a half-smile on her lips. Her impulse was to
jump up, dot one of her quick courtesies, and say: "I am
a fugitive slave. Please, sir, don't give *me* up to any of
those distinguished gentlemen."

Mr. Green noticed her glance, and mistook it for distaste
of his theme. "Pardon me, ladies," said he, "for introducing a subject tabooed in polite society. I called for a
very different purpose. One novelty remains for me in
Rome. I have never seen the statues of the Vatican by
torchlight. Some Americans are forming a party for that
purpose to-morrow evening, and if you would like to join
them, it will give me great pleasure to be your escort."

Flora, being appealed to, expressed acquiescence, and
Mrs. Delano replied: "We will accept your invitation with
pleasure. I have a great predilection for sculpture."

"Finding myself so fortunate in one request encourages
me to make another," rejoined Mr. Green. "On the evening following Norma is to be brought out, with a new
prima donna, from whom great things are expected. I
should be much gratified if you would allow me to procure
tickets and attend upon you."

Flora's face lighted up at once. "I see what my musical daughter wishes," said Mrs. Delano. "We will therefore lay ourselves under obligations to you for two evenings'
entertainment."

The gentleman, having expressed his thanks, bade them
good evening.

Flora woke up the next morning full of pleasant anticipations. When Mrs. Delano looked in upon her, she found
her already dressed, and busy with a sketch of the dancing
couple from Frascati. " I cannot make them so much alive
as I wish," said she, " because they are not in motion. No
picture can give the gleamings of the arrow or the whirl-
ings of the veil. I wish we could dress like Italians. How
I should like to wear a scarlet bodice, and a veil fastened
with a silver arrow."

" If we remained till Carnival, you might have that
pleasure," replied Mrs. Delano ; " for everybody masquer-
ades as they like at that time. But I imagine you would
hardly fancy my appearance in scarlet jacket, with laced
sleeves, big coral necklace, and long ear-rings, like that old
Contadina we met riding on a donkey."

Flora laughed. " To think of Mamita Lila in such costume ! " exclaimed she. " The old Contadina would make
a charming picture ; but a picture of the Campagna, sleepy
with purple haze, would be more like you."

" Am I then so sleepy ? " inquired her friend.

" O, no, not sleepy. You know I don't mean that. But
so quiet ; and always with some sort of violet or lilac cloud
for a dress. But here comes Carlina to call us to breakfast," said she, as she laid down her crayon, and drummed
the saltarello on her picture while she paused a moment to
look at it.

As Mrs. Delano wished to write letters, and Flora expected a teacher in drawing, it was decided that they should
remain at home until the hour arrived for visiting the Vatican. " We have been about sight-seeing so much," said
Mrs. Delano, " that I think it will be pleasant to have a
quiet day." Flora assented ; but as Mrs. Delano wrote,

she could not help smiling at her ideas of quietude. Sometimes rapid thumps on the tambourine might be heard, indicating that the saltarello was again in rehearsal. If a *piffero* strolled through the street, the monotonous drone of his bagpipe was reproduced in most comical imitation; and anon there was a gush of bird-songs, as if a whole aviary were in the vicinity. Indeed, no half-hour passed without audible indication that the little recluse was in merry mood.

At the appointed time Mr. Green came to conduct them to the Vatican. They ascended the wide slopes, and passed through open courts into long passages lined with statues, and very dimly lighted with occasional lamps. Here and there a marble figure was half revealed, and looked so spectral in the gloaming that they felt as if they were entering the world of spirits. Several members of the party preceded them, and all seemed to feel the hushing influence, for they passed on in silence, and stepped softly as they entered the great Palace of Art. The torch-bearers were soon in readiness to illuminate the statues, which they did by holding a covered light over each, making it stand out alone in the surrounding darkness, with very striking effects of light and shadow. Flora, who was crouched on a low seat by the side of Mrs. Delano, gazed with a reverent, half-afraid feeling on the thoughtful, majestic looking Minerva Medica. When the graceful vision of Venus Anadyomene was revealed, she pressed her friend's hand, and the pressure was returned. But when the light was held over a beautiful Cupid, the face looked out from the gloom with such an earnest, childlike expression, that she forgot the presence of strangers, and impulsively exclaimed, " O Mamita, how lovely ! "

A gentleman some little distance in front of them turned

toward them suddenly, at the sound of her voice ; and a movement of the torch-bearer threw the light full upon him for an instant. Flora hid her face in the lap of Mrs. Delano, who attributed the quick action to her shame at having spoken so audibly. But placing her hand caressingly on her shoulder, she felt that she was trembling violently. She stooped toward her, and softly inquired, " What is the matter, dear ? "

Flora seized her head with both hands, and, drawing it closer, whispered : " Take me home, Mamita ! Do take me right home ! "

Wondering what sudden caprice had seized the emotional child, she said, " Why, are you ill, dear ? "

Flora whispered close into her ear: " No, Mamita. But Mr. Fitzgerald is here."

Mrs. Delano rose very quietly, and, approaching Mr. Green, said: " My daughter is not well, and we wish to leave. But I beg you will return as soon as you have conducted us to the carriage."

But though he was assured by both the ladies that nothing alarming was the matter, when they arrived at their lodgings he descended from the driver's seat to assist them in alighting. Mrs. Delano, with polite regrets at having thus disturbed his pleasure, thanked him, and bade him good evening. She hurried after Flora, whom she found in her room, weeping bitterly. " Control your feelings, my child," said she. " You are perfectly safe here in Italy."

" But if he saw me, it will make it so very unpleasant for you, Mamita."

" He could n't see you ; for we were sitting in very deep shadow," replied Mrs. Delano. " But even if he had seen you, I should know how to protect you."

" But what I am thinking of," said Floracita, still weeping, " is that he may have brought Rosa with him, and I can't run to her this very minute. I *must* see her! I *will* see her! If I have to tell ever so many *fibititas* about the reason of my running away."

" I would n't prepare any *fibititas* at present," rejoined Mrs. Delano. " I always prefer the truth. I will send for Mr. Percival, and ask him to ascertain whether Mr. Fitzgerald brought a lady with him. Meanwhile, you had better lie down, and keep as quiet as you can. As soon as I obtain any information, I will come and tell you."

When Mr. Percival was informed of the adventure at the Vatican, he sallied forth to examine the lists of arrivals; and before long he returned with the statement that Mr. and Mrs. Fitzgerald were registered among the newcomers. " Flora would, of course, consider that conclusive," said he ; " but you and I, who have doubts concerning that clandestine marriage, will deem it prudent to examine further."

" If it should prove to be her sister, it will be a very embarrassing affair," rejoined Mrs. Delano.

Mr. Percival thought it very unlikely, but said he would ascertain particulars to-morrow.

With that general promise, without a knowledge of the fact already discovered, Flora retired to rest ; but it was nearly morning before she slept.

CHAPTER XVIII.

THOUGH Flora had been so wakeful the preceding night, she tapped at Mrs. Delano's door very early the next morning. "Excuse me for coming before you were dressed," said she; "but I wanted to ask you how long you think it will be before Mr. Percival can find out whether Mr. Fitzgerald has brought Rosa with him."

"Probably not before noon," replied Mrs. Delano, drawing the anxious little face toward her, and imprinting on it her morning kiss. "Last evening I wrote a note to Mr. Green, requesting him to dispose of the opera tickets to other friends. Mr. Fitzgerald is so musical, he will of course be there; and whether your sister is with him or not, you will be in too nervous a state to go to any public place. You had better stay in your room, and busy yourself with books and drawings, till we can ascertain the state of things. I will sit with you as much as I can; and when I am absent you must try to be a good, quiet child."

"I will try to be good, because I don't want to trouble you, Mamita Lila; but you know I can't be quiet in my mind. I did long for the opera; but unless Mr. Fitzgerald brought Rosa with him, and I could see her before I went, it would almost kill me to hear Norma; for every part of it is associated with her."

After breakfast, Mrs. Delano sat some time in Flora's room, inspecting her recent drawings, and advising her to work upon them during the day, as the best method of restraining restlessness. While they were thus occupied,

Carlina brought in a beautiful bouquet for Miss Delano, accompanied with a note for the elder lady, expressing Mr. Green's great regret at being deprived of the pleasure of their company for the evening.

"I am sorry I missed seeing him," thought Mrs. Delano; "for he is always so intimate with Southerners, I dare say he would know all about Mr. Fitzgerald; though I should have been at a loss how to introduce the inquiry."

Not long afterward Mr. Percival called, and had what seemed to Flora a very long private conference with Mrs. Delano. The information he brought was, that the lady with Mr. Fitzgerald was a small, slight figure, with yellowish hair and very delicate complexion.

"That is in all respects the very opposite of Flora's description of her sister," rejoined Mrs. Delano.

Their brief conversation on the subject was concluded by a request that Mr. Percival would inquire at Civita Vecchia for the earliest vessels bound either to France or England.

Mrs. Delano could not at once summon sufficient resolution to recount all the particulars to Flora; to whom she merely said that she considered it certain that her sister was not with Mr. Fitzgerald.

"Then why can't I go right off to the United States to-day?" exclaimed the impetuous little damsel.

"Would you then leave Mamita Lila so suddenly?" inquired her friend; whereupon the emotional child began to weep and protest. This little scene was interrupted by Carlina with two visiting-cards on a silver salver. Mrs. Delano's face flushed unusually as she glanced at them. She immediately rose to go, saying to Flora: "I must see these people; but I will come back to you as soon as I can. Don't leave your room, my dear."

In the parlor, she found a gentleman and lady, both handsome, but as different from each other as night and morning. The lady stepped forward and said : " I think you will recollect me ; for we lived in the same street in Boston, and you and my mother used to visit together."

"Miss Lily Bell," rejoined Mrs. Delano, offering her hand. "I had not heard you were on this side the Atlantic."

"Not Miss Bell now, but Mrs. Fitzgerald," replied the fair little lady. " Allow me to introduce you to Mr. Fitzgerald."

Mrs. Delano bowed, rather coldly ; and her visitor continued : "I was so sorry I did n't know you were with the Vatican party last night. Mr. Green told us of it this morning, and said you were obliged to leave early, on account of the indisposition of Miss Delano. I hope she has recovered, for Mr. Green has told me so much about her that I am dying with curiosity to see her."

" She is better, I thank you, but not well enough to see company," replied Mrs. Delano.

" What a pity she will be obliged to relinquish the opera to-night!" observed Mr. Fitzgerald. "I hear she is very musical; and they tell wonderful stories about this new *prima donna*. They say she has two more notes in the altissimo scale than any singer who has been heard here, and that her sostenuto is absolutely marvellous."

Mrs. Delano replied politely, expressing regret that she and her daughter were deprived of the pleasure of hearing such a musical genius. After some desultory chat concerning the various sights in Rome, the visitors departed.

" I 'm glad your call was short," said Mr. Fitzgerald. " That lady is a perfect specimen of Boston ice."

Whereupon his companion began to rally him for want of gallantry in saying anything disparaging of Boston.

Meanwhile Mrs. Delano was pacing the parlor in a disturbed state of mind. Though she had foreseen such a contingency as one of the possible consequences of adopting Flora, yet when it came so suddenly in a different place, and under different circumstances from any she had thought of, the effect was somewhat bewildering. She dreaded the agitation into which the news would throw Flora, and she wanted to mature her own future plans before she made the announcement. So, in answer to Flora's questions about the visitors, she merely said a lady from Boston, the daughter of one of her old acquaintances, had called to introduce her husband. After dinner, they spent some time reading Tasso's Aminta together; and then Mrs. Delano said : " I wish to go and have a talk with Mr. and Mrs. Percival. I have asked him to inquire about vessels at Civita Vecchia ; for, under present circumstances, I presume you would be glad to set out sooner than we intended on that romantic expedition in search of your sister."

" O, thank you ! thank you !" exclaimed Flora, jumping up and kissing her.

" I trust you will not go out, or sing, or show yourself at the windows while I am gone," said Mrs. Delano ; " for though Mr. Fitzgerald can do you no possible harm, it would be more agreeable to slip away without his seeing you."

The promise was readily and earnestly given, and she proceeded to the lodgings of Mr. and Mrs. Percival in the next street. After she had related the experiences of the morning, she asked what they supposed had become of Rosabella.

"It is to be hoped she does not continue her relation with that base man if she knows of his marriage," said Mrs. Percival; "for that would involve a moral degradation painful for you to think of in Flora's sister."

"If she has ceased to interest his fancy, very likely he may have sold her," said Mr. Percival; "for a man who could entertain the idea of selling Flora, I think would sell his own Northern wife, if the law permitted it and circumstances tempted him to it."

"What do you think I ought to do in the premises?" inquired Mrs. Delano.

"I would hardly presume to say what you ought to do," rejoined Mrs. Percival; "but I know what I should do, if I were as rich as you, and as strongly attached to Flora."

"Let me hear what you would do," said Mrs. Delano. The prompt reply was: "I would go in search of her. And if she was sold, I would buy her and bring her home, and be a mother to her."

"Thank you," said Mrs. Delano, warmly pressing her hand. "I thought you would advise what was kindest and noblest. Money really seems to me of very little value, except as a means of promoting human happiness. And in this case I might perhaps prevent moral degradation, growing out of misfortune and despair."

After some conversation concerning vessels that were about to sail, the friends parted. On her way homeward, she wondered within herself whether they had any suspicion of the secret tie that bound her so closely to these unfortunate girls. "I ought to do the same for them without that motive," thought she; "but should I?"

Though her call had not been very long, it seemed so to Flora, who had latterly been little accustomed to solitude.

She had no heart for books or drawing. She sat listlessly watching the crowd on Monte Pincio; — children chasing each other, or toddling about with nurses in bright-red jackets; carriages going round and round, ever and anon bringing into the sunshine gleams of gay Roman scarfs, or bright autumnal ribbons fluttering in the breeze. She had enjoyed few things more than joining that fashionable promenade to overlook the city in the changing glories of sunset. But now she cared not for it. Her thoughts were far away on the lonely island. As sunset quickly faded into twilight, carriages and pedestrians wound their way down the hill. The noble trees on its summit became solemn silhouettes against the darkening sky, and the monotonous trickling of the fountain in the court below sounded more distinct as the street noises subsided. She was growing a little anxious, when she heard soft footfalls on the stairs, which she at once recognized and hastened to meet. " O, you have been gone so long!" she exclaimed. Happy, as all human beings are, to have another heart so dependent on them, the gratified lady passed her **arm** round the waist of the loving child, and they ascended to their rooms like two confidential school-girls.

After tea, Mrs. Delano said, " Now I will keep my promise of telling you all I have discovered." Flora ran to an ottoman by her side, and, leaning on her lap, looked up eagerly into her face. " You must try not to be excitable, my dear," said her friend; " for I have some unpleasant news to tell **you**."

The expressive eyes, that were gazing wistfully into hers while she spoke, at once assumed that startled, melancholy look, strangely in contrast with their laughing shape. Her friend was so much affected by it that she hardly knew how to proceed with her painful task. At last Flora murmured, "Is she dead?"

"I have heard no such tidings, darling," she replied. "But Mr. Fitzgerald has married a Boston lady, and they were the visitors who came here this morning."

Flora sprung up and pressed her hand on her heart, as if a sharp arrow had hit her. But she immediately sank on the ottoman again, and said in tones of suppressed agitation : "Then he has left poor Rosa. How miserable she must be! She loved him so! O, how wrong it was for me to run away and leave her! And only to think how I have been enjoying myself, when she was there all alone, with her heart breaking! Can't we go to-morrow to look for her, dear Mamita?"

"In three days a vessel will sail for Marseilles," replied Mrs. Delano. "Our passage is taken ; and Mr. and Mrs. Percival, who intended to return home soon, are kind enough to say they will go with us. I wish they could accompany us to the South ; but he is so well known as an Abolitionist that his presence would probably cause unpleasant interruptions and delays, and perhaps endanger his life."

Flora seized her hand and kissed it, while tears were dropping fast upon it. And at every turn of the conversation, she kept repeating, "How wrong it was for me to run away and leave her!"

"No, my child," replied Mrs. Delano, "you did right in coming to me. If you had stayed there, you would have made both her and yourself miserable, beside doing what was very wrong. I met Mr. Fitzgerald once on horseback, while I was visiting at Mr. Welby's plantation ; but I never fairly saw him until to-day. He is so very handsome, that, when I looked at him, I could not but think it rather remarkable he did not gain a bad power over you by his insinuating flattery, when you were so very young and inexperienced."

The guileless little damsel looked up with an expression of surprise, and said : " How *could* I bear to have him make love to *me*, when he was Rosa's husband? He is so handsome and fascinating, that, if he had loved me instead of Rosa, in the beginning, I dare say I should have been as much in love with him as she was. I did dearly love him while he was a kind brother; but I could n't love him *so*. It would have killed Rosa if I had. Besides, he told falsehoods; and papa taught us to consider that as the meanest of faults. I have heard him tell Rosa he never loved anybody but her, when an hour before he had told me he loved me better than Rosa. What could I do but despise such a man? Then, when he threatened to sell me, I became dreadfully afraid of him." She started up, as if struck by a sudden thought, and exclaimed wildly, " What if he has sold Rosa?"

Her friend brought forward every argument and every promise she could think of to pacify her; and when she had become quite calm, they sang a few hymns together, and before retiring to rest knelt down side by side and prayed for strength and guidance in these new troubles.

Flora remained a long time wakeful, thinking of Rosa deserted and alone. She had formed many projects concerning what was to be seen and heard and done in Rome; but she forgot them all. She did not even think of the much-anticipated opera, until she heard from the street snatches of Norma, whistled or sung by the dispersing audience. A tenor voice passed the house singing, *Vieni*

10 *   o

in Roma. " Ah," thought she, " Gerald and I used to sing that duet together.   And in those latter days how languishingly he used to look at me, behind her back, while he sang passionately, ' *Ah, deh cedi, cedi a me!*'   And poor cheated Rosa would say, ' Dear Gerald, how much heart you put into your voice!'   O shame, shame!   What *could* I do but run away?   Poor Rosa!   How I wish I could hear her sing ' Casta Diva,' as she used to do when we sat gazing at the moon shedding its soft light over the pines in that beautiful lonely island."

And so, tossed for a long while on a sea of memories, she finally drifted into dream-land.

CHAPTER XIX.

WHILE Flora was listlessly gazing at Monte Pincio from the solitude of her room in the Via delle Quattro Fontane, Rosabella was looking at the same object, seen at a greater distance, over intervening houses, from her high lodgings in the Corso. She could see the road winding like a ribbon round the hill, with a medley of bright colors continually moving over it. But she was absorbed in revery, and they floated round and round before her mental eye, like the revolving shadows of a magic lantern.

She was announced to sing that night, as the new Spanish *prima donna*, La Señorita Rosita Campaneo ; and though she had been applauded by manager and musicians at the rehearsal that morning, her spirit shrank from the task. Recent letters from America had caused deep melancholy ; and the idea of singing, not *con amore*, but as a performer before an audience of entire strangers, filled her with dismay. She remembered how many times she and Flora and Gerald had sung together from Norma ; and an oppressive feeling of loneliness came over her. Returning from rehearsal, a few hours before, she had seen a young Italian girl, who strongly reminded her of her lost sister. " Ah ! " thought she, " if Flora and I had gone out into the world together, to make our own way, as Madame first intended, how much sorrow and suffering I might have been spared ! " She went to the piano, where the familiar music of Norma lay open before her, and from the depths of her

saddened soul gushed forth, " *Ah, bello a me Ritorno.*" The
last tone passed sighingly away, and as her hands lingered
on the keys, she murmured, " Will my heart pass into it
there, before that crowd of strange faces, as it does here?"

" To be sure it will, dear," responded Madame, who had
entered softly and stood listening to the last strains.

" Ah, if all would hear with *your* partial ears!" replied Rosabella, with a glimmering smile. " But they
will not. And I may be so frightened that I shall lose my
voice."

" What have you to be afraid of, darling?" rejoined Madame. " It was more trying to sing at private parties of
accomplished musicians, as you did in Paris; and especially
at the palace, where there was such an *élite* company. Yet
you know that Queen Amelia was so much pleased with
your performance of airs from this same opera, that she
sent you the beautiful enamelled wreath you are to wear to-
night."

" What I was singing when you came in wept itself out
of the fulness of my heart," responded Rosabella. " This
dreadful news of Tulee and the baby unfits me for anything. Do you think there is no hope it may prove un-
true?"

" You know the letter explicitly states that my cousin
and his wife, the negro woman, and the white baby, all died
of yellow-fever," replied Madame. " But don't reproach
me for leaving them, darling. I feel badly enough about
it, already. I thought it would be healthy so far out of
the city; and it really seemed the best thing to do with the
poor little *bambino,* until we could get established somewhere."

" I did not intend to reproach you, my kind friend,"

answered Rosa. "I know you meant it all for the best. But I had a heavy presentiment of evil when you first told me they were left. This news makes it hard for me to keep up my heart for the efforts of the evening. You know I **was induced** to enter upon this operatic career mainly by the hope of educating that poor child, and providing well for the old age of you and Papa Balbino, as I have learned to call my good friend, the Signor. **And** poor Tulee, too, — how much I intended to do for her! No mortal **can** ever know what she was to me in **the darkest** hours of my life."

"Well, poor Tulee's troubles are all over," rejoined Madame, with a sigh; "and *bambinos* escape a great deal of suffering by going out of this wicked world. For, between you and I, dear, I don't believe one word about the innocent little souls staying in purgatory on account of not being baptized."

"O, my friend, if you only *knew!*" exclaimed Rosa, in a wild, despairing tone. But she instantly checked herself, and said: "I will try not to think of it; for if I do, I shall spoil my voice; and Papa Balbino would be dreadfully mortified **if** I failed, after he had taken so much pains to have me brought out."

"That is right, darling," rejoined Madame, patting her on the shoulder. "I will go away, and leave you to rehearse."

Again and again **Rosa sang the** familiar airs, trying to put soul into them, by imagining how she would feel if she were in Norma's position. Some of the emotions she knew by her own experience, and those she sang with her deepest feeling.

"If I could only keep the same visions before me that I

have here alone, I should sing well to-night," she said to
herself; "for now, when I sing 'Casta Diva,' I seem to be
sitting with my arm round dear little Flora, watching the
moon as it rises above the dark pines on that lonely
island."

At last the dreaded hour came. Rosa appeared on the
stage with her train of priestesses. The orchestra and the
audience were before her; and she knew that Papa and
Mamma Balbino were watching her from the side with anxious hearts. She was very pale, and her first notes were
a little tremulous. But her voice soon became clear and
strong; and when she fixed her eyes on the moon, and
sang "Casta Diva," the fulness and richness of the tones
took everybody by surprise.

" *Bis! Bis!* " cried the audience; and the chorus was not
allowed to proceed till she had sung it a second and third
time. She courtesied her acknowledgments gracefully.
But as she retired, ghosts of the past went with her; and
with her heart full of memories, she seemed to weep in
music, while she sang in Italian, " Restore to mine afflic-
tion one smile of love's protection." Again the audience
shouted, " *Bis! Bis!* "

The duet with Adalgisa was more difficult; for she had
not yet learned to be an actress, and she was embarrassed
by the consciousness of being an object of jealousy to the
seconda donna, partly because she was *prima*, and partly
because the tenor preferred her. But when Adalgisa
sang in Italian the words, " Behold him! " she chanced to
raise her eyes to a box near the stage, and saw the faces
of Gerald Fitzgerald and his wife bending eagerly toward
her. She shuddered, and for an instant her voice failed
her. The audience were breathless. Her look, her atti-

tude, her silence, her tremor, all seemed inimitable acting. A glance at the foot-lights and at the orchestra recalled the recollection of where she was, and by a strong effort she controlled herself; though there was still an agitation in her voice, which the audience and the singers thought to be the perfection of acting. Again she glanced at Fitzgerald, and there was terrible power in the tones with which she uttered, in Italian, "Tremble, perfidious one! Thou knowest the cause is ample."

Her eyes rested for a moment on Mrs. Fitzgerald, and with a wonderful depth of pitying sadness, she sang, "O, how his art deceived thee!"

The wish she had formed was realized. She was enabled to give voice to her own emotions, forgetful of the audience for the time being. And even in subsequent scenes, when the recollection of being a performer returned upon her, her inward excitation seemed to float her onward, like a great wave.

Once again her own feelings took her up, like a tornado, and made her seem a wonderful actress. In the scene where Norma is tempted to kill her children, she fixed her indignant gaze full upon Fitzgerald, and there was an indescribable expression of stern resolution in her voice, and of pride in the carriage of her queenly head, while she sang: "Disgrace worse than death awaits them. Slavery? No! never!"

Fitzgerald quailed before it. He grew pale, and slunk back in the box. The audience had never seen the part so conceived, and a few criticised it. But her beauty and her voice and her overflowing feeling carried all before her; and this, also, was accepted as a remarkable inspiration of theatrical genius.

When the wave of her own excitement was subsiding, the magnetism of an admiring audience began to affect her strongly. With an outburst of fury, she sang, "War! War!" The audience cried, "*Bis! Bis!*" and she sang it as powerfully the second time.

What it was that had sustained and carried her through that terrible ordeal, she could never understand.

When the curtain dropped, Fitzgerald was about to rush after her; but his wife caught his arm, and he was obliged to follow. It was an awful penance he underwent, submitting to this necessary restraint; and while his soul was seething like a boiling caldron, he was obliged to answer evasively to Lily's frequent declaration that the superb voice of this Spanish *prima donna* was exactly like the wonderful voice that went wandering round the plantation, like a restless ghost.

Papa and Mamma Balbino were waiting to receive the triumphant *cantatrice*, as she left the stage. "*Brava! Brava!*" shouted the Signor, in a great fever of excitement; but seeing how pale she looked, he pressed her hand in silence, while Madame wrapped her in shawls. They lifted her into the carriage as quickly as possible, where her head drooped almost fainting on Madame's shoulder. It required them both to support her unsteady steps, as they mounted the stairs to their lofty lodging. She told them nothing that night of having seen Fitzgerald; and, refusing all refreshment save a sip of wine, she sank on the bed utterly exhausted.

CHAPTER XX.

SHE slept late the next day, and woke with a feeling of utter weariness of body and prostration of spirit. When her dressing-maid Giovanna came at her summons, she informed her that a gentleman had twice called to see her, but left no name or card. "Let no one be admitted to-day but the manager of the opera," said Rosa. "I will dress now; and if Mamma Balbino is at leisure, I should like to have her come and talk with me while I breakfast."

"Madame has gone out to make some purchases," replied Giovanna. "She said she should return soon, and charged me to keep everything quiet, that you might sleep. The Signor is in his room waiting to speak to you."

"Please tell him I have waked," said Rosa; "and as soon as I have dressed and breakfasted, ask him to come to me."

Giovanna, who had been at the opera the preceding evening, felt the importance of her mission in dressing the celebrated Señorita Rosita Campaneo, of whose beauty and gracefulness everybody was talking. And when the process was completed, the *cantatrice* might well have been excused if she had thought herself the handsomest of women. The glossy dark hair rippled over her forehead in soft waves, and the massive braids behind were intertwisted with a narrow band of crimson velvet, that glowed like rubies where the sunlight fell upon it. Her morning wrapper of fine crimson merino, embroidered with gold-colored silk, was singularly becoming to her complexion, softened as the contact was by a white lace collar fastened at the throat with a golden pin. But though she was seated before the mirror, and though her own Spanish taste had chosen the strong contrast of bright colors, she took no notice of the effect produced. Her face was turned toward the window, and as she gazed on the morning sky, all unconscious of its translucent brilliancy of blue, there was an inward-looking expression in her luminous eyes that would have made the fortune of an artist, if he could have reproduced her as a Sibyl. Giovanna looked at her with surprise, that a lady could be so handsome and so beautifully dressed, yet not seem to care for it. She lingered a moment contemplating the superb head with an exultant look, as if it were a picture of her own painting, and then she went out noiselessly to bring the breakfast-tray.

The Señorita Campaneo ate with a keener appetite than she had ever experienced as Rosabella the recluse; for the forces of nature, exhausted by the exertions of the preceding evening, demanded renovation. But the services of the cook were as little appreciated as those of the dressing-maid; the luxurious breakfast was to her simply food. The mirror was at her side, and Giovanna watched curiously to see whether she would admire the effect of the crimson velvet gleaming among her dark hair. But she never once glanced in that direction. When she had eaten sufficiently, she sat twirling her spoon and looking into the depths of her cup, as if it were a magic mirror revealing all the future.

She was just about to say, "Now you may call Papa Balbino," when Giovanna gave a sudden start, and exclaimed, "Signorita! a gentleman!"

And ere she had time to look round, Fitzgerald was kneeling at her feet. He seized her hand and kissed it passionately, saying, in an agony of entreaty: "O Rosabella, do say you forgive me! I am suffering the tortures of the damned."

The irruption was so sudden and unexpected, that for an instant she failed to realize it. But her presence of mind quickly returned, and, forcibly withdrawing the hand to which he clung, she turned to the astonished waiting-maid and said quite calmly, "Please deliver *immediately* the message I spoke of."

Giovanna left the room and proceeded directly to the adjoining apartment, where Signor Balbino was engaged in earnest conversation with another gentleman.

Fitzgerald remained kneeling, still pleading vehemently for forgiveness.

"Mr. Fitzgerald," said she, "this audacity is incredible. I could not have imagined it possible you would presume ever again to come into my presence, after having sold me to that infamous man."

"He took advantage of me, Rosa. I was intoxicated with wine, and knew not what I did. I could not have done it if I had been in my senses. I have always loved you as I never loved any other woman; and I never loved you so wildly as now."

"Leave me!" she exclaimed imperiously. "Your being here does me injury. If you have any manhood in you, leave me!"

He strove to clutch the folds of her robe, and in frenzied tones cried out: "O Rosabella, don't drive me from you! I can't live without —"

A voice like a pistol-shot broke in upon his sentence: "Villain! Deceiver! What are you doing here? Out of the house this instant!"

Fitzgerald sprung to his feet, pale with rage, and encountered the flashing eyes of the Signor. "What right have *you* to order me out of the house?" said he.

"I am her adopted father," replied the Italian; "and no man shall insult her while I am alive."

"So *you* are installed as her protector!" retorted Fitzgerald, sneeringly. "You are not the first gallant I have known to screen himself behind his years."

"By Jupiter!" vociferated the enraged Italian; and he made a spring to clutch him by the throat.

Fitzgerald drew out a pistol. With a look of utter distress, Rosa threw herself between them, saying, in imploring accents, "*Will* you go?"

At the same moment, a hand rested gently on the Signor's shoulder, and a manly voice said soothingly, "Be calm, my friend." Then, turning to Mr. Fitzgerald, the gentleman continued: "Slight as our acquaintance is, sir, it authorizes me to remind you that scenes like this are unfit for a lady's apartment."

Fitzgerald slowly replaced his pistol, as he answered coldly: "I remember your countenance, sir, but I don't recollect where I have seen it, nor do I understand what right you have to intrude here."

"I met you in New Orleans, something more than four years ago," replied the stranger; "and I was then introduced to you by this lady's father, as Mr. Alfred King of Boston."

"O, I remember," replied Fitzgerald, with a slight curl of his lip. "I thought you something of a Puritan then; but it seems *you* are her protector also."

Mr. King colored to the temples; but he replied calmly: "I know not whether Miss Royal recognizes me; for

I have never seen her since the evening we spent so delightfully at her father's house."

"I do recognize you," replied Rosabella; "and as the son of my father's dearest friend, I welcome you."

She held out her hand as she spoke, and he clasped it for an instant. But though the touch thrilled him, he betrayed no emotion. Relinquishing it with a respectful bow, he turned to Mr. Fitzgerald, and said: "You have seen fit to call me a Puritan, and may not therefore accept me as a teacher of politeness; but if you wish to sustain the character of a cavalier, you surely will not remain in a lady's house after she has requested you to quit it."

With a slight shrug of his shoulders, Mr. Fitzgerald took his hat, and said, "Where ladies command, I am of course bound to obey."

As he passed out of the door, he turned toward Rosabella, and, with a low bow, said, "*Au revoir!*"

The Signor was trembling with anger, but succeeded in smothering his half-uttered anathemas. Mr. King compressed his lips tightly for a moment, as if silence were a painful effort. Then, turning to Rosa, he said: "Pardon my sudden intrusion, Miss Royal. Your father introduced me to the Signor, and I last night saw him at the opera. That will account for my being in his room to-day." He glanced at the Italian with a smile, as he added: "I heard very angry voices, and I thought, if there was to be a duel, perhaps the Signor would need a second. You must be greatly fatigued with exertion and excitement. Therefore, I will merely congratulate you on your brilliant success last evening, and wish you good morning."

"I *am* fatigued," she replied; "but if I bid you good morning now, it is with the hope of seeing you again soon.

The renewal of acquaintance with one whom my dear father loved is too pleasant to be willingly relinquished."

"Thank you," he said. But the simple words were uttered with a look and tone so deep and earnest, that she felt the color rising to her cheeks.

"Am I then still capable of being moved by such tones?" she asked herself, as she listened to his departing footsteps, and, for the first time that morning, turned toward the mirror and glanced at her own flushed countenance.

"What a time you've been having, dear!" exclaimed Madame, who came bustling in a moment after. "Only to think of Mr. Fitzgerald's coming here! His impudence goes a little beyond anything I ever heard of. Was n't it lucky that Boston friend should drop down from the skies, as it were, just at the right minute; for the Signor's such a flash-in-the-pan, there's no telling what might have happened. Tell me all about it, dear."

"I will tell you about it, dear mamma," replied Rosa; "but I must beg you to excuse me just now; for I am really very much flurried and fatigued. If you had n't gone out, I should have told you this morning, at breakfast, that I saw Mr. and Mrs. Fitzgerald at the opera, and that I was singing at them in good earnest, while people thought I was acting. We will talk it all over some time; but now I must study, for I shall have hard work to keep the ground I have gained. You know I must perform again to-night. O, how I dread it!"

"You are a strange child to talk so, when you have turned everybody's head," responded Madame.

"Why should I care for everybody's head?" rejoined the successful *cantatrice*. But she thought to herself: "I shall not feel, as I did last night, that I am going to sing

merely to strangers. There will be *one* there who heard
me sing to my dear father. I must try to recall the intonations that came so naturally last evening, and see whether
I can act what I then felt. She seated herself at the piano,
and began **to** sing, " *Oh, di qual sei tu vittima.*" Then,
shaking her head slowly, she murmured : " No ; it does n't
come. I must trust to the inspiration of the moment. But
it is a comfort to know they will not *all* be strangers."

   *   *   *   *   *

    Mr. King took an opportunity that same day to call **on**
Mr. Fitzgerald. He was very haughtily received ; but,
without appearing to notice it, he opened his errand by
saying, " I have come to speak with you concerning Miss
Royal."

    " All I have to say to you, sir," replied Mr. Fitzgerald,
" is, that neither you nor any other man can induce me to
give up my pursuit of her. I will follow her wherever she
goes."

    " What possible advantage can you gain by such **a**
course ? " inquired his visitor. " Why uselessly expose
yourself to disagreeable notoriety, which must, of course,
place Mrs. Fitzgerald in a mortifying position ? "

    " How do you know my perseverance would be useless ? "
asked Fitzgerald. " Did she send you to tell me so ? "

    " She does not know of my coming," replied Mr. King.
" I have told you that my acquaintance with Miss Royal
is very slight. But you will recollect that I met her in
the freshness of her young life, when she was surrounded
by all the ease and elegance that a father's wealth and tenderness could bestow ; and it was unavoidable that her
subsequent misfortunes should excite my sympathy. She
has never told me anything of her own history, but from

others I know all the particulars. It is not my purpose to allude to them; but after suffering all she *has* suffered, now that she has bravely made a standing-place for herself, and has such an arduous career before her, I appeal to your sense of honor, whether it is generous, whether it is manly, to do anything that will increase the difficulties of her position."

"It is presumptuous in you, sir, to come here to teach me what is manly," rejoined Fitzgerald.

"I merely presented the case for the verdict of your own conscience," answered his visitor; "but I will again take the liberty to suggest for your consideration, that if you persecute this unfortunate young lady with professions you know are unwelcome, it must necessarily react in a very unpleasant way upon your own reputation, and consequently upon the happiness of your family."

"You mistook your profession, sir. You should have been a preacher," said Fitzgerald, with a sarcastic smile. "I presume you propose to console the lady for her misfortunes; but let me tell you, sir, that whoever attempts to come between me and her will do it at his peril."

"I respect Miss Royal too much to hear her name used in any such discussion," replied Mr. King. "Good morning, sir."

"The mean Yankee!" exclaimed the Southerner, as he looked after him. "If he were a gentleman he would have challenged me, and I should have met him like a gentleman; but one does n't know what to do with such cursed Yankee preaching."

He was in a very perturbed state of mind. Rosabella had, in fact, made a much deeper impression on him than any other woman had ever made. And now that he saw

her the bright cynosure of all eyes, fresh fuel was heaped
on the flickering flame of his expiring passion. Her dis-
dain piqued his vanity, while it produced the excitement
of difficulties to be overcome. He was exasperated beyond
measure, that the beautiful woman who had depended solely
upon him should now be surrounded by protectors. And
if he could regain no other power, he was strongly tempted
to exert the power of annoyance. In some moods, he
formed wild projects of waylaying her, and carrying her
off by force. But the Yankee preaching, much as he despised it, was not without its influence. He felt that it
would be most politic to keep on good terms with his rich
wife, who was, besides, rather agreeable to him. He concluded, on the whole, that he would assume superiority to
the popular enthusiasm about the new *prima donna ;* that
he would coolly criticise her singing and her acting, while
he admitted that she had many good points. It was a hard
task he undertook ; for on the stage Rosabella attracted
him with irresistible power, to which was added the magnetism of the admiring audience. After the first evening,
she avoided looking at the box where he sat ; but he had
an uneasy satisfaction in the consciousness that it was impossible she could forget he was present and watching
her.

The day after the second appearance of the Señorita
Campaneo, Mrs. Delano was surprised by another call from
the Fitzgeralds.

"Don't think we intend to persecute you," said the little
lady. "We merely came on business. We have just
heard that you were to leave Rome very soon ; but Mr.
Green seemed to think it could n't be so soon as was said."

"Unexpected circumstances make it necessary for me to

11   r

return sooner than I intended," replied Mrs. Delano. "I
expect to sail day after to-morrow."

"What a pity your daughter should go without hearing
the new *prima donna!*" exclaimed Mrs. Fitzgerald. "She
is really a remarkable creature. Everybody says she is as
beautiful as a houri. And as for her voice, I never heard
anything like it, except the first night I spent on Mr. Fitzgerald's plantation. There was somebody wandering about
in the garden and groves who sang just like her. Mr. Fitzgerald did n't seem to be much struck with the voice, but I
could never forget it."

"It was during our honeymoon," replied her husband;
"and how could I be interested in any other voice, when I
had yours to listen to?"

His lady tapped him playfully with her parasol, saying:
"O, you flatterer! But I wish I could get a chance to
speak to this Señorita. I would ask her if she had ever
been in America."

"I presume not," rejoined Mr. Fitzgerald. "They say
an Italian musician heard her in Andalusia, and was so
much charmed with her voice that he adopted her and
educated her for the stage; and he named her Campaneo,
because there is such a bell-like echo in her voice sometimes. Do you think, Mrs. Delano, that it would do your
daughter any serious injury to go with us this evening?
We have a spare ticket; and we would take excellent
care of her. If she found herself fatigued, I would attend
upon her home any time she chose to leave."

"It would be too exciting for her nerves," was Mrs.
Delano's laconic answer.

"The fact is," said Mrs. Fitzgerald, "Mr. Green has
told us so much about her, that we are extremely anxious

to be introduced to her. He says she has n't half seen Rome, and he wishes she could join our party. I wish we could persuade you to leave her with us. I can assure you Mr. Fitzgerald is a most agreeable and gallant protector to ladies. And then it is such a pity, when she is so musical, that she should go without hearing this new *prima donna*."

"Thank you," rejoined Mrs. Delano; "but we have become so much attached to each other's society, that I don't think either of us could be happy separated. Since she cannot hear this musical wonder, I shall not increase her regrets by repeating your enthusiastic account of what she has missed."

"If you had been present at her *début*, you would n't wonder at my enthusiasm," replied the little lady. "Mr. Fitzgerald is getting over the fever a little now, and undertakes to criticise. He says she overacted her part; that she 'tore a passion to tatters,' and all that. But I never saw him so excited as he was then. I think she noticed it; for she fixed her glorious dark eyes directly upon our box while she was singing several of her most effective passages."

"My dear," interrupted her husband, "you are so opera-mad, that you are forgetting the object of your call."

"True," replied she. "We wanted to inquire whether you were certainly going so soon, and whether any one had engaged these rooms. We took a great fancy to them. What a desirable situation! So sunny! Such a fine view of Monte Pincio and the Pope's gardens!"

"They were not engaged last evening," answered Mrs. Delano.

"Then you will secure them immediately, won't you, dear?" said the lady, appealing to her spouse.

With wishes that the voyage might prove safe and pleasant, they departed. Mrs. Delano lingered a moment at the window, looking out upon St. Peter's and the Etruscan Hills beyond, thinking the while how strangely the skeins of human destiny sometimes become entangled with each other. Yet she was unconscious of half the entanglement.

CHAPTER XXI.

THE engagement of the Señorita Rosita Campaneo was for four weeks, during which Mr. King called frequently and attended the opera constantly. Every personal interview, and every vision of her on the stage, deepened the impression she made upon him when they first met. It gratified him to see that, among the shower of bouquets she was constantly receiving, his was the one she usually carried; nor was she unobservant that he always wore a fresh rose. But she was unconscious of his continual guardianship, and he was careful that she should remain so. Every night that she went to the opera and returned from it, he assumed a dress like the driver's, and sat with him on the outside of the carriage, — a fact known only to Madame and the Signor, who were glad enough to have a friend at hand in case Mr. Fitzgerald should attempt any rash enterprise. Policemen were secretly employed to keep the *cantatrice* in sight, whenever she went abroad for air or recreation. When she made excursions out of the city in company with her adopted parents, Mr. King was always privately informed of it, and rode in the same direction; at a sufficient distance, however, not to be visible to her, or to excite gossiping remarks by appearing to others to be her follower. Sometimes he asked himself: "What would my dear prudential mother say, to see me leaving my business to agents and clerks, while I devote my life to the service of an opera-singer? — an opera-singer, too, who has twice been on the verge of being sold as a slave, and

who has been the victim of a sham marriage!" But
though such queries jostled against conventional ideas received from education, they were always followed by the
thought: "My dear mother has gone to a sphere of wider
vision, whence she can look down upon the merely external
distinctions of this deceptive world. Rosabella must be
seen as a pure, good soul, in eyes that see as the angels do;
and as the defenceless daughter of my father's friend, it is
my duty to protect her." So he removed from his more
eligible lodgings in the Piazza di Spagna, and took rooms
in the Corso, nearly opposite to hers, where day by day he
continued his invisible guardianship.

He had reason, at various times, to think his precautions
were not entirely unnecessary. He had several times seen
a figure resembling Fitzgerald's lurking about the opera-
house, wrapped in a cloak, and with a cap very much
drawn over his face. Once Madame and the Signor, having descended from the carriage, with Rosa, to examine the
tomb of Cecilia Metella, were made a little uneasy by the
appearance of four rude-looking fellows, who seemed bent
upon lurking in their vicinity. But they soon recognized
Mr. King in the distance, and not far from him the disguised policemen in his employ. The fears entertained by
her friends were never mentioned to Rosa, and she appeared to feel no uneasiness when riding in daylight with
the driver and her adopted parents. She was sometimes a
little afraid when leaving the opera late at night; but there
was a pleasant feeling of protection in the idea that a friend
of her father's was in Rome, who knew better than the Signor how to keep out of quarrels. That recollection also
operated as an additional stimulus to excellence in her art.
This friend had expressed himself very highly gratified by

her successful *début*, and that consideration considerably increased her anxiety to sustain herself at the height she had attained. In some respects that was impossible; for the thrilling circumstances of the first evening could not again recur to set her soul on fire. Critics generally said she never equalled her first acting; though some maintained that what she had lost in power she had gained in a more accurate conception of the character. Her voice was an unfailing source of wonder and delight. They were never weary of listening to that volume of sound, so full and clear, so flexible in its modulations, so expressive in its intonations.

As the completion of her engagement drew near, the manager was eager for its renewal; and finding that she hesitated, he became more and more liberal in his offers. Things were in this state, when Mr. King called upon Madame one day while Rosa was absent at rehearsal. "She is preparing a new aria for her last evening, when they will be sure to encore the poor child to death," said Madame. "It is very flattering, but very tiresome; and to my French ears their '*Bis! Bis!*' sounds too much like a hiss."

"Will she renew her engagement, think you?" inquired Mr. King.

"I don't know certainly," replied Madame. "The manager makes very liberal offers; but she hesitates. She seldom alludes to Mr. Fitzgerald, but I can see that his presence is irksome to her; and then his sudden irruption into her room, as told by Giovanna, has given rise to some green-room gossip. The tenor is rather too assiduous in his attentions, you know; and the *seconda donna* is her enemy, because she has superseded her in his affections.

These things make her wish to leave Rome; but I tell her she will have to encounter very much the same anywhere."

"Madame," said the young man, "you stand in the place of a mother to Miss Royal; and as such, I have a favor to ask of you. Will you, without mentioning the subject to her, enable me to have a private interview with her to-morrow morning?"

"You are aware that it is contrary to her established rule to see any gentleman, except in the presence of myself or Papa Balbino. But you have manifested so much delicacy, as well as friendliness, that we all feel the utmost confidence in you." She smiled significantly as she added: "If I slip out of the room, as it were by accident, I don't believe I shall find it very difficult to make my peace with her."

Alfred King looked forward to the next morning with impatience; yet when he found himself, for the first time, alone with Rosabella, he felt painfully embarrassed. She glanced at the fresh rose he wore, but could not summon courage to ask whether roses were his favorite flowers. He broke the momentary silence by saying: "Your performances here have been a source of such inexpressible delight to me, Miss Royal, that it pains me to think of such a thing as a last evening."

"Thank you for calling me by that name," she replied. "It carries me back to a happier time. I hardly know myself as La Señorita Campaneo. It all seems to me so strange and unreal, that, were it not for a few visible links with the past, I should feel as if I had died and passed into another world."

"May I ask whether you intend to renew your engagement?" inquired he.

She looked up quickly and earnestly, and said, "What would you advise me?"

"The brevity of our acquaintance would hardly warrant my assuming the office of adviser," replied he modestly.

The shadow of a blush flitted over her face, as she answered, in a bashful way: "Excuse me if the habit of associating you with the memory of my father makes me forget the shortness of our acquaintance. Beside, you once asked me if ever I was in trouble to call upon you as I would upon a brother."

"It gratifies me beyond measure that you should remember my offer, and take me at my word," responded he. "But in order to judge for you, it is necessary to know something of your own inclinations. Do you enjoy the career on which you have entered?"

"I should enjoy it if the audience were all my personal friends," answered she. "But I have lived such a very retired life, that I cannot easily become accustomed to publicity; and there is something I cannot exactly define, that troubles me with regard to operas. If I could perform only in pure and noble characters, I think it would inspire me; for then I should represent what I at least wish to be; but it affects me like a discord to imagine myself in positions which in reality I should scorn and detest."

"I am not surprised to hear you express this feeling," responded he. "I had supposed it must be so. It seems to me the *libretti* of operas are generally singularly ill conceived, both morally and artistically. Music is in itself so pure and heavenly, that it seems a desecration to make it the expression of vile incidents and vapid words. But is the feeling of which you speak sufficiently strong to induce

11 *

you to retire from the brilliant career now opening before you, and devote yourself to concert-singing?"

"There is one thing that makes me hesitate," rejoined she. "I wish to earn money fast, to accomplish certain purposes I have at heart. Otherwise, I don't think I care much for the success you call so brilliant. It is certainly agreeable to feel that I delight the audience, though they are strangers; but their cries of '*Bis! Bis!*' give me less real pleasure than it did to have Papasito ask me to sing over something that he liked. I seem to see him now, as he used to listen to me in our flowery parlor. Do you remember that room, Mr. King?"

"Do I *remember* it?" he said, with a look and emphasis so earnest that a quick blush suffused her eloquent face. "I see that room as distinctly as you can see it," he continued. "It has often been in my dreams, and the changing events of my life have never banished it from my memory for a single day. How *could* I forget it, when my heart there received its first and only deep impression. I have loved you from the first evening I saw you. Judging that your affections were pre-engaged, I would gladly have loved another, if I could; but though I have since met fascinating ladies, none of them have interested me deeply."

An expression of pain passed over her face while she listened, and when he paused she murmured softly, "I am sorry."

"Sorry!" echoed he. "Is it then impossible for me to inspire you with sentiments similar to my own?"

"I am sorry," she replied, "because a first, fresh love, like yours, deserves better recompense than it could receive from a bruised and worn-out heart like mine. I can never experience the illusion of love again. I have suffered too deeply."

"I do not wish you to experience the *illusion* of love again," he replied. "But my hope is that the devotion of my life may enable you to experience the true and tender *reality*." He placed his hand gently and timidly upon hers as he spoke, and looked in her face earnestly.

Without raising her eyes she said, "I suppose you are aware that my mother was a slave, and that her daughters inherited her misfortune."

"I am aware of it," he replied. "But that only makes me ashamed of my country, not of her or of them. Do not, I pray you, pain yourself or me by alluding to any of the unfortunate circumstances of your past life, with the idea that they can depreciate your value in my estimation. From Madame and the Signor I have learned the whole story of your wrongs and your sufferings. Fortunately, my good father taught me, both by precept and example, to look through the surface of things to the reality. I have seen and heard enough to be convinced that your own heart is noble and pure. Such natures cannot be sullied by the unworthiness of others; they may even be improved by it. The famous Dr. Spurzheim says, he who would have the best companion for his life should choose a woman who has suffered. And though I would gladly have saved you from suffering, I cannot but see that your character has been elevated by it. Since I have known you here in Rome, I have been surprised to observe how the young romantic girl has ripened into the thoughtful, prudent woman. I will not urge you for an answer now, my dear Miss Royal. Take as much time as you please to reflect upon it. Meanwhile, if you choose to devote your

fine musical genius to the opera, I trust you will allow me
to serve you in any way that a brother could under similar circumstances. If you prefer to be a concert-singer,
my father had a cousin who married in England, where
she has a good deal of influence in the musical world. I
am sure she would take a motherly interest in you, both
for your own sake and mine. Your romantic story, instead
of doing you injury in England, would make you a great
lioness, if you chose to reveal it."

"I should dislike that sort of attention," she replied
hastily. "Do not suppose, however, that I am ashamed of
my dear mother, or of her lineage; but I wish to have any
interest I excite founded on my own merits, not on any
extraneous circumstance. But you have not yet advised
me whether to remain on the stage or to retire from it."

"If I presumed that my opinion would decide the point,"
rejoined he, "I should be diffident about expressing it in a
case so important to yourself."

"You are very delicate," she replied. "But I conjecture that you would be best pleased if I decided in favor
of concert-singing."

While he was hesitating what to say, in order to leave
her in perfect freedom, she added: "And so, if you will
have the goodness to introduce me to your relative, and
she is willing to be my patroness, I will try my fortune in
England. Of course she ought to be informed of my
previous history; but I should prefer to have her consider
it strictly confidential. And now, if you please, I will say,
Au revoir; for Papa Balbino is waiting for some instructions on matters of business."

She offered her hand with a very sweet smile. He
clasped it with a slight pressure, bowed his head upon it

for an instant, and said, with deep emotion: "Thank you,
dearest of women. You send me away a happy man; for
hope goes with me."

When the door closed after him, she sank into a chair,
and covered her face with both her hands. "How different
is his manner of making love from that of Gerald,"
thought she. "Surely, I can trust *this* time. O, if I was
only worthy of such love!"

Her revery was interrupted by the entrance of Madame
and the Signor. She answered their inquisitive looks by
saying, rather hastily, "When you told Mr. King the particulars
of my story, did you tell him about the poor little
bambino I left in New Orleans?"

Madame replied, "I mentioned to him how the death of
the poor little thing afflicted you."

Rosa made no response, but occupied herself with selecting
some pieces of music connected with the performance
at the opera.

The Signor, as he went out with the music, said, "Do
you suppose she did n't want him to know about the *bambino?*"

"Perhaps she is afraid he will think her heartless for
leaving it," replied Madame. "But I will tell her I took
all the blame on myself. If she is so anxious about his
good opinion, it shows which way the wind blows."

The Señorita Rosita Campaneo and her attendants had
flitted, no one knew whither, before the public were informed
that her engagement was not to be renewed. Rumor
added that she was soon to be married to a rich American,
who had withdrawn her from the stage.

"Too much to be monopolized by one man," said Mr.
Green to Mr. Fitzgerald. "Such a glorious creature belongs
to the world."

"Who is the happy man?" inquired Mrs. Fitzgerald.

"They say it is King, that pale-faced Puritan from Boston," rejoined her husband. "I should have given her credit for better taste."

In private, he made all possible inquiries; but merely succeeded in tracing them to a vessel at Civita Vecchia, bound to Marseilles.

To the public, the fascinating *prima donna*, who had rushed up from the horizon like a brilliant rocket, and disappeared as suddenly, was only a nine-days wonder. Though for some time after, when opera-goers heard any other *cantatrice* much lauded, they would say: "Ah, you should have heard the Campaneo! Such a voice! She rose to the highest D as easily as she breathed. And such glorious eyes!"

CHAPTER XXII.

WHILE Rosabella was thus exchanging the laurel crown for the myrtle wreath, Flora and her friend were on their way to search the places that had formerly known her. Accompanied by Mr. Jacobs, who had long been a steward in her family, Mrs. Delano passed through Savannah, without calling on her friend Mrs. Welby, and in a hired boat proceeded to the island. Flora almost flew over the ground, so great was her anxiety to reach the cottage. Nature, which pursues her course with serene indifference to human vicissitudes, wore the same smiling aspect it had worn two years before, when she went singing through the woods, like Cinderella, all unconscious of the beneficent fairy she was to meet there in the form of a new Mamita. Trees and shrubs were beautiful with young, glossy foliage. Pines and firs offered their aromatic incense to the sun. Birds were singing, and bees gathering honey from the wild-flowers. A red-headed woodpecker was hammering away on the umbrageous tree under which Flora used to sit while busy with her sketches. He cocked his head to listen as they approached, and, at first sight of them, flew up into the clear blue air, with undulating swiftness. To Flora's great disappointment, they found all the doors fastened; but Mr. Jacobs entered by a window and opened one of them. The cottage had evidently been deserted for a considerable time. Spiders had woven their tapestry in all the corners. A pane had apparently been cut out of the window their attendant had opened, and it afforded free passage to the birds. On a bracket of shell-work, which Flora had made to support a vase of flowers, was a deserted nest, bedded in soft green moss, which hung from it in irregular streamers and festoons.

"How pretty!" said Mrs. Delano. "If the little creature had studied the picturesque, she could n't have devised anything more graceful. Let us take it, bracket and all, and carry it home carefully."

"That was the very first shell-work I made after we came from Nassau," rejoined Flora. "I used to put fresh flowers on it every morning, to please Rosa. Poor Rosa! Where *can* she be?"

She turned away her head, and was silent for a moment. Then, pointing to the window, she said: "There's that dead pine-tree I told you I used to call Old Man of the Woods. He is swinging long pennants of moss on his arms, just as he did when I was afraid to look at him in the moonlight."

She was soon busy with a heap of papers swept into a corner of the room she used to occupy. They were covered with sketches of leaves and flowers, and embroidery-patterns, and other devices with which she had amused herself in those days. Among them she was delighted to find the head and shoulders of Thistle, with a garland round his neck. In Rosa's sleeping-room, an old music-book, hung with cobwebs, leaned against the wall.

"O Mamita Lila, I am glad to find this!" exclaimed Flora. "Here is what Rosa and I used to sing to dear papa when we were ever so little. He always loved old-fashioned music. Here are some of Jackson's canzonets, that were his favorites." She began to hum, "Time has not thinned my flowing hair." "Here is Dr. Arne's

'Sweet Echo.' Rosa used to play and sing that beautifully. And here is what he always liked to have us sing
to him at sunset. We sang it to him the very night before
he died." She began to warble, " Now Phœbus sinketh
in the west." " Why, it seems as if I were a little girl
again, singing to Papasito and Mamita," said she.

Looking up, she saw that Mrs. Delano had covered her
face with her handkerchief; and closing the music-book,
she nestled to her side, affectionately inquiring what had
troubled her. For a little while her friend pressed her
hand in silence.

" O darling," said she, " what a strange, sad gift is memory! I sang that to your father the last time we ever saw
the sunset together; and perhaps when he heard it he
used to see me sometimes, as plainly as I now see him. It
is consoling to think he did not quite forget me."

" When we go home, I will sing it to you every evening
if you would like it, Mamita Lila," said Flora.

Her friend patted her head fondly, and said: " You must
finish your researches soon, darling; for I think we had
better go to Magnolia Lawn to see if Tom and Chloe can
be found."

" How shall we get there? It's too far for you to walk,
and poor Thistle's gone," said Flora.

" I have sent Mr. Jacobs to the plantation," replied Mrs.
Delano, " and I think he will find some sort of vehicle.
Meanwhile, you had better be getting together any little
articles you want to carry away."

As Flora took up the music-book, some of the loose
leaves fell out, and with them came a sketch of Tulee's
head, with the large gold hoops and the gay turban.
" Here's Tulee!" shouted Flora. " It isn't well drawn,

Q

but it *is* like her. I 'll make a handsome picture from it, and frame it, and hang it by my bedside, where I can see it every morning. Dear, good Tulee! How she jumped up and kissed us when we first arrived here. I suppose she thinks I am dead, and has cried a great deal about little **Missy** Flory. O, what would n't I give to see her!"

She had peeped about everywhere, and was becoming very much dispirited with the desolation, when **Mr.** Jacobs came back with a mule and a small cart, which he said **was the** best conveyance he could procure. The jolting over hillocks, and the occasional grunts of the mule, made it an amusing ride; but it was a fruitless one. The plantation negroes were sowing cotton, but all Mr. Fitzgerald's household servants were leased out in Savannah during his **absence in Europe.** The white villa at Magnolia Lawn peeped out from its green surroundings; but the jalousies were closed, and **the tracks on the** carriage-road were obliterated by rains.

Hiring a negro to go with them to take back the cart, they made the best **of** their way **to the** boat, which was waiting for them. Fatigued and disconsolate with their fruitless search, they **felt little** inclined to talk as they glided **over** the bright **waters.** The negro boatmen frequently broke in upon the silence with some simple, wild **melody, which they sang in perfect** unison, dipping their oars in rhythm. When Savannah came in sight, they urged the boat faster, and, improvising words to suit the occasion, they **sang in** brisker strains:—

> " Row, darkies, row!
>   See de sun down dar am creepin';
> Row, darkies, row!
>   Hab white ladies in yer keepin';
> Row, darkies, row!"

With the business they had on hand, Mrs. Delano preferred not to seek her friends in the city, and they took lodgings at a hotel. Early the next morning, Mr. Jacobs was sent out to ascertain the whereabouts of Mr. Fitzgerald's servants; and Mrs. Delano proposed that, during his absence, they should drive to The Pines, which she described as an extremely pleasant ride. Flora assented, with the indifference of a preoccupied mind. But scarcely had the horses stepped on the thick carpet of pine foliage with which the ground was strewn, when she eagerly exclaimed, "Tom! Tom!" A black man, mounted on the seat of a carriage that was passing them, reined in his horses and stopped.

"Keep quiet, my dear," whispered Mrs. Delano to her companion, "till I can ascertain who is in the carriage."

"Are you Mr. Fitzgerald's Tom?" she inquired.

"Yes, Missis," replied the negro, touching his hat.

She beckoned him to come and open her carriage-door, and, speaking in a low voice, she said: "I want to ask you about a Spanish lady who used to live in a cottage, not far from Mr. Fitzgerald's plantation. She had a black servant named Tulee, who used to call her Missy Rosy. We went to the cottage yesterday, and found it shut up. Can you tell us where they have gone?"

Tom looked at them very inquisitively, and answered, "Dunno, Missis."

"We are Missy Rosy's friends, and have come to bring her some good news. If you can tell us anything about her, I will give you this gold piece."

Tom half stretched forth his hand to take the coin, then drew it back, and repeated, "Dunno, Missis."

Flora, who felt her heart rising in her throat, tossed back her veil, and said, "Tom, don't you know me?"

The negro started as if a ghost had risen before him.

"Now tell me where Missy Rosy has gone, and who went with her," said she, coaxingly.

"Bress yer, Missy Flory! *am* yer alive!" exclaimed the bewildered negro.

Flora laughed, and, drawing off her glove, shook hands with him. "Now you know I'm alive, Tom. But don't tell anybody. Where's Missy Rosy gone."

"O Missy," replied Tom, "dar am heap ob tings to tell."

Mrs. Delano suggested that it was not a suitable place; and Tom said he must go home with his master's carriage. He told them he had obtained leave to go and see his wife Chloe that evening; and he promised to come to their hotel first. So, with the general information that Missy Rosy and Tulee were safe, they parted for the present.

Tom's communication in the evening was very long, and intensely interesting to his auditors; but it did not extend beyond a certain point. He told of Rosa's long and dangerous illness; of Chloe's and Tulee's patient praying and nursing; of the birth of the baby; of the sale to Mr. Bruteman; and of the process by which she escaped with Mr. Duroy. Further than that he knew nothing. He had never been in New Orleans afterward, and had never heard Mr. Fitzgerald speak of Rosa.

At that crisis in the conversation, Mrs. Delano summoned Mr. Jacobs, and requested him to ascertain when a steamboat would go to New Orleans. Flora kissed her hand, with a glance full of gratitude. Tom looked at her in a very earnest, embarrassed way, and said: "Missis, am yer one ob dem Ab-lish-nishts dar in de Norf, dat Massa swars 'bout?"

Mrs. Delano turned toward Flora with a look of perplexity, and, having received an interpretation of the question, she smiled as she answered: "I rather think I am half an Abolitionist, Tom. But why do you wish to know?"

Tom went on to state, in "lingo" that had to be frequently explained, that he wanted to run away to the North, and that he could manage to do it if it were not for Chloe and the children. He had been in hopes that Mrs. Fitzgerald would have taken her to the North to nurse her baby while she was gone to Europe. In that case, he intended to follow after; and he thought some good people would lend them money to buy their little ones, and, both together, they could soon work off the debt. But this project had been defeated by Mrs. Bell, who brought a white nurse from Boston, and carried her infant grandson back with her.

"Yer see, Missis," said Tom, with a sly look, "dey tinks de niggers don't none ob 'em wants dare freedom, so dey nebber totes 'em whar it be."

Ever since that disappointment had occurred, he and his wife had resolved themselves into a committee of ways and means, but they had not yet devised any feasible mode of escape. And now they were thrown into great consternation by the fact that a slave-trader had been to look at Chloe, because Mr. Fitzgerald wanted money to spend in Europe, and had sent orders to have some of his negroes sold.

Mrs. Delano told him she did n't see how she could help him, but she would think about it; and Flora, with a sideway inclination of the head toward her, gave Tom an expressive glance, which he understood as a promise to persuade her. He urged the matter no further, but asked what time it was. Being told it was near nine o'clock, he said he must hasten to Chloe, for it was not allowable for negroes to be in the street after that hour.

He had scarcely closed the door, before Mrs. Delano said, " If Chloe is sold, I must buy her."

" I thought you would say so," rejoined Flora.

A discussion then took place as to ways and means, and a strictly confidential letter was written to a lawyer from the North, with whom Mrs. Delano was acquainted, requesting him to buy the woman and her children for her, if they were to be sold.

It happened fortunately that a steamer was going to New Orleans the next day. Just as they were going on board, a negro woman with two children came near, and, dropping a courtesy, said: " Skuse, Missis. Dis ere 's Chloe. Please say Ise yer nigger! Do, Missis!"

Flora seized the black woman's hand, and pressed it, while she whispered: " Do, Mamita! They 're going to sell her, you know."

She took the children by the hand, and hurried forward without waiting for an answer. They were all on board before Mrs. Delano had time to reflect. Tom was nowhere to be seen. On one side of her stood Chloe, with two little ones clinging to her skirts, looking at her imploringly with those great fervid eyes, and saying in suppressed tones, "Missis, dey 's gwine to sell me away from de chillen"; and on the other side was Flora, pressing her hand, and entreating, " Don't send her back, Mamita! She was *so* good to poor Rosa."

" But, my dear, if they should trace her to me, it would be a very troublesome affair," said the perplexed lady.

"They won't look for her in New Orleans. They'll think she's gone North," urged Flora.

During this whispered consultation, Mr. Jacobs approached with some of their baggage. Mrs. Delano stopped him, and said: "When you register our names, add a negro servant and her two children."

He looked surprised, but bowed and asked no questions. She was scarcely less surprised at herself. In the midst of her anxiety to have the boat start, she called to mind her former censures upon those who helped servants to escape from Southern masters, and she could not help smiling at the new dilemma in which she found herself.

The search in New Orleans availed little. They alighted from their carriage a few minutes to look at the house where Flora was born. She pointed out to Mrs. Delano the spot whence her father had last spoken to her on that merry morning, and the grove where she used to **pelt him** with oranges; but neither of them cared to enter the house, now that everything was so changed. Madame's house was occupied by strangers, who knew nothing of the **pre-** vious tenants, except that they were said to have gone to Europe to live. They drove to Mr. Duroy's, and found strangers there, who said the former occupants had all died of yellow-fever, — the lady and gentleman, a negro woman, and a white baby. Flora was bewildered to find every link with her past broken and gone. She had not lived long enough to realize that the traces of human lives often disappear from cities as quickly as the ocean closes over the tracks of vessels. Mr. Jacobs proposed searching for some one who had **been** in Mr. Duroy's employ; and with that intention, they returned to the city. As they were passing a house where a large bird-cage hung in the open window, Flora heard the words, "*Petit blanc, mon bon frère! Ha! ha!*"

She called out to Mr. Jacobs, "Stop! Stop!" and pushed at the carriage door, in her impatience to get out.

"What *is* the matter, my child?" inquired Mrs. Delano.

"That's Madame's parrot," replied she; and an instant after she was ringing at the door of the house. She told the servant they wished to make some inquiries concerning Signor and Madame Papanti, and Monsieur Duroy; and she and Mrs. Delano were shown in to wait for the lady of the house. They had no sooner entered, than the parrot flapped her wings and cried out, "*Bon jour, joli petit diable!*" And then she began to whistle and warble, twitter and crow, through a ludicrous series of noisy variations. Flora burst into peals of laughter, in the midst of which the lady of the house entered the room. "Excuse me, Madame," said she. "This parrot is an old acquaintance of mine. I taught her to imitate all sorts of birds, and she is showing me that she has not forgotten my lessons."

"It will be impossible to hear ourselves speak, unless I cover the cage," replied the lady.

"Allow me to quiet her, if you please," rejoined Flora. She opened the door of the cage, and the bird hopped on her arm, flapping her wings, and crying, "*Bon jour! Ha! ha!*"

"*Taisez vous, jolie Manon,*" said Flora soothingly, while she stroked the feathery head. The bird nestled close and was silent.

When their errand was explained, the lady repeated the same story they had already heard about Mr. Duroy's family.

" Was the black woman who died there named Tulee ? " inquired Flora.

" I never heard her name but once or twice," replied the lady. " It was not a common negro name, and I think that was it. Madame Papanti had put her and the baby there to board. After Mr. Duroy died, his son came home from Arkansas to settle his affairs. My husband, who was one of Mr. Duroy's clerks, bought some of the things at auction ; and among them was that parrot."

" And what has become of Signor and Madame Papanti ? " asked Mrs. Delano.

The lady could give no information, except that they had returned to Europe. Having obtained directions where to find her husband, they thanked her, and wished her good morning.

Flora held the parrot up to the cage, and said, " *Bon jour, jolie Manon !* "

" *Bon jour !* " repeated the bird, and hopped upon her perch.

After they had entered the carriage, Flora said : " How melancholy it seems that everybody is gone, except *Jolie Manon !* How glad the poor thing seemed to be to see me ! I wish I could take her home."

" I will send to inquire whether the lady will sell her," replied her friend.

" O Mamita, you will spoil me, you indulge me so much," rejoined Flora.

Mrs. Delano smiled affectionately, as she answered : " If you were very spoilable, dear, I think that would have been done already."

" But it will be such a bother to take care of Manon," said Flora.

12

"Our new servant Chloe can do that," replied Mrs. Delano. "But I really hope we shall get home without any further increase of our retinue."

From the clerk information was obtained that he heard Mr. Duroy tell Mr. Bruteman that a lady named Rosabella Royal had sailed to Europe with Signor and Madame Papanti in the ship Mermaid. He added that news afterward arrived that the vessel foundered at sea, and all on board were lost.

With this sorrow on her heart, Flora returned to Boston. Mr. Percival was immediately informed of their arrival, and hastened to meet them. When the result of their researches was told, he said: "I should n't be disheartened yet. Perhaps they did n't sail in the Mermaid. I will send to the New York Custom-House for a list of the passengers."

Flora eagerly caught at that suggestion; and Mrs. Delano said, with a smile: "We have some other business in which we need your help. You must know that I am involved in another slave case. If ever a quiet and peace-loving individual was caught up and whirled about by a tempest of events, I am surely that individual. Before I met this dear little Flora, I had a fair prospect of living and dying a respectable and respected old fogy, as you irreverent reformers call discreet people. But now I find myself drawn into the vortex of abolition to the extent of helping off four fugitive slaves. In Flora's case, I acted deliberately, from affection and a sense of duty; but in this second instance I was taken by storm, as it were. The poor woman was aboard before I knew it, and I found myself too weak to withstand her imploring looks and Flora's pleading tones." She went on to describe the services

Chloe had rendered to Rosa, and added: "I will pay any expenses necessary for conveying this woman to a place of safety, and supplying all that is necessary for her and her children, until she can support them ; but I do not feel as if she were safe here."

"If you will order a carriage, I will take them directly to the house of Francis Jackson, in Hollis Street," said Mr. Percival. "They will be safe enough under the protection of that honest, sturdy friend of freedom. His house is the depot of various subterranean railroads ; and I pity the slaveholder who tries to get on any of his tracks. He finds himself 'like a toad under a harrow, where ilka tooth gies him a tug,' as the Scotch say."

While waiting for the carriage, Chloe and her children were brought in. Flora took the little ones under her care, and soon had their aprons filled with cakes and sugar-plums. Chloe, unable to restrain her feelings, dropped down on her knees in the midst of the questions they were asking her, and poured forth an eloquent prayer that the Lord would bless these good friends of her down-trodden people.

When the carriage arrived, she rose, and, taking Mrs. Delano's hand, said solemnly : " De Lord bress yer, Missis ! De Lord bress yer ! I seed yer once fore ebber I knowed yer. I seed yer in a vision, when I war prayin' to de Lord to open de free door fur me an' my chillen. Ye war an angel wid white shiny wings. Bress de Lord ! 'T war Him dat sent yer. — An' now, Missy Flory, de Lord bress yer ! Ye war allers good to poor Chloe, down dar in de prison-house. Let me gib yer a kiss, little Missy."

Flora threw her arms round the bended neck, and promised to go and see her wherever she was.

When the carriage rolled away, emotion kept them both silent for a few minutes. " How strange it seems to me now," said Mrs. Delano, " that I lived so many years without thinking of the wrongs of these poor people ! I used to think prayer-meetings for slaves were very fanatical and foolish. It seemed to me enough that they were included in our prayer for ' all classes and conditions of men ' ; but after listening to poor Chloe's eloquent outpouring, I am afraid such generalizing will sound rather cold."

" Mamita," said Flora, " you know you gave me some money to buy a silk dress. Are you willing I should use it to buy clothes for Chloe and her children ? "

" More than willing, my child," she replied. " There is no clothing so beautiful as the raiment of righteousness."

The next morning, Flora went out to make her purchases. Some time after, Mrs. Delano, hearing voices near the door, looked out, and saw her in earnest conversation with Florimond Blumenthal, who had a large parcel in his arms. When she came in, Mrs. Delano said, " So you had an escort home ? "

" Yes, Mamita," she replied ; " Florimond would bring the parcel, and so we walked together."

" He was very polite," said Mrs. Delano ; " but ladies are not accustomed to stand on the doorstep talking with clerks who bring bundles for them."

. " I did n't think anything about that," rejoined Flora. " He wanted to know about Rosa, and I wanted to tell him. Florimond seems just like a piece of my old home, because he loved papa so much. Mamita Lila, did n't you say papa was a poor clerk when you and he first began to love one another ? "

" Yes, my child," she replied ; and she kissed the bright,

innocent face that came bending over her, looking so frankly into hers.

When she had gone out of the room, Mrs. Delano said
to herself, "That darling child, with her strange history
and unworldly ways, is educating me more than I can educate her."

A week later, Mr. and Mrs. Percival came, with tidings
that no such persons as Signor and Madame Papanti were
on board the Mermaid; and they proposed writing letters
of inquiry forthwith to consuls in various parts of Italy
and France.

Flora began to hop and skip and clap her hands. But
she soon paused, and said, laughingly: "Excuse me, ladies
and gentlemen. Mamita often tells me I was brought up
in a bird-cage; and I ask her how then can she expect me
to do anything but hop and sing. Excuse me. I forgot
Mamita and I were not alone."

"You pay us the greatest possible compliment," rejoined
Mr. Percival.

And Mrs. Percival added, "I hope you will always forget it when we are here."

"Do you really wish it?" asked Flora, earnestly. "Then
I will."

And so, with a few genial friends, an ever-deepening attachment between her and her adopted mother, a hopeful
feeling at her heart about Rosa, Tulee's likeness by her
bedside, and Madame's parrot to wish her *Bon jour!*
Boston came to seem to her like a happy home.

CHAPTER XXIII.

ABOUT two months after their return from the South,
Mr. Percival called one evening, and said: "Do you
know Mr. Brick, the police-officer? I met him just now, and
he stopped me. 'There's plenty of work for you Abolitionists
now-a-days,' said he. 'There are five Southerners at the
Tremont, inquiring for runaways, and cursing Garrison.
An agent arrived last night from Fitzgerald's plantation, —
he that married Bell's daughter, you know. He sent for me
to give me a description of a nigger that had gone off in a
mysterious way to parts unknown. He wanted me to try
to find the fellow, and, of course, I did; for I always calculate to do my duty, as the law directs. So I went immediately to Father Snowdon, and described the black
man, and informed him that his master had sent for him, in
a great hurry. I told him I thought it very likely he was
lurking somewhere in Belknap Street; and if he would
have the goodness to hunt him up, I would call, in the
course of an hour or two, to see what luck he had.'"

"Who is Father Snowdon?" inquired Mrs. Delano.

"He is the colored preacher in Belknap Street Church,"
replied Mr. Percival, "and a remarkable man in his way.
He fully equals Chloe in prayer; and he is apt to commend the ship Buzzard to the especial attention of the
Lord. The first time I entered his meeting, he was saying,
in a loud voice, 'We pray thee, O Lord, to bless her
Majesty's good ship, the Buzzard; and if there's a slave-
trader now on the coast of Africa, we pray thee, O

Lord, to blow her straight under the lee of the Buzzard.' He has been a slave himself, and he has perhaps helped off more slaves than any man in the country. I doubt whether Garrick himself had greater power to disguise his countenance. If a slaveholder asks him about a slave, he is the most stolid-looking creature imaginable. You would n't suppose he understood anything, or ever *could* understand anything. But if he meets an Abolitionist a minute after, his black face laughs all over, and his roguish eyes twinkle like diamonds, while he recounts how he 'come it' over the Southern gentleman. That bright soul of his is a jewel set in ebony."

" It seems odd that the police-officer should apply to *him* to catch a runaway," said Mrs. Delano.

" That 's the fun of it," responded Mr. Percival. "The extinguishers are themselves taking fire. The fact is, Boston policemen don't feel exactly in their element as slave-hunters. They are too near Bunker Hill; and on the Fourth of July they are reminded of the Declaration of Independence, which, though it is going out of fashion, is still regarded by a majority of the people as a venerable document. Then they have Whittier's trumpet-tones ringing in their ears, —

' No slave hunt in *our* borders! no pirate on *our* strand!
No fetters in the Bay State! no slave upon *our* land!'"

" How did Mr. Brick describe Mr. Fitzgerald's runaway slave?" inquired Flora.

" He said he was tall and very black, with a white scar over his right eye."

" That 's Tom!" exclaimed she. " How glad Chloe will be! But I wonder he did n't come here the first thing.

We could have told him how well she was getting on in New Bedford."

"Father Snowdon will tell him all about that," rejoined Mr. Percival. "If Tom was in the city, he probably kept him closely hidden, on account of the number of Southerners who have recently arrived; and after the hint the police-officer gave him, he doubtless hustled him out of town in the quickest manner."

"I want to hurrah for that policeman," said Flora; "but Mamita would think I was a very rude young lady, or rather that I was no lady at all. But perhaps you'll let me *sing* hurrah, Mamita?"

Receiving a smile for answer, she flew to the piano, and, improvising an accompaniment to herself, she began to sing hurrah! through all manner of variations, high and low, rapidly trilled and slowly prolonged, now bursting full upon the ear, now receding in the distance. It was such a lively fantasia, that it made Mr. Percival laugh, while Mrs. Delano's face was illuminated by a quiet smile.

In the midst of the merriment, the door-bell rang. Flora started from the piano, seized her worsted-work, and said, "Now, Mamita, I'm ready to receive company like a pink of propriety." But the change was so sudden, that her eyes were still laughing when Mr. Green entered an instant after; and he again caught that archly demure expression which seemed to him so fascinating. The earnestness of his salutation was so different from his usual formal politeness, that Mrs. Delano could not fail to observe it. The conversation turned upon incidents of travel after they had parted so suddenly. "I shall never cease to regret," said he, "that you missed hearing La Señorita Campaneo.

She was a most extraordinary creature. Superbly handsome; and do you know, Miss Delano, I now and then
caught a look that reminded me very much of you. Unfortunately, you have lost your chance to hear her. For
Mr. King, the son of our Boston millionnaire, who has lately
been piling up money in the East, persuaded her to quit
the stage when she had but just started in her grand career. All the musical world in Rome were vexed with
him for preventing her re-engagement. As for Fitzgerald,
I believe he would have shot him if he could have found
him. It was a purely musical disappointment, for he was
never introduced to the fascinating Señorita; but he fairly
pined upon it. I told him the best way to drive off the
blue devils would be to go with me and a few friends to
the Grotta Azzura. So off we started to Naples, and
thence to Capri. The grotto was one of the few novelties
remaining for me in Italy. I had heard much of it, but the
reality exceeded all descriptions. We seemed to be actually under the sea in a palace of gems. Our boat glided
over a lake of glowing sapphire, and our oars dropped
rubies. High above our heads were great rocks of sapphire, deepening to lapis-lazuli at the base, with here and
there a streak of malachite."

" It seems like Aladdín's Cave," remarked Flora.

" Yes," replied Mr. Green; " only it was Aladdin's Cave
undergoing a wondrous ' sea change.' A poetess, who writes
for the papers under the name of Melissa Mayflower, had
fastened herself upon our party in some way; and I suppose she felt bound to sustain the reputation of the quill.
She said the Nereids must have built that marine palace, and decorated it for a visit from fairies of the rain-
bow."

"That was a pretty thought," said Flora. "It sounds like 'Lalla Rookh.'"

"It was a pretty thought," rejoined the gentleman, "but can give you no idea of the unearthly splendor. I thought how you would have been delighted if you had been with our party. I regretted your absence almost as much as I did at the opera. But the Blue Grotto, wonderful as it was, did n't quite drive away Fitzgerald's blue devils, though it made him forget his vexations for the time. The fact is, just as we started he received a letter from his agent, informing him of the escape of a negro woman and her two children ; and he spent most of the way back to Naples swearing at the Abolitionists."

Flora, the side of whose face was toward him, gave Mrs. Delano a furtive glance full of fun ; but he saw nothing of the mischief in her expressive face, except a little whirlpool of a dimple, which played about her mouth for an instant, and then subsided. A very broad smile was on Mr. Percival's face, as he sat examining some magnificent illustrations of the Alhambra. Mr. Green, quite unconscious of the by-play in their thoughts, went on to say, "It is really becoming a serious evil that Southern gentlemen have so little security for that species of property."

"Then you consider women and children *property?*" inquired Mr. Percival, looking up from his book.

Mr. Green bowed with a sort of mock deference, and replied: "Pardon me, Mr. Percival, it is so unusual for gentlemen of your birth and position to belong to the Abolition troop of rough-riders, that I may be excused for not recollecting it."

"I should consider my birth and position great misfortunes, if they blinded me to the plainest principles of truth and justice," rejoined Mr. Percival.

The highly conservative gentleman made no reply, but rose to take leave.

" Did your friends the Fitzgeralds return with you?" inquired Mrs. Delano.

"No," replied he. "They intend to remain until October. Good evening, ladies. I hope soon to have the pleasure of seeing you again." And with an inclination of the head toward Mr. Percival, he departed.

" Why did you ask him that question?" said Flora. " Are you afraid of anything?"

"Not in the slightest degree," answered Mrs. Delano. "If, without taking much trouble, we can avoid your being recognized by Mr. Fitzgerald, I should prefer it, because I do not wish to have any conversation with him. But now that your sister's happiness is no longer implicated, there is no need of caution. If he happens to see you, I shall tell him you sought my protection, and that he has no legal power over you."

The conversation diverged to the Alhambra and Washington Irving; and Flora ended the evening by singing the Moorish ballad of "Xarifa," which she said always brought a picture of Rosabella before her eyes.

The next morning, Mr. Green called earlier than usual. He did not ask for Flora, whom he had in fact seen in the street a few minutes before. " Excuse me, Mrs. Delano, for intruding upon you at such an unseasonable hour," said he. " I chose it because I wished to be sure of seeing you alone. You must have observed that I am greatly interested in your adopted daughter."

" The thought has crossed my mind," replied the lady;

"but I was by no means certain that she interested you more than a very pretty girl must necessarily interest a gentleman of taste."

"Pretty!" repeated he. "That is a very inadequate word to describe the most fascinating young lady I have ever met. She attracts me so strongly, that I have called to ask your permission to seek her for a wife."

Mrs. Delano hesitated for a moment, and then answered, "It is my duty to inform you that she is not of high family on the father's ˌside; and on the mother's, she is scarcely what you would deem respectable."

"Has she vulgar, disagreeable relations, who would be likely to be intrusive?" he asked.

"She has no relative, near or distant, that I know of," replied the lady.

"Then her birth is of no consequence," he answered. "My family would be satisfied to receive her as your daughter. I am impatient to introduce her to my mother and sisters, who I am sure will be charmed with her."

Mrs. Delano was embarrassed, much to the surprise of her visitor, who was accustomed to consider his wealth and social position a prize that would be eagerly grasped at. After watching her countenance for an instant, he said, somewhat proudly: "You do not seem to receive my proposal very cordially, Mrs. Delano. Have you anything to object to my character or family?"

"Certainly not," replied the lady. "My doubts are concerning my daughter."

"Is she engaged, or partially engaged, to another?" he inquired.

"She is not," rejoined Mrs. Delano; "though I imagine she is not quite 'fancy free.'"

"Would it be a breach of confidence to tell me who has been so fortunate as to attract her?"

"Nothing of the kind has ever been confided to me," answered the lady. "It is merely an imagination of my own, and relates to a person unknown to you."

"Then I will enter the lists with my rival, if there is one," said he. "Such a prize is not to be given up without an effort. But you have not yet said that I have your consent."

"Since you are so persistent," rejoined Mrs. Delano, "I will tell you a secret, if you will pledge your honor, as a gentleman, never to repeat it, or hint at it, to any mortal."

"I pledge my honor," he replied, "that whatever you choose to tell me shall be sacred between us."

"It is not pleasant to tell the story of Flora's birth," responded she; "but under present circumstances it seems to be a duty. When I have informed you of the facts, you are free to engage her affections if you can. On the paternal side, she descends from the French gentry and the Spanish nobility; but her mother was a quadroon slave, and she herself was sold as a slave."

Mr. Green bowed his head upon his hand, and spoke no word. Drilled to conceal his emotions, he seemed outwardly calm, though it cost him a pang to relinquish the captivating young creature, who he felt would have made his life musical, though by piquant contrast rather than by harmony. After a brief, troubled silence, he rose and walked toward the window, as if desirous to avoid looking the lady in the face. After a while, he said, slowly, "Do you deem it quite right, Mrs. Delano, to pass such a counterfeit on society?"

"I have attempted to pass no counterfeit on society," she

replied, with dignity. "Flora is a blameless and accomplished young lady. Her beauty and vivacity captivated me before I knew anything of her origin ; and in the same way they have captivated you. She was alone in the world, and I was alone ; and we adopted each other. I have never sought to introduce her into society ; and so far as relates to yourself, I should have told you these facts sooner if I had known the state of your feelings ; but so long as they were not expressed, it would scarcely have been delicate for me to take them for granted."

"Very true," rejoined the disenchanted lover. "You certainly had a right to choose a daughter for yourself; though I could hardly have imagined that any amount of attraction would have overcome *such* obstacles in the mind of a lady of your education and refined views of life. Excuse my using the word ' counterfeit.' I was slightly disturbed when it escaped me."

"It requires no apology," she replied. "I am aware that society would take the same view of my proceeding that you do. As for my education, I have learned to consider it as, in many respects, false. As for my views, they have been greatly modified by this experience. I have learned to estimate people and things according to their real value, not according to any merely external accidents."

Mr. Green extended his hand, saying : "I will bid you farewell, Mrs. Delano ; for, under existing circumstances, it becomes necessary to deny myself the pleasure of again calling upon you. I must seek to divert my mind by new travels, I hardly know where. I have exhausted Europe, having been there three times. I have often thought I should like to look on the Oriental gardens and bright waters of Damascus. Everything is so wretchedly new, and so disagreeably fast, in this country! It must be refreshing to see a place that has known no changes for three thousand years."

They clasped hands with mutual adieus; and the unfortunate son of wealth, not knowing what to do in a country full of noble work, went forth to seek a new sensation in the slow-moving caravans of the East.

A few days afterward, when Flora returned from taking a lesson in oil-colors, she said: "How do you suppose I have offended Mr. Green? When I met him just now, he touched his hat in a very formal way, and passed on, though I was about to speak to him."

"Perhaps he was in a hurry," suggested Mrs. Delano.

"No, it was n't that," rejoined Flora. "He did just so day before yesterday, and he can't always be in a hurry. Besides, you know he is never in a hurry; he is too much of a gentleman."

Her friend smiled as she answered, "You are getting to be quite a judge of aristocratic manners, considering you were brought up in a bird-cage."

The young girl was not quite so ready as usual with a responsive smile. She went on to say, in a tone of perplexity: "What *can* have occasioned such a change in his manner? You say I am sometimes thoughtless about politeness. Do you think I have offended him in any way?"

"Would it trouble you very much if you had?" inquired Mrs. Delano.

"Not *very* much," she replied; "but I should be sorry if he thought me rude to him, when he was so very polite to us in Europe. What is it, Mamita? I think you know something about it."

"I did not tell you, my child," replied she, "because I thought it would be unpleasant. But you keep no secrets from me, and it is right that I should be equally open-hearted with you. Did you never suspect that Mr. Green was in love with you?"

"The thought never occurred to me till he called here that first evening after his return from Europe. Then, when he took my hand, he pressed it a little. I thought it was rather strange in such a formal gentleman; but I did not mention it to you, because I feared you would think me vain. But if he is in love with me, why don't he tell me so? And why does he pass me without speaking?"

Her friend replied: "He deemed it proper to tell me first, and ask my consent to pay his addresses to you. As he persisted very urgently, I thought it my duty to tell him, under the seal of secrecy, that you were remotely connected with the colored race. The announcement somewhat disturbed his habitual composure. He said he must deny himself the pleasure of calling again. He proposes to go to Damascus, and there I hope he will forget his disappointment."

Flora flared up as Mrs. Delano had never seen her. She reddened to the temples, and her lip curled scornfully. "He is a mean man!" she exclaimed. "If he thought that I myself was a suitable wife for his serene highness, what had my great-grandmother to do with it? I wish he had asked me to marry him. I should like to have him know I never cared a button about him; and that, if I didn't care for him, I should consider it more shameful to sell myself for his diamonds, than it would have been to have been sold for a slave by papa's creditors when I couldn't help myself. I am glad you don't feel like going into parties, Mamita; and if you ever do feel like it, I hope you will leave me at home. I don't want to be introduced to any of these cold, aristocratic Bostonians."

"Not all of them cold and aristocratic, darling," replied Mrs. Delano. "Your Mamita is one of them; and she is becoming less cold and aristocratic every day, thanks to a little Cinderella who came to her singing through the woods, two years ago."

"And who found a fairy godmother," responded Flora, subsiding into a tenderer tone. "It *is* ungrateful for me to say anything against Boston; and with such friends as the Percivals too. But it does seem mean that Mr. Green, if he really liked me, should decline speaking to me because my great-grandmother had a dark complexion. I never knew the old lady, though I dare say I should love her if I did know her. Madame used to say Rosabella inherited pride from our Spanish grandfather. I think I have some of it, too; and it makes me shy of being introduced to your stylish acquaintance, who might blame you if they knew all about me. I like people who do know all about me, and who like me because I am I. That's one reason why I like Florimond. He admired my mother, and loved my father; and he thinks just as well of me as if I had never been sold for a slave."

"Do you always call him Florimond?" inquired Mrs. Delano.

"I call him Mr. Blumenthal before folks, and he calls me Miss Delano. But when no one is by, he sometimes calls me Miss Royal, because he says he loves that name, for the sake of old times; and then I call him Blumen, partly for short, and partly because his cheeks are so pink, it comes natural. He likes to have me call him so. He says Flora is the *Göttinn der Blumen* in German, and so I am the Goddess of Blumen.

Mrs. Delano smiled at these small scintillations of wit, which in the talk of lovers sparkle to them like diamond-dust in the sunshine.

"Has he ever told you that he loved *you* as well as your name?" asked she.

"He never said so, Mamita; but I think he does," rejoined Flora.

"What reason have you to think so?" inquired her friend.

"He wants very much to come here," replied the young lady; "but he is extremely modest. He says he knows he is not suitable company for such a rich, educated lady as you are. He is taking dancing-lessons, and lessons on the piano, and he is studying French and Italian and history, and all sorts of things. And he says he means to make a mint of money, and then perhaps he can come here sometimes to see me dance, and hear me play on the piano."

"I by no means require that all my acquaintance should make a mint of money," answered Mrs. Delano. "I am very much pleased with the account you give of this young Blumenthal. When you next see him, give him my compliments, and tell him I should be happy to become acquainted with him."

Flora dropped on her knees and hid her face in her friend's lap. She did n't express her thanks in words, but she cried a little.

"This is more serious than I supposed," thought Mrs. Delano.

A fortnight afterward, she obtained an interview with Mr. Goldwin, and asked, "What is your estimate of that young Mr. Blumenthal, who has been for some time in your employ?"

"He is a modest young man, of good habits," answered the merchant; "and of more than common business capacity."

"Would you be willing to receive him as a partner?" she inquired.

"The young man is poor," rejoined Mr. Goldwin; "and we have many applications from those who can advance some capital."

"If a friend would loan him ten thousand dollars for twenty years, and leave it to him by will in case she should die meanwhile, would that be sufficient to induce you?" said the lady.

"I should be glad to do it, particularly if it obliges you, Mrs. Delano," responded the merchant; "for I really think him a very worthy young man."

"Then consider it settled," she replied. "But let it be an affair between ourselves, if you please; and to him you may merely say that a friend of his former employer and benefactor wishes to assist him."

When Blumenthal informed Flora of this unexpected good-fortune, they of course suspected from whom it came; and they looked at each other, and blushed.

Mrs. Delano did not escape gossiping remarks. "How she has changed!" said Mrs. Ton to Mrs. Style. "She used to be the most fastidious of exclusives; and now she has adopted nobody knows whom, and one of Mr. Goldwin's clerks seems to be on the most familiar footing there. I should have no objection to invite the girl to my parties, for she is Mrs. Delano's *adoptée*, and she would really be an ornament to my rooms, besides being very convenient as an accomplished musician; but, of course, I don't wish my daughters to be introduced to that nobody of a clerk."

"She has taken up several of the Abolitionists too," rejoined Mrs. Style. "My husband looked into an anti-slavery meeting the other evening, partly out of curiosity to hear what Garrison had to say, and partly in hopes of obtaining some clew to a fugitive slave that one of his Southern friends had written to him about. And who should he see there, of all people in the world, but Mrs. Delano and her *adoptée*, escorted by that young clerk. Think of her, with her dove-colored silks and violet gloves, crowded and jostled by Dinah and Sambo! I expect the next thing we shall hear will be that she has given a negro party."

"In that case, I presume she will choose to perfume her embroidered handkerchiefs with musk, or pachouli, instead of her favorite breath of violets," responded Mrs. Ton.

And, smiling at their wit, the fashionable ladies parted, to quote it from each other as among the good things they had recently heard.

Only the faint echoes of such remarks reached Mrs. Delano; though she was made to feel, in many small ways, that she had become a black sheep in aristocratic circles. But these indications passed by her almost unnoticed, occupied as she was in earnestly striving to redeem the mistakes of the past by making the best possible use of the present.

PART SECOND.

CHAPTER XXIV.

AN interval of nineteen years elapsed, bringing with
them various changes to the personages of this story.
A year after Mr. Fitzgerald's return from Europe, a feud
sprang up between him and his father-in-law, Mr. Bell,
growing out of his dissipated and spendthrift habits. His
intercourse with Boston was consequently suspended, and
the fact of Flora's existence remained unknown to him.
He died nine years after he witnessed the dazzling apparition of Rosa in Rome, and the history of his former relation to her was buried with him, as were several other
similar secrets. There was generally supposed to be something mysterious about his exit. Those who were acquainted with Mr. Bell's family were aware that the marriage had been an unhappy one, and that there was an
obvious disposition to hush inquiries concerning it. Mrs.
Fitzgerald had always continued to spend her summers
with her parents; and having lost her mother about the
time of her widowhood, she became permanently established at the head of her father's household. She never
in any way alluded to her married life, and always dis-
missed the subject as briefly as possible, if any stranger
touched upon it. Of three children, only one, her eldest,
remained. Time had wrought changes in her person.

Her once fairy-like figure was now too short for its fulness, and the blue eyes were somewhat dulled in expression; but the fair face and the paly-gold tresses were still very pretty.

When she had at last succeeded in obtaining an introduction to Flora, during one of her summer visits to Boston, she had been very much captivated by her, and was disposed to rally Mr. Green about his diminished enthusiasm, after he had fallen in love with a fair cousin of hers; but that gentleman was discreetly silent concerning the real cause of his disenchantment.

Mrs. Delano's nature was so much deeper than that of her pretty neighbor, that nothing like friendship could grow up between them; but Mrs. Fitzgerald called occasionally, to retail gossip of the outer world, or to have what she termed a musical treat.

Flora had long been Mrs. Blumenthal. At the time of her marriage, Mrs. Delano said she was willing to adopt a son, but not to part with a daughter; consequently, they formed one household. As years passed on, infant faces and lisping voices came into the domestic circle, — fresh little flowers in the floral garland of Mamita Lila's life. Alfred Royal, the eldest, was a complete reproduction, in person and character, of the grandfather whose name he bore. Rosa, three years younger, was quite as striking a likeness of her namesake. Then came two little ones, who soon went to live with the angels. And, lastly, there was the five-year-old pet, Lila, who inherited her father's blue eyes, pink cheeks, and flaxen hair.

These children were told that their grandfather was a rich American merchant in New Orleans, and their grandmother a beautiful and accomplished Spanish lady; that their grandfather failed in business and died poor; that his friend Mrs. Delano adopted their mother; and that they had a very handsome Aunt Rosa, who went to Europe with some good friends, and was lost at sea. It was not deemed wise to inform them of any further particulars, till time and experience had matured their characters and views of life.

Applications to American consuls, in various places, for information concerning Signor and Madame Papanti had proved unavailing, in consequence of the Signor's change of name; and Rosabella had long ceased to be anything but a very tender memory to her sister, whose heart was now completely filled with new objects of affection. The bond between her and her adopted mother strengthened with time, because their influence on each other was mutually improving to their characters. The affection and gayety of the young folks produced a glowing atmosphere in Mrs. Delano's inner life, as their mother's tropical taste warmed up the interior aspect of her dwelling. The fawn-colored damask curtains had given place to crimson; and in lieu of the silvery paper, the walls were covered with bird-of-paradise color, touched with golden gleams. The centre-table was covered with crimson, embroidered with a gold-colored garland; and the screen of the gas-light was a gorgeous assemblage of bright flowers. Mrs. Delano's lovely face was even more placid than it had been in earlier years; but there was a sunset brightness about it, as of one growing old in an atmosphere of love. The ash-colored hair, which Flora had fancied to be violet-tinged, was of a silky whiteness now, and fell in soft curls about the pale face.

On the day when I again take up the thread of this

story, she was seated in her parlor, in a dress of silvery
gray silk, which contrasted pleasantly with the crimson
chair. Under her collar of Honiton lace was an amethys-
tine ribbon, fastened with a pearl pin. Her cap of rich
white lace, made in the fashion of Mary Queen of Scots,
was very slightly trimmed with ribbon of the same color,
and fastened in front with a small amethyst set with pearls.
For fanciful Flora had said: "Dear Mamita Lila, don't
have *every*thing about your dress cold white or gray. Do
let something violet or lilac peep out from the snow, for
the sake of 'auld lang syne.'"

The lady was busy with some crochet-work, when a
girl, apparently about twelve years old, came through the
half-opened folding-doors, and settled on an ottoman at her
feet. She had large, luminous dark eyes, very deeply
fringed, and her cheeks were like ripened peaches. The
dark mass of her wavy hair was gathered behind into what
was called a Greek cap, composed of brown network
strewn with gold beads. Here and there very small, thin
dark curls strayed from under it, like the tendrils of a delicate vine; and nestling close to each ear was a little dark,
downy crescent, which papa called her whisker when he
was playfully inclined to excite her juvenile indignation.

"See!" said she. "This pattern comes all in a tangle.
I have done the stitches wrong. Will you please to help
me, Mamita Lila?"

Mrs. Delano looked up, smiling as she answered, "Let
me see what the trouble is, Rosy Posy."

Mrs. Blumenthal, who was sitting opposite, noticed with
artistic eye what a charming contrast of beauty there was
between that richly colored young face, with its crown of
dark hair, and that pale, refined, symmetrical face, in its

frame of silver. "What a pretty picture I could make, if
I had my crayons here," thought she. "How gracefully
the glossy folds of Mamita's gray dress fall over Rosa's
crimson merino."

She was not aware that she herself made quite as charming a picture. The spirit of laughter still flitted over her
face, from eyes to dimples ; her shining black curls were
lighted up with a rope of cherry-colored chenille, hanging
in a tassel at her ear ; and her graceful little figure showed
to advantage in a neatly fitting dress of soft brown merino,
embroidered with cherry-colored silk. On her lap was little Lila, dressed in white and azure, with her fine flaxen
curls tossed about by the motion of riding to "Banbury
Cross." The child laughed and clapped her hands at every
caper ; and if her steed rested for a moment, she called out
impatiently, "More agin, mamma ! "

But mamma was thinking of the picture she wanted to
make, and at last she said : "We sha' n't get to Banbury
Cross to-day, Lila Blumen ; so you must fall off your horse,
darling, and nursey will take you, while I go to fetch my
crayons." She had just taken her little pet by the hand to
lead her from the room, when the door-bell rang. "That's
Mrs. Fitzgerald," said she. "I know, because she always
rings an *appoggiatura*. Rosen Blumen, take sissy to the
nursery, please."

While the ladies were interchanging salutations with
their visitor, Rosa passed out of the room, leading her little
sister by the hand. "I declare," said Mrs. Fitzgerald,
"that oldest daughter of yours, Mrs. Blumenthal, bears a
striking resemblance to the *cantatrice* who was turning
everybody's head when I was in Rome. You missed
hearing her, I remember. Let me see, what was her

13   s

nomme de guerre? I forget; but it was something that sig
nified a bell, because there was a peculiar ringing in her
voice. When I first saw your daughter, she reminded me
of somebody I had seen; but I never thought who it was
till now. I came to tell you some news about the fascinating Señorita; and I suppose that brought the likeness to
my mind. You know Mr. King, the son of our rich old
merchant, persuaded her to leave the stage to marry him.
They have been living in the South of France for some
years, but he has just returned to Boston. They have
taken rooms at the Revere House, while his father's house
is being fitted up in grand style for their reception. The
lady will of course be a great lioness. She is to make her
first appearance at the party of my cousin, Mrs. Green.
The winter is so nearly at an end, that I doubt whether
there will be any more large parties this season; and I
would n't fail of attending this one on any account, if it
were only for the sake of seeing her. She was the handsomest creature I ever beheld. If you had ever seen her,
you would consider it a compliment indeed to be told that
your Rosa resembles her."

"I should like to get a glimpse of her, if I could without
the trouble of going to a party," replied Mrs. Blumenthal.

"I will come the day after," rejoined Mrs. Fitzgerald,
"and tell you how she was dressed, and whether she
looks as handsome in the parlor as she did on the stage."

After some more chat about reported engagements, and
the probable fashions for the coming season, the lady took
her leave.

When she was gone, Mrs. Delano remarked: "Mrs.
King must be very handsome if she resembles our Rosa.
But I hope Mrs. Fitzgerald will not be so injudicious as to

talk about it before the child. She is free from vanity, and I earnestly wish she may remain so. By the way, Flora, this Mr. King is your father's namesake, — the one who, you told me, called at your house in New Orleans, when you were a little girl."

"I was thinking of that very thing," rejoined Mrs. Blumenthal, "and I was just going to ask you his Christian name. I should like to call there to take a peep at his handsome lady, and see whether he would recollect me. If he did, it would be no matter. So many years have passed, and I am such an old story in Boston, that nobody will concern themselves about me."

"I also should be rather pleased to call," said Mrs. Delano. "His father was a friend of mine; and it was through him that I became acquainted with your father. They were inseparable companions when they were young men. Ah, how long ago that seems! No wonder my hair is white. But please ring for Rosa, dear. I want to arrange her pattern before dinner."

"There 's the door-bell again, Mamita!" exclaimed Flora; "and a very energetic ring it is, too. Perhaps you had better wait a minute."

The servant came in to say that a person from the country wanted to speak with Mrs. Delano; and a tall, stout man, with a broad face, full of fun, soon entered. Having made a short bow, he said, "Mrs. Delano, I suppose?"

The lady signified assent by an inclination of the head.

"My name's Joe Bright," continued he. "No relation of John Bright, the bright Englishman. Wish I was. I come from Northampton, ma'am. The keeper of the Mansion House told me you wanted to get board there in some private family next summer; and I called to tell you that

I can let you have half of my house, furnished or not, just as you like. As I'm plain Joe Bright the blacksmith, of course you won't find lace and damask, and such things as you have here."

"All we wish for," rejoined Mrs. Delano, "is healthy air and wholesome food for the children."

"Plenty of both, ma'am," replied the blacksmith. "And I guess you'll like my wife. She ain't one of the kind that raises a great dust when she sweeps. She's a still sort of body; but she knows a deal more than she tells for."

After a description of the accommodations he had to offer, and a promise from Mrs. Delano to inform him of her decision in a few days, he rose to go. But he stood, hat in hand, looking wistfully toward the piano. "Would it be too great a liberty, ma'am, to ask which of you ladies plays?" said he.

"I seldom play," rejoined Mrs. Delano, "because my daughter, Mrs. Blumenthal, plays so much better."

Turning toward Flora, he said, "I suppose it would be too much trouble to play me a tune?"

"Certainly not," she replied; and, seating herself at the piano, she dashed off, with voice and instrument, "The Campbells are coming, Oho! Oho!"

"By George!" exclaimed the blacksmith. "You was born to it, ma'am; that's plain enough. Well, it was just so with me. I took to music as a Newfoundland pup takes to the water. When my brother Sam and I were boys, we were let out to work for a blacksmith. We wanted a fiddle dreadfully; but we were too poor to buy one; and we couldn't have got much time to play on't if we had had one, for our boss watched us as a weasel watches mice. But we were bent on getting music somehow. The boss always had plenty of iron links of all sizes, hanging in a row, ready to be made into chains when wanted. One day, I happened to hit one of the links with a piece of iron I had in my hand. 'By George! Sam,' said I, 'that was Do.' 'Strike again,' says he. 'Blow! Sam, blow!' said I. I was afraid the boss would come in and find the iron cooling in the fire. So he kept blowing away, and I struck the link again. 'That's Do, just as plain as my name's Sam,' said he. A few days after, I said, 'By George! Sam, I've found Sol.' 'So you have,' said he. 'Now let *me* try. Blow, Joe, blow!' Sam, he found Re and La. And in the course of two months we got so we could play Old Hundred. I don't pretend to say we could do it as glib as you run over the ivory, ma'am; but it was Old Hundred, and no mistake. And we played Yankee Doodle, first rate. We called our instrument the Harmolinks; and we enjoyed it all the more because it was our own invention. I tell you what, ma'am, there's music hid away in everything, only we don't know how to bring it out."

"I think so," rejoined Mrs. Blumenthal. "Music is a sleeping beauty, that needs the touch of a prince to waken her. Perhaps you will play something for us, Mr. Bright?" She rose and vacated the music-stool as she spoke.

"I should be ashamed to try my clumsy fingers in your presence, ladies," he replied. "But I'll sing the Star-spangled Banner, if you will have the goodness to accompany me."

She reseated herself, and he lifted up his voice and sang. When he had done, he drew a long breath, wiped the perspiration from his face with a bandana handkerchief, and laughed as he said: "I made the screen of your gas-light shake, ma'am. The fact is, when I sing *that*, I *have* to put all my heart into it."

"And all your voice, too," rejoined Mrs. Blumenthal.

"O, no," answered he, "I could have put on a good deal more steam, if I had n't been afraid of drowning the piano. I'm greatly obliged to you, ladies; and I hope I shall have the pleasure of hearing you again in my own house. I should like to hear some more now, but I've stayed too long. My wife agreed to meet me at a store, and I don't know what she'll say to me."

"Tell her we detained you by playing to you," said Mrs. Blumenthal.

"O, that would be too much like Adam," rejoined he. "I always feel ashamed to look a woman in the face, after reading that story. I always thought Adam was a mean cuss to throw off all the blame on Eve." With a short bow, and a hasty "Good morning, ladies," he went out.

His parting remark amused Flora so much, that she burst into one of her musical peals of laughter; while her more cautious friend raised her handkerchief to her mouth, lest their visitor should hear some sound of mirth, and mistake its import.

"What a great, beaming face!" exclaimed Flora. "It looks like a sunflower. I have a fancy for calling him Monsieur Girasol. What a pity Mr. Green had n't longed for a musical instrument, and been too poor to buy one. It would have done him so much good to have astonished himself by waking up a tune in the Harmolinks."

"Yes," responded Mrs. Delano, "it might have saved him the trouble of going to Arabia Petræa or Damascus, in search of something new. What do you think about accepting Mr. Bright's offer?"

" O, I hope we shall go, Mamita. The children would be delighted with him. If Alfred had been here this morning, he would have exclaimed, ' Is n't he jolly ? ' "

" I think things must go cheerfully where such a sunflower spirit presides," responded Mrs. Delano. " And he is certainly sufficiently *au naturel* to suit you and Florimond."

" Yes, he bubbles over," rejoined Flora. " It is n't the fashion ; but I like folks that bubble over."

Mrs. Delano smiled as she answered : " So do I. And perhaps you can guess who it was that made me in love with bubbling over ? "

Flora gave a knowing smile, and dotted one of her comic little courtesies. " I don't see what makes you and Florimond like me so well," said she. " I 'm sure I 'm neither wise nor witty."

" But something better than either," replied Mamita.

The vivacious little woman said truly that she was neither very wise nor very witty ; but she was a transparent medium of sunshine ; and the commonest glass, filled with sunbeams, becomes prismatic as a diamond.

CHAPTER XXV.

MRS. GREEN'S ball was *the* party of the season. Five hundred invitations were sent out, all of them to people unexceptionable for wealth, or fashion, or some sort of high distinction, political, literary, or artistic. Smith had received *carte blanche* to prepare the most luxurious and elegant supper possible. Mrs. Green was resplendent with diamonds; and the house was so brilliantly illuminated, that the windows of carriages traversing that part of Beacon Street glittered as if touched by the noonday sun. A crowd collected on the Common, listening to the band of music, and watching the windows of the princely mansion, to obtain glimpses through its lace curtains of graceful figures revolving in the dance, like a vision of fairy-land seen through a veil of mist.

In that brilliant assemblage, Mrs. King was the centre of attraction. She was still a Rose Royal, as Gerald Fitzgerald had called her twenty-three years before. A very close observer would have noticed that time had slightly touched her head; but the general effect of the wavy hair was as dark and glossy as ever. She had grown somewhat stouter, but that only rendered her tall figure more majestic. It still seemed as if the fluid Art, whose harmonies were always flowing through her soul, had fashioned her form and was swaying all its motions; and to this natural gracefulness was now added that peculiar stylishness of manner, which can be acquired only by familiar intercourse with elegant society. There was nothing foreign in her accent, but the modulations of her voice were so musical, that English, as she spoke it, seemed all vowels and liquid consonants. She had been heralded as La Señorita, and her dress was appropriately Spanish. It was of cherry-colored satin, profusely trimmed with black lace. A mantilla of very rich transparent black lace was thrown over her head, and fastened on one side with a cluster of red fuchsias, the golden stamens of which were tipped with small diamonds. The lace trimming on the corsage was looped up with a diamond star, and her massive gold bracelets were clasped with diamonds.

Mr. Green received her with great *empressement ;* evidently considering her the " bright particular star" of the evening. She accepted her distinguished position with the quietude of one accustomed to homage. With a slight bow she gave Mr. Green the desired promise to open the ball with him, and then turned to answer another gentleman, who wished to obtain her for the second dance. She would have observed her host a little more curiously, had she been aware that he once proposed to place her darling Floracita at the head of that stylish mansion.

Mrs. King's peculiar style of beauty and rich foreign dress attracted universal attention ; but still greater admiration was excited by her dancing, which was the very soul of music taking form in motion ; and as the tremulous diamond drops of the fuchsias kept time with her graceful movements, they sparkled among the waving folds of her black lace mantilla, like fire-flies in a dark night. She was, of course, the prevailing topic of conversation ; and when Mr. Green was not dancing, he was called upon to repeat, again and again, the account of her wonderful *début* in the opera at Rome. In the midst of one of these recitals, Mrs.

13 *

Fitzgerald and her son entered ; and a group soon gathered round that lady, to listen to the same story from her lips. It was familiar to her son; but he listened to it with quickened interest, while he gazed at the beautiful opera-singer winding about so gracefully in the evolutions of the dance.

Mr. King was in the same set with his lady, and had just touched her hand, as the partners crossed over, when he noticed a sudden flush on her countenance, succeeded by deadly pallor.   Following the direction her eye had taken, he saw a slender, elegant young man, who, with some variation in the fashion of dress, seemed the veritable Gerald Fitzgerald to whom he had been introduced in the flowery parlor so many years ago.   His first feeling was pain, that this vision of her first lover had power to excite such lively emotion in his wife ; but his second thought was, " He recalls her first-born son."

Young Fitzgerald eagerly sought out Mr. Green, and said : " Please introduce me the instant this dance is ended, that I may ask her for the next.   There will be so many trying to engage her, you know."

He was introduced accordingly.   The lady politely acceded to his request, and the quick flush on her face was attributed by all, except Mr. King, to the heat produced by dancing.

When her young partner took her hand to lead her to the next dance, she stole a glance toward her husband, and he saw that her soul was troubled.   The handsome couple were " the observed of all observers "; and the youth was so entirely absorbed with his mature partner, that not a little jealousy was excited in the minds of young ladies. When he led her to a seat, she declined the numerous invi-

tations that crowded upon her, saying she should dance no
more that evening. Young Fitzgerald at once professed a
disinclination to dance, and begged that, when she was sufficiently rested, she would allow him to lead her to the
piano, that he might hear her sing something from Norma, by which she had so delighted his mother, in Rome.

"Your son seems to be entirely devoted to the queen of
the evening," said Mr. Green to his cousin.

"How can you wonder at it?" replied Mrs. Fitzgerald.
"She is such a superb creature!"

"What was her character in Rome?" inquired a lady
who had joined the group.

"Her stay there was very short," answered Mrs. Fitzgerald. "Her manners were said to be unexceptionable.
The gentlemen were quite vexed because she made herself
so inaccessible."

The conversation was interrupted by La Campaneo's
voice, singing, "*Ah, bello a me ritorno.*" The orchestra
hushed at once, and the dancing was suspended, while the
company gathered round the piano, curious to hear the remarkable singer. Mrs. Fitzgerald had long ceased to allude to what was once her favorite topic, — the wonderful
resemblance between La Señorita's voice and a mysterious
voice she had once heard on her husband's plantation. But
she grew somewhat pale as she listened; for the tones recalled that adventure in her bridal home at Magnolia Lawn,
and the fair moonlight vision was followed by dismal spec-
tres of succeeding years. Ah, if all the secret histories
and sad memories assembled in a ball-room should be at
once revealed, what a judgment night it would be!

Mrs. King had politely complied with the request to
sing, because she was aware that her host and the company

would be disappointed if she refused; but it was known only to her own soul how much the effort cost her. She bowed rather languidly to the profuse compliments which followed her performance, and used her fan as if she felt oppressed.

" Fall back ! " said one of the gentlemen, in a low voice. " There is too great a crowd round her."

The hint was immediately obeyed, and a servant was requested to bring iced lemonade. She soon breathed more freely, and tried to rally her spirits to talk with Mr. Green and others concerning European reminiscences. Mrs. Fitzgerald drew near, and signified to her cousin a wish to be introduced; for it would have mortified her vanity, when she afterward retailed the gossip of the ball-room, if she had been obliged to acknowledge that she was not presented to *la belle lionne.*

" If you are not too much fatigued," said she, " I hope you will allow my son to sing a duet with you. He would esteem it such an honor ! I assure you he has a fine voice, and he is thought to sing with great expression, especially '*M' odi ! Ah, m' odi !* ' "

The young gentleman modestly disclaimed the compliment to his musical powers, but eagerly urged his mother's request. As he bent near the *cantatrice,* waiting for her reply, her watchful husband again noticed a quick flush suffusing her face, succeeded by deadly pallor. Gently moving young Fitzgerald aside, he said in a low tone, " Are you not well, my dear ? "

She raised her eyes to his with a look of distress, and replied : " No, I am not well. Please order the carriage."

He took her arm within his, and as they made their way

through the crowd she bowed gracefully to the right and left, in answer to the lamentations occasioned by her departure. Young Fitzgerald followed to the hall door to offer, in the name of Mrs. Green, a beautiful bouquet, enclosed within an arum lily of silver filigree. She bowed her thanks, and, drawing from it a delicate tea-rose, presented it to him. He wore it as a trophy the remainder of the evening; and none of the young ladies who teased him for it succeeded in obtaining it.

When Mr. and Mrs. King were in the carriage, he took her hand tenderly, and said, "My dear, that young man recalled to mind your infant son, who died with poor Tulee."

With a heavy sigh she answered, "Yes, I am thinking of that poor little baby."

He held her hand clasped in his; but deeming it most kind not to intrude into the sanctum of that sad and tender memory, he remained silent. She spoke no other word as they rode toward their hotel. She was seeing a vision of those two babes, lying side by side, on that dreadful night when her tortured soul was for a while filled with bitter hatred for the man she had loved so truly.

Mrs. Fitzgerald and her son were the earliest among the callers the next day. Mrs. King happened to rest her hand lightly on the back of a chair, while she exchanged salutations with them, and her husband noticed that the lace of her hanging sleeve trembled violently.

"You took everybody by storm last evening, Mrs. King, just as you did when you first appeared as Norma," said the loquacious Mrs. Fitzgerald. "As for you, Mr. King, I don't know but you would have received a hundred challenges, if gentlemen had known you were going to carry off the prize. So sly of you, too! For I always heard you were entirely indifferent to ladies."

"Ah, well, the world don't always know what it's talking about," rejoined Mr. King, smiling. Further remarks were interrupted by the entrance of a young girl, whom he took by the hand, and introduced as "My daughter Eulalia."

Nature is very capricious in the varieties she produces by mixing flowers with each other. Sometimes the different tints of each are blended in a new color, compounded of both; sometimes the color of one is delicately shaded into the other; sometimes one color is marked in distinct stripes or rings upon the other; and sometimes the separate hues are mottled and clouded. Nature had indulged in one of her freaks in the production of Eulalia, a maiden of fifteen summers, the only surviving child of Mr. and Mrs. King. She inherited her mother's tall, flexile form, and her long dark eyelashes, eyebrows, and hair; but she had her father's large blue eyes, and his rose-and-white complexion. The combination was peculiar, and very handsome; especially the serene eyes, which looked out from their dark surroundings like clear blue water deeply shaded by shrubbery around its edges. Her manners were a little shy, for her parents had wisely forborne an early introduction to society. But she entered pleasantly enough into some small talk with Fitzgerald about the skating parties of the winter, and a new polka that he thought she would like to practise.

Callers began to arrive rapidly. There was a line of carriages at the door, and still it lengthened. Mrs. King received them all with graceful courtesy, and endeavored to say something pleasing to each; but in the midst of it all, she never lost sight of Gerald and Eulalia. After a short time she beckoned to her daughter with a slight motion of her fan, and spoke a few words to her aside. The young girl left the room, and did not return to it. Fitzgerald, after interchanging some brief remarks with Mr. King about the classes at Cambridge, approached the *cantatrice*, and said in lowered tones: " I tried to call early with the hope of hearing you sing. But I was detained by business for grandfather; and even if you were graciously inclined to gratify my presumptuous wish, you will not be released from company this morning. May I say, *Au revoir ?* "

" Certainly," she replied, looking up at him with an expression in her beautiful eyes that produced a glow of gratified vanity. He bowed good morning, with the smiling conviction that he was a great favorite with the distinguished lady.

When the last caller had retired, Mrs. King, after exchanging some general observations with her husband concerning her impressions of Boston and its people, seated herself at the window, with a number of Harper's Weekly in her hand; but the paper soon dropped on her lap, and she seemed gazing into infinity. The people passing and repassing were invisible to her. She was away in that lonely island home, with two dark-haired babies lying near her, side by side.

Her husband looked at her over his newspaper, now and then; and observing her intense abstraction, he stepped softly across the room, and, laying his hand gently upon her head, said: " Rosa, dear, do memories trouble you so much that you regret having returned to America ? "

Without change of posture, she answered: " It matters

not where we are. We must always carry ourselves with us." Then, as if reproaching herself for so cold a response to his kind inquiry, she looked up at him, and, kissing his hand, said: "Dear Alfred! Good angel of my life! I do not deserve such a heart as yours."

He had never seen such a melancholy expression in her eyes since the day she first encouraged him to hope for her affection. He made no direct allusion to the subject of her thoughts, for the painful history of her early love was a theme they mutually avoided; but he sought, by the most assiduous tenderness, to chase away the gloomy phantoms that were taking possession of her soul. In answer to his urgent entreaty that she would express to him unreservedly any wish she might form, she said, as if thinking aloud: "Of course they buried poor Tulee among the negroes; but perhaps they buried the baby with Mr. and Mrs. Duroy, and inscribed something about him on the gravestone."

"It is hardly probable," he replied; "but if it would give you satisfaction to search, we will go to New Orleans."

"Thank you," rejoined she; "and I should like it very much if you could leave orders to engage lodgings for the summer somewhere distant from Boston, that we might go and take possession as soon as we return."

He promised compliance with her wishes; but the thought flitted through his mind, "Can it be possible the young man fascinates her, that she wants to fly from him?"

"I am going to Eulalia now," said she, with one of her sweet smiles. "It will be pleasanter for the dear child when we get out of this whirl of society, which so much disturbs our domestic companionship."

As she kissed her hand to him at the door, he thought to

himself, "Whatever this inward struggle may be, she will remain true to her pure and noble character."

Mrs. Fitzgerald, meanwhile, quite unconscious that the flowery surface she had witnessed covered such agitated depths, hastened to keep her promise of describing the party to Mrs. Delano and her daughter.

"I assure you," said she, "La Señorita looked quite as handsome in the ball-room as she did on the stage. She is stouter than she was then, but not so 'fat and forty' as I am. Large proportions suit her stately figure. As for her dress, I wish you could have seen it. It was splendid, and wonderfully becoming to her rich complexion. It was completely Spanish, from the mantilla on her head to the black satin slippers with red bows and brilliants. She was all cherry-colored satin, black lace, and diamonds."

"How I should like to have seen her!" exclaimed Mrs. Blumenthal, whose fancy was at once taken by the bright color and strong contrast of the costume.

But Mrs. Delano remarked: "I should think her style of dress rather too *prononcé* and theatrical; too suggestive of Fanny Elsler and the Bolero."

"Doubtless it would be so for you or I," rejoined Mrs. Fitzgerald. "Mother used to say you had a poet lover, who called you the twilight cloud, violet dissolving into lilac. And when I was a young lady, some of my admirers compared me to the new moon, which must, of course, appear in azure and silver. But I assure you Mrs. King's conspicuous dress was extremely becoming to her style of face and figure. I wish I had counted how many gentlemen quoted, 'She walks in beauty like the night.' It became really ridiculous at last. Gerald and I called upon her this morning, and we found her handsome in the parlor by daylight, which is a trying test to the forties, you know. We were introduced to their only daughter, Eulalia, — a very peculiar-looking young miss, with sky-blue eyes and black eyelashes, like some of the Circassian beauties I have read off. Gerald thinks her almost as handsome as her mother. What a fortune that girl will be! But I have promised ever so many people to tell them about the party; so I must bid you good by."

When the door closed after her, Flora remarked, "I never heard of anybody but my Mamita who was named Eulalia."

"Eulalia was a Spanish saint," responded Mrs. Delano; "and her name is so very musical that it would naturally please the ear of La Señorita."

"My curiosity is considerably excited to see this stylish lady," said Flora.

"We will wait a little, till the first rush of visitors has somewhat subsided, and then we will call," rejoined Mrs. Delano.

They called three days after, and were informed that Mr. and Mrs. King had gone to New Orleans.

CHAPTER XXVI.

STRANGE contrasts occur in human society, even where there is such a strong tendency toward equality as there is in New England. A few hours before Queen Fashion held her splendid court in Beacon Street, a vessel from New Orleans called "The King Cotton" approached Long Wharf in Boston. Before she touched the pier, a young man jumped on board from another vessel close by. He went directly up to the captain, and said, in a low, hurried tone: "Let nobody land. You have slaves on board. Mr. Bell is in a carriage on the wharf waiting to speak to you."

Having delivered this message, he disappeared in the same direction that he came.

This brief interview was uneasily watched by one of the passengers, a young man apparently nineteen or twenty years old. He whispered to a yellow lad, who was his servant, and both attempted to land by crossing the adjoining vessel. But the captain intercepted them, saying, "All must remain on board till we draw up to the wharf."

With desperate leaps, they sprang past him. He tried to seize them, calling aloud, "Stop thief! Stop thief!" Some of his sailors rushed after them. As they ran up State Street, lads and boys, always ready to hunt anything, joined in the pursuit. A young black man, who was passing down the street as the crowd rushed up, saw the yellow lad race by him, panting for breath, and heard him cry, "Help me!"

The crowd soon turned backward, having caught the fugitives. The black man hurried after, and as they were putting them on board the vessel he pushed his way close to the yellow lad, and again heard him say, " Help me! I am a slave."

The black man paused only to look at the name of the vessel, and then hastened with all speed to the house of Mr. Willard Percival. Almost out of breath with his hurry, he said to that gentleman: " A vessel from New Orleans, named ' The King Cotton,' has come up to Long Wharf. They 've got two slaves aboard. They was chasing 'em up State Street, calling out, ' Stop thief!' and I heard a mulatto lad cry, ' Help me!' I run after 'em; and just as they was going to put the mulatto lad aboard the vessel, I pushed my way close up to him, and he said, ' Help me! I 'm a slave.' So I run fast as I could to tell you."

" Wait a moment till I write a note to Francis Jackson, which you must carry as quick as you can," said Mr. Percival. " I will go to Mr. Sewall for a writ of *habeas corpus.*"

While this was going on, the captain had locked the fugitives in the hold of his vessel, and hastened to the carriage, which had been waiting for him at a short distance from the wharf.

" Good evening, Mr. Bell," said he, raising his hat as he approached the carriage door.

" Good evening, Captain Kane," replied the gentleman inside. " You 've kept me waiting so long, I was nearly out of patience."

" I sent you word they 'd escaped, sir," rejoined the captain. " They gave us a run; but we 've got 'em fast

enough in the hold. One of 'em seems to be a white man.
Perhaps he 's an Abolitionist, that 's been helping the nigger off. It 's good enough for him to be sent back to the
South. If they get hold of him there, he 'll never have a
chance to meddle with gentlemen's property again."

"They 're both slaves," replied Mr. Bell. "The tele-
gram I received informed me that one would pass himself for a white man. But, captain, you must take 'em
directly to Castle Island. One of the officers there will
lock 'em up, if you tell them I sent you. And you can't
be off too quick; for as likely as not the Abolitionists will
get wind of it, and be raising a row before morning.
There 's no safety for property now-a-days."

Having given these orders, the wealthy merchant bade
the captain good evening, and his carriage rolled away.

The unhappy fugitives were immediately taken from the
hold of the vessel, pinioned fast, and hustled on board a
boat, which urged its swift way through the waters to
Castle Island, where they were safely locked up till further
orders.

"O George, they 'll send us back," said the younger
one. "I wish we war dead."

George answered, with a deep groan: "O how I have
watched the North Star! thinking always it pointed to a
land of freedom. O my God, is there *no* place of refuge
for the slave?"

"*You* are so white, you could have got off, if you had n't
brought *me* with you," sobbed the other.

"And what good would freedom do me without you,
Henny?" responded the young man, drawing his companion closer to his breast. "Cheer up, honey! I 'll try
again; and perhaps we 'll make out better next time."

He tried to talk hopefully; but when yellow Henny, in her boy's dress, cried herself to sleep on his shoulder, his tears dropped slowly on her head, while he sat there gazing at the glittering stars, with a feeling of utter discouragement and desolation.

That same evening, the merchant who was sending them back to bondage, without the slightest inquiry into their case, was smoking his amber-lipped meerschaum, in an embroidered dressing-gown, on a luxurious lounge; his daughter, Mrs. Fitzgerald, in azure satin and pearls, was meandering through the mazes of the dance; and his exquisitely dressed grandson, Gerald, was paying nearly equal homage to Mrs. King's lambent eyes and the sparkle of her diamonds.

When young Fitzgerald descended to a late breakfast, the morning after the great party, his grandfather was lolling back in his arm-chair, his feet ensconced in embroidered slippers, and resting on the register, while he read the Boston Courier.

"Good morning, Gerald," said he, "if it be not past that time of day. If you are sufficiently rested from last night's dissipation, I should like to have you attend to a little business for me."

"I hope it won't take very long, grandfather," replied Gerald; "for I want to call on Mrs. King early, before her rooms are thronged with visitors."

"That opera-singer seems to have turned your head, though she is old enough to be your mother," rejoined Mr. Bell.

"I don't know that my head was any more turned than others," answered the young man, in a slightly offended tone. "If you call to see her, sir, as mother says you intend to do, perhaps she will make *you* feel as if you had a young head on your shoulders."

"Likely as not, likely as not," responded the old gentleman, smiling complacently at the idea of re-enacting the beau. "But I wish you to do an errand for me this morning, which I had rather not put in writing, for fear of accidents, and which I cannot trust verbally to a servant. I got somewhat chilled waiting in a carriage near the wharf, last evening, and I feel some rheumatic twinges in consequence. Under these circumstances, I trust you will excuse me if I ask the use of your young limbs to save my own."

"Certainly, sir," replied Gerald, with thinly disguised impatience. "What is it you want me to do?"

"Two slaves belonging to Mr. Bruteman of New Orleans, formerly a friend of your father, have escaped in my ship, 'The King Cotton.' The oldest, it seems, is a head carpenter, and would bring a high price. Bruteman values them at twenty-five hundred dollars. He is my debtor to a considerable amount, and those negroes are mortgaged to me. But independently of that circumstance, it would be very poor policy, dealing with the South as I do, to allow **negroes to** be brought away in my vessels with impunity. Besides, there is a heavy penalty in all the Southern States, if the thing is proved. You see, Gerald, it is every way for my interest to make sure of returning those negroes; and your interest is somewhat connected with mine, seeing that the small pittance saved from the wreck of your father's property is quite insufficient to supply your rather expensive wants."

"I think I have been reminded of that often enough, sir, to be in no danger of forgetting it," retorted the youth, reddening **as he spoke.**

"Then you will perhaps think it no great hardship to transact a little business for me now and then," coolly rejoined the grandfather. "I shall send orders to have these negroes sold as soon as they arrive, and the money transmitted to me; for when they once begin to run away, the disease is apt to become chronic."

"Have you seen them, sir," inquired Gerald.

"No," replied the merchant. "That would have been unpleasant, without being of any use. When a disagreeable duty is to be done, the quicker it is done the better. Captain Kane took 'em down to Castle Island last night; but it won't do for them to stay there. The Abolitionists will ferret 'em out, and be down there with their devilish *habeas corpus.* I want you to go on board 'The King Cotton,' take the captain aside, and tell him, from me, to remove them forthwith from Castle Island, keep them under strong guard, and skulk round with them in the best hiding-places he can find, until a ship passes that will take them to New Orleans. Of course, I need not caution you to be silent about this affair, especially concerning the slaves being mortgaged to me. If that is whispered abroad, it will soon get into the Abolition papers that I am a man-stealer, as those rascals call the slaveholders."

The young man obeyed his instructions to the letter; and having had some difficulty in finding Captain Kane, he was unable to dress for quite so early a call at the Revere House as he had intended. "How much trouble these niggers give us!" thought he, as he adjusted his embroidered cravat, and took his fresh kid gloves from the box.

*   *   *   *   *

When Mr. Blumenthal went home to dine that day, the ladies of the household noticed that he was unusually serious. As he sat after dinner, absently playing a silent tune on the table-cloth, his wife touched his hand with her napkin, and said, "*What* was it so long ago, Florimond?"

He turned and smiled upon her, as he answered: "So my fingers were moving to the tune of 'Long, long ago,' were they? I was not conscious of it, but my thoughts were with the long ago. Yesterday afternoon, as I was passing across State Street, I heard a cry of 'Stop thief!' and I saw them seize a young man, who looked like an Italian. I gave no further thought to the matter, and pursued the business I had in hand. But to-day I have learned that he was a slave, who escaped in 'The King Cotton' from New Orleans. I seem to see the poor fellow's terrified look now; and it brings vividly to mind something dreadful that came very near happening, long ago, to a person whose complexion is similar to his. I was thinking how willingly I would then have given the services of my whole life for a portion of the money which our best friend here has enabled me to acquire."

"What *was* the dreadful thing that was going to happen, papa?" inquired Rosa.

"That is a secret between mamma and I," he replied. "It is something not exactly suitable to talk with little girls about, Rosy Posy." He took her hand, as it lay on the table, and pressed it affectionately, by way of apology for refusing his confidence.

Then, looking at Mrs. Delano, he said: "If I had only known the poor fellow was a slave, I might, perhaps, have done something to rescue him. But the Abolitionists are doing what can be done. They procured a writ of *habeas corpus*, and went on board 'The King Cotton'; but they could neither find the slaves nor obtain any informa-

14

tion from the captain. They are keeping watch on all vessels bound South, in which Mr. Goldwin and I are assisting them. There are at least twenty spies out on the wharves."

"I heartily wish you as much success as I have had in that kind of business," replied Mrs. Delano with a smile.

"O, I do hope they 'll be rescued," exclaimed Flora. "How shameful it is to have such laws, while we keep singing, in the face of the world, about 'the land of the free, and the home of the brave.' I don't mean to sing that again; for it 's false."

"There 'll come an end to this some time or other, as surely as God reigns in the heavens," rejoined Blumenthal.

*　　*　　*　　*　　*

Two days passed, and the unremitting efforts of Mr. Percival and Mr. Jackson proved unavailing to obtain any clew to the fugitives. After an anxious consultation with Samuel E. Sewall, the wisest and kindest legal adviser in such cases, they reluctantly came to the conclusion that nothing more could be done without further information. As a last resort, Mr. Percival suggested a personal appeal to Mr. Bell.

"Rather a forlorn hope that," replied Francis Jackson. "He has named his ship for the king that rules over us all, trampling on freedom of petition, freedom of debate, and even on freedom of locomotion."

"We will try," said Mr. Percival. "It is barely possible we may obtain some light on the subject."

Early in the evening they accordingly waited upon the merchant at his residence. When the servant informed him that two gentlemen wished to see him on business,

he laid aside his meerschaum and the Courier, and said,
" Show them in."

Captain Kane had informed him that the Abolitionists
were " trying to get up a row "; but he had not anticipated
that they would call upon him, and it was an unpleasant
surprise when he saw who his visitors were. He bowed
stiffly, and waited in silence for them to explain their business.

" We have called," said Mr. Percival, " to make some
inquiries concerning two fugitives from slavery, who, it is
said, were found on board your ship, ' The King Cotton.' "

" I know nothing about it," replied Mr. Bell. " My
captains understand the laws of the ports they sail from ;
and it is their business to see that those laws are respected."

" But," urged Mr. Percival, " that a man is *claimed* as a
slave by no means proves that he *is* a slave. The law
presumes that every man has a right to personal liberty,
until it is proved otherwise ; and in order to secure a fair
trial of the question, the writ of *habeas corpus* has been
provided."

" It 's a great disgrace to Massachusetts, sir, that she
puts so many obstacles in the way of enforcing the laws of
the United States," replied Mr. Bell.

" If your grandson should be claimed as a slave, I rather
think you would consider the writ of *habeas corpus* a wise
and just provision," said the plain-speaking Francis Jackson. " It is said that this young stranger, whom they
chased as 'a thief, and carried off as a slave, had a complexion no darker than his."

" I take it for granted," added Mr. Percival, " that you
do not wish for a state of things that would make every

man and woman in Massachusetts liable to be carried off as slaves, without a chance to prove their right to freedom."

Mr. Bell answered, in tones of suppressed anger, his face all ablaze with excitement, "If I could choose *who* should be thus carried off, I would do the Commonwealth a service by ridding her of a swarm of malignant fanatics." ;

"If you were to try that game," quietly rejoined Francis Jackson, "I apprehend you would find some of the fire of '76 still alive under the ashes."

"A man is strongly tempted to argue," said Mr. Percival, "when he knows that all the laws of truth and justice and freedom are on his side; but we did not come here to discuss the subject of slavery, Mr. Bell. We came to appeal to your own good sense, whether it is right or safe that men should be forcibly carried from the city of Boston without any process of law."

"I stand by the Constitution," answered Mr. Bell, doggedly. "I don't presume to be wiser than the framers of that venerable document."

"That is evading the question," responded Mr. Percival. "There is no question before us concerning the framers of the Constitution. The simple proposition is, whether it is right or safe for men to be forcibly carried from Boston without process of law. Two strangers *have* been thus abducted; and you say it is your captain's business. You know perfectly well that a single line from you would induce your captain to give those men a chance for a fair trial. Is it not your duty so to instruct him?"

A little thrown off his guard, Mr. Bell exclaimed: "And give an Abolition mob a chance to rescue them? I shall do no such thing."

"It is not the Abolitionists who get up mobs," rejoined

Francis Jackson. "Garrison was dragged through the streets for writing against slavery; but when Yancey of Alabama had the use of Faneuil Hall, for the purpose of defending slavery, no Abolitionist attempted to disturb his speaking."

A slight smile hovered about Mr. Percival's lips; for it was well known that State Street and Ann Street clasped hands when mobs were wanted, and that money changed palms on such occasions; and the common rumor was that Mr. Bell's purse had been freely used.

The merchant probably considered it an offensive insinuation, for his face, usually rubicund from the effects of champagne and oysters, became redder, and his lips were tightly compressed; but he merely reiterated, "I stand by the Constitution, sir."

"Mr. Bell, I must again urge it upon your conscience," said Mr. Percival, "that you are more responsible than the captain in this matter. Your captains, of course, act under your orders, and would do nothing contrary to your expressed wishes. Captain Kane has, doubtless, consulted you in this business."

"That's none of your concern, sir," retorted the irascible merchant. "My captains know that I think Southern gentlemen ought to be protected in their property; and that is sufficient. I stand by the Constitution, sir. I honor the reverend gentleman who said he was ready to send his mother or his brother into slavery, if the laws required it. That's the proper spirit, sir. You fanatics, with your useless abstractions about human rights, are injuring trade, and endangering the peace of the country. You are doing all you can to incite the slaves to insurrection. I don't pretend to be wiser than the framers of the Constitution, sir.

I don't pretend to be wiser than Daniel Webster, sir, who said in Congress that he 'would support, to the fullest extent, any law Southern gentlemen chose to frame for the recovery of fugitive slaves.'"

"I wish you a better conscience-keeper," rejoined Francis Jackson, rising as he spoke. "I don't see, my friend, that there's any use in staying here to talk any longer. There's none so deaf as those that *won't* hear."

Mr. Percival rose at this suggestion, and "Good evening" was exchanged, with formal bows on both sides. But sturdy Francis Jackson made no bow, and uttered no "Good evening." When they were in the street, and the subject was alluded to by his companion, he simply replied: "I've pretty much done with saying or doing what I don't mean. It's a pity that dark-complexioned grandson of his could n't be carried off as a slave. That might, perhaps, bring him to a realizing sense of the state of things."

CHAPTER XXVII.

A FEW days past the middle of the following May, a carriage stopped before the house of Mr. Joseph Bright, in Northampton, and Mrs. Delano, with all the Blumenthal family, descended from it. Mr. Bright received them at the gate, his face smiling all over. "You're welcome, ladies," said he. "Walk in! walk in! Betsey, this is Mrs. Delano. This is Mrs. Bright, ladies. Things ain't so stylish here as at your house; but I hope you'll find 'em comfortable."

Mrs. Bright, a sensible-looking woman, with great moderation of manner, showed them into a plainly furnished, but very neat parlor.

"O, how pleasant this is!" exclaimed Mrs. Blumenthal, as she looked out of one of the side-windows.

The children ran up to her repeating: "How pleasant! What a nice hedge, mamma! And see that wall all covered with pretty flowers!"

"Those are moss-pinks," said Mrs. Bright. "I think they are very ornamental to a wall."

"Did you plant them?" inquired Rosa.

"O, no," said Mr. Bright, who was bringing in various baskets and shawls. "That's not our garden; but we have just as much pleasure looking at it as if it was. A great Southern nabob lives there. He made a heap o' money selling women and children, and he's come North to spend it. He's a very pious man, and deacon of the church." The children began to laugh; for Mr. Bright drawled out his words in solemn tones, and made his broad face look very comical by trying to lengthen it. "His name is Still-ham," added he, "but I call him Deacon Steal'em."

As he passed out, Rosa whispered to her mother, "What does he mean about a deacon's selling women and children?"

Before an answer could be given, Mr. Bright reappeared with a bird-cage. "I guess this is a pretty old parrot," said he.

"Yes, she is quite old," replied Mrs. Delano. "But we are all attached to her; and our house being shut up for the summer, we were unwilling to trust her with strangers."

The parrot, conscious of being talked about, turned up her head sideways, and winked her eye, without stirring from the corner of the cage, where she was rolled up like a ball of feathers. Then she croaked out an English phrase, which she had learned of the children, "Polly wants a cacker."

"She shall have a cracker," said good-natured Mr. Bright; and Rosa and little Lila were soon furnished with a cracker and a lump of sugar for Poll.

In a short time they were summoned to tea; and after enjoying Mrs. Bright's light bread and sweet butter, they saw no more of their host and hostess for the evening. In the morning the whole family were up before the hour appointed for breakfast, and were out in the garden, taking a look at the environments of their new abode. As Mrs. Blumenthal was walking among the bushes, Mr. Bright's beaming face suddenly uprose before her, from where he was stooping to pluck up some weeds.

"Good morning, ma'am," said he. "Do hear that old thief trying to come Paddy over the Lord!"

As he spoke, he pointed his thumb backward toward

Deacon Stillham's house, whence proceeded a very loud
and monotonous voice of prayer.

Mrs. Blumenthal smiled as she inquired, "What did
you mean by saying he sold women and children?"

"Made his money by slave-trading down in Carolina,
ma'am. I reckon a man has to pray a deal to get himself
out of that scrape; needs to pray pretty loud too, or the
voice of women screaming for their babies would get to
the throne afore him. He don't like us over and above
well, 'cause we're Abolitionists. But there's Betsey calling me; I must n't stop here talking."

Mrs. Blumenthal amused her companions by a repetition
of his remarks concerning the Deacon. She was much entertained by their host's original style of bubbling over, as
she termed it. After breakfast she said: "There he is in
the garden. Let's go and talk with him, Florimond."

And taking her parasol, she went out, leaning on her
husband's arm.

"So you are an Abolitionist?" said Mr. Blumenthal, as
they stopped near their host.

Mr. Bright tossed his hat on a bush, and, leaning on his
hoe, sang in a stentorian voice: "I am an Abolitionist; I
glory in the name. — There," said he, laughing, "I let out
all my voice, that the Deacon might hear. He can pray
the loudest; but I reckon I can sing the loudest. I'll tell
you what first made me begin to think about slavery. You
see I was never easy without I could be doing something
in the musical way, so I undertook to teach singing. One
winter, I thought I should like to run away from Jack
Frost, and I looked in the Southern papers to see if any
of 'em advertised for a singing-master. The first thing
my eye lighted on was this advertisement: —

14 *   U

" ' Run away from the subscriber a stout mulatto slave, named Joe; has light sandy hair, blue eyes, and ruddy complexion; is intelligent, and will pass himself for a white man. I will give one hundred dollars' reward to whoever will seize him and put him in jail.'

" ' By George!' said I, 'that's a description of *me*. I did n't know before that I was a mulatto. It 'll never do for me to go *there*.' So I went to Vermont to teach. I told 'em I was a runaway slave, and showed 'em the advertisement that described me. Some of 'em believed me till I told 'em it was a joke. Well, it is just as bad for those poor black fellows as it would have been for me; but that blue-eyed Joe seemed to bring the matter home to me. It set me to thinking about slavery, and I have kept thinking ever since."

" Not exactly such a silent thinking as the apothecary's famous owl, I judge," said Mrs. Blumenthal.

" No," replied he, laughing. " I never had the **Quaker** gift of gathering into the stillness, that 's a fact. But I reckon even that 'pothecary's owl would n't be silent if he could hear and understand all that Betsey has told me about the goings-on down South. Before I married her, she went there to teach; but she 's a woman o' feeling, and she could n't stand it long. But, dear me, if I believed Deacon Steal'em's talk, I should think it was just about the pleasantest thing in the world to be sold; and that the niggers down South had nothing 'pon earth to do but to lick treacle and swing on a gate. Then he proves it to be a Divine institution from Scripture, chapter and verse. You may have noticed, perhaps, that such chaps are always mighty well posted up about the original designs of Providence; especially as to who 's foreordained to be kept down. He says God cussed Ham, and the niggers are the descendants of Ham. I told him if there was an estate of Ham's left unsettled, I reckoned 't would puzzle the 'cutest lawyer to hunt up the rightful heirs."

" I think so," rejoined Mr. Blumenthal, smiling; " especially when they've become so mixed up that they advertise runaway negroes with sandy hair, blue eyes, and ruddy complexion."

" When the Deacon feels the ground a little shaky under him," resumed Mr. Bright, he leans on his minister down in Carolina, who, he says, is a Northern man, and so pious that folks come from far and near to get him to pray for rain in a dry time; thinking the prayers of such a godly man will be sure to bring down the showers. He says that man preached a sermon that proved niggers were born to be servants of servants unto their brethren. I told him I did n't doubt that part of the prophecy was fulfilled about their serving their *brethren ;* and I showed him the advertisement about sandy hair and blue eyes. But as for being servants of *servants,* I never heard of slaveholders serving anybody except — a chap whose name it ain't polite to mention before ladies. As for that preacher, he put me in mind of a minister my father used to tell of. He 'd been to a wedding, and when he come home he could n't light his lamp. After trying a long spell he found out that the extinguisher was on it. I told the deacon that ministers down South had put an extinguisher on their lamp, and could n't be expected to raise much of a light from it to guide anybody's steps."

" Some of the Northern ministers are not much better guides, I think," rejoined Mr. Blumenthal.

" Just so," replied his host; " 'cause they 've got the same extinguisher on ; and ain't it curious to see 'em puff-

ing and blowing at the old lamp ? I get 'most tired of
talking common sense and common feeling to the Deacon.
You can't get it into him, and it won't stay on him. You
might as well try to heap a peck o' flax-seed. He keeps
eating his own words, too ; though they don't seem to agree
with him, neither. He maintains that the slaves are perfectly contented and happy ; and the next minute, if you
quote any of their cruel laws, he tells you they are obliged
to make such laws or else they would rise and cut their
masters' throats. He says blacks and whites won't mix
any more than oil and water; and the next minute he
says if the slaves are freed they 'll marry our daughters.
I tell him his arguments are like the Kilkenny cats, that
ate one another up to the tip o' their tails. The Deacon is sensible enough, too, about many other subjects ;
but he nor no other man can saw straight with a crooked
saw."

"It 's an old saying," rejoined Blumenthal, " that, when
men enter into a league with Satan, he always deserts
them at the tightest pinch ; and I 've often observed he 's
sure to do it where arguments pinch."

"I don't wonder you are far from being a favorite with
the Deacon," remarked Flora ; " for, according to your own
account, you hit him rather hard."

"I suppose I do," rejoined Mr. Bright. "I 'm always in
earnest myself; and when I 'm sure I 'm in the right, I
always drive ahead. I soon get out o' patience trying to
twist a string that ain't fastened at nary eend, as an old
neighbor of my father used to say. I suppose some of us
Abolitionists *are* a little rough at times ; but I reckon the
coarsest of us do more good than the false prophets that
prophesy smooth things."

"You said Mrs. Bright had been a teacher in the South. What part of the South was it?" inquired Mrs. Blumenthal.

"She went to Savannah to be nursery governess to Mrs. Fitzgerald's little girl," replied he. "But part of the time she was on an island where Mr. Fitzgerald had a cotton plantation. I dare say you've heard of him, for he married the daughter of that rich Mr. Bell who lives in your street. He died some years ago; at least they suppose he died, but nobody knows what became of him."

Flora pressed her husband's arm, and was about to inquire concerning the mystery, when Mrs. Delano came, hand in hand with Rosa and Lila, to say that she had ordered the carriage and wanted them to be in readiness to take a drive.

They returned to a late dinner; and when they rose from a long chat over the dessert, Mr. Bright was not to be found, and his wife was busy; so further inquiries concerning Mr. Fitzgerald's fate were postponed. Mr. Blumenthal proposed a walk on Round Hill; but the children preferred staying at home. Rosa had a new tune she wanted to practise with her guitar; and her little sister had the promise of a story from Mamita Lila. So Mr. Blumenthal and his wife went forth on their ramble alone. The scene from Round Hill was beautiful with the tender foliage of early spring. Slowly they sauntered round from point to point, pausing now and then to look at the handsome villages before them, at the blooming peach-trees, the glistening river, and the venerable mountains, with feathery crowns of violet cloud.

Suddenly a sound of music floated on the air; and they stood spell-bound, with heads bowed, as if their souls were hushed in prayer. When it ceased, Mr. Blumenthal drew a long breath, and said, "Ah! that was our Mendelssohn."

"How exquisitely it was played," observed his wife, "and how in harmony it was with these groves! It sounded like a hymn in the forest."

They lingered, hoping again to hear the invisible musician. As they leaned against the trees, the silver orb of the moon ascended from the horizon, and rested on the brow of Mount Holyoke; and from the same quarter whence Mendelssohn's "Song without Words" had proceeded, the tones of "Casta Diva" rose upon the air. Flora seized her husband's arm with a quick, convulsive grasp, and trembled all over. Wondering at the intensity of her emotion, he passed his arm tenderly round her waist and drew her closely to him. Thus, leaning upon his heart, she listened with her whole being, from the inmost recesses of her soul, throughout all her nerves, to her very fingers' ends. When the sounds died away, she sobbed out: "O, how like Rosa's voice! It seemed as if she had risen from the dead."

He spoke soothingly, and in a few minutes they descended the hill and silently wended their way homeward. The voice that had seemed to come from another world invested the evening landscape with mystical solemnity. The expression of the moon seemed transfigured, like a great clairvoyant eye, reflecting light from invisible spheres, and looking out upon the external world with dreamy abstraction.

When they arrived at their lodgings, Flora exclaimed "O Mamita Lila, we have heard such heavenly music, and a voice so wonderfully like Rosa's! I don't believe I shall sleep a wink to-night."

"Do you mean the Aunt Rosa I was named for?" inquired her daughter.

"Yes, Rosen Blumen," replied her mother; "and I wish you had gone with us, that you might have an idea what a wonderful voice she had."

This led to talk about old times, and to the singing of various airs associated with those times. When they retired to rest, Flora fell asleep with those tunes marching and dancing through her brain; and, for the first time during many years, she dreamed of playing them to her father, while Rosabella sang.

The next morning, when the children had gone out to ramble in the woods with their father, her memory being full of those old times, she began to say over to the parrot some of the phrases that formerly amused her father and Rosabella. The old bird was never talkative now; but when urged by Flora, she croaked out some of her familiar phrases.

"I'm glad we brought *pauvre Manon* with us," said Mrs. Blumenthal. "I think she seems livelier since she came here. Sometimes I fancy she looks like good Madame Guirlande. Those feathers on her head make me think of the bows on Madame's cap. Come, *jolie Manon*, I'll carry you out doors, where the sun will shine upon you. You like sunshine, don't you, Manon?"

She took the cage, and was busy fastening it on the bough of a tree, when a voice from the street said, "*Bon jour, jolie Manon!*"

The parrot suddenly flapped her wings, gave a loud laugh, and burst into a perfect tornado of French and Spanish phrases: "*Bon jour! Buenos dias! Querida mia! Joli diable! Petit blanc! Ha! ha!*"

Surprised at this explosion, Mrs. Blumenthal looked round to discover the cause, and exclaiming, "*Oh ciel!*" she turned deadly pale, and rushed into the house.

"What *is* the matter, my child? inquired Mrs. Delano, anxiously.

"O Mamita, I've seen Rosa's ghost," she replied, sinking into a chair.

Mrs. Delano poured some cologne on a handkerchief, and bathed her forehead, while she said, "You were excited last night by the tune you used to hear your sister sing; and it makes you nervous, dear."

While she was speaking, Mrs. Bright entered the room, saying, "Have you a bottle of sal volatile you can lend me? A lady has come in, who says she is a little faint."

"I will bring it from my chamber," replied Mrs. Delano. She left the room, and was gone some time. When she returned, she found Mrs. Blumenthal leaning her head on the table, with her face buried in her hands. "My child, I want you to come into the other room," said Mrs. Delano. "The lady who was faint is the famous Mrs. King, from Boston. She is boarding on Round Hill, and I suppose it was her voice you heard singing. She said she had seen a lady come into this house who looked so much like a deceased relative that it made her feel faint. Now don't be excited, darling; but this lady certainly resembles the sketch you made of your sister; and it is barely possible —"

Before she could finish the sentence, Flora started up, and flew into the adjoining room. A short, quick cry, "O Floracita!" "O Rosabella!" and they were locked in each other's arms.

After hugging and kissing, and weeping and laughing by

turns, Mrs. King said : "That **must** have been Madame's parrot. The sight of her made me think of old times, and I said, '*Bon jour, jolie Manon!*' Your back was toward me, and I should have passed on, if **my** attention had not been arrested by her wild outpouring of French and Spanish. I suppose she knew my voice."

"Bless the dear old bird!" exclaimed Flora. "It was she who brought us together again at last. She shall come in to see you."

They went out to bring in their old pet. But *jolie Manon* was lying on the floor of her cage, with eyes closed and wings outstretched. The joyful surprise had been too much for her feeble old nerves. **She was dead.**

CHAPTER XXVIII.

SO you *are* alive!" exclaimed Rosa, holding her sister back a little, and gazing upon her face with all her soul in her eyes.

"Yes, very *much* alive," answered Flora, with a smile that brought out all her dimples.

"But do tell me," said Rosa, "how you came to go away so strangely, and leave me to mourn for you as if you were dead."

The dimples disappeared, and a shadow clouded Flora's expressive eyes, as she replied: "It would take a long while to explain all that, *sistita mia*. We will talk it over another time, please."

Rosa sighed as she pressed her sister's hand, and said: "Perhaps I have already conjectured rightly about it, Floracita. My eyes were opened by bitter experiences after we were parted. Some time I will explain to you how I came to run to Europe in such a hurry, with Madame and the Signor."

"But tell me, the first thing of all, whether Tulee is dead," rejoined Flora.

"You know Madame was always exceedingly careful about expense," responded Rosa. "Mrs. Duroy was willing to board Tulee for her work, and Madame thought it was most prudent to leave her there till we got established in Europe, and could send for her; and just when we were expecting her to rejoin us, letters came informing us that Mr. and Mrs. Duroy and Tulee all died of yellow-fever.

It distresses me beyond measure to think of our having left poor, faithful Tulee."

"When we found out that Mr. Fitzgerald had married another wife," replied Flora, "my new Mamita kindly volunteered to go with me in search of you and Tulee. We went to the cottage, and to the plantation, and to New Orleans. Everybody I ever knew seemed to be dead or gone away. But Madame's parrot was alive, and her chattering led me into a stranger's house, where I heard that you were lost at sea on your way to Europe; and that Tulee, with a white baby she had charge of, had died of yellow-fever. Was that baby yours, dear?"

Rosa lowered her eyes, and colored deeply, as she answered: "That subject is very painful to me. I can never forgive myself for having left Tulee and that poor little baby."

Flora pressed her sister's hand in silence for a moment, and then said: "You told me Madame and the Signor were alive and well. Where are they?"

"They lived with us in Provence," replied Rosa. "But when we concluded to return to America, the Signor expressed a wish to end his days in his native country. So Mr. King purchased an estate for them near Florence, and settled an annuity upon them. I had a letter from Madame a few days ago, and she writes that they are as happy as rabbits in clover. The Signor is getting quite old; and if she survives him, it is agreed that she will come and end her days with us. How it will delight her heart to hear that you are alive! What a strange fortune we have had! It seems that Mr. King always loved me, from the first evening that he spent at our house. Do you remember how you laughed because he offered to help us if ever we were in trouble? He knew more about us then than we knew about ourselves; and he afterward did help me out of very great troubles. I will tell you all about it some time. But first I want to know about you. Who is this new Mamita that you speak of?"

" O, it was wonderful how she came to me when I had the greatest need of a friend," answered Flora. "You must know that she and Papasito were in love with each other when they were young; and she is in love with his memory now. I sometimes think his spirit led her to me. I will show you a picture I have made of Papasito and Mamita as guardian angels, placing a crown of violets and lilies of the valley on the head of my new Mamita. When I had to run away, she brought me to live with her in Boston; and there I met with an old acquaintance. Do you remember Florimond Blumenthal?"

"The good German boy that Papasito took such an interest in?" inquired Rosa. "To be sure I remember him."

" Well, he's a good German boy now," rejoined Flora; "and I'm Mrs. Blumenthal."

"Is it possible?" exclaimed Rosa. "You look so exactly as you did when you were such a merry little elf, that I never thought to inquire whether you were married. In the joy of this sudden meeting, I forgot how many years had passed since we saw each other."

" You will realize how long it has been when you see my children," rejoined Flora. "My oldest, Alfred Royal, is fitting for college. He is the image of *cher Papa*; and you will see how Mamita Lila doats upon him. She must have loved Papasito very much. Then I had a daughter that died in a few days; then I had my Rosen Blumen, and you will see who she looks like; then some more came and went to the angels. Last of all came little Lila, who looks just like her father, — flaxen hair, pink cheeks, and great German forget-me-nots for eyes."

"How I shall love them all!" exclaimed Rosa. "And you will love our Eulalia. I had a little Alfred and a little Flora. They came to us in Provence, and we left their pretty little bodies there among the roses."

The sisters sat folded in each other's arms, their souls wandering about among memories, when Mr. Blumenthal returned from his long ramble with the children. Then, of course, there was a scene of exclamations and embraces. Little Lila was shy, and soon ran away to take refuge in Mamita's chamber; but Rosen Blumen was full of wonder and delight that such a grand, beautiful lady was the Aunt Rosa of whom she had heard so much.

"Mamita Lila has stayed away all this time, out of regard to our privacy," said Flora; "but now I am going to bring her."

She soon returned, arm in arm with Mrs. Delano. Mr. Blumenthal took her hand respectfully, as she entered, and said: "This is our dear benefactress, our best earthly friend."

"My guardian angel, my darling Mamita," added Flora.

Mrs. King eagerly stepped forward, and folded her in her arms, saying, in a voice half stifled with emotion, "Thank God and you for all this happiness."

While they were speaking together, Flora held a whispered consultation with her husband, who soon went forth in search of Mr. King, with strict injunctions to say merely that an unexpected pleasure awaited him. He hastened to obey the summons, wondering what it could mean. There was no need of introducing him to his new-found relative. The moment he entered the room, he exclaimed, " Why, Floracita!"

" So you knew me?" she said, clasping his hand warmly.

" To be sure I did," he answered. " You are the same little fairy that danced in the floral parlor."

" O, I 'm a sober matron now," said she, with a comic attempt to look demure about the mouth, while her eyes were laughing. " Here is my daughter Rosa; and I have a tall lad, who bears two thirds of your regal name."

The happy group were loath to separate, though it was only to meet again in the evening at Mr. King's lodgings on Round Hill. There, memories and feelings, that tried in vain to express themselves fully in words, found eloquent utterance in music.

Day after day, and evening after evening, the sisters met, with a hunger of the heart that could not be satisfied. Their husbands and children, meanwhile, became mutually attached. Rosen Blumen, richly colored with her tropical ancestry and her vigorous health, looked upon her more ethereal cousin Eulalia as a sort of angel, and seemed to worship her as such. Sometimes she accompanied her sweet, bird-like voice with the guitar; sometimes they sang duets together; and sometimes one played on the piano, while the other danced with Lila, whose tiny feet kept time to the music, true as an echo. Not unfrequently, the pretty little creature was called upon to dance a *pas seul;* for she had improvised a dance for herself to the tune of Yankee Doodle, and it was very amusing to see how emphatically she stamped the rhythm.

While the young people amused themselves thus, Flora often brought forward her collection of drawings, which Rosa called the portfolio of memories.

There was the little fountain in their father's garden, the lonely cottage on the island, the skeleton of the dead pine-tree, with the moon peeping through its streamers of moss, and Thistle with his panniers full of flowers. Among the variety of foreign scenes, Mrs. King particularly admired the dancing peasants from Frascati.

"Ah," said Flora, "I see them now, just as they looked when we passed them on our beautiful drive to Albano. It was the first really merry day I had had for a long time. I was just beginning to learn to enjoy myself without you. It was very selfish of me, dear Rosa, but I was forgetful of you, that day. And, only to think of it! if it had not been for that unlucky apparition of Mr. Fitzgerald, I should have gone to the opera and seen you as Norma."

"Very likely we should both have fainted," rejoined Rosa, "and then the manager would have refused to let La Campaneo try her luck again. But what is this, Floracita?"

"That is a group on Monte Pincio," she replied. "I sketched it when I was shut up in my room, the day before you came out in the opera."

"I do believe it is Madame and the Signor and I," responded Rosa. "The figures and the dresses are exactly the same; and I remember we went to Monte Pincio that morning, on my return from rehearsal."

"What a stupid donkey I was, not to know you were so near!" said Flora. "I should have thought my fingers would have told me while I was drawing it."

"Ah," exclaimed Rosa, "here is Tulee!" Her eyes moistened while she gazed upon it. "Poor Tulee!" said she, "how she cared for me, and comforted me, during those dark and dreadful days! If it had n't been for her

and Chloe, I could never have lived through that trouble.
When I began to recover, she told me how Chloe held my
hand hour after hour, and prayed over me without ceasing.
I believe she prayed me up out of the grave. She said
our Mamita appeared to her once, and told her she was
my guardian angel; but if it had really been our Mamita,
I think she would have told her to tell me you were alive,
Mignonne. When Alfred and I went South, just before
we came here, we tried to find Tom and Chloe. We intend to go to New Bedford soon to see them. A glimpse
of their good-natured black faces would give me more
pleasure than all the richly dressed ladies I saw at Mrs.
Green's great party."

"Very likely you'll hear Tom preach when you'go to
New Bedford," rejoined Flora, "for he is a Methodist
minister now ; and Chloe, they say, is powerful in prayer
at the meetings. I often smile when I think about the
manner of her coming away. It was so funny that my
quiet, refined Mamita Lila should all at once become a
kidnapper. But here is Rosen Blumen. Well, what now,
Mignonne ? "

"Papa says Lila is very sleepy, and we ought to be
going home," replied the young damsel.

"Then we will kiss good night, *sistita mia*," said Mrs.
Blumenthal ; "and you will bring Eulalia to us to-morrow."

On their return home, Mr. Bright called to them over
the garden fence. "I've just had a letter from your
neighbor, Mrs. Fitzgerald," said he. "She wants to know
whether we can accommodate her, and her father, and her
son with lodgings this summer. I'm mighty glad we can
say we've let all our rooms ; for that old Mr. Bell treats
mechanics as if he thought they all had the small-pox, and

he was afraid o' catching it. So different from you, Mr. Blumenthal, and Mr. King! You ain't afraid to take hold of a rough hand without a glove on. How is Mrs. King? Hope she 's coming to-morrow. If the thrushes and bobolinks could sing human music, and put human feeling into it, her voice would beat 'em all. How romantic that you should come here to Joe Bright's to find your sister, that you thought was dead."

When they had courteously answered his inquiries, he repeated a wish he had often expressed, that somebody would write a story about it. If he had been aware of all their antecedents, he would perhaps have written one himself; but he only knew that the handsome sisters were orphans, separated in youth, and led by a singular combination of circumstances to suppose each other dead.

15

CHAPTER XXIX.

WHEN the sisters were alone together, the next day after dinner, Flora said, "Rosa, dear, does it pain you very much to hear about Mr. Fitzgerald?"

"No; that wound has healed," she replied. "It is merely a sad memory now."

"Mrs. Bright was nursery governess in his family before her marriage," rejoined Flora. "I suppose you have heard that he disappeared mysteriously. I think she may know something about it, and I have been intending to ask her; but your sudden appearance, and the quantity of things we have had to say to each other, have driven it out of my head. Do you object to my asking her to come in and tell us something about her experiences?"

"I should be unwilling to have her know we were ever acquainted with Mr. Fitzgerald," responded Mrs. King.

"So should I," said Flora. "It will be a sufficient reason for my curiosity that Mrs. Fitzgerald is our acquaintance and neighbor."

And she went out to ask her hostess to come and sit with them. After some general conversation, Flora said: "You know Mrs. Fitzgerald is our neighbor in Boston. I have some curiosity to know what were your experiences in her family."

"Mrs. Fitzgerald was always very polite to me," replied Mrs. Bright; "and personally I had no occasion to find fault with Mr. Fitzgerald, though I think the Yankee schoolma'am was rather a bore to him. The South is a

beautiful part of the country.   I used to think the sea-
island, where they spent most of the summer, was as beautiful as Paradise before the fall; but I never felt at home
there.   I did n't like the state of things.   It 's my theory
that everybody ought to help in doing the work of the
world.   There 's a great . deal to be done, ladies, and it
don't seem right that some backs should be broken with
labor, while others have the spine complaint for want of
exercise.   It did n't agree with my independent New England habits to be waited upon so much.   A negro woman
named Venus took care of my room.   The first night I
slept at the plantation, it annoyed me to see her kneel
down to take off my stockings and shoes.   I told her she
might go, for I could undress myself.   She seemed surprised ; and I think her conclusion was that I was no lady.
But all the negroes liked me.   They had got the idea,
somehow, that Northern people were their friends, and
were doing something to set them free."

"Then they generally wanted their freedom, did they?"
inquired Flora.

"To be sure they did," rejoined Mrs. Bright.   "Did
you ever hear of anybody that liked being a slave?"

Mrs. King asked whether Mr. Fitzgerald was a hard
master.

"I don't think he was," said their hostess.   "I have
known him to do very generous and kind things for his
servants.   But early habits had made him indolent and
selfish, and he left the overseer to do as he liked.   Besides,
though he was a pleasant gentleman when sober, he was
violent when he was intoxicated ; and he had become much
addicted to intemperance before I went there.   They said
he had been a very handsome man ; but he was red and

bloated when I knew him. He had a dissipated circle of
acquaintances, who used to meet at his house in Savannah,
and gamble with cards till late into the night; and the
liquor they drank often made them very boisterous and
quarrelsome.   Mrs. Fitzgerald never made any remark,
in my presence, about these doings; but I am sure they
troubled her, for I often heard her walking her chamber
long after she had retired for the night. Indeed, they
made such an uproar, that it was difficult to sleep till they
were gone. Sometimes, after they had broken up, I heard
them talking on the piazza; and their oaths and obscene
jests were shocking to hear; yet if I met any of them the
next day, they appeared like courtly gentlemen. When
they were intoxicated, niggers and Abolitionists seemed
always to haunt their imaginations. I remember one night
in particular. I judged by their conversation that they
had been reading in a Northern newspaper some discussion
about allowing slaveholders to partake of the sacrament.
Their talk was a strange tipsy jumble. If Mr. Bright had
heard it, he would give you a comical account of it. As
they went stumbling down the steps, some were singing
and some were swearing. I heard one of them bawl out,
'God damn their souls to all eternity, they 're going to
exclude us from the communion-table.' When I first told
the story to Mr. Bright, I said d—— their souls; but he
said that was all a sham, for everybody knew what d——
stood for, and it was just like showing an ass's face to
avoid speaking his name. So I have spoken the word
right out plain, just as I heard it. It was shocking talk to
hear, and you may think it very improper to repeat it, ladies; but I have told it to give you an idea of the state of
things in the midst of which I found myself.

Mrs. King listened in sad silence. The Mr. Fitzgerald of this description was so unlike the elegant young gentleman who had won her girlish love, that she could not recognize him as the same person.

"Did Mr. Fitzgerald die before you left?" inquired Flora.

"I don't know when or how he died," replied Mrs. Bright; "but I have my suspicions. Out of regard to Mrs. Fitzgerald, I have never mentioned them to any one but my husband; and if I name them to you, ladies, I trust you will consider it strictly confidential."

They promised, and she resumed.

"I never pried into the secrets of the family, but I could not help learning something about them, partly from my own observation, and inferences drawn therefrom, and partly from the conversation of Venus, my talkative waiting-maid. She told me that her master married a Spanish lady, the most beautiful lady that ever walked the earth; and that he conveyed her away secretly somewhere after he married the milk-face, as she called Mrs. Fitzgerald. Venus was still good-looking when I knew her. From her frequent remarks I judge that, when she was young, her master thought her extremely pretty; and she frequently assured me that he was a great judge 'ob we far sex.' She had a handsome mulatto daughter, whose features greatly resembled his; and she said there was good reason for it. I used to imagine Mrs. Fitzgerald thought so too; for she always seemed to owe this handsome Nelly a grudge. Mr. Fitzgerald had a body-servant named Jim, who was so genteel that I always called him 'Dandy Jim o' Caroline.' Jim and Nelly were in love with each other; but their master, for reasons of his own, forbade their meeting together.

Finding that Nelly tried to elude his vigilance, he sold Jim
to a New Orleans trader, and the poor girl almost cried her
handsome eyes out. A day or two after he was sold, Mr.
Fitzgerald and his lady went to Beaufort on a visit, and
took their little son and daughter with them. The walls
of my sleeping-room were to be repaired, and I was told to
occupy their chamber during their absence. The evening
after they went away, I sat up rather late reading, and
when I retired the servants were all asleep. As I sat before the looking-glass, arranging my hair for the night, I
happened to glance toward the reflection of the bed, which
showed plainly in the mirror; and I distinctly saw a dark
eye peeping through an opening in the curtains. My heart
was in my throat, I assure you; but I had the presence of
mind not to cry out or to jump up. I continued combing
my hair, occasionally glancing toward the eye. If it be one
of the negroes, thought I, he surely cannot wish to injure
me, for they all know I am friendly to them. I tried to
collect all my faculties, to determine what it was best to do.
I reflected that, if I alarmed the servants, he might be driven
to attack me in self-defence. I began talking aloud to myself, leisurely taking off my cuffs and collar as I did so, and
laying my breastpin and watch upon the table. 'I wish
Mr. and Mrs. Fitzgerald were not going to stay so long at
Beaufort,' said I. 'It is lonesome here, and I don't feel
at home in this chamber. I sha'n't sleep if I go to bed; so
I think I'll read a little longer.' I looked round on the
table and chairs, and added: 'There, now! I've left my
book down stairs, and must go for it.' I went down to the
parlor and locked myself in. A few minutes afterward I
saw a dark figure steal across the piazza; and, unless the
moonlight deceived me, it was Dandy Jim. I wondered at it,

because I thought he was on his way to New Orleans. Of course, there was no sleep for me that night. When the household were all astir, I went to the chamber again. My watch and breastpin, which I had left on purpose, were still lying on the table. It was evident that robbery had not been the object. I did not mention the adventure to any one. I pitied Jim, and if he had escaped, I had no mind to be the means of his recapture. Whatever harm he had intended, he had not done it, and there was no probability that he would loiter about in that vicinity. I had reason to be glad of my silence; for the next day an agent from the slave-trader arrived, saying that Jim had escaped, and that they thought he might be lurking near where his wife was. When Mr. and Mrs. Fitzgerald returned, they questioned Nelly, but she averred that she had not seen Jim, or heard from him since he was sold. Mr. Fitzgerald went away on horseback that afternoon. The horse came back in the evening with an empty saddle, and he never returned. The next morning Nelly was missing, and she was never found. I thought it right to be silent about my adventure. To have done otherwise might have produced mischievous results to Jim and Nelly, and could do their master no good. I searched the woods in every direction, but I never came upon any trace of Mr. Fitzgerald, except the marks of footsteps near the sea, before the rising of the tide. I had made arrangements to return to the North about that time; but Mrs. Fitzgerald's second son was seized with fever, and I stayed with her till he was dead and buried. Then we all came to Boston together. About a year after, her little daughter, who had been my pupil, died."

"Poor Mrs. Fitzgerald!" said Flora. "I have heard

her allude to her lost children, but I had no idea she had suffered so much."

"She did suffer," replied Mrs. Bright, "though not so deeply as some natures would have suffered in the same circumstances. Her present situation is far from being enviable. Her father is a hard, grasping man, and he was greatly vexed that her splendid marriage turned out to be such a failure. It must be very mortifying to her to depend upon him mainly for the support of herself and son. I pitied her, and I pitied Mr. Fitzgerald too. He was selfish and dissipated, because he was brought up with plenty of money, and slaves to obey everything he chose to order. That is enough to spoil any man."

Rosa had listened with downcast eyes, but now she looked up earnestly and said, "That is a very kind judgment, Mrs. Bright, and I thank you for the lesson."

"It is a just judgment," replied their sensible hostess. "I often tell Mr. Bright we cannot be too thankful that we were brought up to wait upon ourselves and earn our own living. You will please to excuse me now, ladies, for it is time to prepare tea."

As she closed the door, Rosa pressed her sister's hand, and sighed as she said, "O, this is dreadful!"

"Dreadful indeed," rejoined Flora. "To think of him as he was when I used to make you blush by singing, '*Petit blanc! mon bon frère!*' and then to think what an end he came to!"

The sisters sat in silence for some time, thinking with moistened eyes of all that had been kind and pleasant in the man who had done them so much wrong.

CHAPTER XXX.

IF young Fitzgerald had not been strongly inclined to spend the summer in Northampton, he would have been urged to it by his worldly-minded mother and grandfather, who were disposed to make any effort to place him in the vicinity of Eulalia King. They took possession of lodgings on Round Hill in June; and though very few weeks intervened before the college vacation, the time seemed so long to Gerald, that he impatiently counted the days. Twice he took the journey for a short visit before he was established as an inmate of his grandfather's household. Alfred Blumenthal had a vacation at the same time, and the young people of the three families were together almost continually. Songs and glees enlivened their evenings, and nearly every day there were boating excursions, or rides on horseback, in which Mr. and Mrs. King and Mr. and Mrs. Blumenthal invariably joined. No familiarity could stale the ever fresh charm of the scenery. The beautiful river, softly flowing in sunlight through richly cultivated meadows, always seemed to Mr. Blumenthal like the visible music of Mendelssohn. Mr. King, who had been in Germany, was strongly reminded of the Rhine and the Black Forest, while looking on that wide level expanse of verdure, with its broad band of sparkling silver, framed in with thick dark woods along the river-range of mountains. The younger persons of the party more especially enjoyed watching Mill River rushing to meet the Connecticut, like an impatient boy let loose for the holidays, shouting, and

15*

laughing, and leaping, on his way homeward. Mrs. Delano
particularly liked to see, from the summit of Mount Holyoke,
the handsome villages, lying so still in the distance, giving
no sign of all the passions, energies, and sorrows that were
seething, struggling, and aching there ; and the great stretch
of meadows, diversified with long, unfenced rows of stately
Indian corn, rich with luxuriant foliage of glossy green, al-
ternating with broad bands of yellow grain, swayed by the
breeze like rippling waves of the sea. These regular lines
of variegated culture, seen from such a height, seemed like
handsome striped calico, which earth had put on for her
working-days, mindful that the richly wooded hills were
looking down upon her picturesque attire. There was
something peculiarly congenial to the thoughtful soul of the
cultured lady in the quiet pastoral beauty of the extensive
scene ; and still more in the sense of serene elevation above
the whole, seeing it all dwindle into small proportions, as the
wisdom of age calmly surveys the remote panorama of life.

These riding parties attracted great attention as they
passed through the streets ; for all had heard the rumor
of their wealth, and all were struck by the unusual amount
of personal beauty, and the distinguished style of dress.
At that time, the Empress Eugenie had issued her imperial
decree that all the world should shine in "barbaric gold," —
a fashion by no means distasteful to the splendor-loving
sisters. Long sprays of Scotch laburnum mingled their
golden bells with the dark tresses of Eulalia and Rosen
Blumen ; a cluster of golden wheat mixed its shining
threads with Flora's black curls ; and a long, soft feather,
like "the raven down of darkness," dusted with gold,
drooped over the edge of Mrs. King's riding-cap, fastened
to its band by a golden star. Even Mrs. Fitzgerald so far

changed her livery of the moon as to wear golden buds
mixed with cerulean flowers. Mrs. Delano looked cool as
evening among them in her small gray bonnet, with a few
violets half hidden in silver leaves. Old Mr. Bell not unfrequently joined in these excursions. His white hair, and
long silky white beard, formed a picturesque variety in the
group; while all recognized at a glance the thorough-bred
aristocrat in his haughty bearing, his stern mouth, his cold,
turquoise eyes, and the clenching expression of his hand.
Mrs. King seemed to have produced upon him the effect
Gerald had predicted. No youthful gallant could have
been more assiduous at her bridle-rein, and he seemed to
envy his grandson every smile he obtained from her beautiful lips.

Both he and Mrs. Fitzgerald viewed with obvious satisfaction the growing intimacy between that young gentleman and Eulalia. "Capital match for Gerald, eh?" said
Mr. Bell to his daughter. "They say King's good for
three millions at least, — some say four."

"And Eulalia is such a lovely, gentle girl!" rejoined
Mrs. Fitzgerald. "I'm very fond of her, and she seems
fond of me; though of course that's on account of my
handsome son."

"Yes, she's a lovely girl," replied the old gentleman;
"and Gerald will be a lucky dog if he wins her. But her
beauty is n't to be compared to her mother's. If I were
Emperor of France, and she were a widow, I know who
would have a chance to become Empress."

But though Mrs. King lived in such an atmosphere of
love, and was the object of so much admiration, with ample
means for indulging her benevolence and her tastes, she
was evidently far from being happy. Flora observed it,

and often queried with her husband what could be the reason. One day she spoke to Mr. King of the entire absence of gayety in her sister, and he said he feared young Mr. Fitzgerald painfully reminded her of her lost son.

Flora reflected upon this answer without being satisfied with it. "It does n't seem natural," said she to her husband. "She parted from that baby when he was but a few weeks old, and he has been dead nearly twenty years. She has Eulalia to love, and a noble husband, who worships the very ground she treads on. It don't seem natural. I wonder whether she has a cancer or some other secret disease."

She redoubled her tenderness, and exerted all her powers of mimicry to amuse her sister. The young folks screamed with laughter to see her perform the shuffling dances of the negroes, or to hear her accompany their singing with imitations of the growling contra-fagotto, or the squeaking fife. In vain she filled the room with mocking-birds, or showed off the accomplishments of the parrot, or dressed herself in a cap with a great shaking bow, like Madame Guirlande's, or scolded in vociferous Italian, like Signor Pimentero. The utmost these efforts could elicit from her sister was a faint, vanishing smile.

Mr. King noticed all this, and was pained to observe that his wife's sadness increased daily. He would not himself have chosen young Fitzgerald as a suitor for his daughter, fearing he might resemble his father in character as he did in person; but he was willing to promote their acquaintance, because the young man seemed to be a favorite with his lady, and he thought that as a son-in-law he might supply the loss of her first-born. But, in their rides and other excursions, he was surprised to observe that Mrs. King assiduously tried to withdraw Mr. Fitzgerald from her daughter, and attach him to herself. Her attentions generally proved too flattering to be resisted; but if the young man, yielding to attractions more suited to his age, soon returned to Eulalia, there was an unmistakable expression of pain on her mother's face. Mr. King was puzzled and pained by this conduct. Entire confidence had hitherto existed between them. Why had she become so reserved? Was the fire of first-love still smouldering in her soul, and did a delicate consideration for him lead her to conceal it? He could not believe it, she had so often repeated that to love the unworthy was a thing impossible for her. Sometimes another thought crossed his mind and gave him exquisite torture, though he repelled it instantly: "Could it possibly be that his modest and dignified wife was in love with this stripling, who was of an age suitable for her daughter?" Whatever this mysterious cloud might be that cast its cold shadow across the sunshine of his home, he felt that he could not endure its presence. He resolved to seek an explanation with his wife, and to propose an immediate return to Europe, if either of his conjectures should prove true. Returning from a solitary walk, during which these ideas had been revolving in his mind, he found her in their chamber kneeling **by the** bedside, sobbing violently. With the utmost tenderness he inquired what had grieved her.

She answered with a wild exclamation, "O Alfred, this *must* be stopped!"

"*What* must be stopped, my dear?" said he.

"Gerald Fitzgerald *must* not court our daughter," **she** replied.

"I thought it would please you, dearest," rejoined he. "The young man has always seemed to be a favorite of yours. I should not have selected him for our Eulalia, for fear the qualities of his father might develop themselves in him; but you must remember that he has not been educated among slaves. I think we can trust to that to make a great difference in his character."

She groaned aloud, and sobbed out: "It *must* be stopped. It will kill me."

He sat down by her side, took her hand, and said very gravely: "Rosa, you have often told me I was your best friend. Why then do you not confide to me what it is that troubles you?"

"O, I cannot! I cannot!" she exclaimed. "I am a guilty wretch." And there came a fresh outburst of sobs, which she stifled by keeping her face hidden in the bed-clothes.

"Rosa," said he, still more gravely, "you *must* tell me the meaning of this strange conduct. If an unworthy passion has taken possession of you, it is your duty to try to conquer it for your own sake, for my sake, for our daughter's sake. If you will confide in me, I will not judge you harshly. I will return to Europe with you, and help you to cure yourself. Tell me frankly, Rosa, do you love this young man?"

She looked up suddenly, and, seeing the extreme sadness of his face, she exclaimed: "O Alfred, if you have thought *that*, I *must* tell you all. I do love Gerald; but it is because he is my own son."

"Your son!" he exclaimed, springing up, with the feeling that a great load was lifted from his heart. He raised her to his bosom, and kissed her tearful face again and again. The relief was so sudden, that for an instant he forgot the strangeness of her declaration. But coming to his senses immediately, he inquired, "How can it be that your son passes for Mrs. Fitzgerald's son? And if it be so, why did you not tell me of it?"

"I ought to have told you when I consented to marry you," she replied. "But your protecting love was so precious to me, that I had not the courage to tell you anything that would diminish your esteem for me. Forgive me, dearest. It is the only wrong I have ever done you. But I will tell you all now; and if it changes your love for me, I must try to bear it, as a just punishment for the wrong I have done. You know how Mr. Fitzgerald deserted me, and how I was stricken down when I discovered that I was his slave. My soul almost parted from my body during the long illness that followed. When I came to my senses, I humbled myself to entreat Mr. Fitzgerald to emancipate me, for the sake of our unborn child. He promised to do it, but he did not. I was a mere wreck when my babe was born, and I had the feeling that I should soon die. I loved the helpless little thing; and every time I looked at him, it gave me a pang to think that he was born a slave. I sent again and again for papers of manumission, but they never came. I don't know whether it was mere negligence on the part of Mr. Fitzgerald, or whether he meant to punish me for my coldness toward him after I discovered how he had deceived me. I was weak in body, and much humbled in spirit, after that long illness. I felt no resentment toward him. I forgave him, and pitied his young wife. The only thing that bound me to life was my child. I wanted to recover my strength, that I might carry him to some part of the world where slavery could not reach him. I was in that state, when Madame sent Mr. Duroy to tell me Mr. Fitzgerald was in debt, and had sold me to that odious Mr. Bruteman, whom he had always represented to me as the filthiest soul alive. I think that incredible cruelty and that horrible danger made me insane. My soul was in a terrible tempest of hatred and revenge. If Mr. Fitzgerald had appeared before me, I should have stabbed him. I never had such feelings before nor since. Unfortunately Chloe had come to the cottage that day, with Mrs. Fitzgerald's babe, and he was lying asleep by the side of mine. I had wild thoughts of killing both the babies, and then killing myself. I had actually risen in search of a weapon, but I heard my faithful Tulee coming to look upon me, to see that all was well, and I lay down again and pretended to be asleep. While I waited for her to cease watching over me, that frightful mood passed away. Thank God, I was saved from committing such horrible deeds. But I was still half frantic with misery and fear. A wild, dark storm was raging in my soul. I looked at the two babes, and thought how one was born to be indulged and honored, while the other was born a slave, liable to be sold by his unfeeling father or by his father's creditors. Mine was only a week the oldest, and was no larger than his brother. They were so exactly alike that I could distinguish them only by their dress. I exchanged the dresses, Alfred ; and while I did it, I laughed to think that, if Mr. Fitzgerald should capture me and the little one, and make us over to Mr. Bruteman, he would sell the child of his Lily Bell. It was not like me to have such feelings. I hope I was insane. Do you think I was ? "

He pressed her to his heart as he replied, " You surely had suffering enough to drive you wild, dearest ; and I do suppose your reason was unsettled by intensity of anguish."

She looked at him anxiously, as she asked, "Then it does not make you love me less?"

"No, darling," he replied; "for I am sure it was not my own gentle Rosa who had such feelings."

"O, how I thank you, dear one, for judging me so charitably," said she. "I hope it was temporary insanity; and always when I think it over, it seems to me it must have been. I fell asleep smiling over the revenge I had taken, and I slept long and heavily. When I woke, my first wish was to change the dresses back again; but Chloe had gone to the plantation with my babe, and Mr. Duroy hurried me on board the boat before sunrise. I told no one what I had done; but it filled me with remorse then, and has troubled me ever since. I resolved to atone for it, as far as I could, by taking the tenderest care of the little changeling, and trying to educate him as well as his own mother could have done. It was that which gave me strength to work so hard for musical distinction; and that motive stimulated me to appear as an opera-singer, though the publicity was distasteful to me. When I heard that the poor little creature was dead, I was tormented with self-reproach, and I was all the more unhappy because I could tell no one of my trouble. Then you came to console and strengthen me with your blessed love, and I grew cheerful again. If the changeling had been living at the time you asked me to marry you, I should have told you all; but the poor little creature was dead, and there seemed to be no necessity of confessing the wrong I had done. It was a selfish feeling. I could n't bear the thought of diminishing the love that was so precious to my wounded heart. I have now told you all, dear husband."

"Your excuse for concealment is very precious to my

w

own heart," he replied. "But I regret you did not tell me while we were in Europe; for then I would not have returned to the United States till I was quite sure all obstacles were removed. You know I never formed the project until I knew Mr. Fitzgerald was dead."

"The American gentleman who informed you of his death led me into a mistake, which has proved disastrous," rejoined she. "He said that Mrs. Fitzgerald lost her husband and son about the same time. I was not aware of the existence of a second son, and therefore I supposed that my first-born had died. I knew that you wanted to spend your old age in your native country, and that you were particularly desirous to have Eulalia marry in New England. The dread I had of meeting my child as the son of another, and seeming to him a stranger, was removed by his death; and though I shed tears in secret, a load was lifted from my heart. But the old story of avenging Furies following the criminal wheresoever he goes seems verified in my case. On the day of Mrs. Green's ball, I heard two gentlemen in the Revere House talking about Mr. Bell; and one of them said to the other that Mrs. Fitzgerald's second son and her daughter had died, and that her oldest son was sole heir to Mr. Bell's property. My first impulse was to tell you all; but because I had so long concealed my fault, it was all the more difficult to confess it then. You had so generously overlooked many disagreeable circumstances connected with my history, that I found it extremely painful to add this miserable entanglement to the list. Still, I foresaw that it must be done, and I resolved to do it; but I was cowardly, and wanted to put off the evil day. You may remember, perhaps, that at the last moment I objected to attending that ball; but you

thought it would be rude to disappoint Mrs. Green, merely
because I felt out of spirits. I went, not dreaming of seeing my son there. I had not looked upon him since the
little black, silky head drooped on my arm while I exchanged the dresses. You may partly imagine what I
suffered. And now he and Eulalia are getting in love
with each other; and I know not what is to be done
When you came in, I was praying for strength to seek
your counsel. What *can* we do, dear? It will be a great
disappointment for you to return to Europe, now that you
have refitted your father's house, and made all your arrangements to spend the remainder of our days here."

"I would do it willingly," he replied, "if I thought it
would avail to separate Gerald and Eulalia. But a voyage to Europe is nothing now-a-days, to people of their
property. I believe he loves the dear girl; and if he did
not, my reputed millions would prevent his grandfather and
his mother from allowing him to lose sight of her. If we
were to build a castle on the top of Mount Himalaya, they
would scale it, you may depend. I see no other remedy
than to tell Gerald that Eulalia is his sister."

"O, I cannot tell him!" exclaimed she. "It would be
so dreadful to have my son hate me! And he *would* hate
me; for I can see that he is very proud."

In very kind and serious tones he replied: "You know,
dear Rosa, that you expressed a wish the other day to go
to the Catholic church in which your mother worshipped,
because you thought confession and penance would be a
comfort. You have wisely chosen me for your confessor,
and if I recommend penance I trust you will think it best
to follow my advice. I see how difficult it would be to tell
all your own and your mother's story to so young a man as
Gerald, and he your own son. I will tell him; and I need

not assure you that you will have a loving advocate to plead your cause with him. But his mother must know why he relinquishes Eulalia, when he has had so much reason to think himself in favor both with her and her parents. Gerald might tell her the mere external facts; but she could appreciate and understand them much better if told, as they would be told, by a delicate and loving woman, who had suffered the wrongs that drove her to madness, and who repented bitterly of the fault she had committed. I think you ought to make a full confession to Mrs. Fitzgerald; and having done that, we ought to do whatever she chooses to prescribe."

"It will be a severe penance," she rejoined; "but I will do whatever you think is right. If I could have all the suffering, I would not murmur. But Gerald will suffer and Eulalia will suffer. And for some weeks I have made you unhappy. How sad you look, dear."

"I am a very happy man, Rosa, compared with what I was before you told me this strange story. But I am very serious, because I want to be sure of doing what is right in these difficult premises. As for Gerald and Eulalia, their acquaintance has been very short, and I don't think they have spoken of love to each other. Their extreme youth is also a favorable circumstance. Rochefoucault says, 'Absence extinguishes small passions, and increases great ones.' My own experience proved the truth of one part of the maxim; but perhaps Gerald is of a more volatile temperament, and will realize the other portion."

"And do you still love me as well as you ever did?" she asked.

He folded her more closely as he whispered, "I do, darling." And for some minutes she wept in silence on his generous breast.

CHAPTER XXXI.

THAT evening young Fitzgerald was closeted two or three hours with Mr. King. Though the disclosure was made with the utmost delicacy and caution, the young man was startled and shocked; for he inherited pride from both his parents, and he had been educated in the prejudices of his grandfather. At first he flushed with indignation, and refused to believe he was so disgraced.

"I don't see that you are disgraced, my young friend," replied Mr. King. "The world might indeed so misjudge, because it is accustomed to look only on externals; but there is no need that the world should know anything about it. And as for your own estimate of yourself, you were Mr. Fitzgerald the gentleman before you knew this singular story, and you are Mr. Fitzgerald the gentleman still."

"I am not so much of a philosopher," rejoined the young man. "I shall not find it easy to endure the double stain of illegitimacy and alliance with the colored race."

Mr. King regarded him with a friendly smile, as he answered: "Perhaps this experience, which you find so disagreeable, may educate you to more wisdom than the schools have done. It may teach you the great lesson of looking beneath the surface into the reality of things, my son. Legally you are illegitimate; but morally you are not so. Your mother believed herself married to your father, and through all the vicissitudes of her life she has proved herself a modest, pure, and noble woman. During twenty years of intimate acquaintance, I have never known her to indulge an unworthy thought, or do a dishonorable action, except that of substituting you for Mr. Fitzgerald's legal heir. And if I have at all succeeded in impressing upon your mind the frantic agony of her soul, desolate and shockingly abused as she was, I think you will agree with me in considering that an excusable offence; especially as she would have repaired the wrong a few hours later, if it had been in her power. With regard to an alliance with the colored race, I think it would be a more legitimate source of pride to have descended from that truly great man, Toussaint L'Ouverture, who was a full-blooded African, than from that unprincipled filibuster called William the Conqueror, or from any of his band of robbers, who transmitted titles of nobility to their posterity. That is the way I have learned to read history, my young friend, in the plain sunlight of truth, unchanged by looking at it through the deceptive colored glasses of conventional prejudice. Only yesterday you would have felt honored to claim my highly accomplished and noble-minded wife as a near relative. She is as highly accomplished and noble-minded a lady to-day as she was yesterday. The only difference is, that to-day you are aware her grandmother had a dark complexion. No human being can be really stained by anything apart from his own character; but if there were any blot resting upon you, it would come from your father. We should remember, however, that He who made man can alone justly estimate man's temptations. For myself, I believe that Mr. Fitzgerald's sins were largely attributable to the system of slavery under which he had the misfortune to be educated. He loved pleasure, he was rich, and he had irresponsible power over many of his fel-

low-beings, whom law and public opinion alike deprived
of protection. Without judging him harshly, let his career
be a warning to you to resist the first enticements to evil ;
and, as one means of doing so, let me advise you never to
place yourself in that state of society which had such a
malign influence upon him."

"Give me time to think," rejoined the young man.
"This has come upon me so suddenly that I feel stunned."

"That I can easily imagine," replied his friend. "But
I wish you to understand distinctly, that it depends entirely
upon Mrs. Fitzgerald and yourself to decide what is to be
done in relation to this perplexing affair. We are ready
to do anything you wish, or to take any position you prescribe for us. You may prefer to pass in society merely as
my young friend, but you are my step-son, you know ; and
should you at any time of your life need my services, you
may rely upon me as an affectionate father."

That word brought cherished hopes to Gerald's mind,
and he sighed as he answered, "I thank you."

"Whatever outward inconveniences may arise from this
state of things," resumed Mr. King, "we prefer to have
them fall upon ourselves. It is of course desirable that
you and my daughter should not meet at present. Your
vacation has nearly expired, and perhaps you will deem it
prudent to return a little sooner than you intended. We
shall remain here till late in the autumn ; and then, if circumstances render it necessary, we will remove Eulalia to
Cuba, or elsewhere, for the winter. Try to bear this disappointment bravely, my son. As soon as you feel suffi-
c.ently calm, I would advise you to seek an interview with
your mother. Her heart yearns for you, and the longer
your meeting is deferred, the more embarrassing it will be."

While this conversation was going on in the parlor, the two mothers of the young man were talking confidentially up stairs. The intense curiosity which Mrs. Fitzgerald had formerly felt was at once renewed when Mrs. King said, " Do you remember having heard any one singing about the house and garden at Magnolia Lawn, the first evening you spent there?"

" Indeed I do," she replied; " and when I first heard you in Rome, I repeatedly said your voice was precisely like that singer's."

" You might well be reminded of it," responded Mrs. King, " for I was the person you heard at Magnolia Lawn, and these are the eyes that peeped at you through the lattice of the veranda."

" But why were you there? And why did you keep yourself invisible?" inquired Mrs. Fitzgerald.

Rosa hesitated a moment, embarrassed how to choose words to convey the unwelcome facts. " My dear lady," said she, " we have both had very sad experiences. On my side, they have been healed by time; and I trust it is the same with you. Will it pain you too much to hear something disparaging to the memory of your deceased husband?"

Mrs. Fitzgerald·colored very deeply, and remained silent.

" Nothing but an imperious necessity would induce me to say what I am about to say," continued Mrs. King; " not only because I am very reluctant to wound your feelings, but because the recital is humiliating and painful to myself. When I peeped at you in your bridal attire, I believed myself to be Mr. Fitzgerald's wife. Our marriage had been kept strictly private, he always assuring me that it was only for a time. But you need not look so alarmed.

I was not his wife. I learned the next morning that I had been deceived by a sham ceremony. And even if it had been genuine, the marriage would not have been valid by the laws of Louisiana, where it was performed; though I did not know that fact at the time. No marriage with a slave is valid in that State. My mother was a quadroon slave, and by the law that 'a child follows the condition of the mother,' I also became a slave."

"*You* a slave!" exclaimed Mrs. Fitzgerald, with unfeigned astonishment. "That is incredible. That goes beyond any of the stories Abolitionists make up to keep the country in agitation."

"Judging by my own experience," rejoined Mrs. King, "I should say that the most fertile imagination could invent nothing more strange and romantic than many of the incidents which grow out of slavery."

She then went on to repeat her story in detail; not accusing Mr. Fitzgerald more than was absolutely necessary to explain the agonized and frantic state of mind in which she had changed the children. Mrs. Fitzgerald listened with increasing agitation as she went on; and when it came to that avowal, she burst out with the passionate exclamation: "Then Gerald is not my son! And I love him so!"

Mrs. King took her hand and pressed it gently as she said: "You can love him still, dear lady, and he will love you. Doubtless you will always seem to him like his own mother. If he takes an aversion to me, it will give me acute pain; but I shall try to bear it meekly, as a part of the punishment my fault deserves."

"If you don't intend to take him from me, what was the use of telling me this dreadful story?" impatiently asked Mrs. Fitzgerald.

16

"I felt compelled to do it on Eulalia's account," responded Mrs. King.

"Ah, yes!" sighed the lady. "How disappointed he will be, poor fellow!" After a brief pause, she added, vehemently: "But whatever you may say, he is *my* son. I never will give him up. He has slept in my arms. I have sung him to sleep. I taught him all his little hymns and songs. He loves me; and I will never consent to take a second place in his affections."

"You shall not be asked to do so, dear lady," meekly replied Mrs. King. "I will, as in duty bound, take any place you choose to assign me."

Somewhat disarmed by this humility, Mrs. Fitzgerald said, in a softened tone: "I pity you, Mrs. King. You have had a great deal of trouble, and this is a very trying situation you are in. But it would break my heart to give up Gerald. And then you must see, of course, what an embarrassing position it would place me in before the world."

"I see no reason why the world should know anything about it," rejoined Mrs. King. "For Gerald's sake, as well as our own, it is very desirable that the secret should be kept between ourselves."

"You may safely trust my pride for that," she replied.

"Do you think your father ought to be included in our confidence," inquired Mrs. King.

"No indeed," she replied, hastily. "He never can bear to hear my poor husband mentioned. Besides, he has had the gout a good deal lately, and is more irritable than usual."

As she rose to go, Mrs. King said: "Then, with the exception of Eulalia, everything remains outwardly as it was.

Can you forgive me? I do believe I was insane with misery; and you don't know how I have been haunted with
remorse."

"You must have suffered terribly," rejoined Mrs. Fitzgerald, evading a direct answer to the question. "But we
had better not talk any more about it now. I am bewildered, and don't know what to think. Only one thing is
fixed in my mind: Gerald is *my* son."

They parted politely, but with coldness on Mrs. Fitzgerald's side. There had arisen in her mind a double dislike toward Mrs. King, as the first love of her husband, and
as the mother of the elegant young man who was to her
an object of pride as well as fondness. But her chagrin
was not without compensation. Mrs. King's superior
wealth and beauty had been felt by her as somewhat over-
shadowing; and the mortifying circumstances she had now
discovered in her history seemed, in her imagination, **to**
bring her down below a level with herself. She and
Gerald sat up late into the night, talking over this strange
disclosure. She was rather jealous of the compassion he
expressed for Mrs. King, and of his admiration for her
manners and character; though they mutually declared,
again and again, that they could realize no change whatever in their relation to each other.

The wise words of Mr. King had not been without their
effect on Gerald. The tumult of emotions gradually subsided, and he began to realize that these external accidents
made no essential change in himself. The next morning
he requested an interview with Mrs. King, **and was** received alone. When he entered, she cast upon him a hesitating, beseeching look; but when he said, "My mother!"
she flew into his arms, and wept upon his neck.

"Then you do not hate me?" she said, in a voice choked with emotion. "You are not ashamed to call me mother?"

"It was only yesterday," he replied, "that I thought with pride and joy of the possibility that I might some day call you by that dear name. If I had heard these particulars without knowing you, they might have repelled me. But I have admired you from the first moment; I have lately been learning to love you; and I am familiar with the thought of being your son."

She raised her expressive eyes to his with such a look of love, that he could not refrain from giving her a filial kiss and pressing her warmly to his heart. "I was so afraid you would regard me with dislike," said she. "You can understand now why it made me so faint to think of singing '*M' odi! Ah, m' odi!*' with you at Mrs. Green's party. How could I have borne your tones of anguish when you discovered that you were connected with the Borgias? And how could I have helped falling on your neck when you sang '*Madre mia*'? But I must not forget that the mother who tended your childhood has the best claim to your affection," she added mournfully.

"I love her, and always shall love her. It cannot be otherwise," rejoined he. "It has been the pleasant habit of so many years. But ought I not to consider myself a lucky fellow to have two such mothers? I don't know how I am to distinguish you. I must call you Rose-mother and Lily-mother, I believe."

She smiled as he spoke, and she said, "Then it has not made you so *very* unhappy to know that you are my son?"

His countenance changed as he replied: "My only unhappiness is the loss of Eulalia. That disappointment I must bear as I can."

"You are both very young," rejoined she; "and perhaps you may see another — "

"I don't want to hear about that now," he exclaimed impetuously, moving hastily toward the window, against which he leaned for a moment. When he turned, he saw that his mother was weeping; and he stooped to kiss her forehead, with tender apologies for his abruptness.

"Thank God," she said, "for these brief moments of happiness with my son."

"Yes, they must be brief," he replied. "I must go away and stay away. But I shall always think of you with affection, and cherish the deepest sympathy for your wrongs and sufferings."

Again she folded him in her arms, and they kissed and blessed each other at parting. She gazed after him wistfully till he was out of sight. "Alas!" murmured she, "he cannot be a son to me, and I cannot be a mother to him." She recalled the lonely, sad hours when she embroidered his baby clothes, with none but Tulee to sympathize with her. She remembered how the little black silky head looked as she first fondled him on her arm; and the tears began to flow like rain. But she roused in a few moments, saying to herself: "This is all wrong and selfish. I ought to be glad that he loves his Lily-mother, that he can live with her, and that her heart will not be made desolate by my fault. O Father of mercies! this is hard to bear. Help me to bear it as I ought!" She bowed her head in silence for a while; then, rising up, she said: "Have I not my lovely Eulalia? Poor child! I must be very tender with her in this trial of her young heart."

She saw there was need to be very tender, when a farewell card was sent the next day, with a bouquet of delicate flowers from Gerald Fitzgerald.

CHAPTER XXXII.

THE next morning after these conversations, Mrs. Blumenthal, who was as yet unconscious of the secret they had revealed, was singing in the garden, while she gathered some flowers for her vases. Mr. Bright, who was cutting up weeds, stopped and listened, keeping time on the handle of his hoe. When Flora came up to him, she glanced at the motion of his fingers and smiled. " Can't help it, ma'am," said he. " When I hear your voice, it's as much as ever I can do to keep from dancing; but if I should do that, I should shock my neighbor the Deacon. Did you see the stage stop there, last night? They've got visitors from Carolina, — his daughter, and her husband and children. I reckon I stirred him up yesterday. He came to my shop to pay for some shoeing he'd had done. So I invited him to attend our anti-slavery meeting to-morrow evening. He took it as an insult, and said he didn't need to be instructed by such sort of men as spoke at our meetings. 'I know some of us are what they call mudsills down South,' said I; 'but it might do you good to go and hear' em, Deacon. When a man's lamp's out, it's better to light it by the kitchen fire than to go blundering about in the dark, hitting himself against everything.' He said we should find it very convenient if we had slaves here; for Northern women were mere beasts of burden. I told him that was better than to be beasts of prey. I thought afterward I wasn't very polite. I don't mean to go headlong against other folks' prejudices; but the fact is, a man never knows with what impetus he *is* going till he comes up against a post. I like to see a man firm as a rock in his opinions. I have a sort of a respect for a *rock*, even if it *is* a little mossy. But when I come across a *post*, I like to give it a shaking, to find out whether it's rotten at the foundation. As to things in general, I calculate to be an obliging neighbor; but I shall keep a lookout on these Carolina folks. If they've brought any blacks with 'em, I shall let 'em know what the laws of Massachusetts are; and then they may take their freedom or not, just as they choose."

"That's right," replied Mrs. Blumenthal; "and when you and the Deacon have another encounter, I hope I shall be near enough to hear it."

As she walked away, tying up her bouquet with a spear of striped grass, she heard him whistling the tune she had been singing. When she returned to the parlor, she seated herself near the open window, with a handkerchief, on which she was embroidering Mrs. Delano's initials. Mr. Bright's remarks had somewhat excited her curiosity, and from time to time she glanced toward Deacon Stillham's grounds. A hawthorn hedge, neatly clipped, separated the two gardens; but here and there the foliage had died away and left small open spaces. All at once, a pretty little curly head appeared at one of these leafy lunettes, and an infantile voice called out, "You're a Bob-o-lith-o-nitht!"

"Do come here, Mamita Lila, and see this little darling," said Flora, laughing.

For a moment she was invisible. Then the cherub face came peeping out again; and this time the little mouth was laughing, when it repeated, "You're a Bob-o-lith-o-nitht."

"Isn't it amusing to hear such an infant trying to abuse

us with a big mouthful of a word, to which she attaches no meaning?" said Mrs. Delano.

Flora beckoned with her hand, and called out, "Come in and see the Bobolithonithts, darling." The little creature laughed and ran away. At that moment, a bright turban was seen moving along above the bushes. Then a black face became visible. Flora sprang up with a quick cry, and rushed out of the room, upsetting her basket, and leaving balls and thimble rolling about the floor. Placing her foot on a stump, she leaped over the hedge like an opera-dancer, and the next moment she had the negro woman in her arms, exclaiming: "Bless you, Tulee! You *are* alive, after all!"

The black woman was startled and bewildered for an instant; then she held her off at arm's length, and looked at her with astonishment, saying: "Bless the Lord! Is it you, Missy Flory? or is it a sperit? Well now, *is* it you, little one?"

"Yes, Tulee; it is I," she replied. "The same Missy Flory that used to plague your life out with her tricks."

The colored woman hugged and kissed, and hugged and kissed, and laughed and cried; ever and anon exclaiming, "Bless the Lord!"

Meanwhile, the playful cherub was peeping at Joe Bright through another hole in the hedge, all unconscious how pretty her little fair face looked in its frame of green leaves, but delighted with her own sauciness, as she repeated, "You're a Bob-o-lith-o-nitht! you're a Bob-o-lith-o-nitht!" When he tried to kiss her, she scampered away, but soon reappeared again to renew the fun.

While this by-play was going on, a white servant came through the Deacon's grounds, and said to Tulee, "Mrs.

Robbem wants you to come to her immediately, and bring Laura."

" I must go now, darling," said Tulee, clasping Flora's hand with a warm pressure.

" Come again quickly," said Flora.

" As soon as I can," she replied, and hurried away with her little charge.

When Mr. Bright offered his hand to help Mrs. Blumenthal over the hedge, he burst into a hearty laugh. " Was n't it funny," said he, " to hear that baby calling us Bob-o-lith-o-niths? They begin education early down South. Before the summer is out she 'll be talking about the cuth o' Ham, and telling the story of Oneshimuth. But they 've found a mare's nest now, Mrs. Blumenthal. The Deacon will be writing to his Carolina friends how the Massachusetts ladies hug and kiss niggers."

Flora smiled as she answered : " I suppose it must seem strange to them, Mr. Bright. But the fact is, that black woman tended me when I was a child ; and I have n't seen her for twenty years."

As soon as she entered the house, she explained the scene to Mrs. Delano, and then said to her daughter : " Now, Rosen Blumen, you may leave your drawing and go to Aunt Rosa, and tell her I want to see her for something special, and she must come as soon as possible. Don't tell her anything more. You may stay and spend the day with Eulalia, if you like."

" How many mysteries and surprises we have," observed Mrs. Delano. " A dozen novels might be made out of your adventures."

The hasty summons found Mrs. King still melancholy with the thought that her newly found son could be no

more to her than a shadow. Glad to have her thoughts
turned in another direction, she sent Rosen Blumen to her
cousin, and immediately prepared to join her sister. Flora,
who was watching for her, ran out to the gate to meet her,
and before she entered the house announced that Tulee
was alive. The little that was known was soon communi-
cated, and they watched with the greatest anxiety for the
reappearance of Tulee. But the bright turban was seen no
more during the forenoon; and throughout the afternoon
no one but the Deacon and his gardener were visible about
the grounds. The hours of waiting were spent by the sisters and Mrs. Delano in a full explanation of the secret
history of Gerald Fitzgerald, and Mrs. King's consequent
depression of spirits. The evening wore away without any
tidings from Tulee. Between nine and ten o'clock they
heard the voice of the Deacon loud in prayer. Joe Bright,
who was passing the open window, stopped to say: " He
means his neighbors shall hear him, anyhow. I reckon he
thinks it 's a good investment for character. He's a cute
manager, the Deacon is ; and a quickster, too, according to
his own account ; for he told me when he made up his
mind to have religion, he was n't half an hour about it.
I 'd a mind to tell him I should think slave-trading religion
was a job done by contract, knocked up in a hurry."

"Mr. Bright," said Flora, in a low voice, "if you see
that colored woman, I wish you would speak to her, and
show her the way in."

The sisters sat talking over their affairs with their husbands, in low tones, listening anxiously meanwhile to every
sound. Mr. and Mrs. King were just saying they thought
it was best to return home, when Mr. Bright opened the
door and Tulee walked in. Of course, there was a general

exclaiming and embracing. There was no need of introducing the husbands, for Tulee remembered them both.
As soon as she could take breath, she said: "I've had *such*
a time to get here! I've been trying all day, and I could n't
get a chance, they kept such watch of me. At last, when
they was all abed and asleep, I crept down stairs softly,
and come out of the back door, and locked it after me."

"Come right up stairs with me," said Rosa. "I want to
speak to you." As soon as they were alone, she said,
"Tulee, where is the baby?"

"Don't know no more than the dead what's become of
the poor little picaninny," she replied. "After ye went
away, Missy Duroy's cousin, who was a sea-captain, brought
his baby with a black nurse to board there, because his
wife had died. I remembered how ye looked at me when ye
said, 'Take good care of the poor little baby.' And I did
try to take good care of him. I toted him about a bit out
doors whenever I could get a chance. One day, just as I
was going back into the house, a gentleman o' horseback
turned and looked at me. I did n't think anything about
it then; but the next day, he come to the house. and he
said I was Mr. Royal's slave, and that Mr. Fitzgerald
bought me. He wanted to know where ye was; and when
I told him ye'd gone over the sea with Madame and the
Signor, he cursed and swore, and said he'd been cheated.
When he went away, Missis Duroy said it was Mr. Bruteman. I did n't think there was much to be 'fraid of, 'cause
ye'd got away safe, and I had free papers, and the picaninny was too small to be sold. But I remembered ye
was always anxious about his being a slave, and I was a
little uneasy. One day when the sea-captain came to see
his baby, he was marking an anchor on his own arm with

a needle and some sort of black stuff; and he said 't would never come out. I thought if they should carry off yer picaninny, it would be more easy to find him again if he was marked. I told the captain I had heard ye call him Gerald; and he said he would mark G. F. on his arm. The poor little thing worried in his sleep while he was doing it, and Missis Duroy scolded at me for hurting him. The next week Massa Duroy was taken with yellow-fever; and then Missis Duroy was taken, and then the captain's baby and the black nurse. I was frighted, and tried to keep the picaninny out doors all I could. One day, when I'd gone a bit from the house, two men grabbed us and put us in a cart. When I screamed, they beat me, and swore at me for a runaway nigger. When I said I was free, they beat me more, and told me to shut up. They put us in the calaboose; and when I told 'em the picaninny belonged to a white lady, they laughed and said there was a great many white niggers. Mr. Bruteman come to see us, and he said we was his niggers. When I showed him my free paper, he said 't want good for anything, and tore it to pieces. O Missy Rosy, that was a dreadful dark time. The jailer's wife did n't seem so hard-hearted as the rest. I showed her the mark on the picaninny's arm, and gave her one of the little shirts ye embroidered; and I told her if they sold me away from him, a white lady would send for him. They did sell me, Missy Rosy. Mr. Robbem, a Caroliny slave-trader bought me, and he's my massa now. I don't know what they did with the picaninny. I did n't know how to write, and I did n't know where ye was. I was always hoping ye would come for me some time; and at last I thought ye must be dead."

"Poor Tulee," said Rosa. "They wrote that Mr. and

Mrs. Duroy and the black woman and the white baby all died of yellow-fever; and we did n't know there was any other black woman there. I 've sent to New Orleans, and I 've been there; and many a cry I 've had, because we could n't find you. But your troubles are all over now. You shall come and live with us."

"But I 'm Mr. Robbem's slave," replied Tulee.

"No, you are not," answered Rosa. "You became free the moment they brought you to Massachusetts."

"Is it really so?" said Tulee, brightening up in look and tone. Then, with a sudden sadness, she added: "I 've got three chil'ren in Carolina. They 've sold two on 'em; but they 've left me my little Benny, eight years old. They would n't have brought me here, if they had n't known Benny would pull me back."

"We 'll buy your children," said Rosa.

"Bless ye, Missy Rosy!" she exclaimed. "Ye 's got the same kind heart ye always had. How glad I am to see ye all so happy!"

"O Tulee!" groaned Rosa, "I can never be happy till that poor little baby is found. I 've no doubt that wicked Bruteman sold him." She covered her face with her hands, and the tears trickled through her fingers.

"The Lord comfort ye!" said Tulee, "I did all I could for yer poor little picaninny."

"I know you did, Tulee," she replied. "But I am *so* sorry Madame did n't take you with us! When she told me she had left you, I was afraid something bad would happen; and I would have gone back for you if I could. But it is too late to talk any more now. Mr. King is waiting for me to go home. Why can't you go with us to-night?"

"I must go back," rejoined Tulee. "I've got the key with me, and I left the picaninny asleep in my bed. I'll come again to-morrow night, if I can."

"Don't say if you can, Tulee," replied Mrs. King. "Remember you are not a slave here. You can walk away at mid-day, and tell them you are going to live with us."

"They'd lock me up and send me back to Caroliny, if I told 'em so," said Tulee. "But I'll come, Missy Rosy."

Rosa kissed the dark cheek she had so often kissed when they were children together, and they parted for the night.

The next day and the next night passed without a visit from Tulee. Mr. and Mrs. Bright, who entered into the affair with the liveliest interest, expressed the opinion that she had been spirited away and sent South. The sisters began to entertain a similar fear; and it was decided that their husbands should call with them the following morning, to have a talk with Mr. and Mrs. Robbem. But not long after breakfast, Tulee stole into the back door with the cherub in her arms.

"O Missy Flory," said she, "I tried to get here last night. But Missis Robbem takes a heap o' care o' me." She said this with a mischievous smile. "When we was at the Astor House, she locked up my clothes in her room, 'cause New York was such a dreadful wicked place, she was 'fraid they'd be stole; and she never let me out o' her sight, for fear the colored waiters in the hotel would be impudent to me. Last night she sent me away up into the cupola to sleep, 'cause she said I could have more room there. And when I'd got the picaninny asleep, and was watching for a chance to steal away, she come all the way up there very softly, and said she'd brought me some hot drink, 'cause I did n't seem to be well. Then she begun to

advise me not to go near the next house. She told me
Abolitionists was very bad people ; that they pretended to
be great friends to colored folks, but all they wanted was
to steal 'em and sell 'em to the West Indies. I told her I
did n't know nothing 'bout Abolitionists ; that the lady I
was hugging and kissing was a New Orleans lady that
I used to wait upon when we was picaninnies. She said
if you had the feelings Southern ladies ought to have, you
would n't be boarding with Abolitionists. When she went
down stairs I did n't dare to come here, for fear she 'd come
up again with some more hot drink. This morning she
told me to walk up street with the picaninny ; and she
watched me till I was out o' sight. But I went round and
round and got over a fence, and come through Massa
Bright's barn."

Mr. and Mrs. King came in as she was speaking ; and
she turned to them, saying anxiously, "Do you think,
Massa, if I don't go back with 'em, they 'll let me have my
chil'ren ? "

" Don't call me Massa," replied Mr. King, " I dislike the
sound of it. Speak to me as other people do. I have no
doubt we shall manage it so that you will have your children. I will lead home this pretty little Tot, and tell them
you are going to stay with us."

With bonbons and funny talk he gained the favor of
Tot, so that she consented to walk with him. Tulee often
applied her apron to her eyes, as she watched the little
creature holding by his finger, and stepping along in childish fashion, turning her toes inward. When she disappeared through the Deacon's front door, she sat down and
cried outright. " I love that little picaninny," sobbed she.
" I 've tended her ever since she was born ; and I love her.

She 'll cry for Tulee. But I does want to be free, and I does want to live with ye, Missy Rosy and Missy Flory."

Mrs. Robbem met Mr. King as soon as he entered her father's door, and said in a tone of stern surprise, " Where is my servant, sir?"

He bowed and answered, " If you will allow me to walk in for a few moments, I will explain my errand." As soon as they were seated he said : " I came to inform you that Tulee does not wish to go back to Carolina ; and that by the laws of Massachusetts she has a perfect right to remain here."

" She 's an ungrateful wench !" exclaimed Mrs. Robbem. " She 's always been treated kindly, and she would n't have thought of taking such a step, if she had n't been put up to it by meddlesome Abolitionists, who are always interfering with gentlemen's servants."

" The simple fact is," rejoined Mr. King, " Tulee used to be the playmate and attendant of my wife when both of them were children. They lived together many years, and are strongly attached to each other."

" If your wife is a Southern lady," replied Mrs. Robbem, " she ought to be above such a mean Yankee trick as stealing my servant from me."

Her husband entered at that moment, and the visitor rose and bowed as he said, " Mr. Robbem, I presume."

He lowered his head somewhat stiffly in reply ; and his wife hastened to say, " The Abolitionists have been decoying Tulee away from us."

Mr. King repeated the explanation he had already made.

" I thought the wench had more feeling," replied Mr. Robbem. " She left children in Carolina. But the fact is, niggers have no more feeling for their young than so many pigs."

"I judge differently," rejoined Mr. King; "and my principal motive for calling was to speak to you about those children. I wish to purchase them for Tulee."

"She shall never have them, sir!" exclaimed the slave-trader, fiercely. "And as for you Abolitionists, all I wish is that we had you down South."

"Differences of opinion must be allowed in a free country," replied Mr. King. "I consider slavery a bad institution, injurious to the South, and to the whole country. But I did not come here to discuss that subject. I simply wish to make a plain business statement to you. Tulee chooses to take her freedom, and any court in Massachusetts will decide that she has a right to take it. But, out of gratitude for services she has rendered my wife, I am willing to make you gratuitous compensation, provided you will enable me to buy all her children. Will you name your terms now, or shall I call again?"

"She shall never have her children," repeated Mr. Robbem; "she has nobody but herself and the Abolitionists to blame for it."

"I will, however, call again, after you have thought of it more calmly," said Mr. King. "Good morning, sir; good morning, madam."

His salutations were silently returned with cold, stiff bows.

A second and third attempt was made with no better success. Tulee grew very uneasy. "They'll sell my Benny," said she. "Ye see they ain't got any heart, 'cause they's used to selling picaninnies."

"What, does this Mr. Robbem carry on the Deacon's old business?" inquired Mr. Bright.

"Yes, Massa," replied Tulee. "Two years ago, Massa Stillham come down to Caroliny to spend the winter, and he was round in the slave-pen as brisk as Massa Robbem, counting the niggers, and telling how many dollars they ought to sell for. He had a dreadful bad fever while he was down there, and I nursed him. He was out of his head half the time, and he was calling out: ‘Going! going! How much for this likely nigger? Stop that wench's squalling for her brat! Carry the brat off!’ It was dreadful to hear him."

"I suppose he calculated upon going to heaven if he died," rejoined Mr. Bright; "and if he 'd gone into the kingdom with such words in his mouth, it would have been a heavenly song for the four-and-twenty elders to accompany with their golden harps."

"They 'll sell my Benny," groaned Tulee; "and then I shall never see him again."

"I have no doubt Mr. King will obtain your children," replied Mr. Bright; "and you should remember that, if you go back South, just as likely as not they will sell him where you will never see him or hear from him."

"I know it, Massa, I know it," answered she.

"I am not your master," rejoined he. "I allow no man to call me master, and certainly not any woman; though I don't belong to the chivalry."

His prediction proved true. The Deacon and his son-in-law held frequent consultations. "This Mr. King is rich as Crœsus," said the Deacon; "and if he thinks his wife owes a debt to Tulee, he 'll be willing to give a round sum for her children. I reckon you can make a better bargain with him than you could in the New Orleans market."

"Do you suppose he 'd give five thousand dollars for the young niggers?" inquired the trader.

"Try him," said the Deacon.

The final result was that the sum was deposited by Mr. King, to be paid over whenever Tulee's children made their appearance; and in due time they all arrived. Tulee was full of joy and gratitude; but Mr. Bright always maintained it was a sin and a shame to pay slave-traders so much for what never belonged to them.

Of course there were endless questions to be asked and answered between the sisters and their faithful servant; but all she could tell threw no further light on the destiny of the little changeling whom she supposed to be Rosa's own child. In the course of these private conversations, it came out that she herself had suffered, as all women must suffer, who have the feelings of human beings, and the treatment of animals. But her own humble little episode of love and separation, of sorrow and shame, was whispered only to Missy Rosy and Missy Flory.

CHAPTER XXXIII.

THE probability that the lost child was alive and in slavery was a very serious complication of existing difficulties. Thinking it prudent to prepare Gerald's mind for any contingencies that might occur, Mr. King proceeded immediately to Boston to have a conference with him. The young man received the news with unexpected composure.

"It will annoy Lily-mother very much," said he, "and on that account I regret it; but so far as I am myself concerned, it would in some respects be a relief to me to get out of the false position in which I find myself. Grandfather Bell has always grumbled about the expense I have been to him in consequence of my father's loss of fortune, and of course that adds to the unpleasantness of feeling that I am practising a fraud upon him. He is just now peculiarly vexed with me for leaving Northampton so suddenly. He considers it an unaccountable caprice of mine, and reproaches me with letting Eulalia slip through my fingers, as he expresses it. Of course, he has no idea how it cuts me. This state of things is producing a great change in my views. My prevailing wish now is to obtain an independent position by my own exertions, and thus be free to become familiar with my new self. At present, I feel as if there were two of me, and that one was an impostor." ·

"I heartily approve of your wish to rely upon your own resources," replied Mr. King; "and I will gladly assist you to accomplish it. I have already said you should be to me as a son, and I stand by my word; but I advise

you, as I would an own son, to devote yourself assiduously
to some business, profession, or art. Never be a gentleman
of leisure. It is the worst possible calling a man can have.
Nothing but stagnation of faculties and weariness of soul
comes of it. But we will talk about *your* plans hereafter.
The urgent business of the present moment is to obtain
some clew to your missing brother. My conscientious wife
will suffer continual anxiety till he is found. I must go to
New Orleans and seek out Mr. Bruteman, to ascertain
whether he has sold him."

"Bruteman!" exclaimed the young man, with sudden
interest. "Was he the one who seized that negro woman
and the child?"

"Yes," rejoined Mr. King. "But why does that excite
your interest?"

"I am almost ashamed to tell you," replied Gerald.
"But you know I was educated in the prejudices of my
father and grandfather. It was natural that I should be
proud of being the son of a slaveholder, that I should despise the colored race, and consider abolition a very vulgar
fanaticism. But the recent discovery that I was myself
born a slave has put me upon my thoughts, and made me a
little uneasy about a transaction in which I was concerned.
The afternoon preceding Mrs. Green's splendid ball, where I
first saw my beautiful Rose-mother, two fugitive slaves arrived here in one of grandfather's ships called 'The King
Cotton.' Mr. Bruteman telegraphed to grandfather about
them, and the next morning he sent me to tell Captain Kane
to send the slaves down to the islands in the harbor, and
keep them under guard till a vessel passed that would take
them back to New Orleans. I did his errand, without be-
stowing upon the subjects of it any more thought or care

than I should have done upon two bales of cotton. At parting, Captain Kane said to me, ' By George, Mr. Fitzgerald, one of these fellows looks so much like you, that, if you were a little tanned by exposure to the sun, I should n't know you apart.' ' That's flattering,' replied I, ' to be compared to a negro.' And I hurried away, being impatient to make an early call upon your lady at the Revere House. I don't suppose I should ever have thought of it again, if your present conversation had not brought it to my mind."

" Do you know whether Mr. Bruteman sold those slaves after they were sent back ? " inquired Mr. King.

" There is one fact connected with the affair which I will tell you, if you promise not to mention it," replied the young man. " The Abolitionists annoyed grandfather a good deal about those runaways, and he is nervously sensitive lest they should get hold of it, and publish it in their papers." Having received the desired promise, he went on to say : " Those slaves were mortgaged to grandfather, and he sent orders to have them immediately sold. I presume Mr. Bruteman managed the transaction, for they were his slaves ; but I don't know whether he reported the name of the purchaser. He died two months ago, leaving his affairs a good deal involved ; and I heard that some distant connections in Mississippi were his heirs."

" Where can I find Captain Kane ? " inquired Mr. King.

" He sailed for Calcutta a fortnight ago," rejoined Gerald.

" Then there is no other resource but to go to New Orleans, as soon as the weather will permit," was the reply.

" I honor your zeal," said the young man. " I wish my own record was clean on the subject. Since I have taken

the case home to myself, I have felt that it was mean and
wrong to send back fugitives from slavery ; but it becomes
painful, when I think of the possibility of having helped to
send back my own brother, — and one, too, whom I have
supplanted in his birthright."

*   *   *   *   *

When Mr. King returned to Northampton, the information he had obtained sent a new pang to the heart of his
wife. " Then he *is* a slave ! " she exclaimed. " And
while the poor fellow was being bound and sent back to
slavery, I was dancing and receiving homage. Verily the
Furies do pursue me. Do you think it is necessary to tell
Mrs. Fitzgerald of this ? "

" In a reverse of cases, I think you would feel that you
ought to be informed of everything," he replied. " But I
will save you from that portion of the pain. It was most
fitting that a woman should make the first part of the disclosure ; but this new light on the subject can be as well
revealed by myself."

" Always kind and considerate," she said. " This news
will be peculiarly annoying to her, and perhaps she will receive it better from you than from me ; for I can see that I
have lost her favor. But you have taught me that it is of
more consequence to *deserve* favor than to *have* it ; and I
shall do my utmost to deserve a kindly estimate from her."

" I confess I am somewhat puzzled by this tangle," rejoined her husband. " But where there is both the will
and the means to repair a wrong, it will be strange if a
way cannot be found."

" I would like to sell my diamonds, and all my other expensive ornaments, to buy that young man," said she.

" That you can do, if it will be any gratification to you,"

he replied; "but the few thousands I have invested in
jewels for you would go but little way toward the full
remuneration I intend to make, if he can be found. We
will send the young people out of the way this evening,
and lay the case before a family council of the elders. I
should like to consult Blumenthal. I have never known a
man whose natural instincts were so true as his; and his
entire freedom from conventional prejudices reminds me
of my good father. I have great reliance also on Mrs.
Delano's delicate perceptions and quiet good sense. And
our lively little Flora, though she jumps to her conclu-
sions, always jumps in a straight line, and usually hits the
point."

As soon as the council was convened, and the subject introduced, Mrs. Blumenthal exclaimed: "Why, Florimond,
those slaves in 'The King Cotton' were the ones you and
Mr. Goldwin tried so hard to help them find."

"Yes," rejoined he; "I caught a hasty glimpse of one
of the poor fellows just as they were seizing him with the
cry of 'Stop thief!' and his Italian look reminded me so
forcibly of the danger Flora was once in, that I was extremely troubled about him after I heard he was a slave.
As I recall him to my mind, I do think he resembled young
Fitzgerald. Mr. Percival might perhaps throw some light
on the subject; for he was unwearied in his efforts to rescue
those fugitives. He already knows Flora's history."

"I should like to have you go to Boston with me and
introduce me to him," said Mr. King.

"That I will do," answered Blumenthal. "I think both
Mr. Bell and Mrs. Fitzgerald would prefer to have it all
sink into unquestioned oblivion; but that does not change
our duty with regard to the poor fellow."

"Do you think they ought to be informed of the present circumstances?" inquired Mr. King.

"If I were in their position, I should think I ought to know all the particulars," replied he; "and the golden rule is as good as it is simple."

"Mrs. Fitzgerald has great dread of her father's knowing anything about it," responded Rosa; "and I have an earnest desire to spare her pain as far as possible. It seems as if she had a right to judge in the premises."

Mrs. Delano took Mr. Blumenthal's view of the subject, and it was decided to leave that point for further consideration. Flora suggested that some difficulties might be removed by at once informing Eulalia that Gerald was her brother. But Mrs. Delano answered: "Some difficulties might be avoided for ourselves by that process; but the good of the young people is a paramount consideration. You know none of them are aware of all the antecedents in their family history, and it seems to me best that they should not know them till their characters are fully formed. I should have no objection to telling them of their colored ancestry, if it did not involve a knowledge of laws and customs and experiences growing out of slavery, which might, at this early age, prove unsettling to their principles. Anything that mystifies moral perceptions is not so easily removed from youthful minds as breath is wiped from a mirror."

"I have that feeling very deeply fixed with regard to our Eulalia," observed Mr. King; "and I really see no need of agitating their young, unconscious minds with subjects they are too inexperienced to understand. I will have a talk with Mrs. Fitzgerald, and then proceed to Boston."

17   Y

Mrs. Fitzgerald received the announcement with much less equanimity than she had manifested on a former occasion. Though habitually polite, she said very abruptly: "I was in hopes I should never be troubled any more with this vulgar subject. Since Mrs. King saw fit to change the children, let her take care of the one she has chosen. Of course, it would be very disagreeable to me to have a son who had been brought up among slaves. If I wished to make his acquaintance, I could not do it without exciting a great deal of remark; and there has already been too much talk about my husband's affairs. But I have no wish to see him. I have educated a son to my own liking, and everybody says he is an elegant young man. If you would cease from telling me that there is a stain in his blood, I should never be reminded of it."

"We thought it right to inform you of everything," rejoined Mr. King, "and leave you to decide what was to be done."

"Then, once for all," said she, "please leave Gerald and me in peace; and do what you choose about the other one. We have had sufficient annoyance already; and I never wish to hear the subject mentioned again."

"I accept your decision," replied Mr. King. "If the unfortunate young man can be found, I will educate him and establish him in business, and do the same for him in all respects that you would have done if he had been your acknowledged heir."

"And keep him at a distance from me," said the perturbed lady; "for if he resembles Gerald so strongly, it would of course give rise to unpleasant inquiries and remarks."

The gentleman bowed, wished her good morning, and

departed, thinking what he had heard was a strange com-
mentary on natural instincts.

Mr. Percival was of course greatly surprised and excited
when he learned the relation which one of the fugitives
in "The King Cotton" bore to Mr. Bell. "We hear a
good deal about poetical justice," said he; "but one rarely
sees it meted out in this world. The hardness of the old
merchant when Mr. Jackson and I called upon him was a
thing to be remembered. He indorsed, with warm approbation, the declaration of the reverend gentleman who professed his willingness to send his mother or brother into
slavery, if the laws of the United States required it."

"If our friend Mr. Bright was with us, he would say the
Lord took him at his word," rejoined Mr. Blumenthal,
smiling.

An earnest discussion ensued concerning the possibilities
of the case, and several days were spent in active investi-
gation. But all the additional light obtained was from a
sailor, who had been one of the boat's crew that conveyed
the fugitives to the islands in the harbor; and all he could
tell was that he heard them call each other George and
Henry. When he was shown a colored photograph, which
Gerald had just had taken for his Rose-mother, he at once
said that was the one named George.

"This poor fellow must be rescued," said Mr. King, after
they returned from their unsatisfactory conference with the
sailor. "Mr. Bell may know who purchased him, and a
conversation with him seems to be the only alternative."

"Judging by my own experience, your task is not to be
envied," rejoined Mr. Percival. "He will be in a tremen-
dous rage. But perhaps the lesson will do him good. I
remember Francis Jackson said at the time, that if his

dark-complexioned grandson should be sent into slavery, it might bring him to a realizing sense of the state of things he was doing his utmost to encourage."

The undertaking did indeed seem more formidable to Mr. King than anything he had yet encountered; but true to his sense of duty he resolved to go bravely through with it.

CHAPTER XXXIV.

THE old merchant received Mr. King with marked politeness; for though he suspected him of anti-slavery proclivities, and despised him for that weakness, he had great respect for a man whose name was as good as gold, and who was the father of such an eligible match as Eulalia.

After some discursive conversation, Mr. King said, " I am desirous to tell you a short story, if you will have patience to listen to it."

" Certainly, sir," replied the old gentleman.

His visitor accordingly began by telling of Mr. Royal's having formed one of those quadroon alliances so common in New Orleans; of his having died insolvent; and of his two handsome octoroon daughters having been claimed as slaves by his creditors.

" What the deuce do you suppose I care about his octoroon daughters?" interrupted Mr. Bell, impatiently. " I was n't one of his creditors."

" Perhaps you will take some interest in it," rejoined Mr. King, "when I tell you that the eldest of them was married to Mr. Gerald Fitzgerald of Savannah, and that she is still living."

" Do you mean the Mr. Fitzgerald who married my daughter Lily?" inquired he.

" I do mean him," was the response.

" It 's false," vociferated Mr. Bell, growing almost purple in the face.

"No, sir, it is not false," replied Mr. King. "But you need not be so much excited. The first marriage did not render the second illegal; first, because a sham ceremony was performed to deceive the inexperienced girl; and secondly, because, according to the laws of the South, any marriage with a slave, however sanctified by religious forms, is utterly void in law."

"I consider such a law a very wise provision," replied the merchant. "It is necessary to prevent the inferior race from being put on an equality with their superiors. The negroes were made to be servants, sir. *You* may be an advocate for amalgamation, but I am not."

"I would simply ask you to observe that the law you so much approve is not a preventive of amalgamation. Mr. Fitzgerald married the daughter of the quadroon. The only effect of the law was to deprive her of a legal right to his support and protection, and to prevent her son from receiving any share of his father's property. By another Southern law, that 'the child shall follow the condition of the mother,' her son became a slave."

"Well, sir, what interest do you suppose I can take in all this?" interrupted the merchant. "It's nothing to me, sir. The South is competent to make her own laws."

Mr. King begged his attention a little longer. He then proceeded to tell how Mr. Fitzgerald had treated the octoroon, at the time of his marriage with Miss Bell; that he had subsequently sold her to a very base man, in payment of a debt; that she, terrified and bewildered by the prospect of such a fate, had, in a moment of frantic revenge, changed her babe for his daughter's; and that consequently the Gerald he had been educating as his grandson was in fact the son of the octoroon, and born a slave.

"Really, sir," said Mr. Bell, with a satirical smile, "that story might sell for something to a writer of sensation novels; but I should hardly have expected to hear it from a sensible gentleman like yourself. Pray, on whose testimony do you expect me to believe such an improbable fiction?"

"On that of the mother herself," replied Mr. King.

With a very contemptuous curl of his lip, Mr. Bell answered: "And you really suppose, do you, that I can be induced to disinherit my grandson on the testimony of a colored woman? Not I, sir. Thank God, I am not infected with this negro mania."

"But you have not asked who the woman is," rejoined Mr. King; "and without knowing that, you cannot judge candidly of the value of her testimony."

"I don't ask, because I don't care," replied the merchant. "The negroes are a lying set, sir; and I am no Abolitionist, that I should go about retailing their lies."

Mr. King looked at him an instant, and then answered, very calmly: "The mother of that babe, whose word you treat so contemptuously, is Mrs. King, my beloved and honored wife."

The old merchant was startled from his propriety; and, forgetful of the gout in his feet, he sprung from his chair, exclaiming, "The Devil!"

Mr. King, without noticing the abrupt exclamation, went on to relate in detail the manner of his first introduction to Miss Royal, his compassion for her subsequent misfortunes, his many reasons for believing her a pure and noble woman, and the circumstances which finally led to their marriage. He expressed his conviction that the children had been changed in a fit of temporary insanity, and dwelt much on

his wife's exceeding anxiety to atone for the wrong, as far
as possible. "I was ignorant of the circumstance," said he,
"until the increasing attraction between Gerald and Eulalia made an avowal necessary. It gives me great pain to
tell you all this; but I thought that, under a reverse of circumstances, I should myself prefer to know the facts. I
am desirous to do my utmost to repair the mischief done by
a deserted and friendless woman, at a moment when she
was crazed by distress and terror; a woman, too, whose
character I have abundant reason to love and honor. If
you choose to disinherit Gerald, I will provide for his future as if he were my own son; and I will repay with interest all the expense you have incurred for him. I hope
that this affair may be kept secret from the world, and that
we may amicably settle it, in such a way that no one will
be materially injured."

Somewhat mollified by this proposal, the old gentleman
inquired in a milder tone, "And where is the young man
who you say is my daughter's son?"

"Until very recently he was supposed to be dead," rejoined Mr. King; "and unfortunately that circumstance led
my wife to think there was no need of speaking to me concerning this affair at the time of our marriage. But we
now have reason to think he may be living; and that is
why I have particularly felt it my duty to make this unpleasant revelation." After repeating Tulee's story, he said,
"You probably have not forgotten that last winter two slaves
escaped to Boston in your ship 'The King Cotton'?"

The old merchant started as if he had been shot.

"Try not to be agitated," said Mr. King. "If we keep
calm, and assist each other, we may perhaps extricate ourselves from this disagreeable dilemma, without any very

disastrous results. I have but one reason for thinking it possible there may be some connection between the lost babe and one of the slaves whom you sent back to his claimant. The two babes were very nearly of an age, and so much alike that the exchange passed unnoticed; and the captain of 'The King Cotton' told Gerald that the eldest of those slaves resembled him so much that he should not know them apart."

Mr. Bell covered his face and uttered a deep groan. Such distress in an old man powerfully excited Mr. King's sympathy; and moving near to him, he placed his hand on his and said: "Don't be so much troubled, sir. This is a bad affair, but I think it can be so managed as to do no very serious harm. My motive in coming to you at this time is to ascertain whether you can furnish me with any clew to that young man. I will myself go in search of him, and I will take him to Europe and have him educated in a manner suitable to his condition, as your descendant and the heir of your property."

The drawn expression of the old merchant's mouth was something painful to witness. It seemed as if every nerve was pulled to its utmost tension by the excitement in his soul. He obviously had to make a strong effort to speak when he said, "Do you suppose, sir, that a merchant of my standing is going to leave his property to negroes?"

"You forget that this young man is pure Anglo-Saxon," replied Mr. King.

"I tell you, sir," rejoined Mr. Bell, "that the mulatto who was with him was his wife; and if he is proved to be my grandson, I'll never see him, nor have anything to do with him, unless he gives her up; not if you educate him with the Prince Royal of France or England. A pretty

17 *

dilemma you have placed me in, sir. My property, it seems, must either go to Gerald, who you say has negro blood in his veins, or to this other fellow, who is a slave with a negro wife."

"But she could be educated in Europe also," pleaded Mr. King; "and I could establish him permanently in lucrative business abroad. By this arrangement —"

"Go to the Devil with your arrangements!" interrupted the merchant, losing all command of himself. "If you expect to arrange a pack of mulatto heirs for *me*, you are mistaken, sir."

He rose up and struck his chair upon the floor with a vengeance, and his face was purple with rage, as he vociferated: "I'll have legal redress for this, sir. I'll expose your wife, sir. I'll lay my damages at a million, sir."

Mr. King bowed and said, "I will see you again when you are more calm."

As he went out, he heard Mr. Bell striding across the room and thrashing the furniture about. "Poor old gentleman!" thought he. "I hope I shall succeed in convincing him how little I value money in comparison with righting this wrong, as far as possible. Alas! it would never have taken place had there not been a great antecedent wrong; and that again grew out of the monstrous evil of slavery."

He had said to the old merchant, "I will see you again when you are calmer." And when he saw him again, he was indeed calm, for he had died suddenly, of a fit produced by violent excitement.

CHAPTER XXXV.

A FEW weeks after the funeral of Mr. Bell, Gerald wrote the following letter to Mr. King: —

"My honored and dear Friend, — Lily-mother has decided to go to Europe this fall, that I may have certain educational advantages which she has planned for me. That is the only reason she assigns; but she is evidently nervous about your investigations, and I think a wish to be out of the country for the present has had some effect in producing this decision. I have not sought to influence her concerning this, or the other important point you wot of. My desire is to conform to her wishes, and promote her happiness in any way she chooses. This it is my duty as well as my pleasure to do. She intends to remain in Europe a year, perhaps longer. I wish very much to see you all; and Eulalia might well consider me a very impolite acquaintance, if I should go without saying good by. If you do not return to Boston before we sail, I will, with your permission, make a short call upon you in Northampton. I thank Rose-mother for her likeness. It will be very precious to me. I wish you would add your own and another; for wherever my lot may be cast, you three will always be among my dearest memories."

"I am glad of this arrangement," said Mr. King. "At their age, I hope a year of separation will prove sufficient."

The Rose-mother covered the wound in her heart, and answered, "Yes, it is best." But the constrained tone of the letter pained her, and excited her mind to that most unsatisfactory of all occupations, the thinking over what might have been. She had visions of her first-born son, as he lay by her side a few hours before Chloe carried him away from her sight; and then there rose before her the fair face of that other son, whose pretty little body was passing into the roses of Provence. Both of them had gone out of her life. Of one she received no tidings from the mysterious world of spirits; while the other was walking within her vision, as a shadow, the reality of which was intangible.

Mr. King returned to Boston with his family in season for Gerald to make the proposed call before he sailed. There was a little heightening of color when he and Eulalia met, but he had drilled himself to perform the part of a polite acquaintance; and as she thought she had been rather negligently treated of late, she was cased in the armor of maidenly reserve.

Both Mr. and Mrs. King felt it to be an arduous duty to call on Mrs. Fitzgerald. That lady, though she respected their conscientiousness, could not help disliking them. They had disturbed her relations with Gerald, by suggesting the idea of another claim upon his affections; and they had offended her pride by introducing the vulgar phantom of a slave son to haunt her imagination. She was continually jealous of Mrs. King; so jealous, that Gerald never ventured to show her the likeness of his Rose-mother. But though the discerning eyes of Mr. and Mrs. King read this in the very excess of her polite demonstrations, other visitors who were present when they called supposed them to be her dearest friends, and envied her the distinguished intimacy.

Such formal attempts at intercourse only increased the cravings of Rosa's heart, and Mr. King requested Gerald to grant her a private interview. Inexpressibly precious were these few stolen moments, when she could venture to call him son, and hear him call her mother. He brought her an enamelled locket containing some of his hair, inscribed with the word "Gerald"; and she told him that to the day of her death she would always wear it next her heart. He opened a small morocco case, on the velvet lining of which lay a lily of delicate silver filigree.

"Here is a little souvenir for Eulalia," said he.

Her eyes moistened as she replied, "I fear it would not be prudent, my son."

He averted his face as he answered: "Then give it to her in my mother's name. It will be pleasant to me to think that my sister is wearing it."

*　　*　　*　　*　　*

A few days after Gerald had sailed for Europe, Mr. King started for New Orleans, taking with him his wife and daughter. An auctioneer was found, who said he had sold to a gentleman in Natchez a runaway slave named Bob Bruteman, who strongly resembled the likeness of Gerald. They proceeded to Natchez and had an interview with the purchaser, who recognized a likeness between his slave Bob and the picture of Gerald. He said he had made a bad bargain of it, for the fellow was intelligent and artful, and had escaped from him two months ago. In answer to his queries, Mr. King stated that, if Bob was the one he supposed, he was a white man, and had friends who wished to redeem him; but as the master had obtained no clew to the runaway, he could of course give none. So their long journey produced no result, except the satisfaction of thinking that the object of their interest had escaped from slavery.

It had been their intention to spend the coldest months at the South, but a volcano had flared up all of a sudden at Harper's Ferry, and boiling lava was rolling all over the land. Every Northern man who visited the South was eyed suspiciously, as a possible emissary of John Brown ; and the fact that Mr. King was seeking to redeem a runaway slave was far from increasing confidence in him. Finding that silence was unsatisfactory, and that he must either indorse slavery or be liable to perpetual provocations to quarrel, he wrote to Mr. Blumenthal to have their house in readiness for their return ; an arrangement which Flora and her children hailed with merry shouts and clapping of hands.

When they arrived, they found their house as warm as June, with Flora and her family there to receive them, backed by a small army of servants, consisting of Tulee, with her tall son and daughter, and little Benny, and Tom and Chloe ; all of whom had places provided for them, either in the household or in Mr. King's commercial establishment. Their tropical exuberance of welcome made him smile. When the hearty hand-shakings were over, he said to his wife, as they passed into the parlor, " It really seemed as if we were landing on the coast of Guinea with a cargo of beads."

" O Alfred," rejoined she, " I am so grateful to you for employing them all ! You don't know, and never *can* know, how I feel toward these dusky friends ; for you never had them watch over you, day after day, and night after night, patiently and tenderly leading you up from the valley of the shadow of death."

He pressed her hand affectionately, and said, " Inasmuch as they did it for you, darling, they did it for me."

This sentiment was wrought into their daily deportment to their servants ; and the result was an harmonious relation between employer and employed, which it was beautiful to witness. But there are skeletons hidden away in the happiest households. Mrs. King had hers, and Tom and Chloe had theirs. The death of Mr. Bell and the absence of Mrs. Fitzgerald left no one in Boston who would be likely to recognize them ; but they knew that the Fugitive Slave Act was still in force, and though they relied upon Mr. King's generosity in case of emergency, they had an uncomfortable feeling of not being free. It was not so with Tulee. She had got beyond Mount Pisgah into the Canaan of freedom ; and her happiness was unalloyed. Mr. King, though kind and liberal to all, regarded her with especial favor, on account of old associations. The golden hoops had been taken from her ears when she was in the calaboose ; but he had presented her with another pair, for he liked to have her look as she did when she opened for him that door in New Orleans, which had proved an entrance to the temple and palace of his life. She felt herself to be a sort of prime minister in the small kingdom, and began to deport herself as one having authority. No empress ever had more satisfaction in a royal heir than she had in watching her Benny trudging to school, with his spelling-book slung over his shoulder, in a green satchel Mrs. King had made for him. The stylishness of the establishment was also a great source of pride to her ; and she often remarked in the kitchen that she had always said gold was none too good for Missy Rosy to walk upon. Apart **from** this consideration, she herself had an Oriental

delight in things that were lustrous and gayly colored.
Tom had learned to read quite fluently, and was accustomed to edify his household companions with chapters
from the Bible on Sunday evenings. The descriptions of
King Solomon's splendor made a lively impression on Tulee's mind. When she dusted the spacious parlors, she
looked admiringly at the large mirrors, the gilded circles
of gas lights, and the great pictures framed in crimson and
gold, and thought that the Temple of Solomon could not
have been more grand. She could scarcely believe Mrs.
Delano was wealthy. "She's a beautiful lady," said she
to Flora; "but if she's got plenty o' money, what makes
her dress so innocent and dull? There's Missy Rosy
now, when *she*'s dressed for company, she looks like the
Queen of Shebee."

One morning Tulee awoke to look out upon a scene
entirely new to her Southern eyes, and far surpassing
anything she had imagined of the splendor of Solomon's
Temple. On the evening previous, the air had been full
of mist, which, as it grew colder, had settled on the trees
of the Common, covering every little twig with a panoply
of ice. A very light snow had fallen softly during the
night, and sprinkled the ice with a feathery fleece. The
trees, in this delicate white vesture, standing up against a
dark blue sky, looked like the glorified spirits of trees.
Here and there, the sun touched them, and dropped a
shower of diamonds. Tulee gazed a moment in delighted
astonishment, and ran to call Chloe, who exclaimed, "They
looks like great white angels, and Ise feared they'll fly
away 'fore Missis gits up."

Tulee was very impatient for the sound of Mrs. King's
bell, and as soon as the first tinkle was heard she rushed

into her dressing-room, exclaiming, "O, do come to the window, Missy Rosy! Sure this is silver land."

Rosa was no less surprised when she looked out upon that wonderful vision of the earth, in its transfigured raiment of snow-glory. "Why. Tulee," said she, "it is diamond land. I've seen splendid fairy scenes in the theatres of Paris, but never anything so brilliant as this."

"I used to think the woods down South, all covered with jess'mines, was the beautifullest thing," responded Tulee; "but, Lors, Missy Rosy, this is as much handsomer as Solomon's Temple was handsomer than a meetin'-house."

But neither the indoor nor the outdoor splendor, nor all the personal comforts they enjoyed, made this favored band of colored people forgetful of the brethren they had left in bondage. Every word about John Brown was sought for and read with avidity. When he was first taken captive, Chloe said: "The angel that let Peter out o' prison ha' n't growed old an' hard o' hearing. If we prays loud enough, he 'll go and open the doors for old John Brown."

Certainly, it was not for want of the colored people's praying loud and long enough, that the prisoner was not supernaturally delivered. They did not relinquish the hope till the 2d of December : and when that sad day arrived, they assembled in their meeting-house to watch and pray. All was silent, except now and then an occasional groan, till the hands of the clock pointed to the moment of the martyr's exit from this world. Then Tom poured forth his soul in a mighty voice of prayer, ending with the agonized entreaty, "O Lord, thou hast taken away our Moses. Raise us up a Joshua!" And all cried, "Amen!"

Chloe, who had faith that could walk the stormiest waves, spoke words of fervent cheer to the weeping con

z

gregation. " I tell ye they ha'n't killed old John Brown," said she; " 'cause they *could n't* kill him. The angel that opened the prison doors for Peter has let him out, and sent him abroad in a different way from what we 'spected ; that 's all."

CHAPTER XXXVI.

THROUGH the following year, the political sky grew ever darker with impending clouds, crinkled with lightning, and vocal with growlings of approaching thunder. The North continued to make servile concessions, which history will blush to record; but they proved unavailing. The arrogance of slaveholders grew by what it fed on. Though a conscientious wish to avoid civil war mingled largely with the selfishness of trade, and the heartless gambling of politicians, all was alike interpreted by them as signs of Northern cowardice. At last, the Sumter gun was heard booming through the gathering storm. Instantly, the air was full of starry banners, and Northern pavements resounded with the tramp of horse and the rolling of artillery wagons. A thrill of patriotic enthusiasm kindled the souls of men. No more sending back of slaves. All our cities became at once cities of refuge; for men had risen above the letter of the Constitution into the spirit of the Declaration of Independence.

Gerald and his Lily-mother arrived in New York to find the social atmosphere all aglow. Under its exciting influence, he wrote to Mr. King: —

"Yesterday, I informed you of our arrival; and now I write to tell you that they are forming a regiment here to march to the defence of Washington, and I have joined it. Lily-mother was unwilling at first. But a fine set of fellows are joining, — all first-class young gentlemen. I told Lily-mother she would be ashamed to have me loiter behind the sons of her acquaintance, and that Mr. Seward said it was only an affair of sixty days. So she has consented. I enclose a letter to Rose-mother, to ask her blessing on my enterprise, which I am quite sure I shall have, together with your own."

Thus, with the unreflecting exhilaration of youth, Gerald went forth to the war, as light of heart as if he had been joining a boat-race or a hunting excursion ; so little did he comprehend that ferocious system of despotism which was fastening its fangs on free institutions with the death-grapple of a bloodhound.

For the next two months, his letters, though hurried, were frequent, and always cheerful ; mostly filled with tri-fling gossipings about camp-life, and affectionate remem-brances to those he had left behind. At last, Mr. King received one of graver import, which ran thus : —

"I have met with a strange adventure. A number of us were on picket duty, with orders to keep a sharp look-out. We went pacing back and forth on our allotted ground, now passing under the shadow of trees, now com-ing out into the moonlight. I walked very erect, feeling myself every inch a soldier. Sometimes I cast scrutinizing glances into groups of shrubbery, and sometimes I gazed absently on the sparkling Potomac, while memory was re-tracing the events of my life, and recalling the dear ones connected with them. Just as I reached a large tree which formed the boundary of my prescribed course, the next sentinel, whose walk began where mine ended, approached the same tree, and before he turned again we met face to face for an instant. I started, and I confess to a momentary feeling of superstition ; for I thought I had seen myself ; and that, you know, is said to be a warning of approaching

death. He could not have seen me very plainly, for I was
in shadow, while he for an instant was clearly revealed by
the moonlight. Anxious to be sure whether I had seen a
vision or a reality, when I again approached the tree I
waited for him; and a second time I saw such a likeness
of myself as I never saw excepting in the mirror. He
turned quickly, and marched away with military prompti-
tude and precision. I watched him for a moment, as his
erect figure alternately dipped into shadow and emerged
into light. I need not tell you what I was thinking of
while I looked; for you can easily conjecture. The third
time we met, I said, ' What is your name?' He replied,
' George Falkner,' and marched away. I write on a drum-
head, in a hurry. As soon as I can obtain a talk with this
duplicate of myself, I will write to you again. But I shall
not mention my adventure to Lily-mother. It would only
make her unhappy."

Another letter, which arrived a week after, contained
merely the following paragraph on the subject that interested them most: —

" We soldiers cannot command our own movements or
our time. I have been able to see G. F. but once, and
then our interview was brief. He seemed very reserved
about himself. He says he came from New York; but his
speech is Southern. He talks about ' toting ' things, and
says he ' disremembers.' I shall try to gain his confidence,
and perhaps I shall be able to draw him out."

A fortnight later he wrote: —

" I have learned from G. F. that the first thing he re-
members of himself is living with an old negress, about ten
miles from New Orleans, with eight other children, of various shades, but none so white as himself. He judges he

was about nine years old when he was carried to New
Orleans, and let out by a rich man named Bruteman to a
hotel-keeper, to black boots, do errands, &c.   One of
the children that the old negress brought up with him
was a mulatto named Henriet.   The boys called her Hen,
he said.   He used to 'tote' her about when she was a
baby, and afterward they used to roll in the mud, and
make mud-pies together.   When Hen was twelve years
old, she was let out to work in the same hotel where he
was.   Soon afterward, Mr. Bruteman put him out to learn
the carpenter's trade, and he soon became expert at it.
But though he earned five or six dollars a week, and
finally nine or ten, he never received any portion of it;
except that now and then Mr. Bruteman, when he counted
his wages, gave him a fip.   I never thought of *this* side
of the question when I used to hear grandfather talk about
the rights of slaveholders; but I feel now, if this had
been my own case, I should have thought it confounded
hard.   He and Hen were very young when they first begun to talk about being married; but he could n't bear the
thoughts of bringing up a family to be slaves, and they
watched for an opportunity to run away.   After several
plans which proved abortive, they went boldly on board
'The King Cotton,' he as a white gentleman, and she disguised as his boy servant.   You know how that attempt
resulted.   He says they were kept two days, with hands
and feet tied, on an island that was nothing but rock.
They suffered with cold, though one of the sailors, who
seemed kind-hearted, covered them with blankets and over-
coats.   He probably did not like the business of guarding
slaves; for one night he whispered to G. F., 'Can't you
swim?'   But George was very little used to the water,

and Hen could n't swim at all. Besides, he said, the sailors had loaded guns, and some of them would have fired
upon them, if they had heard them plunge; and even if
by a miracle they had gained the shore, he thought they
would be seized and sent back again, just as they were in
Boston.

"You may judge how I felt, while I listened to this.
I wanted to ask his forgiveness, and give him all my money, and my watch, and my ring, and everything. After
they were carried back, Hen was sold to the hotel-keeper
for six hundred dollars, and he was sold to a man in
Natchez for fifteen hundred. After a while, he escaped in
a woman's dress, contrived to open a communication with
Hen, and succeeded in carrying her off to New York.
There he changed his woman's dress, and his slave name
of Bob Bruteman, and called himself George Falkner.
When I asked him why he chose that name, he rolled up
his sleeve and showed me G. F. marked on his arm. He
said he did n't know who put them there, but he supposed
they were the initials of his name. He is evidently impressed by our great resemblance. If he asks me directly
whether I can conjecture anything about his origin, I hardly know how it will be best to answer. Do write how
much or how little I ought to say. Feeling unsafe in
the city of New York, and being destitute of money, he
applied to the Abolitionists for advice. They sent him to
New Rochelle, where he let himself to a Quaker, called
Friend Joseph Houseman, of whom he hired a small hut.
There, Hen, whom he now calls Henriet, takes in washing
and ironing, and there a babe has been born to them.
When the war broke out he enlisted; partly because he
thought it would help him to pay off some old scores with

slaveholders, and partly because a set of rowdies in the
village of New Rochelle said he was a white man, and
threatened to mob him for living with a nigger wife.
While they were in New York city, he and Henriet were
regularly married by a colored minister. He said he did
it because he hated slavery and could n't bear to live as
slaves did. I heard him read a few lines from a newspaper, and he read them pretty well. He says a little boy,
son of the carpenter of whom he learned his trade, gave
him some instruction, and he bought a spelling-book for
himself. He showed me some beef-bones, on which he
practises writing with a pencil. When he told me how
hard he had tried to get what little learning he had, it made
me ashamed to think how many cakes and toys I received
as a reward for studying my spelling-book. He is teach-
ing an old negro, who waits upon the soldiers. It is funny
to see how hard the poor old fellow tries, and to hear what
strange work he makes of it. It must be ' that stolen waters are sweet,' or slaves would never take so much more
pains than I was ever willing to take to learn to spell out
the Bible. Sometimes I help G. F. with his old pupil;
and I should like to have Mrs. Blumenthal make a sketch
of us, as I sit on the grass in the shade of some tree, helping the old negro hammer his syllables together. My
New York companions laugh at me sometimes ; but I have
gained great favor with G. F. by this proceeding. He is
such an ingenious fellow, that he is always in demand to
make or mend something. When I see how skilful he is
with tools, I envy him. I begin to realize what you once
told me, and which did not please me much at the time,
that being a fine gentleman is the poorest calling a man
can devote himself to.

" I have written this long letter under difficulties, and at various times. I have omitted many particulars, which I will try to remember in my next. Enclosed is a note for Rose-mother. I hold you all in most affectionate remembrance."

Soon after the reception of this letter, news came of the defeat at Bull Run, followed by tidings that Gerald was among the slain. Mr. King immediately waited upon Mrs. Fitzgerald to offer any services that he could render, and it was agreed that he should forthwith proceed to Washington with her cousin, Mr. Green. They returned with a long wooden box, on which was inscribed Gerald's name and regiment. It was encased in black walnut without being opened, for those who loved him dreaded to see him, marred as he was by battle. It was carried to Stone Chapel, where a multitude collected to pay the last honors to the youthful soldier. A sheathed sword was laid across the coffin, on which Mrs. Fitzgerald placed a laurel wreath. Just above it, Mrs. King deposited a wreath of white roses, in the centre of which Eulalia timidly laid a white lily. A long procession followed it to Mount Auburn, with a band playing Beethoven's Funeral March. Episcopal services were performed at the grave, which friends and relatives filled with flowers ; and there, by the side of Mr. Bell, the beautiful young man was hidden away from human sight. Mr. King's carriage had followed next to Mrs. Fitzgerald's ; a circumstance which the public explained by a report that the deceased was to have married his daughter. Mrs. Fitzgerald felt flattered to have it so understood, and she never contradicted it. After her great disappointment in her husband, and the loss of her other children, all the affection she was capable of feeling had

18

centred in Gerald. But hers was not a deep nature, and the world held great sway over it. She suffered acutely when she first heard of her loss; but she found no small degree of soothing compensation in the praises bestowed on her young hero, in the pomp of his funeral, and the general understanding that he was betrothed to the daughter of the quatro-millionnaire.

The depth of Mrs. King's sorrow was known only to Him who made the heart. She endeavored to conceal it as far as possible, for she felt it to be wrong to cast a shadow over the home of her husband and daughter. Gerald's likeness was placed in her chamber, where she saw it with the first morning light; but what were her reveries while she gazed upon it was told to no one. Custom, as well as sincere sympathy, made it necessary for her to make a visit of condolence to Mrs. Fitzgerald. But she merely took her hand, pressed it gently, and said, "May God comfort you." "May God comfort you, also," replied Mrs. Fitzgerald, returning the pressure; and from that time henceforth the name of Gerald was never mentioned between them.

After the funeral it was noticed that Alfred Blumenthal appeared abstracted, as if continually occupied with grave thoughts. One day, as he stood leaning against the window, gazing on the stars and stripes that floated across the street, he turned suddenly and exclaimed: "It is wrong to be staying here. I ought to be fighting for that flag. I *must* supply poor Gerald's place."

Mrs. Delano, who had been watching him anxiously, rose up and clasped him round the neck, with stronger emotion than he had ever seen her manifest. "*Must* you go, my son?" she said.

He laid his hand very gently on her head as he replied:
" Dearest Mamita, you always taught me to obey the voice
of duty; and surely it is a duty to help in rescuing Liberty
from the bloody jaws of this dragon Slavery."

She lingered an instant on his breast, then, raising her
tearful face, she silently pressed his hand, while she looked
into those kind and honest eyes, that so strongly reminded
her of eyes closed long ago. " You are right, my son,"
murmured she; " and may God give you strength."

Turning from her to hide the swelling of his own heart,
Alfred saw his mother sobbing on his father's bosom.
" Dearest mamma," said he, " Heaven knows it is hard for
me. Do not make it harder."

" It takes the manhood out of him to see you weep, darling," said Mr. Blumenthal. " Be a brave little woman,
and cheerfully give your dearest and best for the country."

She wiped her eyes, and, fervently kissing Alfred's hand,
replied, " I will. May God bless you, my dear, my only
son!"

His father clasped the other hand, and said, with forced
calmness: " You are right, Alfred. God bless you! And
now, dear Flora, let us consecrate our young hero's resolution by singing the Battle Song of Körner."

She seated herself at the piano, and Mrs. Delano joined
in with her weak but very sweet voice, while they sang,
" Father! I call on thee." But when they came to the
last verse, the voices choked, and the piano became silent.
Rosen Blumen and Lila came in and found them all weeping; and when their brother pressed them in his arms and
whispered to them the cause of all this sorrow, they cried
as if their hearts were breaking. Then their mother summoned all her resolution, and became a comforter. While

their father talked to them of the nobility and beauty of self-sacrifice, she kissed them and soothed them with hopeful words. Then, turning to Mrs. Delano, she tenderly caressed her faded hair, while she said : " Dearest Mamita, I trust God will restore to us our precious boy. I will paint his picture as St. George slaying the dragon, and you shall hang it in your chamber, in memory of what he said to you."

Alfred, unable to control his emotions, hid himself in the privacy of his own chamber. He struck his hand wildly against his forehead, exclaiming, " O my country, great is the sacrifice I make for thee ! " Then, kneeling by the bed where he had had so many peaceful slumbers, and dreamed so many pleasant dreams, he prayed fervently that God would give him strength according to his need.

And so he went forth from his happy home, self-consecrated to the cause of freedom. The women now had but one absorbing interest and occupation. All were eager for news from the army, and all were busy working for the soldiers.

CHAPTER XXXVII.

WHEN Mr. King returned from his mournful journey to Washington, he said to his wife: "I saw George Falkner, and was pleased with him. His resemblance to poor Gerald is wonderful. I could see no difference, except a firmer expression of the mouth, which I suppose is owing to his determined efforts to escape from slavery. Of course, he has not Gerald's gracefulness; but his bearing seemed manly, and there was no obvious stamp of vulgarity upon him. It struck me that his transformation into a gentleman would be an easy process. I was glad our interview was a hurried one, and necessarily taken up with details about Gerald's death. It seems he carried him off in his own arms when he was wounded, and that he did his utmost to stanch the blood. Gerald never spoke after the bullet struck him, though he pressed his hand, and appeared to try to say something. When he opened his vest to dress the wound, he found this."

Rosa looked at it, groaned out, "Poor Gerald!" and covered her face. It was the photograph of Eulalia, with the upper part shot away. Both remained for some time with their heads bowed in silence.

After a while, Mr. King resumed: "In answer to Mr. Green's inquiries concerning the mutilated picture, I replied that it was a likeness of my daughter; and he answered that he had heard a marriage was thought of between them. I was glad he happened to say that, for it will make it seem natural to George that I should take a lively interest in him on Gerald's account. The funeral, and Alfred's departure for the army, have left me little time to arrange my thoughts on that subject. But I have now formed definite plans, that I propose we should this evening talk over at Blumenthal's."

When the sisters met, and the girls had gone to another room to talk over their lessons, and imagine what Alfred was then doing, Mr. King began to speak of George Falkner.

Rosa said: "My first wish is to go to New Rochelle and bring home Henriet. She ought to be educated in a degree somewhat suitable to her husband's prospects. I will teach her to read and write, and give her lessons on the piano."

"I think that would prove too much for your finely attuned musical nerves," rejoined her husband.

"Do you suppose you are going to make *all* the sacrifices?" responded she, smiling. "It is n't at all like you to wish to engross everything to yourself."

"Rosa has a predilection for penance," remarked Flora; "and if she listens daily to a beginner knocking the scales up hill and down hill, I think it will answer instead of walking to Jerusalem with peas in her shoes."

"Before I mention my plans, I should like to hear your view of the subject, Blumenthal," said Mr. King.

His brother-in-law replied: "I think Rosa is right about taking charge of Henriet and educating her. But it seems to me the worst thing you could do for her or her husband would be to let them know that they have a claim to riches. Sudden wealth is apt to turn the heads of much older people than they are; and having been brought up as slaves, their danger would be greatly increased. If Henriet could be employed to sew for you, she might be gratified with easy work and generous wages, while you watched over her morals, and furnished her with opportunities to improve her mind. If George survives the war, some employment with a comfortable salary might be provided for him, with a promise to advance him according to his industry and general good habits. How does that strike you, Mamita?"

"I agree perfectly with you," rejoined Mrs. Delano. "I think it would be far more prudent to have their characters formed by habits of exertion and self-reliance, before they are informed that they are rich."

"It gratifies me to have my own judgment thus confirmed," said Mr. King. "You have given the outlines of a plan I had already formed. But this judicious process must not, of course, deprive the young man of a single cent that is due to him. You are aware that Mr. Bell left fifty thousand dollars to his grandson, to be paid when he was twenty-two years of age. I have already invested that sum for George, and placed it in the care of Mr. Percival, with directions that the interest shall be added to it from that date. The remainder of Mr. Bell's property, with the exception of some legacies, was unreservedly left to his daughter. I have taken some pains to ascertain the amount, and I shall add a codicil to my will leaving an equal sum to George. If I survive Mrs. Fitzgerald, the interest on it will date from her decease; and I shall take the best legal advice as to the means of securing her property from any claims, by George or his heirs, after they are informed of the whole story, as they will be whenever Mrs. Fitzgerald dies."

"You are rightly named Royal King," rejoined Mr. Blumenthal, "you do things in such princely style."

"In a style better than that of most royal kings," replied

he, "for it is simply that of an honest man. If this entanglement had never happened, I should have done as much for Gerald ; and let me do what I will, Eulalia will have more money than is good for her. Besides, I rather expect this arrangement will prove a benefit to myself. I intend to employ the young man as one of my agents in Europe ; **and if he shows as much** enterprise and perseverance in business as he did in escaping from slavery, he will prove an excellent partner for me when increasing **years diminish my** own energies. I would gladly adopt him, and have him live with us ; but I doubt whether such a great and sudden change of condition would prove salutary, and his having a colored wife would put obstructions in his way entirely beyond our power to remove. But the strongest objection to it is, that such an arrangement would greatly annoy Mrs. Fitzgerald, whose happiness we are bound to consult in every possible way."

"Has she been informed that the young man is found?" inquired Mrs. Delano.

"No," replied Mr. King. "It occurred very near the time of Gerald's death ; and we deem it unkind to disturb her mind about it for some months to come."

*   *   *   *   *

The next week, Mr. and Mrs. King started for New York, and thence proceeded to New Rochelle. Following the directions they had received, they hired a carriage at the steamboat-landing, to convey them to a farm-house a few miles distant. As they approached the designated place, they saw a slender man, in drab-colored clothes, lowering a bucket into the well. Mr. King alighted, and inquired, "Is this Mr. Houseman's farm, sir?"

"My name is Joseph Houseman," replied the Quaker.
"I am usually called Friend Joseph."

Mr. King returned to the carriage, and saying, " This is the place," he assisted his lady to alight. Returning to the farmer, he said : " We have come to ask you about a young colored woman, named Henriet Falkner. Her husband rendered service to a dear young friend of ours in the army, and we would be glad to repay the obligation by kindness to her."

" Walk in," said the Quaker. He showed them into a neat, plainly furnished parlor. " Where art thou from ? " he inquired.

" From Boston," was the reply.

" What is thy name ? "

" Mr. King."

" All men are called Mister," rejoined the Quaker. " What is thy given name ? "

" My name is Alfred Royal King ; and this is my wife, Rosa King."

" Hast thou brought a letter from the woman's husband ? " inquired Friend Joseph.

" No," replied Mr. King. " I saw George Falkner in Washington, a fortnight ago, when I went to seek the body of our young friend ; but I did not then think of coming here. If you doubt me, you can write to William Lloyd Garrison or Wendell Phillips, and inquire of them whether Alfred R. King is capable of deceiving."

" I like thy countenance, Friend Alfred, and I think thou art honest," rejoined the Quaker ; " but where colored people are concerned, I have known very polite and fair-spoken men to tell falsehoods."

Mr. King smiled as he answered : " I commend your caution, Friend Joseph. I see how it is. You suspect we may be slaveholders in disguise. But slaveholders are just

now too busy seeking to destroy this Republic to have any
time to hunt fugitives ; and when they have more leisure,
my opinion is they will find that occupation gone."

" I should have more hope of that," replied the farmer,
" if there was not so much pro-slavery here at the North.
And thee knows that the generals of the United States are
continually sending back fugitive slaves to bleed under the
lash of their taskmasters."

" I honor your scruples, Friend Joseph," responded Mr.
King ; " and that they may be completely removed, we
will wait at the Metropolitan in New York until you have
received letters from Mr. Garrison and Mr. Phillips. And
lest you should think I may have assumed the name of
another, I will give you these to enclose in your letter."
He opened his pocket-book and took out two photographs.

" I shall ask to have them sent back to me," replied the
farmer ; " for I should like to keep a likeness of thee and
thy Rosa. They will be pleasant to look upon. As soon
as I receive an answer, Friend Alfred, I will call upon thee
at the Metropolitan."

" We shall be pleased to see you, Friend Joseph," said
Rosa, with one of her sweetest smiles, which penetrated
the Quaker's soul, as sunshine does the receptive earth.
Yet, when the carriage had rolled away, he harnessed his
sleek horses to the wagon, and conveyed Henriet and her
babe to the house of a Friend at White Plains, till he ascertained whether these stylish-looking strangers were what
they professed to be.

A few days afterward, Friend Joseph called at the Metropolitan. When he inquired for the wealthy Bostonian,
the waiter stared at his plain dress, and said, "Your card,
sir."

" I have no card," replied the farmer. " Tell him Friend Joseph wishes to see him."

The waiter returned, saying, " Walk this way, sir," and showed him into the elegant reception-room.

As he sat there, another servant, passing through, looked at him, and said, " All gentlemen take off their hats in this room, sir."

" That may be," quietly replied the Quaker; " but all *men* do not, for thee sees I keep mine on."

The entrance of Mr. King, and his cordial salutation, made an impression on the waiters' minds; and when Friend Joseph departed, they opened the door very obsequiously.

The result of the conference was that Mr. and Mrs. King returned to Boston with Henriet and her little one.

Tulee had proved in many ways that her discretion might be trusted; and it was deemed wisest to tell her the whole story of the babe, who had been carried to the calaboose with her when Mr. Bruteman's agent seized her. This confidence secured her as a firm friend and ally of Henriet, while her devoted attachment to Mrs. King rendered her secrecy certain. When black Chloe saw the new-comer learning to play on the piano, she was somewhat jealous because the same privilege had not been offered to her children. " I did n't know Missy Rosy tought thar war sech a mighty difference 'tween black an' brown," said she. " I don't see nothin' so drefful pooty in dat ar molasses color."

" Now ye shut up," rejoined Tulee. " Missy Rosy knows what she 's 'bout. Ye see Mr. Fitzgerald was in love with Missy Eulaly; an' Henret's husban' took care o' him when he was dying. Mr. King is going to send him 'cross the water on some gran' business, to pay him for 't; and Missy Rosy wants his wife to be 'spectable out there 'moug strangers."

Henriet proved good-natured and unassuming, and, with occasional patronage from Tulee, she was generally able to keep her little boat in smooth water.

When she had been there a few months Mr. King enclosed to Mrs. Fitzgerald the letters Gerald had written about George; and a few days afterward he called to explain fully what he had done, and what he intended to do. That lady's dislike for her rival was much diminished since there was no Gerald to excite her jealousy of divided affection. There was some perturbation in her manner, but she received her visitor with great politeness; and when he had finished his statement she said: "I have great respect for your motives and your conduct; and I am satisfied to leave everything to your good judgment and kind feelings. I have but one request to make. It is that this young man may never know he is my son."

"Your wishes shall be respected," replied Mr. King. "But he so strongly resembles Gerald, that, if you should ever visit Europe again, you might perhaps like to see him, if you only recognized him as a relative of your husband."

The lady's face flushed as she answered promptly: "No, sir. I shall never recognize any person as a relative who has a colored wife. Much as I loved Gerald, I would never have seen him again if he had formed such an alliance; not even if his wife were the most beautiful and accomplished creature that ever walked the earth."

"You are treading rather closely upon *me*, Mrs. Fitzgerald," rejoined Mr. King, smiling.

The lady seemed embarrassed, and said she had forgotten Mrs. King's origin.

"Your son's wife is not so far removed from a colored ancestry as mine is," rejoined Mr. King; "but I think you would soon forget her origin, also, if you were in a country where others did not think of it. I believe our American prejudice against color is one of what Carlyle calls 'the phantom dynasties.'"

"It may be so," she replied coldly; "but I do not wish to be convinced of it."

And Mr. King bowed good morning.

A week or two after this interview, Mrs. Fitzgerald called upon Mrs. King; for, after all, she felt a certain sort of attraction in the secret history that existed between them; and she was unwilling to have the world suppose her acquaintance had been dropped by so distinguished a lady. By inadvertence of the servant at the door, she was shown into the parlor while Henriet was there, with her child on the floor, receiving directions concerning some muslin flounces she was embroidering. Upon the entrance of a visitor, she turned to take up her infant and depart. But Mrs. King said, "Leave little Hetty here, Mrs. Falkner, till you bring my basket for me to select the floss you need."

Hetty, being thus left alone, scrambled up, and toddled toward Mrs. King, as if accustomed to an affectionate reception. The black curls that clustered round her yellow face shook, as her uncertain steps hastened to a place of refuge; and when she leaned against her friend's lap, a pretty smile quivered on her coral lips, and lighted up her large dark eyes.

Mrs. Fitzgerald looked at her with a strange mixture of feelings.

"Don't you think she's a pretty little creature?" asked Mrs. King.

"She might be pretty if the yellow could be washed off," replied Mrs. Fitzgerald.

"Her cheeks are nearly the color of your hair," rejoined Mrs. King; "and I always thought that beautiful."

Mrs. Fitzgerald glanced at the mirror, and sighed as she said: "Ah, yes. My hair used to be thought very pretty when I was young; but I can see that it begins to fade."

When Henriet returned and took the child, she looked at her very curiously. She was thinking to herself, "What *would* my father say?" But she asked no questions, and made no remark.

She had joined a circle of ladies who were sewing and knitting for the soldiers; and after some talk about the difficulty she had found in learning to knit socks, and how fashionable it was for everybody to knit now, she rose to take leave.

CHAPTER XXXVIII.

THE months passed on, and brought ever-recurring demands for more soldiers. Mr. King watched the progress of the struggle with the deepest anxiety.

One day, when he had seen a new regiment depart for the South, he returned home in a still more serious mood than was now habitual to him. After supper, he opened the Evening Transcript, and read for a while. Then turning to his wife, who sat near him knitting for the army, he said, " Dear Rosabella, during all the happy years that I have been your husband, you have never failed to encourage me in every good impulse, and I trust you will strengthen me now."

With a trembling dread of what was coming, she asked, " What is it, dear Alfred."

" Rosa, this Republic *must* be saved," replied he, with solemn emphasis. " It is the day-star of hope to the toiling masses of the world, and it *must* not go out in darkness. It is not enough for me to help with money. I ought to go and sustain our soldiers by cheering words and a brave example. It fills me with shame and indignation when I think that all this peril has been brought upon us by that foul system which came so near making a wreck of *you*, my precious one, as it has wrecked thousands of pure and gentle souls. I foresee that this war is destined, by mere force of circumstances, to rid the Republic of that deadly incubus. Rosa, are you not willing to give me up for the safety of the country, and the freedom of your mother's race ? "

She tried to speak, but utterance failed her. After a struggle with herself, she said: "Do you realize how hard is a soldier's life? You will break down under it, dear Alfred; for you have been educated in ease and luxury."

"My education is not finished," replied he, smiling, as he looked round on the elegant and luxurious apartment. "What are all these comforts and splendors compared with the rescue of my country, and the redemption of an oppressed race? What is my life, compared with the life of this Republic? Say, dearest, that you will give me willingly to this righteous cause."

"Far rather would I give my own life," she said. "But I will never seek to trammel your conscience, Alfred."

They spoke together tenderly of the past, and hopefully of the future; and then they knelt and prayed together.

Some time was necessarily spent in making arrangements for the comfort and safety of the family during his absence; and when those were completed, he also went forth to rescue Liberty from the jaws of the devouring dragon. When he bade farewell to Flora's family, he said: "Look after my precious ones, Blumenthal; and if I never return, see to it that Percival carries out all my plans with regard to George Falkner."

Eight or ten weeks later, Alfred Blumenthal was lying in a hospital at Washington, dangerously wounded and burning with fever. His father and mother and Mrs. Delano immediately went to him; and the women remained until the trembling balance between life and death was determined in his favor. The soldier's life, which he at first dreaded, had become familiar to him, and he found a terrible sort of excitement in its chances and dangers. Mrs.

Delano sighed to observe that the gentle expression of his countenance, so like the Alfred of her memory, was changing to a sterner manhood. It was harder than the first parting to send him forth again into the fiery hail of battle; but they put strong constraint upon themselves, and tried to perform bravely their part in the great drama.

That visit to his suffering but uncomplaining son made a strong impression on the mind of Mr. Blumenthal. He became abstracted and restless. One evening, as he sat leaning his head on his hand, Flora said, "What are you thinking of, Florimond?"

He answered: "I am thinking, dear, of the agony I suffered when I had n't money to save you from the auction-block; and I am thinking how the same accursed system is striving to perpetuate and extend itself. The Republic has need of all her sons to stop its ravages; and I feel guilty in staying here, while our Alfred is so heroically offering up his young life in the cause of freedom."

"I have dreaded this," she said. "I have seen for days that it was coming. But, O Florimond, it is hard."

She hid her face in his bosom, and he felt her heart beat violently, while he talked concerning the dangers and duties of the time. Mrs. Delano bowed her head over the soldier's sock she was knitting, and tears dropped on it while she listened to them.

The weight that lay so heavily upon their souls was suddenly lifted up for a time by the entrance of Joe Bright. He came in with a radiant face, and, bowing all round, said, "I've come to bid you good by; I'm going to defend the old flag." He lifted up his voice and sang,

"'T is the star-spangled banner, O long may it wave!"

Flora went to the piano, and accompanied him with instrument and voice. Her husband soon struck in ; and Rosen Blumen and Lila left their lessons to perform their part in the spirit-stirring strain. When they had sung the last line, Mr. Bright, without pausing to take breath, struck into " Scots wha hae wi' Wallace bled," and they followed his lead. He put on all his steam when he came to the verse,

> " By our country's woes and pains,
> By our sons in servile chains,
> We will drain our dearest veins,
> But they *shall* be free ! "

He emphasized the word *shall*, and brought his clenched hand down upon the table so forcibly, that the shade over the gas-light shook.

In the midst of it, Mrs. Delano stole out of the room. She had a great respect and liking for Mr. Bright, but he was sometimes rather too demonstrative to suit her taste. He was too much carried away with enthusiasm to notice her noiseless retreat, and he went on to the conclusion of his song with unabated energy. All earnestness is magnetic. Mr. and Mrs. Blumenthal, and even the children, caught his spirit. When the song ended, Mr. Blumenthal drew a long breath, and said : " One needs strong lungs to accompany you, Mr. Bright. You sang that like the tramp of a regiment."

" And you blazed away like an explosion of artillery," rejoined he.

" The fact is," replied Blumenthal, " the war spirit pervades the air, and I've caught it. I'm going to join the army."

" Are you ? " exclaimed Mr. Bright, seizing his hand

with so tight a grip that it made him wince. "I hope you'll be my captain."

Mr. Blumenthal rubbed his hand, and smiled as he said, "I pity the Rebel that you get hold of, Mr. Bright."

"Ask your pardon. Ask your pardon," rejoined he. "But speaking of the tramp of a regiment, here it goes!" And he struck up "John Brown's Hallelujah." They put their souls into it in such a manner, that the spirit of the brave old martyr seemed marching all through it.

When it came to a conclusion, Mr. Bright remarked: "Only to think how that incendiary song is sung in Boston streets, and in the parlors too, when only little more than a year ago a great mob was yelling after Wendell Phillips, for speaking on the anniversary of John Brown's execution. I said then the fools would get enough of slavery before they'd done with it; and I reckon they're beginning to find it out, not only the rowdies, but the nabobs that set 'em on. War ain't a blessing, but it's a mighty great teacher; that's a fact. No wonder the slavites hated Phillips. He aims sure and hits hard. No use in trying to pass off shams upon *him*. If you bring him anything that ain't real mahogany, his blows'll be sure to make the veneering fly. But I'm staying too long. I only looked in to tell you I was going." He glanced round for Mrs. Delano, and added: "I'm afraid I sung too loud for that quiet lady. The fact is, I'm full of fight."

"That's what the times demand," replied Mr. Blumenthal.

They bade him "Good night," and smiled at each other to hear his strong voice, as it receded in the distance, still singing, "His soul is marching on."

"Now I will go to Mamita," said Flora. "Her gentle

spirit suffers in these days. This morning, when she saw a company of soldiers marching by, and heard the boys hurrahing, she said to me so piteously, 'O Flora, these are wild times.' Poor Mamita! she's like a dove in a tornado."

" *You* seemed to be strong as an eagle while you were singing," responded her husband.

"I felt like a drenched humming-bird when Mr. Bright came in," rejoined she; "but he and the music together lifted me up into the blue, as your Germans say."

"And from that height can you say to me, 'Obey the call of duty, Florimond'?"

She put her little hand in his and answered, "I can. May God protect us all!"

Then, turning to her children, she said: "I am going to bring Mamita; and presently, when I go away to be alone with papa a little while, I want you to do everything to make the evening pleasant for Mamita. You know she likes to hear you sing, 'Now Phœbus sinketh in the west.'"

"And I will play that Nocturne of Mendelssohn's that she likes so **much**," replied Rosen Blumen. "She says I play it almost as well as Aunt Rosa."

"And she likes to hear me sing, 'Once on a time there was a king,'" said Lila. "She says she heard *you* singing it in the woods a long time ago, when she had n't anybody to call her Mamita."

"Very well, my children," replied their mother. "Do everything you can to make Mamita happy; for there will never be such another Mamita."

*   *   *   *   *

During the anxious months that followed Mr. Blumenthal's departure, the sisters and their families were almost daily at the rooms of the Sanitary Commission, sewing, packing, or writing. Henriet had become expert with the sewing-machine, and was very efficient help; and even Tulee, though far from skilful with her needle, contrived to make dozens of hospital slippers, which it was the pride of her heart to deliver to the ladies of the Commission. Chloe added her quota of socks, often elephantine in shape, and sometimes oddly decorated with red tops and toes; but with a blessing for "the boys in blue" running through all the threads. There is no need to say how eagerly they watched for letters, and what a relief it was to recognize the writing of beloved hands, feeling each time that it might be the last.

Mr. King kept up occasional correspondence with the officers of George Falkner's company, and sent from time to time favorable reports of his bravery and good habits. Henriet received frequent letters from him, imperfectly spelled, but full of love and loyalty.

Two years after Mr. King left his happy home, he was brought back with a Colonel's shoulder-strap, but with his right leg gone, and his right arm in a sling. When the first joy of reunion had expressed itself in caresses and affectionate words, he said to Rosa, "You see what a cripple you have for a husband."

"I make the same reply the English girl did to Commodore Barclay," she replied; "'You're dear as ever to me, so long as there's body enough to hold the soul.'"

Eulalia wept tears of joy on her father's neck, while Flora, and Rosen Blumen, and Lila clasped their arms round him, and Tulee stood peeping in at the door, waiting for her turn to welcome the hero home.

"Flora, you see my dancing days are over," said the Colonel.

"Never mind, I'll do your dancing," she replied.
"Rosen Blumen, play uncle's favorite waltz."

She passed her arm round Eulalia, and for a few moments they revolved round the room to the circling music. She had so long been called the life of the family, that she tried to keep up her claim to the title. But her present mirthfulness was assumed; and it was contrary to her nature to act a part. She kissed her hand to her brother-in-law, and smiled as she whirled out of the room; but she ran up stairs and pressed the tears back, as she murmured to herself, "Ah, if I could only be sure Florimond and Alfred would come back, even mutilated as he is!"

CHAPTER XXXIX.

ANOTHER year brought with it what was supposed to be peace, and the army was disbanded. Husband and son returned alive and well, and Flora was her young self again. In the exuberance of her joy she seemed more juvenile than her girls; jumping from husband to son and from son to husband, kissing them and calling them all manner of pet names; embracing Mrs. Delano at intervals, and exclaiming, "O Mamita, here we are all together again! I wish my arms were long enough to hug you all at once."

"I thank God, my child, for your sake and for my own," replied Mrs. Delano. She looked at Alfred, as she spoke, and the affectionate glance he returned filled her heart with a deep and quiet joy. The stern shadow of war vanished from his face in the sunshine of home, and she recognized the same gentle expression that had been photographed on her memory long years ago.

When the family from Beacon Street came, a few minutes later, with welcomes and congratulations, Alfred bestowed a different sort of glance on his cousin Eulalia, and they both blushed; as young people often do, without knowing the reason why. Rosen Blumen and Lila had been studying with her the language of their father's country; and when the general fervor had somewhat abated, the girls manifested some disposition to show off the accomplishment. "Do hear them calling Alfred *Mein lieber bruder*," said Flora to her husband, "while Rosa and I

are sprinkling them all with pet names in French and
Spanish. What a polyglot family we are! as *cher papa*
used to say. But, Florimond, did you notice anything peculiar in the meeting between Alfred and Eulalia?"

"I thought I did," he replied.

"How will Brother King like it?" she asked. "He
thinks very highly of Alfred; but you know he has a theory against the marriage of cousins."

"So have I," answered Blumenthal; "but nations and
races have been pretty thoroughly mixed up in the ancestry of our children. What with African and French, Spanish, American, and German, I think the dangers of too close
relationship are safely diminished."

"They are a good-looking set, between you and I," said
Flora; "though they *are* oddly mixed up. See Eulalia,
with her great blue eyes, and her dark eyebrows and eyelashes. Rosen Blumen looks just like a handsome Italian
girl. No one would think Lila Blumen was her sister,
with her German blue eyes, and that fine frizzle of curly
light hair. Your great-grandmother gave her the flax, and
I suppose mine did the frizzling."

This side conversation was interrupted by Mr. King's
saying: "Blumenthal, you have n't asked for news concerning Mrs. Fitzgerald. You know Mr. Green has been a
widower for some time. Report says that he finds in her
company great consolation for the death of her cousin."

"That's what I call a capital arrangement," said Flora;
"and I did n't mean any joke about their money, either.
Won't they sympathize grandly? Won't she be in her
element? Top notch. No end to balls and parties; and
a coat of arms on the coach."

"The news made me very glad," observed Rosa; "for

the thought of her loneliness always cast a shadow over my happiness."

"Even *they* have grown a little during the war," rejoined Mr. King. "Nabob Green, as they call him, did actually contribute money for the raising of colored regiments. He so far abated his prejudice as to be willing that negroes should have the honor of being shot in his stead; and Mrs. Fitzgerald agreed with him. That was a considerable advance, you must admit."

They went on for some time talking over news, public and private; not omitting the prospects of Tom's children, and the progress of Tulee's. But such family chats are like the showers of manna, delicious as they fall, but incapable of preservation.

The first evening the families met at the house in Beacon Street, Mr. Blumenthal expressed a wish to see Henriet, and she was summoned. The improvement in her appearance impressed him greatly. Having lived three years with kindly and judicious friends, who never reminded her, directly or indirectly, that she was a black sheep in the social flock, her faculties had developed freely and naturally; and belonging to an imitative race, she readily adopted the language and manners of those around her. Her features were not handsome, with the exception of her dark, liquid-looking eyes; and her black hair was too crisp to make a soft shading for her brown forehead. But there was a winning expression of gentleness in her countenance, and a pleasing degree of modest ease in her demeanor. A map, which she had copied very neatly, was exhibited, and a manuscript book of poems, of her own selection, written very correctly, in a fine flowing hand.

"Really, this is encouraging," said Mr. Blumenthal, as

19   B B

she left the room. "If half a century of just treatment
and free schools can bring them all up to this level, our
battles will not be in vain, and we shall deserve to rank
among the best benefactors of the country; to say nothing
of a corresponding improvement in the white population."

"Thitherward is Providence leading us," replied Mr.
King. "Not unto us, but unto God, be all the glory.
We were all of us working for better than we knew."

*   *   *   *   *

Mr. King had written to George Falkner, to inform him
of a situation he had in store for him at Marseilles, and to
request a previous meeting in New York, as soon as he
could obtain his discharge from the army; being in this, as
in all other arrangements, delicately careful to avoid giving
annoyance to Mrs. Fitzgerald. In talking this over with
his wife, he said: "I consider it a duty to go to Marseilles
with him. It will give us a chance to become acquainted
with each other; it will shield him from possible imperti-
nences on the passage, on Henriet's account; and it will be
an advantage to him to be introduced as my friend to the
American Consul, and some commercial gentlemen of my
acquaintance."

"I am to go with you, am I not?" asked Rosa. "I am
curious to see this young man, from whom I parted, so
unconscious of all the strange future, when he was a baby
in Tulee's arms."

"I think you had better not go, dear," he replied;
"though the loss of your company will deprive me of a
great pleasure. Eulalia would naturally wish to go with
us; and as she knows nothing of George's private history,
it would be unwise to excite her curiosity by introducing
her to such a striking likeness of Gerald. But she might

stay with Rosen Blumen while you go to New York and remain with me till the vessel sails. If I meet with no accidents, I shall return in three months; for I go merely to give George a fair start, though, when there, I shall have an eye to some other business, and take a run to Italy to look in upon our good old friends, Madame and the Signor."

The journey to New York was made at the appointed time, in company with Henriet **and her** little one. George had risen to the rank of lieutenant in the army, and had acquired a military bearing that considerably increased the manliness of his appearance. He was browned by exposure to sun and wind; but he so strongly resembled her handsome Gerald, that Rosa longed to clasp him to her heart. His wife's appearance evidently took him by surprise. "How you have changed!" he exclaimed. "What a lady you are! I can hardly believe this is the little Hen I used to make mud pies with."

She laughed as she answered: "You are changed, too. If I have improved, it is owing to these kind friends. Only think of it, George, though Mrs. King is such a handsome and grand lady, she always called me Mrs. Falkner."

Mrs. King **made** several appropriate parting presents to Henriet and little Hetty. To George she gave a gold watch, **and a very** beautiful colored photograph of Gerald, **in a morocco case, as a souvenir of** their brief friendship in the army.

Mr. King availed himself of every hour of the voyage to gain the confidence of the young man, and to instil some salutary lessons into his very receptive mind. After they had become well acquainted, he said: "I have made an estimate of what I think it will be necessary for you to spend for rent, food, and clothing; also of what I think it would be wise for you to spend in improving your education, and for occasional amusements. I have not done this in the spirit of dictation, my young friend, but merely with the wish of helping you by my greater experience of life. It is important that you should learn to write a good commercial hand, and also acquire, as soon as possible, a very thorough knowledge of the French language. For these you should employ the best teachers that can be found. Your wife can help you in many ways. She has learned to spell correctly, to read with fluency and expression, and to play quite well on the piano. You will find it very profitable to read good books aloud to each other. I advise you not to go to places of amusement oftener than once a fortnight, and always to choose such places as will be suitable and pleasant for your wife. I like that young men in my employ should never taste intoxicating drinks, or use tobacco in any form. Both those habits are expensive, and I have long ago abjured them as injurious to health."

The young man bowed, and replied, "I will do as you wish in all respects, sir; I should be very ungrateful if I did not."

"I shall give you eight hundred dollars for the first year," resumed Mr. King; "and shall increase your salary year by year, according to your conduct and capabilities. If you are industrious, temperate, and economical, there is no reason why you should not become a rich man in time; and it will be wise for you to educate yourself, your wife, and your children, with a view to the station you will have it in your power to acquire. If you do your best, you may rely upon my influence and my fatherly interest to help you all I can."

The young man colored, and, after a little embarrassed hesitation, said: "You spoke of a fatherly interest, sir; and that reminds me that I never had a father. May I ask whether you know anything about my parents?"

Mr. King had anticipated the possibility of such a question, and he replied: "I will tell you who your father was, if you will give a solemn promise never to ask a single question about your mother. On that subject I have given a pledge of secrecy which it would be dishonorable for me to break. Only this much I will say, that neither of your parents was related to me in any degree, or connected with me in any way."

The young man answered, that he was of course very desirous to know his whole history, but would be glad to obtain any information, and was willing to give the required promise, which he would most religiously keep.

Mr. King then went on to say: "Your father was Mr. Gerald Fitzgerald, a planter in Georgia. You have a right to his name, and I will so introduce you to my friends, if you wish it. He inherited a handsome fortune, but lost it all by gambling and other forms of dissipation. He had several children by various mothers. You and the Gerald with whom you became acquainted were brothers by the father's side. You are unmixed white; but you were left in the care of a negro nurse, and one of your father's creditors seized you both, and sold you into slavery. Until a few months before you were acquainted with Gerald, it was supposed that you died in infancy; and for that reason no efforts were made to redeem you. Circumstances which I am not at liberty to explain led to the discovery that you were living, and that Gerald had learned your history as a slave. I feel the strongest sympathy with your misfortunes, and cherish a lively gratitude for your kindness to my young friend Gerald. All that I have told you is truth; and if it were in my power, I would most gladly tell you the *whole* truth."

The young man listened with the deepest interest; and, having expressed his thanks, said he should prefer to be called by his father's name; for he thought he should feel more like a man to bear a name to which he knew that he had a right.

   *   *   *   *   *

When Mr. King again returned to his Boston home, as soon as the first eager salutations were over, he exclaimed: "How the room is decorated with vines and flowers! It reminds me of that dear floral parlor in New Orleans.".

"Did n't you telegraph that you were coming? And is it not your birthday?" inquired his wife.

He kissed her, and said: "Well, Rosabella, I think you may now have a tranquil mind; for I believe things have been so arranged that no one is very seriously injured by that act of frenzy which has caused you so much suffering. George will not be deprived of any of his pecuniary rights; and he is in a fair way to become more of a man than he would have been if he had been brought up in luxury. He and Henriet are as happy in their prospects as two mortals well can be. Gerald enjoyed his short life; and was more bewildered than troubled by the discovery that he had two mothers. Eulalia was a tender, romantic memory to him; and such, I think, he has become to our child. I don't believe Mrs. Fitzgerald suffered much more than annoyance. Gerald was always the same to her as a son; and if he had been really so, he would probably have gone to the war, and have run the same chance of being killed."

" Ah, Alfred," she replied, " I should never have found my way out of that wretched entanglement if it had not been for you. You have really acted toward me the part of Divine Providence. It makes me ashamed that I have not been able to do anything in atonement for my own fault, except the pain I suffered in giving up my Gerald to his Lily-mother. When I think how that poor babe became enslaved by my act, I long to sell my diamonds, and use the money to build school-houses for the freedmen."

" Those diamonds seem to trouble you, dearest," rejoined he, smiling. " I have no objection to your selling them. You become them, and they become you; but I think school-houses will shine as brighter jewels in the better world."

Here Flora came in with all her tribe; and when the welcomes were over, her first inquiries were for Madame and the Signor.

" They are well," replied Mr. King, "and they seem to be as contented as tabbies on a Wilton rug. They show signs of age, of course. The Signor has done being peppery, and Madame's energy has visibly abated; but her mind is as lively as ever. I wish I could remember half the stories she repeated about the merry pranks of your childhood. She asked a great many questions about *Jolie Manon ;* and she laughed till she cried while she described, in dramatic style, how you crazed the poor bird with imitations, till she called you *Joli petit diable.*"

" How I wish I had known mamma then ! How funny she must have been !" exclaimed Lila.

" I think you have heard some performances of hers that were equally funny," rejoined Mrs. Delano. " I used to be entertained with a variety of them ; especially when we were in Italy. If any of the *pifferari* went by, she would imitate the drone of their bagpipes in a manner irresistibly comic. And if she saw a peasant-girl dancing, she forthwith went through the performance to the life."

"Yes, Mamita," responded Flora; "and you know I fancied myself a great musical composer in those days, — a sort of feminine Mozart; but the *qui vive* was always the key I composed in."

"I used to think the fairies helped you about that, as well as other things," replied Mrs. Delano.

"I think the fairies help her now," said Mr. Blumenthal; "and well they may, for she is of their kith and kin."

This playful trifling was interrupted by the sound of the folding-doors rolling apart; and in the brilliantly lighted adjoining room a tableau became visible, in honor of the birthday. Under festoons of the American flag, surmounted by the eagle, stood Eulalia, in ribbons of red, white, and blue, with a circle of stars round her head. One hand upheld the shield of the Union, and in the other the scales of Justice were evenly poised. By her side stood Rosen Blumen, holding in one hand a gilded pole surmounted by a liberty-cap, while her other hand rested protectingly on the head of Tulee's Benny, who was kneeling and looking upward in thanksgiving.

Scarcely had the vision appeared before Joe Bright's voice was heard leading invisible singers through the tune "Hail to the Chief," which Alfred Blumenthal accompanied with a piano. As they sang the last line the striped festoons fell and veiled the tableau. Then Mr. Bright, who had returned a captain, appeared with his company, consisting of Tom and Chloe with their children, and Tulee with her children, singing a parody composed by himself, of which the chorus was: —

> " Blow ye the trumpet abroad o'er the sea,
>   Columbia has triumphed, the negro is free !
>   Praise to the God of our fathers ! 't was He,
>   Jehovah, that triumphed, Columbia, through thee."

To increase the effect, the director of ceremonies had
added a flourish of trumpets behind the scenes.

Then the colored band came forward, hand in hand, and
sang together, with a will, Whittier's immortal " Boat
Song " : —

> " We own de hoe, we own de plough,
>   We own de hands dat hold ;
>   We sell de pig, we sell de cow ;
>   But nebber *chile* be sold.
>   De yam will grow, de cotton blow,
>   We 'll hab de rice an' corn :
>   O, nebber you fear, if nebber you hear
>   De driver blow his horn ! "

All the family, of all ages and colors, then joined in
singing " The Star-spangled Banner "; and when Mr.
King had shaken hands with them all, they adjourned to the
breakfast-room, where refreshments were plentifully provided.

At last Mr. Bright said : " I don't want to bid you good
night, friends ; but I must. I don't generally like to go
among Boston folks. Just look at the trees on the Common. They 're dying because they 've rolled the surface
of the ground so smooth. That 's just the way in Boston,
I reckon. They take so much pains to make the surface
smooth, that it kills the roots o' things. But when I come
here, or go to Mrs. Blumenthal's, I feel as if the roots o'
things wa'n't killed. Good night, friends. I have n't enjoyed myself so well since I found Old Hundred and
Yankee Doodle in the Harmolinks."

The sound of his whistling died away in the streets; the young people went off to talk over their festival; the colored troop retired to rest; and the elders of the two families sat together in the stillness, holding sweet converse concerning the many strange experiences that had been so richly crowned with blessings.

A new surprise awaited them, prepared by the good taste of Mr. Blumenthal. A German Liederkrantz in the hall closed the ceremonies of the night with Mendelssohn's "Song of Praise."

THE END.

Cambridge : Stereotyped and Printed by Welch, Bigelow, & Co.